I0545420

SPRITE

A THOMAS IRONCUTTER NOVEL

DAVID ACHORD

SEVEREDPRESS

SPRITE: A THOMAS IRONCUTTER NOVEL

Copyright © 2023 David Achord
Copyright © 2023 by Severed Press

WWW.SEVEREDPRESS.COM

All rights reserved. No part of this book may be
reproduced or transmitted in any form or by any
electronic or mechanical means, including
photocopying, recording or by any information and
retrieval system, without the written permission of
the publisher and author, except where permitted by law.
This novel is a work of fiction. Names,
characters, places and incidents are the product of
the author's imagination, or are used fictitiously.
Any resemblance to actual events, locales or persons,
living or dead, is purely coincidental.

ISBN: 978-1-922861-59-7

All rights reserved.

CHAPTER 1

It was Friday morning, the beginning of the Labor Day weekend, and I could hardly keep my eyes open. The fatigue was deep, brought upon by being awake for over twenty-four hours, most of it spent driving. I'd broken my new rule of only smoking one cigar every other day. It took me a minute to add it up, but I believed I'd smoked four already. Nicotine over caffeine. Caffeine required restroom stops and I didn't want that. The sooner I got this over with, the better.

The crazy dream finally convinced me to do something. I'd been having a lot of them the past few months. Two days it happened again, but this one was different. In this dream, I was having conversations with people I knew and loved, and who were terribly dead.

First it was Uncle Mike, then my father, my wife, Simone, Lilith, and finally Mick. That was the part of the dream I remembered the most vividly. We were sitting in his cigar bar. The fat bastard had an enormous stogie lit up, the biggest I'd ever seen. He inhaled deeply and blew all the smoke in my face before peering at me through the thick blue haze and speaking.

"When are you going to do something about it, you dumb Dago?" he demanded.

When I awoke, my sheets were soaked in perspiration. I rolled out of bed, stripped it, and took the linens to the utility room. Loading the washer, I went into the kitchen and started a pot of coffee. Sitting there, I tried to remember all of the dream, what everyone had said, but Mick's single sentence was the only thing I could recall. I thought it all over while I sipped my coffee. I'd been having a lot of dreams like this lately.

It was the curse, it had to be.

I'm a realistic man. A man who does not believe in ghosts, psychics, or other superstitious silliness. A curse? That was a trope in a cheesy low budget movie, not real life. But things had been strange lately. The intensity of this latest dream pushed me into deciding on something I'd been mulling over for a few weeks now.

Finishing my coffee, I got my phone, scrolled through the contact list, and found Kalina's number. Her voice was groggy, like I had awakened her. No surprise, it was five in the morning.

"Thomas?"

"Yeah, it's me. Can we talk?" I asked.

And that's how it started. I told her that even though I didn't believe in the damned curse her great aunt had put on me, I was open to suggestions of how I might be rid of it. We talked a little. She said she'd get back to me and called back an hour later.

"Come to Chicago," she directed.

I didn't hesitate. I cleaned up, filled Tommy Boy's food bowl, packed an overnight bag, and took off. I was knocking on her door seven hours later. Kalina greeted me wearing nothing but a loosely tied white silk bathrobe. The physical traits she shared with Lilith were easily recognizable. Sooty black hair, pale olive toned skin, dark eyes. Nice teeth, but they would've looked better had she worn braces when she was a kid. She was around ten or twenty pounds heavier than Lilith, but it was in all the right places.

"Come on in," she said and led me to the den. Two older women were sitting on a couch, silently appraising me with sour stares.

"This is my grandmother and her sister." She gestured toward the second woman. "She's the one who put the curse on you," she said.

"You killed my Ivan," the woman huffed in thickly accented English.

I felt like I had to defend myself. "If you mean Wolf, I didn't kill him. A cop shot him."

"You were there," she retorted while waving a wrinkled finger at me and continuing to give me the stink eye.

"Yeah, I was there." I turned to Kalina. "Okay, tell me what's going on."

"I need to go to Atlanta and pick up some heirlooms. They're priceless and there are other people who want them. So, we need you to go with me and act as my bodyguard."

The great aunt spoke to Kalina in a foreign language. Kalina nodded and turned back to me. "She said you will need to kill anyone who interferes."

I stared a moment. "Heirlooms, huh? You wouldn't lie to me, would you?"

"What do you mean?" she asked.

"I'm not going to help you mule drugs," I said.

"No, it's not drugs, I promise you," Kalina replied.

I continued with the long hard stare before responding. "Alright, I'll do it. Two conditions. Number one, no matter what, the curse is lifted."

Kalina nodded. "What's the second condition?"

"If it's drugs, I'll personally turn you in," I declared.

She shook her head vigorously. "It's not drugs."

"Fine, get dressed, let's get going."

It was a lot of driving, and I did most of it, but the heirlooms were retrieved and transported safely back to Chicago. Kalina's great aunt led us to the back yard where she performed some sort of ritual before spitting on the ground at my feet. Kalina grinned and informed me I was now curse free. I thanked them and was backing out of their driveway before they thought to put another curse on me.

It was a long drive home. At one point, the fatigue was so bad I almost ran off the road. I took an hour nap at a rest area, which helped, but not much. After what seemed to be an eternity, I spotted the exit that would lead me to my house and veered onto it.

"Not long now," I muttered.

I was looking forward to nothing more than crawling into my bed for nine or ten hours of uninterrupted sleep, but when I saw the dark blue Dodge Durango with blacked out windows parked at the gate of my driveway, I knew sleep was going to have to wait.

CHAPTER 2

The driver got out first and eyed me with an arrogant, baleful stare. I recognized him immediately. I parked and exited my SUV.

"Why hello, Georgie," I greeted as a second man exited the Durango.

Georgie was George Thompson, a somewhat dimwitted detective who was employed by the Rutherford County Sheriff's Office. I didn't like him, and he certainly did not like me. He also hated to be called Georgie, which is why I made a point of using that moniker every time I saw him. The corners of his mouth turned down and he looked me up and down. When he spotted the Springfield 45 on my hip, he made a face like he was seeing a ticking time bomb.

"What are you doing armed?" he asked.

"That's a stupid question, Georgie, I always go armed." I didn't bother explaining how carry permits worked. I had one, even though it was no longer a requirement in Tennessee.

"Tell me why you're here or hit the road. I have better things to do," I demanded.

I guess he had a spark or two in his brain. He realized that yes, it was perfectly legal for me to carry, and he was in Davidson County, which was not his lawful jurisdiction. But then his look of consternation turned to a sneer.

"Damn, Ironcutter, you look like hell. Have you been out all night boozing it up? You ought to get yourself into a treatment program."

"What can I say, your mother's insatiable," I said.

It angered him, but to my surprise, he regained his composure and offered a small smile. He hooked a thumb toward the other man.

"This is Hayden Westlake. You may have heard of him."

I glanced at Hayden Westlake. He was a lean man with a slight paunch, I guessed him in his early forties, a touch under six feet, and wearing a custom-tailored suit that had an impeccable fit. He extended his hand as he approached.

"Pleased to meet you, Mister Ironcutter."

I shook it, but my gut was telling me he was being insincere. This wasn't a friendly visit, and he had no intention of being my friend. He continued speaking.

"I'm an assistant district attorney with the United States Attorney's Office," he said.

"That's Federal Attorney General, Tommy Boy," Georgie drawled out. I guess he thought I was ignorant of the difference between state and federal. Perhaps he thought he was scaring me. I ignored him and focused on Hayden.

"Nice to meet you, I guess, and call me Thomas. Tommy Boy is the name of my cat. What brings the two of you here?"

"May we go somewhere and sit?" he asked. "Your house perhaps?"

He gave me a pleasant smile when he asked, but I detected an undercurrent of disdain, hostility. The man considered me an enemy, and I had no idea why. Even though I was dead tired, my gut told me it would be in my best interests to find out what they wanted.

"Sure. When the gate opens, take the drive and park out front," I directed.

Getting back in my vehicle, I activated the gate and followed them. When we'd parked, I opened the front door and let Tommy Boy out. He looked everyone over and rubbed up against my leg before meandering out into the front yard. I pointed at my rocking chairs.

"We can sit here. I would offer you something to drink, but all I have is water," I said, which wasn't true, but they didn't need to know that.

"Nothing for me, thank you," Hayden said. Georgie grunted and lit a cigarette before sitting.

"Alright, let's not bother with any small talk, tell me what brings the two of you here today," I repeated. Hayden cleared his throat.

"Yes, let's get to it. We recently made a series of arrests. The suspects are all members of an outlaw biker gang known as the Satan's Dogs," he said.

I paused a moment before responding. I began having a bad feeling. Why were they coming to me to talk about the Satan's Dogs? Only a few people knew about my interaction with those knuckleheads. I gave a noncommittal answer.

"I believe I saw that on the news."

Hayden nodded, as if he expected this answer.

"Yes, good. So, why are we here? We are following up on loose ends. Detective Thompson has informed me that you were formerly a police officer."

"I was," I answered.

"Excellent," Hayden said with a smile that reminded me of a used car salesman. "As for your question, I am the prosecuting attorney in their case and I am interviewing people who have had contact with members of the Satan's Dogs in an attempt to gain a little insight about them, perhaps information that will help in the prosecution of these individuals. With your background and experience, I believe you could be a valuable source of information about them. Wouldn't you agree, Detective Thompson?"

Georgie bobbed his head. "You still have a cop's nose, Ironcutter, I'll admit that. I bet you're like me, you can have one single conversation with a person and learn more about them in a minute than a common everyday civilian could in a month."

He was laying it on thick. Now I was certain I was smelling a rat. I couldn't figure out why Georgie was involved though. He wasn't federal, he was a lowly, semi-competent detective in a county that was located immediately south of Nashville. It seemed odd. My first thought was to respond with some kind of smartassed remark, but instead, I offered a thoughtful nod.

"I appreciate that," I said, and then frowned. "I'm not sure I can help though. I don't believe I've ever met any of the Satan's Dogs. The only outlaw bikers I know are a couple of guys who are members of a club called the Baroques, but that's it. As far as I know, there is no relationship between the two clubs."

Hayden eyed me a moment before giving a tacit nod to Georgie. Georgie dutifully pulled out a piece of paper from a manila folder he was carrying and handed it over to me. It was a color printout of a man's mug photo. I instantly recognized the piece of shit, although I didn't know his real name.

I first met Bang-Bang one summer night when he and two of his biker brothers came to my house and assaulted me. I later had a talk with him at a dive bar in Smyrna. Those were my only two contacts with him. Nothing else. No clandestine meetings, no conspiratorial plans, nothing.

So, what were these two men doing? There was some other dynamic at play. Playing dumb and proceeding with caution was warranted here. I gave a casual gesture toward the picture.

"Who is he?" I asked.

"Don't you know?" Georgie asked.

"Can't say I do," I replied.

"His legal name is Samuel Todd," Hayden said.

"He goes by Bang-Bang," Georgie added. "He's the president of the Satan's Dogs."

I gratuitously gave the photo another thoughtful stare before handing it back to Georgie.

"I'm drawing a blank," I said.

"Are you certain?" Hayden asked.

"My memory isn't perfect, maybe I've bumped into him sometime in the past, but I don't remember him," I replied.

"You were seen with him in a bar back in June," Georgie said.

There it is. I'd been asking myself how they were connecting me to Bang-Bang and Georgie unwittingly provided the answer. The time I sat with Bang-Bang in Mona's Paradise. They obviously didn't know about the night Bang-Bang and two of his biker brothers paid a visit to me at my house. They wanted information and they made it clear they were going to beat it out of me. A fight did indeed occur. I can't say I won, but they learned the hard way not to mess with me.

The second, and last, interaction with Bang-Bang happened one afternoon in Smyrna. I'd been surveilling their biker club for most of the day. When Bang-Bang drove out on his bike, I drove up beside him and invited him for a beer. We met at a place called Mona's Paradise.

We only talked about two things. The arson of my garage and Flaky's murder charge. I later found out the Dogs had nothing to do with the arson, and Flaky had taken a manslaughter plea. So, what was it then? My mind was racing through a myriad of questions, but I did not dare ask any. Instead, I frowned, as if in deep, confused thought. I caught Hayden eyeing me.

"You seem lost in thought, Thomas."

I shrugged. "I'm searching my memory but I'm still drawing a blank and I can't remember the last time I patronized any bar in Smyrna, not since the Omni Hut closed down, and that's been a while now. Are you guys certain you have the right person?"

Georgie scoffed. Hayden continued staring. I gave a helpless shrug.

"I don't know what else to say. Your source is either mistaken or they have some kind of ulterior motive going on and they're purposely lying to you. Besides, the way you two are acting, you're not being honest with me about the real purpose of your visit."

When I said it, Hayden stared, his poker face set in stone. Georgie glanced over at Hayden, who acted like he didn't notice, and then smirked.

"We have you on surveillance video, bub," he declared.

I kept my own poker face. I'm sure his little trick had worked on other people, causing them to admit some sort of culpability, but not me. I shrugged again.

"I don't know how that can be unless it's somehow been created. You know how it is with computers these days. You can fabricate anything. I saw a video the other day of Kennedy and Hitler in a threesome with Marilyn Monroe. I don't know how, but it looked real."

Georgie scowled and then glanced at Hayden again, looking for guidance. Hayden's smile had disappeared, replaced with a somber gaze.

"Are you aware it is a federal crime to lie in an investigation?" he asked.

"I've heard that," I said.

It was sort of true, but under this scenario, any kind of obstruction law would not apply. I wasn't going to say it though, let them think they were smarter than me. Hayden waited to see if I had anything else to say, but I merely stared.

I guess my façade worked, at least for now. He slapped his knees lightly and stood. I stood as well. The smile returned and he ran a hand down his tie.

"Well then, it appears we were mistaken. Since you don't remember knowing Mister Todd, our time here is for naught. We'll be going now. It was nice to meet you, Thomas Ironcutter. I'm sure we'll speak again."

He extended his hand again, like we had developed a harmonious friendship during this ten-minute conversation. I accepted and shook it. Georgie didn't bother. Instead, he lingered behind as Hayden walked to the car. He was smirking as he stared at me, like he had a secret.

"Is there something you want to say, Georgie?" I asked.

He glanced again at Hayden, who was getting into the Durango and not paying attention to us. Georgie leaned closer. "The next time I see you, I'll be charging your ass with murder."

He said it quietly, like he was wishing me a fond farewell, but it was undeniably a threat. I could have asked him what he meant by it, but before I had a chance, he abruptly turned and walked to their car.

I watched them on my phone and made sure the security gate closed properly as they drove away. Putting my phone in my pocket, I walked inside, locked the doors, and set my alarm. I was tired, dead tired, but it was going to take a few before I could wind down enough to sleep. I'd never admit it to him, but Georgie's veiled threat unnerved me.

Sitting at my desk, I booted up my laptop and began searching the internet. Although I didn't have the computer skills my buddy Ronald had, it only took a couple of minutes to find what I was looking for. The Daily News Journal, Murfreesboro's quaint daily paper, had an article of a man who had died after being found unconscious on the bathroom floor of a bar in Smyrna.

There was a follow-up article in which none other than Detective George Thompson was interviewed about the incident. He declared the incident a murder and even said, "We are actively pursuing leads in this brutal murder and have identified a person of interest."

Senseless? Murder? I wondered how he reached those conclusions. This was odd. Yeah, I'd knocked the hell out of a punk who'd tried to bean me in the head with a beer bottle in the men's room. He fell to the floor, unconscious. There were no eyewitnesses and I left immediately after. I guess when he hit his head it had killed him.

I thought back to Georgie's smug expression when he told me he was going to pin a murder charge on me. Hell, I bet he even had a copy of the newspaper article framed and hanging on his wall. He was out to get me, no doubt.

The bigger question, why was a federal prosecutor involved? I was so fatigued I couldn't even come up with a viable hypothesis.

"I guess I'll find out when they come arrest me," I muttered and headed to bed.

CHAPTER 3

Ronald had recently shown me a neat little trick with my phone. It had a do not disturb function. When it was turned on, the phone did not ring, and all incoming calls automatically went directly to voicemail. Plus, you could program in numbers that would bypass the do not disturb and ring anyway. I only had a couple of numbers that bypassed it. One of them was Marti. She was calling now.

"What are you doing? You sound like I woke you up," she said.

I glanced at the clock. It looked like I'd only slept for four hours.

"Yeah, I've been out of town and drove all night. What's up?" I asked.

"I'm calling to remind you about tomorrow. You promised you'd come."

She was referring to a potluck dinner at Mick's Place. It was a custom that Mick had started a few years ago. On Labor Day, the regulars would get together. It usually happened on Monday, but this year the regulars took a vote and decided to have it on Saturday.

"Yeah, I should be able to make it," I said.

"Please don't be a no-show, Thomas," she pleaded. "I really need you here for moral support. Besides, I'm having some problems with the books, and I want you to look it over."

I held in a sigh. After Mick died, his wife closed the business. All she wanted to do was move back to Korea to be with her family. Marti approached me and asked if I would finance her purchase of the bar. I talked it out with Kim and found Mick had actually owned the property, a prime piece of commercial real estate near I-65. I bought it all for under market value and Marti took over Mick's Place.

"Alright, I'll be there around six, but I'm not staying long," I said.

"Thanks, Thomas. The regulars keep asking why you don't hang out anymore. They'll be glad to see you. I will too."

After hanging up, I thought about going back to sleep but decided I'd rather go play in my shop. I got cleaned up, dressed in some old jeans and a tee shirt before fixing a large glass of iced water. As soon as I walked in my shop, I felt a little better. I had plans of spending the entire weekend in it. I'd made a lot of progress, but there was still work to be done, and working on things helped me think.

Number one on my mind was the death of the idiot who had attacked me in the dive bar. I'd put him to sleep with a hard right fist to the chin, but that's not what killed him. I remembered the sound of his head hitting the floor. It was dirty linoleum tile, but I suspected the subfloor was concrete.

Maybe I should have stuck around, it was a clear case of self-defense, but I didn't want to be subjected to the subsequent investigation. Now I was in a pickle. I had a sudden thought while I was wiring up the subpanel for the air compressor. Finishing it, I wiped my hands and called an old friend, Harvey Wilson, the former sheriff of Rutherford County.

"Hey Harvey, how are you?" I asked.

"Good buddy, what're you up to?"

"I have a favor to ask."

"If it involves cucumbers and KY jelly, I ain't interested," he replied with a guffaw.

"Nothing like that this time," I said. "I need to get some information on a barroom fight, but I need it on the down low."

"That's a little bit vague, buddy. You want to fill me in?" he asked.

"I'll do what I can, my client is fuzzy on the details, but there was a little incident in a biker bar located in the Smyrna city limits. It's called…"

He cut me off. "Mona's Paradise."

"You know of it?" I asked.

"Yep. I went to high school with the owner, Mona. She was a year younger than me. We had some good times together."

"With Mona?" I asked, remembering how rough she looked.

"Yep. Back in the day she was a good-looking little filly with a blue-ribbon backside. Life hasn't been kind to her, but trust me, at one time she was beautiful."

"Okay, if you say so. Anyway, my client thinks he has information on a fight or something that occurred there back in June. I'm having trouble finding out anything about it, but I think that idiot George Thompson is assigned the case. It seems weird because the bar is in Smyrna city limits."

"If it was something serious, like a murder, the sheriff's department may have exercised jurisdiction and taken over the investigation," he said.

"That's probably it," I said.

"Hmm, yeah, that's something I might be able to do. Let me make some phone calls and I'll get back to you."

I clicked over to the incoming call. It was my friend and erstwhile car restoration partner, Bubba.

"Hey, are you at home?" he asked.

"Yeah, why?" I asked.

"Nate has a job for us. He wants us to fix up a car. It's going to be an anniversary present for his wife."

"What kind of car?"

"Some kind of foreign car," he said. "How about I load it on the tow truck and bring it over? We can look it over and decide if we want to do it."

It was the last thing I wanted to do. All I wanted this weekend was to be alone in my shop. But Nate Askew was like Harvey, he was one of the few friends who didn't turn their back on me when I'd been accused of murdering my wife.

"Yeah, bring it on by," I found myself saying.

He showed up five minutes later, which told me he was already on the way before he called. Parking, he got out, walked around to the rollback portion of the truck, and unhooked the bungee cords that were holding a tarp in place.

"Are you familiar with this kind of car?" he asked.

I was, although I'd not seen one in a while. It was an Austin Healey Sprite, a small, two-door convertible made in Britain.

"Where did he find it?" I asked.

"It was his wife's car back when she was a teenager," Bubba said.

I hopped up on the tow truck and inspected it closer.

"It's a 1964 Mark III," I told Bubba.

"Is that a good one?" he asked.

"I don't think they're high on the collector's list, but it's a unique car. Let's have a look under the hood."

It looked like the original engine, an underpowered four-cylinder. Not something that I'd buy, but that didn't matter. What mattered was the condition. It was grimy, but I didn't see any of the telltale signs that an idiot had worked on it.

"He said it still runs, but the transmission is acting up and it runs a little hot," Bubba said.

I closed the hood and looked under it. My inspection was cursory, but I didn't see any frame damage or deep rust. That was a good sign. I hopped down and brushed my hands off.

"What does he want us to do, exactly?"

"He said he wanted us to go over the drivetrain and undercarriage. He said you know how to rebuild transmissions, is that true?"

"Yeah, that one will be easy. Finding the parts will be hard but rebuilding it is no problem. I saw a coolant leak around the water pump, that's probably why it's running hot. If there's no surprises, we can get this knocked out in a month or two. Did he tell you what his budget is?"

"He thinks three thousand will take care of everything, but if you find any surprises, let him know," he said.

I stared at it a minute. I didn't care anything about fixing up someone else's car, but like I said, Nate had been a good friend.

"I think that's doable. I'm not sure about the price though. Let me get us something to drink and we'll talk it over."

Bubba admired my shop while I got us both glasses of tea. I realized I was famished, but if I fixed dinner with Bubba here, I'd be obligated to fix enough for him, and all I wanted to do was have some time by myself.

Bubba was inspecting the two-post lift when I walked back in the shop. He looked over and grinned.

"Man, you've done a lot to this man-cave," he exclaimed.

"I still have more to do. Finishing everything up is my weekend project."

His grin faltered. "I could help you, if you need me to."

"No, Bubba. I appreciate the offer, but to be honest, all I want this weekend is a little peace and solitude."

His grin returned. "Okay, no problem. In fact, my wife has all these plans for the weekend, and she'd be pissed if I was here rather than home with the family."

"Your family is the most important thing in your life," I said, knowing that I had no family of my own.

Bubba nodded in somber agreement. We talked a little more and made tentative arrangements to start on the car first thing Tuesday morning. After he left, I put the Sprite on the lift and gave the undercarriage a more thorough inspection. There was some surface rust, but nothing overwhelming, and I did not find any evidence of it being involved in any kind of accident. Everything was manual. No computers, no fancy electronics. It was going to be pretty easy to fix this one up.

I locked up the shop, and intended to fix a good meal, but I was too tired. Instead, I ate a couple of sandwiches and watched a little TV before going to bed early. I fell asleep in a manner of seconds and to my relief, had no nightmares.

CHAPTER 4

I arrived at the fitness center promptly at six. The scant number of cars in the parking lot was a good sign. Most people seemed to have other plans for the Labor Day weekend, which meant the gym wasn't going to be crowded and I could get in a serious workout.

Recently, I'd made some life changing decisions. On the day of Mick's funeral, all the pallbearers went to a bar close to the cemetery and got sideways drunk. Me included. I took a long hard look at myself in the mirror the next morning and it wasn't a pretty sight. The face staring back at me looked like hell. It was at that moment I knew that unless I changed my lifestyle, I was going to end up like my friend, and I wasn't ready for that.

I joined a fitness center that same day and worked out religiously. In addition, I minded my diet and had cut back significantly on both cigars and alcohol. Morning was the best time to work out. Less of a crowd but there were regulars who also preferred the morning hours. I always ignored them and kept to myself.

I was still stiff after being cramped in a car for several hours, so I opted for an all-around workout where I hit each muscle group and worked up a good sweat. I decided to finish up with a few minutes on one of the speed bags. There were three of them lined up along the far wall. Ironically, I'd never seen anyone using them.

I chose the one in the middle and soon had a good rhythm going. I was about twenty seconds into it when I caught movement out of my peripheral vision. Someone had walked up and was watching me. I ignored them and kept going. When I finally stopped, I was breathing heavily, and my arms were like rubber.

"How do you do that?"

I turned to the person who had spoken. It was a woman in her twenties, as in barely older than the legal age to drink. She was cute, blonde, fairly fit but skinny. She probably didn't weigh more than a hundred pounds.

"It takes practice," I replied curtly. I didn't know this girl and wasn't in the mood to engage in conversation.

"Can you show me?" she asked with a grin, revealing braces. Did I say she was around twenty-one? More like still a teenager, which made

14

me feel old. I shrugged it off, decided not to be an ass, and gave a small smile in return.

"Yeah, sure. There are different techniques, I'll show you a simple one."

I adjusted the height of the speed bag for her and then instructed her to mimic me as I slowly began working the adjacent bag. She struggled with it, and if I were interested, I would've helped her more. But I wasn't, and I had things to do. When she paused, I gave her another small smile.

"Keep at it, you'll have it down in no time," I encouraged and walked off.

I rushed through some stretching and had made it to the parking lot when I heard her calling out.

"Hey."

I was inclined to ignore her and keep walking, but I stopped and put on a friendly face.

"Thanks for showing me how to do that. Were you a boxer once? You look like you could've been."

"No, nothing like that. Keep practicing and you'll be better at it than I ever was."

"I don't know. I couldn't seem to get the timing down and my arms got tired within seconds." She gave a pouty-face smile. She probably thought she was being flirtatious. If I were twenty years younger, it would've been.

"My name's Danica." She stuck her hand out. I responded with my own extended hand.

"I'm Thomas. It's nice to meet you but I'm a little rushed for time."

"Oh, I understand, I…"

She was interrupted by someone shouting from across the parking lot.

"What is this shit?"

We both turned to the source. A young man with his chest puffed out and arms bowed like he was Popeye was purposely striding toward us. Another kid with sagging pants was following close behind.

"Oh, shit," Danica stammered. When I looked at her, her face was as white as a sheet.

I sighed and my jaw clenched. It was going to be another repeat of a similar incident that'd happened to me not too long ago. This young man was not much older than Danica. He was at least four inches shorter than me, but he had muscle. The kind you get when you spend a lot of time on the weights and supplemented it with steroids.

"I asked a goddamned question," he growled as he approached.

"Vince, what are you doing here?" she asked.

He ignored her and mean-mugged me. "Are you messing with my girlfriend?"

"I'm your ex-girlfriend, Vince, and I can talk to whoever I want," Danica snapped. "You don't own me."

This started a back and forth between the two of them. My first inclination was to walk to my car and leave, but if Vince hurt this little girl, I'd regret walking away.

Both men were young and fit. I didn't want a confrontation, especially now that I knew I was a murder suspect. Even so, I subtly shifted my feet and loosened the grip I had on my bag. Vince argued with Danica a moment longer before focusing on me.

"You've messed with the wrong man's girl, old man. Are you ready for me to whip your ass?"

I frowned. "I'm sorry, my hearing's not so good. Did you say you wanted to lick my ass?"

His friend let out a laugh before he could help himself. Vince's eyes widened and he closed the distance between us. He possibly wrestled back in high school, which for him was probably last year. He was going to get close and then try to throw me down for a little ground and pound. I wasn't going to let him.

As soon as he got close enough, I dropped my bag and hit him with a one-two combination. His knees instantly buckled, and he began stumbling backward. I managed to grab one of his arms and broke his fall somewhat. Luckily, his head did not bounce off the asphalt. He wasn't fully unconscious, but he was addled.

I quickly straightened and squared off with his friend. Thankfully, he didn't want to fight. He put his hands out and shook his head. I pointed at Vince.

"Take care of dumbass. When he comes to, tell him he's got a lot of growing up to do and next time I won't be so nice." I picked up my workout bag and resumed walking to my SUV. Danica came running after me.

"Holy shit," she gushed and stared at me in goofy-eyed amazement. "I've never seen anything like that before. I knew you were a fighter. I wish I could do that."

I ignored her, got in my car, and left the parking lot as quickly as I could without spinning my tires. I was mad. If the curse had been lifted, why was I still getting into these situations? Then the other voice in my head told me if I still had the curse, I'd be in the back of an ambulance right now, or worse.

Arriving home, I went straight to my shop. The only way I was going to calm myself, without lighting up a cigar and slurping down some

Scotch, was to find work. I opened the bay doors and looked around, contemplating what I wanted to do. It was a warm day, upper eighties, and it was hot inside the shop. A commercial ceiling fan was still boxed up and lying off to the side.

"Well, why don't you install it, dumbass?" I said to myself and began unpackaging it.

It took me three hours before I bolted on the last rotor. I was already sweaty from the gym and now I was soaked. I smiled in satisfaction when I flipped the switch and watched the fan come to life.

"Definitely calls for a reward," I said. I went inside, got a cigar, and poured myself a big glass of iced tea. I started to walk back outside but noticed a missed call. It was from Harvey. I immediately called him back.

"Well, this is an odd one," he began.

"How so?" I asked.

"Mona said one of her regulars, a guy by the name of Perry Goforth, was found unconscious in the men's room of the bar. An ambulance hauled him off and that was the last of it, or so she thought. A month later a detective comes swaggering in and began questioning her about it and telling her Perry was murdered."

"Is there any surveillance video?" I asked.

"Nah. She's got a cheap system that isn't too good. Besides, it has a thirty day overwrite," he said.

I nodded to myself in understanding. The cheaper surveillance systems had limited memory and would only store data for thirty days. On day thirty-one, the software begins overwriting. It was the first good news I heard about this nonsense, but then, Harvey burst my bubble.

"They asked her who was present in the bar that day. She didn't remember until they reminded her that Bang-Bang was there. She goes on to say how she remembered a big guy that looked like a mafia enforcer drinking a beer with Bang-Bang. They showed her a photographic lineup. Now, I don't have the skinny, but rumor has it she didn't pick anyone until good ole Detective Thompson helped her out." He paused. "What's going on, Thomas? Or do I want to know?"

I held in a sigh. "All I'll say is, if anything happened, I'm sure it was a case of self-defense," I said.

There was a long pause before Harvey spoke. "I understand. Anyway, the person I talked to said George is going around bragging that he has a big case in the works that's going federal and will make national news."

"That sounds like him. Why'd you ever hire him?" I asked.

"Because his bucktooth uncle is a county commissioner. I needed the votes. He got promoted to detective after I was voted out of office, which tells me his uncle sold out to my competition."

"He's a piece of work," I said.

Harvey agreed. "Yeah, he's an idiot. I never did like him. I'm keeping all my inquiries lowkey, but if you need anything else, let me know."

"I appreciate it, Harvey."

"In the meantime, let me think on this a little bit and maybe I can come up with something that'll make this go away," he said.

After hanging up, I saw it was time for me to clean up and head to Mick's Place. Honestly, the only thing I wanted to do was padlock my gate and hide in my shop, but I made a promise to Marti.

CHAPTER 5

I was so preoccupied I almost drove out in front of a car as I exited my driveway. They laid on their horn as they sped past. Sure, I wasn't paying attention, but they were probably doing around seventy, which was thirty over the speed limit. I made sure there were no other knuckleheads speeding down the road and pulled out.

If it was Georgie's intention to play mind games with that little statement he made yesterday, he'd succeeded. It occupied most of my thoughts. I relived that day at Mona's Paradise once again.

I'd met Bang-Bang there and talked to him about my shop being burned down, among other things. It turned out that nobody from the Satan's Dogs had anything to do with the arson, but I didn't know that at the time.

When our conversation was over, I went to the restroom before driving home. That's when a punk walked in, made some kind of derogatory remark, and tried to bash me in the head with a beer bottle. I had instinctively ducked, swiveled, and drove a right cross into his chin. It was a good punch. His feet flew up in the air and he hit the floor like a sack of day-old dog turds. I still remember the noise his head made when it hit the linoleum. He was out like a light.

I had hurriedly put the little soldier back in my pants and looked him over before walking out. Nobody seemed to be paying any attention to me. Not even Bang-Bang. He'd seemingly forgotten all about me and was flirting with some buxom barfly.

The man didn't know me, but I had no doubt the reason he attacked me was because he had overheard Bang-Bang mentioning I was an ex-cop. The alcohol no doubt fueled his courage and animosity toward cops, and maybe he thought he'd take a cheap shot while I was taking a leak and then brag about it to his friends.

And now he was dead.

During my career as a homicide detective, I had assisted in the investigation of two different fights which we had dubbed one-punch homicides. In both instances, the punch wasn't what killed the victim, it was the impact of their head against a hard object or surface. One of them was the asphalt parking lot. The other one was the hard corner of a bar. The impact caused their brains to swell and bleed. Intracranial hematoma is the technical phrase, and unless it's treated quickly, the victim will die.

I sighed deeply. Did Georgie really have enough evidence to charge me with murder?

I couldn't dwell on it. I had other matters to think about. I wanted a stress-free Labor Day week. Hell, I wanted a stress-free month. That was the whole reason for contacting Kalina and getting that damn curse lifted.

What was I supposed to think about that now? Was the curse really lifted? If it was, why was I a murder suspect? I absently rubbed my pinky finger. Due to the recent application of a razor blade to it, I had permanent nerve damage on the pad and tip. Sometimes it felt like little needles were being poked into it.

I felt certain that any reasonable jury would agree that it was a clear case of self-defense, but I didn't want it to come to that. I could certainly afford the Goldman to represent me, but the billable hours alone would eat away my savings.

"So, what's he got on me?" I mused.

Georgie could most likely be able to prove I was in the bar on the afternoon the victim was found, but there were no actual eyewitnesses to the incident. That being said, was there anyone who could testify that they saw me walking out of the restroom shortly after the punk walked in? I thought of that one man that was walking into the restroom as I was leaving. Had he been interviewed? Could he positively identify me? I didn't know.

I tried to put it all out of my mind as I drove into the parking lot of Mick's Place. I was greeted with a chorus of hellos when I entered, which surprised me. I thought of myself as more of an inconspicuous customer, and not someone who people looked forward to seeing. Marti squealed with delight as she ran over and grabbed me in a tight hug. She then whispered in my ear.

"If you don't mind, let's look over the books before you start drinking," she suggested.

"Yeah, sure," I replied.

I didn't tell her I had no intention of spending the entire night here getting sloshed. My plan, which was not going to be altered by her pressing her big breasts up against me, was to be home in bed no later than ten o'clock.

After engaging in small talk with some of the regulars, Marti beckoned for me to follow her back to the office. She closed the door behind us and motioned for me to take a seat in front of her computer monitor.

"I'm having trouble reconciling a couple of beer vendor's bills," she said.

I looked it over, even though computers and spreadsheets weren't my strongest suit. Even so, I found the problem in only a couple of minutes.

"You're being double billed," I said and then walked her through it. When she understood, she breathed a sigh of relief.

"Thanks, Thomas. It's been driving me nuts."

"No problem, but you have to pay close attention to these rascals. Some vendors are managed by unscrupulous assholes, and they'll try to sneak stuff by you. Put a stop to it right now, otherwise they'll keep doing it."

"Yeah, you're right." She then dropped her head and began rubbing her eyes.

"What else is wrong?" I asked.

She emitted a long sigh. "I've been putting in fourteen-hour days since I reopened the place. After I close, I spend another two hours here working on the books and I never seem to get caught up." She sighed again and I thought she was going to start crying.

I reached over and gave her a hug, which may have been a mistake. She buried her head in the crook of my neck and began loudly sobbing. I held her tighter. She smelled like perfume and cigar smoke, which, under other circumstances, would have been a powerful aphrodisiac.

"It's going to be alright," I assured her.

"I don't know, Thomas. I think I'm over my head."

My heart went out to her. She'd had a hard life, growing up. Her father was a deadbeat, and her mother wasn't much better. She grew up poor, which led her in the direction of stripping for a living as soon as she turned eighteen. That'll make a girl grow up fast. Owning her own business was her first opportunity to make something of herself and at that moment she probably thought she was failing. I held her and waited for the sobs to subside before speaking.

"You're overdoing it," I said.

"What do you mean?"

"You're trying to do it all yourself and you're spreading yourself too thin. The first thing you need to do is hire a bookkeeper. That alone will free up ten to fifteen hours a week, right?"

"Yeah, I guess so," she murmured.

"Maybe you should also hire someone part-time that can help out on the weekends."

"I don't think I can afford one right now. With this new anti-work movement going around, everyone wants twice the minimum wage, and that doesn't count their tips."

"We'll figure it out," I said.

"You have to help me, Thomas," she implored.

"It goes without saying I'm going to help you. I promised that at the beginning, right?"

She bit her lower lip. "You've practically stopped coming in and hanging out. It's like you don't want to be here."

"It's not you," I said. "I was smoking and drinking too much. When Mick died, it was a wakeup call."

She slowly nodded. "I guess I understand, but you can still hang out here. You don't have to drink and smoke."

I smiled. "I suppose I could."

We talked some more and soon she was back to her old self. I realized that when she pressed up against me and sweet-talked me into straightening out the walk-in humidor. Although it took me a little over an hour, I didn't mind. I wanted Marti to be successful, but honestly, if she folded and closed the business, I'd still come out ahead. I'd already had two offers to buy the property. One of them tried to lowball me, but one was a semi legitimate offer of twenty grand higher than I paid for it. That offer alone let me know if I had to, I could sell this property for a nice profit. I chuckled to myself as I rearranged some boxes.

"Thomas Ironcutter, businessman. Who would've thunk it?"

When I finished, I admired my work for a moment before walking out of the humidor and joining the regulars, a few of whom were already well into their cups. Wally was in the middle of telling a story about how Mick had kept crop-dusting him one evening after they'd eaten some potluck chili.

I joined in with a few of my own stories. Everyone wanted me to retell the story of how he'd saved my life one night, and I obliged them. I limited myself to only a single beer and was out the door well before nine.

It was pleasant weather out, and on a night like this it wasn't unusual for me to ride around in my old Cadillac, smoking a cigar and enjoying the ride, but not anymore. Although my Ford SUV was newer, smoother riding, and had a far superior sound system, it wasn't the same.

I was about to drive off when I spotted a man walking across the parking lot. I recognized him about the same time he spotted me. He was walking toward the door, but then abruptly changed direction and began purposely striding toward me. I rolled down my window and unholstered my handgun.

CHAPTER 6

He stopped when he was a couple of feet from my car door. "You're just the man I've been looking for. Do you remember me?" he asked.

"I do. Last time I saw you, you were laid out on the floor. That was after you tried to sucker punch me."

Damned if that didn't sound familiar. It seems like I was a magnet for people trying to sucker punch me.

"Yeah, well, that was all wrong," he said.

"I suppose that's one way of looking at it, but I'll go ahead and warn you right now, I'm not in the mood for any stupid little games. You try anything, the first bullet is going in your sack."

I then raised my gun, rested the barrel across the window frame of the door, and aimed it toward his groin. His eyes widened and he immediately raised his hands.

"Whoa! Hey, I'm not trying to start anything."

"What do you want then?" I asked.

"I heard you were a private investigator and I need your help."

His response surprised me. Like I mentioned, the last time the two of us interacted, he tried to sucker punch me. I was sitting inside with a group of people, including his girlfriend, a busty brunette by the name of Felicity. He seemed to think I was putting the moves on his woman. He was a big guy, taller than me by about an inch, and he had some muscle on him. Rough looking though, like he was a little too friendly with the bottle and other substances. He was currently unshaven, and his features were drawn. He hadn't been sleeping well.

"Help with what?" I asked.

"You remember Felicity?" he responded.

"Yeah, what about her?"

"She's missing, and everybody thinks I killed her."

I stared at him, wondering if he was bullshitting me or something. "Missing?"

"Yeah, and everybody, even the cops, think I killed her," he repeated.

Did he kill her? I didn't know, but I knew what he was about to ask. He was going to ask me to help find her. I already knew what my answer was. My limited interaction with both him and Felicity was enough to know I wanted nothing to do with either of them. I was about to say so, but before I could speak, his next words hit home.

"Please, man. I didn't do anything to her, but nobody believes me. I need help and I don't know what else to do."

Like I said, his words had an effect on me. It wasn't that long ago when people thought I had murdered my wife. I stared at him a moment more before speaking. "You see that table over there?" I motioned at one of the outdoor tables on the sidewalk. "Go over there and sit. Put your hands on the table and leave them there."

He frowned in confusion but did as I said. Once he was seated, I holstered my handgun, got out, and walked over to him. Taking the chair on the opposite side of him, I pulled it a few feet away from the table and sat.

"I'm not agreeing to help you, you probably can't afford me anyway, but I'll listen to what you have to say. I'll warn you now, if I smell bullshit, I'm walking back to my car and leaving." He nodded once. "I never did get your name."

"Art Bell, just like that dude on the radio," he said.

I gave a slight grunt. Art Bell was once a famous late-night talk radio host. He'd developed a huge following by discussing the paranormal, aliens, and other bizarre stuff. I loved listening to him.

"Are you related to him?" I asked.

Art snorted. "Nah. I'm asked that all the time, but there's no relation."

"Alright, tell me what's going on."

"So, me and Felicity, we got this thing. Some days she loves me, some days she hates me. Anyway, we've been seeing each other off and on for the past six months or so. A couple of days ago, she comes by my apartment with her two kids. They stayed the night. And, yeah, before you ask, we had a few drinks and smoked some nug that was pretty strong."

"Nug?" I asked.

He stared. "Yeah, nug. High-grade weed. You know, marijuana."

"Alright."

"Yeah, it was good stuff. It knocked me out. The next thing I know, the sun is up, and her older kid was shaking me and telling me he was hungry. Are you gonna get all antsy if I help myself to a cigarette?"

"Are you armed right now?" I asked.

"No, man," he replied.

"Go ahead then."

I'm not a gullible person and didn't blindly believe him. I watched him closely as he fished a pack and a lighter out of his pocket. He held the pack out, offering me one. I shook my head and waited as he lit one and inhaled deeply.

"Alright, keep going," I prodded.

His face tightened slightly. "It's not the first time she's done this to me. One time, she left the kids with me for two days. But I also thought she maybe went out to McDonalds or somewhere to get us all breakfast. I looked out at the parking lot and didn't see her car, so I tried calling her, but she'd left her phone at my place. I fixed the kids some cereal and sat there for an hour or two waiting on her. Eventually, it was time for me to go to work. She knew my schedule, so she should've come back. I couldn't leave the kids alone, so I ended up calling in and taking a sick day."

"Why didn't you call their father or maybe the grandparents?" I asked.

Art shook his head. "I don't know any of them people and her phone is password locked, so I couldn't look at her contact list or anything. So, anyway, later that evening her phone rings and I'm able to answer. It was her mother. I explain what happened, and the next thing I know, the bitch shows up at the apartment with the cops."

"When was that?"

"Two days ago," he said. "Later that day, the cops come back, only this time there's a detective with them and he had a search warrant. He wanted to question me, but I lawyered up."

"Do you really have a lawyer?" I asked.

"I talked to one, a guy by the name of Bart Waters. After I explained everything, he suggested I give you a call."

That one surprised me. Bart Waters. All the cops called him Bart the Watery Fart. He was a local attorney who was known for his big mouth and crazy antics. The last time he and I interacted, he had threatened to, in his words, ruin me.

"What exactly did he tell you to do?" I asked.

"He said once they find her body I'll probably get charged with murder and that I needed to go ahead and start preparing a defense."

"Alright, but why did he suggest giving me a call?" I asked.

"I told him I thought she was still alive, and I wanted to find her. I know it sounds funny, but I love that crazy woman and want her back. I told him that and he said if anyone could find her, it would be you."

I sat in silence, taking it all in and considered my best course of action. Normally, I would have lit a cigar to help with the thinking process, but I'd already had one for the day and that was my limit. When I faced him, he was staring back at me with a brooding expression.

"My starting fee is one thousand for the first week, plus expenses, and I don't guarantee any results. Can you afford that?"

He continued staring a moment, probably thinking I was ripping him off. I didn't care. After a couple of seconds, he slowly reached into his hip pocket and pulled out his wallet, whereupon he started counting off one-hundred-dollar bills. When he was finished, he handed it over to me.

"Do you want a formal contract written up? I can do it at home and email it to you."

"I don't care anything about that. Just find Felicity."

"Alright, you have officially hired me, so anything you tell me from here on out will be in total confidence. I have a lot of questions to ask you."

"Alright," he said with a singular nod.

We talked for thirty more minutes while I got the specifics from him. When I told him I had enough to get started, he stood and stared a moment before walking off. I watched as he got into his truck and bark the tires as he exited the parking lot.

I pocketed the money and stood. I caught Marti staring through the window at me. I gave her a wink before leaving. I called Percy as I drove.

"Is Felicity Turnbow your case?" I asked, although I already knew the answer.

"Yes, she is. She went missing after visiting with her boyfriend. She left her kids with him. Her car is missing and there's been no activity on her bank account or credit cards. The boyfriend probably killed her, but so far, no body has been found. Why?"

"He's hired me to help him," I said,

"Oh?"

I explained everything, including the night he tried to sucker punch me.

"What's your take on him?" Percy asked.

"Oh, he's probably not thinking beyond tomorrow. It's only a matter of time until he steps on his dick and ends up in prison again," I said.

"Yeah, that's a good analysis. He's a convicted felon with an extensive record, mostly drugs and assaults. He has three kids by three different women, all of whom have permanent orders of protection against him."

"Damn, how does he pay child support?" I asked.

"He's a truck driver for UPS. Believe it or not, those boys and girls make respectable money."

I thought about those one-hundred dollar bills he plunked down on the table. "Yeah, I guess they do."

"So, you're taking his case?" he asked.

"I've taken his money, so I guess I'll help you hunt around for the body."

"Good, I could use some help. The chief says there's no money in the budget for more than one missing person detective and my overtime has been restricted," he said.

"Sounds about right. Have you talked to her kids?"

"Yeah. They said their mom took them over to Art's about five. They know this because the news was on when they walked in. They ordered pizza from Papa John's for dinner and watched TV and at some point both of them fell asleep on the couch. When they woke up the next morning, their mother was gone. There was no fight or arguing. They also said Art and his mom smoked something that smelled awful."

I shook my head in disgust. Personally, I didn't care about marijuana and its legality, but smoking anything in the close proximity of kids was wrong on many levels. My opinion of Art and Felicity sank even further.

"Did the search warrant yield anything?" I asked.

"Nope, only some drug residue. We tried Luminol with negative results. The place wasn't very clean, so he had not cleaned up any crime scene."

"What's your take on it, big guy?" I asked.

"It's a strange one. I'm going to interview two of her friends in the morning. Marley and Melanie Henderson."

"Yeah, I know them. They're nice people, even though they're the ones who introduced me to Felicity. Would you mind if I tag along with you?"

"Not at all. It'll be like old times," he said.

I had to chuckle. I went through the academy with Percy, and we had worked in the homicide unit together, but he'd always been a lone wolf. He'd never had a partner. There was a reason for his aloofness, which I didn't learn until years later.

"Alright, let's meet for breakfast in the morning," I suggested. Percy agreed.

After arriving home, I did some work on the computer, mostly taking notes about the incident at Mona's, and was about to go to bed when my phone rang. Looking at the caller ID, I saw it was Kalina. I started to let it go to voicemail, but then decided to answer.

"How's it going?" she asked.

"All is good, I suppose. How about you?"

"Not so good on this end," she said.

"Do I want to ask?"

"My idiot boyfriend and idiot brother have been arrested for drug trafficking. The narcs padlocked our tattoo shop and seized all the assets," she said.

"I'm sorry to hear that."

"I have to get away from here for a while. Would it be okay to come down and visit for a couple of days?"

I hesitated. I thought I'd seen the last of Kalina Ratkovich and the rest of her family, which I believed was a good thing. Still, she was a decent person and my relationship with Lilith created a soft spot.

"Is it only you?" I asked.

"Only me. Things are pretty messed up here. I only want a place to hang out for a few days without any drama. Maybe you can take me to visit Lilith's grave."

I thought it over a moment. "Alright, sure. When are you coming down?"

CHAPTER 7

I met Percy at a Waffle House restaurant located near the south precinct. We used to eat there frequently when we worked together. We ordered our usuals and engaged in small talk. I was tempted to tell him about the fight at Mona's, but I refrained from doing so. Sometimes, it was better not to include your friends in your personal issues, and he did not need to be dragged into my problem.

After breakfast, we headed to Marley and Mel's house. Since it was Sunday of the Labor Day weekend, I hoped they were home and not spending the day kayaking down the Harpeth River, which was a favorite pastime for them. Mel opened the door wearing her green, two-tone uniform for the animal shelter.

"Well, hey, Thomas. This is a surprise," she said.

I pointed at the uniform. "Do you have to work today?"

She gave a smile. "Hell, the animals don't know it's a holiday. They still need to be cared for."

Marley walked to the door while we were talking. He was wearing sweatpants and a Mario Brothers tee shirt.

"Hey, Thomas, what brings you here?" he asked.

I introduced them to Percy and informed them we were investigating Felicity's disappearance. Their grins evaporated.

"She's really missing this time?" Marley asked.

"It looks that way. Detective Trotter has some questions; may we come in?"

"Oh, yes, of course," he said.

Marley led us to his office, which was meant to be a spare bedroom by the builder. It was decorated the way you'd expect a computer geek to decorate an office, all kinds of electronic knickknacks, along with some scratching posts for the cats, but his server system was nowhere near Ronald's system.

Percy went through the list of typical missing person questions. Both of them answered dutifully. The last time they saw Felicity was three days prior.

"She's flighty sometimes," Mel said. "She's gone missing before but always turned up after a couple of days."

"What caused her to go missing the last time?" Percy asked.

"Well, the official story is she had been under a lot of stress and needed to get away for a couple of days, but she later confided to me she'd met a guy and he flew her to Miami for a weekend of debauchery."

"She referred to it as the C and O weekend," Marley said. "Cocaine and orgies."

"Has she done that before?" Percy asked.

Mel made an unapproving face. "Yeah, she did it to her ex once or twice."

"Does she work?" I asked.

Marley snorted. His wife gave him a look before answering.

"The last time I know of her actually working was when I got her a job at the animal shelter. She lasted two days and never went back. She claimed she was allergic to the animals."

"I'd say it's more like she's allergic to work," Marley quipped.

Mel gave him another look, but reluctantly nodded. "That was three months ago. She hasn't had a job since. She lives off child support and government assistance. Art gives her money from time to time as well. Oh, and sometimes she's successful in cajoling money from her ex."

"More like extorting," Marley murmured. Mel gave another reluctant nod.

Percy went on to ask them if they knew of anyone who would want to hurt her. Mel responded that the only person in her life she felt would hurt her would be Art.

"Yeah, he's hot headed," Marley agreed.

He asked a few more questions about Art before eventually moving on to the other man in her life.

"You mentioned her ex. Do you know him?"

Mel nodded her head. "I've met him, but I don't really know him. He's a nice enough guy in a dull boring sort of way. All he does is work."

Percy jotted a few notes and then paused in thought, which allowed me to jump in.

"Okay, you two probably know her better than most, so help us out. Who can we talk to? There has to be others who she's acquainted with."

The two of them looked at each other in concern. Marley shrugged. Mel pursed her lips before responding.

"Thomas, I honestly think we are her only two friends. I've known her since high school. She was a sweet girl back then, a little high strung, but a good friend." She then frowned and shrugged. "Somewhere along the line her moral compass went haywire. She's ruined all her other friendships."

30

"If it weren't for Mel, I definitely wouldn't have anything to do with her," Marley added.

"Is she the type who would abandon her kids?" Percy asked.

Mel scrunched up her face and voiced her doubts while Marley subtly leaned back out of his wife's peripheral vision and gave a slight nod of the head.

We thanked them for their time and next met with Felicity's ex-husband, who agreed to speak with us, but only if we met somewhere other than his house or his business. We ultimately agreed to meet back at the Waffle House where we'd had breakfast.

Gene Turnbow was a plain looking man with a receding hairline who looked chronically stressed and depressed. He might've played football back in high school, but he'd gone to seed years ago and was now at least fifty pounds overweight. And he was only thirty-six. I moved over so he could sit in the booth.

"Look, I'll make this simple for you guys. I have no clue where she is. I'll say this, it's not the first time she's pulled this stunt. She'll go on and on about how her kids are the most important thing in her life, and then she'll go off on a lark for a few days."

"We understand she pulled this stunt on you once or twice," Percy said.

"Yes, she did, but that didn't sway that bitch of a divorce judge. She gave Felicity full custody and child support, plus five years of alimony, all of which worked out to be about forty-five percent of my income. You don't think I'm working on the Labor Day weekend because I want to, do you? Ask me what I'm doing after I leave my main job? I'll be doing Uber. Sounds like a fun way to spend Labor Day, right? In addition to the fifty hours a week I put in my regular job, I Uber three days a week. The rate I'm going, I'll be lucky if I live to be forty."

I could see the pain etched in the lines of his face as he spoke. Did something happen where he was pushed over the edge and killed her in a moment of blind rage? It could've happened, but my gut told me he wasn't involved in her disappearance. If Percy felt the same way, he didn't show it.

"When was the last time you saw her?" Percy asked.

"Three weeks ago, this past Saturday," he said. "I went to her house to pick up the kids for visitation, but she demanded a thousand dollars or else I couldn't have them." He paused, gritting his teeth. "You want to know something? This woman has ruined my life. The only reason I haven't stuck a gun in my mouth is my kids. If she turns up dead tomorrow, I won't shed a single tear, but I didn't do anything to her and I never would. I'd never do that to my kids. Now I have to find a way of getting them from their grandmother, and that won't be easy. She's every bit as crazy as her daughter."

He took a sip of coffee, checked the time on his cell phone and sighed. "I've got to get back to work."

"We appreciate you meeting with us," Percy said.

He scooted out of the booth, which was not easy for him, stood, and paused a moment, staring at both of us thoughtfully. "You gentlemen have been cordial and polite, but I don't want to speak to you guys anymore without an attorney present." His lips tightened and I could see his jaw muscles flexing. He started to say something else, but then gestured at the unfinished cup.

"Thanks for the coffee."

He walked out of the restaurant. I watched him drive away in an older model Chevy.

"What do you think?" I asked Percy.

"My gut says he's probably thought about killing her many times, but he didn't do it."

"Yeah, me too," I said. "What about the mother? What does she have to say?"

"She's one of those bitter, cynical types, all men are evil, etcetera, etcetera. She's mad at Felicity because now she's stuck with the two grandkids. I suggested taking them to the father, but she was adamantly against it. She's convinced he has his bags packed and at the first opportunity he's going to take them out of the country, or some such nonsense. Before I left, she asked me how she could go about getting child support from him."

"Alright, what's next for you?" I asked.

Before he could answer, his phone buzzed. He pulled it out, read a text message, and scowled. "Well, it looks like I'm heading back to the office. Bartlett has called an emergency meeting."

"On Sunday?" I asked. He nodded. "About this case?" I asked.

"No, another case. It's a double murder that happened in West Nashville a couple of weeks ago. A couple, male and female, were found murdered in their car. An anonymous tip came in yesterday stating they were attempting to blackmail an ex-boyfriend of hers that is worth several million, and that's what got them killed. He apparently hired two men to come up to Nashville and murder them." He gave me a look. "A precinct detective was originally assigned to it, but now that the murder-for-hire plot has been discovered and the suspects identified, guess who has taken over the case?"

I smirked. "Our little buddy, Ian Poston."

"Yep. He convinced Bartlett that this case should be top priority, hence the reason for the meeting. I'm thinking I am going to be sidetracked off my other open cases, including this one."

I nodded my understanding. That's the way it often went, cases got prioritized and missing person cases had the lowest priority. Unless they were somebody famous or important.

"No worries," I said. "I'll keep at it, and if I learn anything, I'll let you know."

"I appreciate it, brother," Percy said.

After leaving the Waffle House, I decided to go to the apartments where Art lived. I knew without asking that Percy had already performed a canvass. Even so, I was going to do the same.

The multi-unit complex was on Bell Road. I guessed around two hundred buildings, which was probably around eight hundred apartments. I knew they'd been built several years ago, but the place was well maintained. Turning in, I parked in the area designated for visitors, got out, and walked around. I was impressed. The parking lot had a fresh coat of sealer, and the grounds were free of litter. A lawn care crew was hard at work and a maintenance man was servicing a HVAC system.

I walked over to the area of parking that was reserved for Art's building. There were two spots with his apartment number professionally painted in white numbers on the pavement. Both were empty. I squatted down beside them staring at the asphalt in an attempt to spot anything out of the ordinary. A blood drop, strands of hair, any possible hint of forensic evidence. But there was nothing.

I slowly stood and continued staring, pondering the feasibility of coming back after dark and spraying the area with Luminol. I texted Percy and asked if it had already been done. It took a couple of minutes for him to respond, and when he did, he had a pdf attached to the text message. When I opened it, I saw that it was a supplemental report from the crime scene tech detailing all the areas where she had attempted Luminol tests, including the parking lot. I nodded in understanding and admiration. Percy was always thorough. Putting my phone away, I turned to see an elderly woman standing near a car and staring at me.

"Good morning, ma'am," I said with a friendly smile.

"Who the hell are you?" she demanded.

"My name is Thomas Ironcutter. I'm investigating the recent disappearance of a woman who was staying with her boyfriend here."

She made a face. "Yeah, I've already been questioned by one of you detectives."

I gave a professional head nod. "That's good. Her boyfriend is awfully worried about her."

She snorted now and motioned me closer to her. When I was within a foot, she leaned forward and spoke in a low voice. "I didn't exactly say it to that other detective, but that man is a rotten, no-good sonofabitch."

I stared in surprise. She smirked, amused at my astonishment.

"Pardon my language, but it's what he is. Every night when he comes home, he takes a piss on the shrubbery over by the stairs, and I can't prove it, but I'm certain he keyed my car a few months ago. I've lived here for five years. Never had a lick of trouble from anyone. I asked him one day not to double-park with that ugly redneck looking truck of his. The next morning there was a big scratch mark running down the side of my car. Look, it's still there."

She pointed toward an older but clean Toyota Corolla that was parked in the reserved spot next to Art's. I could clearly see a scratch mark running down the passenger side.

"That wasn't very nice," I remarked.

"Damn right, it wasn't," she agreed. "I complained to management to get some surveillance cameras for the parking lot, but I don't know if they'll ever do it."

I nodded. A lot of the newer apartment complexes now had cameras everywhere, and she was right, this place could use a few as well.

"Can I show you a picture?" I asked and retrieved my phone without waiting for an answer. I pulled up a picture of Felicity and handed my phone to her.

"Have you seen her recently?" I asked.

"Yeah, I've seen her. She walks around with her chest stuck out like those tits are the crown jewels."

I chuckled. "Yes, she does. When is the last time you saw her?"

"The day before she disappeared, like I told that other detective. Don't y'all ever talk to each other?"

I offered a humble smile. "We do, but we aren't perfect."

"Well, she had two kids with her. Now, I know what you're going to ask because that other detective has already asked. No, I didn't notice anything strange, and I didn't see them arguing or anything like that."

"Is your apartment next to theirs?" I asked.

"Yes, it is. I will say he's normally a quiet person. Plays his stereo every morning before he goes to work, but that's it. I didn't hear any kind of commotion if that's what you're wondering, and I didn't see her leave. You people think she's been murdered, don't you?"

"It's hard to say, but she's definitely missing," I replied. "Are there any other neighbors you think I should talk to?"

She frowned a moment and then motioned me closer. "You didn't hear this from me, but the rumor is the people who live down there on the corner unit sell drugs. Now, I'm not saying that because they're black, that's just what I heard."

"Alright, thank you for your time, ma'am."

I didn't care if the people she referred to were drug dealers, but if they were, they'd be extremely reluctant to talk. I still looked too much like a cop to simply knock on their door and pretend to be hip, and down, and whatever else they called it these days, but I was going to try to talk to them. A young man with long twists in his hair, or braids, or whatever they were called, answered the door. If my appearance unnerved him, he didn't show it.

"Hello, my name is Thomas Ironcutter. I am assisting in the investigation of a missing woman. Would you mind if I spoke to you about it?"

"I don't know anything about a missing person. Who is it?" he asked.

"Her name is Felicity Turnbow. She's the girlfriend of the gentleman who lives over there," I said, pointing at the building where Art lived. The man responded with a shrug. I tried a different tact.

"Listen, I'm not a cop. I'm a private investigator and was hired by her boyfriend. He implied he bought his nug here."

The man's eyes widened slightly. My wild guess was on the money.

"Man, I don't know anything about that missing woman," he said.

"But you've seen her around, right?" I asked. He answered with a shrug. "When's the last time you saw her?"

"I don't know, maybe a couple of days ago. She was with him."

"Were they getting along?"

"Yeah, I guess so. They weren't fighting or anything if that's what you're asking," he said. "I don't know anything else."

He was getting antsy, so I didn't push it. "Okay, I appreciate it."

I fished a business card out of my wallet. "Here's my card. If you can think of anything, I'd appreciate a call."

He gave a slight grin and shut the door. At least he didn't throw my card back at me. I called Art as I was walking back to my SUV. I didn't want to call him. I didn't like the man, but I had accepted his money, so I needed to keep him in the loop.

"Hello, Art, this is Thomas Ironcutter."

"Hey dude, I'm glad you called me back so quickly. How's the case going?" he asked. I could hear the sounds of road traffic in the background and assumed he was driving.

"It's not going well. I've spoken with the detective assigned to the case."

"Yeah? What'd he say, other than he thinks I did it?" he asked.

"Honestly, Art, it's not looking good for you. You have a history of domestic violence and other charges that would indicate you have anger issues. One could speculate that you got upset with Felicity and your temper got the best of you."

There was a moment where all I could hear was a horn honking and some cussing. "Alright, sorry about that. People around here don't know how to drive. So, what were you saying?"

"I'm saying you're looking like a good murder suspect." I was being blunt, but that was intentional. "Listen, I don't think I'm going to be able to help you. Your best bet is pay your attorney and let him guide you. I've only spent a few hours on this, so you're entitled to a partial refund."

"No, fuck that," he said angrily. "I want you to clear my name."

"I'm not sure I can do that," I said.

"You gotta help me, dude. I don't have anyone else on my side."

I was about to tell him I wasn't on his side either, but back when I was suspected of murdering my wife, I could count on one hand how many people were on my side. I sat there thinking it over for so long he asked me if I'd hung up on him.

"No, I'm still here." I paused another few seconds, sighed, and then responded. "Alright, I'll finish out the time you've paid me for and then we'll see where we're at."

"Alright, I appreciate it," he said.

"Do I understand correctly; her car is a white Kia Sorento?" I asked.

"Yeah. It's easy to spot. She was drunk one night and backed into something. It has a big dent in the bumper on the passenger side."

"Is there anywhere she might be staying at? Maybe a friend nobody else knows about?"

"Not that I know of," Art said. "She had her little secrets and she liked to tell tall tales, so I guess she could be anywhere."

I thought a moment and asked him a question designed to see how truthful he was.

"What kind of relationship did she have with her ex-husband?" I asked.

"She hated him, and if you were to listen to her, he was an evil SOB who ruined her life, but I happen to know he caught her cheating, that's why he divorced her. I listened in on a phone call one night where she cussed him like a dog, but he kept his cool the whole time. Much better than I would've done. She's tried to talk me into kicking his ass a few times, but I never did."

"What did they argue about?" I asked.

"It was always about money. She'd use those two kids as pawns to get money out of him. He has his own business and according to her, he hides his profits, so he doesn't have to pay his fair share of child support." He laughed without humor. "You know, when we first hooked up, she told me he was a deadbeat who refused to pay child support. I found out later that was a lie. He's always made his payments."

He confirmed what I already knew about the ex-husband, and he unknowingly raised his credibility with me.

"Alright, if you can think of anything else, any friend or acquaintance to speak to, anywhere to look for her, give me a call," I said.

"Alright, dude."

"And stop calling me dude," I said and hung up.

The man irritated me, no doubt about it, but unfortunately, he was my client, and I had a duty to my client.

"Okay, *dude*, you better be worth it," I muttered.

CHAPTER 8

The former sheriff of Rutherford County, Harvey Wilson, called me as I was driving home. "I've learned a little bit more. Do you have time to talk?" he asked.

"Absolutely," I replied.

"One of Perry's friends found him on the floor in the men's room. An ambulance and a uniformed cop responded. They deduced he was drunk and slipped. The cop didn't even take a report. So, he dies a day later, and it's originally classified as accidental. That's why it was assigned to George. Everyone is beginning to understand how inept he is, so they give him the meaningless work. All the other detectives are busy with other cases. You know, real cases. This is the part where you ask me about the other cases."

"Alright, what about the other cases?" I asked.

"They've recently found two dump jobs, two women that lived in the county and had been reported missing. For some reason, the current sheriff wants it kept under wraps. So far, he's been able to keep it out of the media. I guess he thinks the public will go into mass hysteria if they find out. So, the only detective working the Goforth case is your fat buddy, and like I said, it started out as a simple accidental death investigation."

"What changed?" I asked.

"Someone is claiming to have witnessed Goforth being assaulted," he said.

That's what I'd suspected, and I had an idea who it was.

"Do you know who?" I asked.

"Now, that's where it gets interesting. The sheriff calls George into his office one day, and after a few minutes, George comes out and hightails it out of there. He comes back a couple of hours later and tells anyone that'll listen that his case is a murder and he's going to bust it wide open. Oh, and then there was the bullshit of how it was going to be national news and all that happy horse shit.

"Oh, and he's already named you as the prime suspect. I don't know what kind of case he thinks he has against you, but I don't think you have much to worry about."

"Yeah, I suppose. Alright, enough about me. I'm currently working a missing female case and so I'm curious about those dump jobs. What can you tell me about them?"

"Two women. Both dumped in rural areas of Rutherford County, and both had evidence of antemortem and postmortem injuries. Sexual assault too. That's all I know."

"Have they been identified?" I asked.

"Not that I'm aware of," Harvey said.

"And no suspects identified either, I bet. Who's the primary?"

"Officially, McAdoo is the primary, but there's some jurisdiction friction going on. The TBI has decided to get involved and it's become a massive clusterfuck. It doesn't help that the sheriff has been playing junior detective as well. Did I ever tell you he didn't even graduate high school? The kid was so stupid that instead of a diploma they gave him a certificate of attendance. The word is he's hamstringing the investigation with all kinds of crazy nonsense. He's even called a psychic hotline."

"Wow, that sounds pathetic. You ought to come out of retirement and run for reelection," I said.

Harvey grunted. "If I did that, my wife would leave me."

I drove home in silence and thought about my latest dilemma. This was not good. As if I were sending out a psychic signal, my phone rang. The caller ID showed the number was from the Federal Government.

"Good afternoon, Thomas. This is Hayden Westlake. How are you?"

The man was polite, I'd give him that, but I didn't bother with any superficial pleasantries. "What can I do for you, Hayden?"

"I would like to meet with you. Without Detective Thompson being present. Would you be agreeable to that?"

My first inclination was to tell him to take a hike, but I had to admit, I was curious. What did he have on me and what did he want from me?

"Alright, I suppose we could," I said. We agreed to meet Tuesday morning at nine sharp.

I stared at my phone after hanging up. "At least I'll get to enjoy Labor Day."

I had a sudden thought and realized Percy had said nothing about Felicity's residence. I called him but it went to voicemail. After a moment, I received a text.

Stuck in a crazy meeting. What's up?

I texted back, asking about the residence.

Searched and processed. Short answer - nothing.

I frowned. I knew Percy was thorough and would not let a crime scene tech do a half-assed search. Even so, I asked for the address. He knew what I was going to do and sent the address a moment later.

What would I do differently? There was a police search and then there was a Thomas Ironcutter search. I checked my kit to ensure I had everything I needed and plugged the address into my map app.

Felicity lived in a condo in an area of Nashville commonly referred to as Brantioch, which was an area in between Antioch and Brentwood. Nobody who lived there called it that. Antioch was synonymous with minorities and blue-collar workers, whereas Brentwood was synonymous with rich white folks. Everyone who lived in Brantioch always adamantly proclaimed they lived in Brentwood and would argue with you vociferously if you dared to correct them.

There was no alarm, and the lockset was a cheap brand you could buy at Walmart. Traces of fingerprint powder were noticeable around it. I used my pick set and had the door opened in seconds. Stepping inside, I softly closed the door and waited, listening for anyone stirring. Satisfied there was nobody home, I began looking.

I started with a slow walk-thru, attempting to take everything in and get a feel for Felicity Turnbow. Genius loci if you will. The condo was a two-story affair. Den, kitchen, dining room, utility room, and a half-bath downstairs. Three small bedrooms were located upstairs, along with a bathroom. The kids' rooms were messy, but they had toys and clothes. Felicity's bedroom was worse. There were clothes everywhere and a brief sniff of the sheets indicated she'd not washed them lately.

The downstairs consisted of a den and kitchen with an adjoining dining area. The furniture was nice but dated. There was a moderate number of dirty dishes stacked in the sink, and the automatic dishwasher was full too. The utility room also had a fair amount of dirty clothes stacked up, but there were some clean clothes still lying in the dryer. They'd been in there long enough to be wrinkled.

She wasn't Suzie Homemaker. If she were single, it wouldn't matter, but she had two kids depending on her. I tried not to be judgmental of people, but the more I learned about Felicity, the more I realized she was not a decent person. I felt sorry for the kids.

My next step was a thorough search. It took me about three hours, and when I was finished, I had nothing. Her nightstand contained a small marijuana pipe and a vibrator, but those were the worse things I found, if one did not count her poor housekeeping. There was no little black blook with damning information, no cryptic notes, nothing. The dry erase board in the kitchen only had dates for children's functions. If she had a tablet or laptop, it was not present. I made a mental note to ask Percy about that.

I spent another hour looking for any hidden nooks or crevices. I even went into the attic and muddled around. I came up empty.

Leaving Felicity's condo, I started walking toward my SUV when a clean late model Dodge Challenger drove in and parked in the reserve spot for the condo next door to Felicity. A hot looking woman clad in spandex shorts and a crop top got out. She looked like she'd been working out. I took a chance and walked over. She had straight, sable brown hair flowing down to her shoulders and the outfit was skintight, showing off an impeccable figure.

"Excuse me," I said as I walked toward her. She glanced back with an impatient stare and dipped a hand into her gym bag, as if she were getting her gun or pepper spray ready for use.

"Hi. I'm a private investigator looking into the disappearance of your neighbor. May I have a moment of your time?"

She continued staring, but at least I'd gotten her to stop walking. "Do you have any identification?"

"Yes, ma'am, I do," I said. I pulled out my wallet, and showed her my State of Tennessee Private Investigator's license. She maintained her distance while she scanned it. I held out my arm to help. When she was finished, she looked up.

"So, what do you want? I've already spoken to a detective. A big guy. Maybe a little bigger than you."

"Yes, ma'am, that sounds like Detective Percy Trotter."

"Yeah, that was his name. I answered all his questions," she said.

"I understand, but if I can ask for your indulgence, I'll only take a couple of minutes of your time," I said it with a smile, hoping my charming manner would work. If it did, she didn't outwardly show it.

"I only have a few minutes, so let me see if I can help speed this up. I don't know her very well, but I don't like her. She's a bitch with a foul mouth, her kids are loud and bratty, and she tried to make a play for my boyfriend not too long ago."

"I'm not surprised," I said before I could catch myself.

She gave a small, tight, grimace. "Yeah. He was staying here while I was gone. I'm a flight attendant and I travel frequently. She seems to think that means she can hit on my boyfriend and let her white trash boyfriend park his white trash truck in my parking spot whenever he wants. And yeah, I've met him. Art something. He's made a pass at me more than once, and for the record, I wouldn't hook up with him if he were the last man on earth."

"Wow, you're to the point," I said in admiration.

She gave me a hint of a smile now. "Oh, I almost forgot, during the timeframe she went missing, I was in Puerto Rico. The last time I saw her was maybe a week before that. I avoid her whenever I can."

"Has she had any other gentleman callers, other than Art?" I asked.

She shook her head. "Not that I know of. Like I said, I'm not home that often. This was my grandmother's condo and the only reason I'm living here is because it's free. The rent in Nashville is sky high and getting worse every day."

"Yes, it is," I agreed. I was still holding my wallet, so I took the opportunity to fish out a business card. "If it's not too much trouble, could you call me if you think of anything?"

I offered the card. She readily took it and stared at it a moment. "Yeah, okay. Is there anything else?"

"I think you've covered it all, but please call if you think of anything else. Day or night," I said with a smile.

She returned my smile with one of her own now. She had flawless teeth that enhanced her attractiveness. Her boyfriend was a lucky man. I thanked her for her time and left before I made a fool of myself.

CHAPTER 9

The Middle Tennessee District Attorney's Office was located at the Estes Kefauver building at Ninth and McGavock, but for some reason they were currently operating out of office located on Church Street. There was a private parking lot across the street, and it wasn't cheap. The thought of having to pay to park and go listen to someone who was about to threaten me with possible imprisonment chaffed my ass.

William Goldman, the grandson of my friend Sherman, drove into the parking lot as I was getting out of my SUV. Arrogant and cocky, he was driving a brand-new blue BMW Model M4. It was a beautiful car, and I had no doubt that with all the upgrades he had on it, it cost him close to a hundred grand. It was a testament to his success as a hotshot lawyer.

He emerged from his car like he owned the world. He was wearing a custom-tailored charcoal gray suit and a pair of handcrafted leather shoes. The sunglasses alone probably cost over a hundred. I was wearing dark gray slacks, a matching sport coat, and a white starched button-down shirt. I thought I looked snappy, but I looked like a bum next to William.

I walked over to him while he was admiring a couple of office girls walking along the sidewalk and grinned when he saw me.

"This is going to be fun," he said.

"If you say so," I replied.

"Stick with what we talked about last night and this will be over quick," he said.

I didn't need his directives, but I knew it made him feel good to have a take charge attitude, so I didn't admonish him.

We walked in the front lobby where two male security guards were sitting behind bulletproof glass. One was doing something on his phone, the other scowled at us like a typical old man with a chronic case of inflamed hemorrhoids. He punched a button on an intercom.

"Help you?" he asked.

"We have an appointment with Hayden Westlake," I said.

"I'll have to give him a call and confirm it," he said.

"Please do, and please tell him if we're kept waiting for longer than five minutes, we're leaving," William declared.

The guard was not amused and stared at William a moment before picking up the phone. When the other party answered, the guard made a point of speaking loudly and said that some punk lawyer was demanding to speak with General Westlake. He listened to the response for a few seconds, hung up, and gave us both another annoyed glare.

"Someone will be here shortly." He then sat back down and made a pointed effort of ignoring us.

We only waited a minute before a young woman opened the interior security door and poked her head through. The security guard took his cue and faced us.

"Empty your pockets of all contents, place them in the bowl, and walk through the scanner," he said.

We complied without argument. Both William and I had been through this process before. Most of our valuables and metal objects were locked in our respective cars. All we had was our key fobs.

"Follow me, please," the lady said. She was an attractive woman in her late twenties, wearing a flattering business outfit, a moderate amount of jewelry, and pretty blonde hair. William attempted to engage her in conversation, but she ignored him. No doubt she had plenty of attorneys vying for her attention.

Exiting the elevator, she led us down a hallway and to a windowless room. "If you will please have a seat, Mister Westlake will be with you shortly."

The room was plain. There were no decorations, only a rectangular table and four chairs. We each chose one and sat on one side of the table. William took it in.

"Nice office," he quipped.

I knew what he meant. This wasn't a meeting. That's why we were in this room instead.

"I've no doubt the young lady is in the monitor room and actively recording us at this very moment." I raised my voice slightly. "Please tell Hayden our time is important and not to be wasted."

There was no physical response, but my statement had the desired effect. Within a minute, Hayden walked into the room. He was accompanied by a gentleman who was a little older than me and wearing a nice, tailored suit. It was almost as nice as William's, which probably cost a grand or more, but his five-hundred-dollar shoes complimented it splendidly.

"Good morning, Thomas, I'm glad you could make it," Hayden said. We shook hands like we were old golfing buddies. William stuck his hand out.

"I'm William Goldman, Thomas's attorney. It's a pleasure to meet you, sir," he said, and I realized he wasn't directing his attention to Hayden, but to the other gentleman.

"Ah, I believe I remember you, William. How's your grandfather?"

"Still alive and kicking," William said with a pleasant smile. Almost as an afterthought, William extended his hand to Hayden. "And it's a pleasure to meet you, sir. Shall we get started?"

"Certainly," Hayden said and the four of us sat.

"Before I allow my client to say anything, I want to know what the purpose of this meeting is all about. That will include you formally stating whether or not you believe my client is suspected of, or being accused of a crime or crimes, and if he is, what are the specifics of the accusations."

Hayden gave his used car salesman smile. "Of course. We will get into all of the specifics."

"Yes, you will start with those specifics, or this meeting is over," William said. He was not returning Hayden's fake smile. He then pulled his sleeve back, revealing a Blancpain watch. It was a beautiful watch and probably cost as much as the car Hayden drove. William made a point of taking a few seconds to look at it before speaking. "I have another appointment at eleven, so please let's not bother with any unnecessary preamble."

Hayden's smile faltered and after a moment he cleared his throat. "Very well. In June of this year, your client, Thomas Ironcutter, was in a business known as Mona's Paradise Bar, located in Smyrna, Tennessee. He followed a man into the restroom, attacked him, and left him seriously injured. The victim lapsed into a coma and later died at a local hospital."

"I see. May I ask if there are any eyewitnesses?" William asked.

"There are," Hayden answered.

William continued. "Did the victim ever make a statement before dying?"

"I'm not at liberty to divulge that information at this time," Hayden said.

William didn't miss a beat. "And physical evidence. Has physical evidence been recovered that connects my client to this alleged crime?"

Hayden stared without emotion. "Would your client be willing to answer a few questions now?"

William stared a moment before sitting back in his chair. When he spoke, it was in an admonishing tone. "You've omitted a few things, Hayden."

Hayden arched an eyebrow. "Such as?"

"Specific answers to my questions. No matter, your lack of candor is all the more telling. I am curious though, why does an alleged barroom homicide in Smyrna, Tennessee have the interest of the Federal District Attorney General?"

Hayden's smile returned. It was a smile of a man who was trying to convince me he was doing me a tremendous favor. "I am personally giving your client a chance to help himself."

"How?" William asked.

"I am sure you are aware of our recent arrests of several members of an outlaw motorcycle club known as the Satan's Dogs," he said.

"I saw it on the news," William said. "Drug trafficking. Fentanyl, if I remember."

"Yes, Fentanyl and heroin," Hayden said.

"Good. I have no doubt you'll obtain guilty verdicts, but what does that have to do with my client?"

Hayden turned slightly and focused on me. "You're facing a murder charge, Thomas. The only reason you are not sitting in jail at this moment is we have directed the local authorities to delay charging you."

"Why?" William asked.

"We are offering a chance for Thomas to avoid a life of daily beatings in prison. Life in general population for an ex-cop is most unpleasant, I've seen the results many times." He paused to let it sink in. He probably thought I was quaking in my shoes at this point. I doubted he'd ever visited a prison in his life. He leaned forward in his chair.

"What we want from you, Thomas, is for you to cultivate friendships with these outlaw bikers. There are several of them who we have not yet arrested and frankly, we need more evidence of their crimes to ensure convictions."

"In exchange for what?" William asked.

A hint of a smile crossed Hayden's lips. "Detective Thompson has a solid case on your client. I'm sure you're a good attorney, William, but a conviction is inevitable. If Thomas works with us, I will guarantee he will be able to serve his sentence at FPC Montgomery."

"FPC Montgomery?" William asked.

"Federal Prison Camp Montgomery," I said. "It's a minimum-security prison located at Maxwell Airforce Base in Montgomery, Alabama."

"Yes, exactly," Hayden said. "Far better than the maximum-security prison here in Nashville, I can assure you. Riverbend Prison, right Thomas? I've no doubt there are a few people still residing there, thanks to you." The car salesman's smile was back. "You were a cop, Thomas. Bad for you if you go to prison but being a former cop could be a good thing in this instance. We have them for trafficking, but we also suspect them of a lot more, and that includes the Baroques."

It was the first time he'd mentioned the Baroques. While I only knew a couple of the Dogs, I knew most of the Baroques. In fact, there was a time when I called a couple of them my friends. Hayden continued.

"There have been rumors that they're engaged in human trafficking as well, but we have very little evidence of this. Thomas, I've already gotten word from people with the FBI. You know how to sniff out human trafficking. This will be a fantastic opportunity for you."

I kept from laughing in his face. He wanted me to be a snitch and was trying to sell it as a fantastic opportunity. I didn't answer and glanced over to my right. William checked his watch again. Maybe he did have other pressing matters. He then glanced at me. I gave him a nod. He stood, which was my cue to stand.

"We will take your request under advisement. Give me a call in a couple of days and I'll let you know. In the meantime, please do not contact my client," William said.

Hayden was apparently convinced his sales pitch, along with the frightful implications of life in prison, would hook me into cooperating. He suddenly realized why we'd even bothered agreeing to meet in the first place was not to look for help, but to find out what he was up to.

"It would be in your client's best interest to cooperate in this investigation. And, I might add, this offer has an expiration date." When he said it, he spoke in a condescending tone, like we were stupid not to take his advice. William was unimpressed.

"Duly noted," he said and checked his watch again.

Hayden declined to make small talk as he escorted us to the lobby. We walked outside in silence. William waited until we were in the parking lot before speaking.

"What do you think?" he asked.

"I'm speculating, but if they had enough to arrest me, they would have already done so," I said.

William nodded. "Yeah, if you were sitting in a nasty jail cell, they'd believe they would have more leverage to get you to cooperate."

"Exactly, and if I ever do get charged and convicted, I doubt they'd honor their agreement," I said. "In any event, if they really do have enough evidence, their failure to get what they wanted from this meeting will compel them to arrest me." William nodded and looked at his watch again. "Alright, I hope this is the correct strategy. I'm sure you have other things to do. I can pay you in cash if you like."

"I've got something else in mind. Follow me," William said and led me to his parked car. Opening it, he reached in and came out with an overstuffed manila envelope.

"What's this?" I asked.

"Subpoenas," he answered with a grin and handed me the envelope. "You get them all served, and I'll consider your fee paid."

I sighed and opened the envelope. "That looks like about a dozen subpoenas."

"Thirteen, to be exact. So, do we have a deal?"

I did some quick mental arithmetic. I was definitely coming out on the short end of the deal, but William was a good person to have in my corner. He was maturing as a lawyer and would no doubt take over his grandfather's law firm one day.

"Alright, I'll get started on them this week," I said.

We shook hands and departed company. I sat in my SUV and looked over the subpoenas. Most of them appeared easy services. I started heading toward Murfreesboro. My phone rang as I drove. It was Bubba.

"You ain't gonna believe what my buddy found," he gushed.

"What's that?" I asked.

"The Kia."

CHAPTER 10

"The Kia? Felicity's Kia? Are you sure?" I asked.

"He sent me pictures of it," Bubba replied. "It matches the description, and even has damage to the bumper. It ain't got no license plate on it and he had to go on a run, so he didn't have time to snap a pic of the VIN, but there can't be too many white Kias out there with a big dent in the bumper. I'll forward these pics to you if you want."

I considered what he said and couldn't argue with his assessment. "Sure. So, where is it?"

"Big Boy's Auto Salvage. You know where that's at?"

I did. It was located off of Briley Parkway near the Cheatham County line. I'd been a customer there many times.

"Weird Harold said go into the main entrance, take the first left into the salvage yard, and then go down about a hundred feet. It's parked by a wrecked school bus."

"Alright, I'm going there now. I'll call you later and let you know," I said.

I had to admit, I was giddy with excitement. I texted Percy.

I may have something big. Will let you know something soon.

I arrived and parked in their front lot ten minutes later. I'd dressed fairly nice for the visit with Hayden Westlake, which meant I wasn't properly attired for a salvage yard. I had a change of clothes in the back, but I didn't bother. I got out and began walking.

This was a pull-a-part salvage yard. That is, you as a customer were allowed to walk around the salvage yard, find the appropriate vehicle, and use your tools to pull parts. You then took your parts to the office and paid for them. You could bring your own tools or pay one of the business employees to assist you. It was a good business model. I'd been a customer enough times to know a few of the employees by name.

I followed the directions Bubba provided. It only took a couple of minutes to find the bus, and then the Kia. I walked up to it and immediately read the VIN. Well, to be honest, I looked inside the car first. Not seeing a dead body crumpled up inside, I then read the VIN and compared it to the VIN info I had stored in my phone. I took a picture of it, along with the VIN, attached them to a text, and sent them to Percy. He called back within a minute.

"Where did you find it?" he asked. I advised him of my location and gave him a synopsis of how it was found. "Alright, hold tight, I'll be there in a few. I'm going to go ahead and have the zone car dispatched."

"Alright, I'll be waiting," I said and disconnected the call.

Out of habit, I looked around. There was someone at the far end of the yard working on something under the hood of a wrecked Escalade, but otherwise there was nobody around. I focused back on the Kia. There were no overt bloodstains, nor were there any post-it notes divulging the location of Felicity. Still, it may contain trace evidence, so I didn't touch it. Stepping back, I admired it for a moment and then gave Bubba a call.

"It looks like I owe Weird Harold the reward," I said.

"He'll be glad to hear that. He looked all over for it. Just between you and me, he has to eat at the Union Mission most evenings because his child support takes all his paycheck."

"Alright, I'm glad it's for a good cause. Text me his info and I'll get it to him right away, and I'll pay him in cash."

After ending the call, I took a few photographs, and on impulse, I dropped down and began viewing the undercarriage. I remembered a case years ago where a woman had backed over a neighbor's child. She panicked and drove off. She was at church when we found her, and she vehemently denied involvement while tightly clutching her bible to her breast with one hand and holding the pastor's hand with the other. There was a minute where we began to believe she was not the culprit. That is, until we inspected the undercarriage of her car. It was not a pleasant sight.

I didn't see anything, but again, there may have been trace evidence present. I heard the sound of a vehicle approaching. I straightened and brushed the dirt off my slacks as two men approached riding a golf cart. They drove directly toward me and stopped about twenty feet away.

I recognized one of them. He was close to my age but looked ten years older. He had a bad haircut, a week-old growth of beard, and grimy work clothes. I'd never seen him without a lit cigarette dangling from his mouth. He'd helped me a time or two when I'd been here getting parts for a car I was working on.

"Hello, Lamar," I said.

He squinted. "Oh, hey, Thomas."

"What the hell are you doing looking under that car?" the other one demanded.

I'd seen him before, but he'd never helped me pull parts. He was always sitting in his office eating something and watching TV. He too was close to my age, but I swear, he easily weighed five hundred pounds. He took up every square inch of the passenger side of the golf cart and it even looked like Lamar didn't have much room for his scrawny ass. It also looked like he had the same barber as Lamar. Normally, I would have been pleasant, courteous, but I took an instant disliking to him. I walked over to him and gave him a hard stare.

"Who the hell is asking?" I demanded back.

"I don't answer questions, boy," he retorted.

"If you want answers, you're going to need to check your tone with me, and I'm not your boy," I said.

He responded with a sneer. "You get your ass out of here now before we bury you out here. Nobody will ever see your ass again."

I glanced over at Lamar, who squirmed in the driver's seat. I fixed my stare back on the butterball.

"I already told you to check your tone with me if you want me to answer your questions. And if you want your fat ass beat to a pulp, go ahead and throw out another threat about burying me out here."

His eyes widened and he looked rattled for a moment, but then he seemed to remember he had something sitting down beside his leg. He sneered again as he pulled out a revolver with his left hand and began bringing it to bear on me.

It was sad, really. The man was so fat he moved like a slug. As he started to point the pistol at me, I deftly reached out and grabbed it around the frame and cylinder. It was a double-action Smith and Wesson. A decent firearm, but if the trigger was not cocked, it was incapable of firing if the cylinder was prevented from rotating, which was exactly what I was doing with my vise tight grip. When he tried to squeeze the trigger, it wouldn't budge.

"Hey!" he exclaimed and then grabbed the gun with both hands and tried to pull it from my grasp.

I responded by flicking a finger into his eye. He chirped in pain. One hand released the grip on the pistol and went to his face, allowing me to wrench the gun away from him. I stepped back out of his reach and inspected his firearm. It was a 357 magnum and loaded with six hollow point cartridges. It was capable of doing a lot of damage to a man.

"So, you were going to shoot me, huh?" I said before unloading it and throwing the gun and bullets as far as I could before grabbing the fat ass and pulling him from the cart.

He flailed at me with his stubby hands, but he was no match. I slapped his face so hard it sounded like a big water balloon splattering against a brick wall. He yelped, stumbled, and fell to the ground. When he did, he flatulated so loudly it sounded like a rusty foghorn. I was mad, but I couldn't help it and started laughing. Lamar chuckled along with me.

"What the hell, Lamar?" I asked.

"I told Earl time and time again not to be pointing that gun at nobody, but he wouldn't listen." He stared down at his fat buddy. "You bit off more than you could chew this time, Earl."

Earl had remained flat on his back, breathing heavily, and staring at the sky. Lamar then focused back on me, wondering what I was going to do next.

"Who the hell is he anyway?" I asked.

Lamar frowned at the question. "Don't you know? He owns this here salvage yard."

"Wonderful," I muttered. I knew now I'd never be pulling parts from here again.

"Yeah, and I'm going to see to it that you go to prison," Earl declared between gasps.

I stared down at Earl. He flipped me the bird as he gasped for breath.

That did not set well with me, but I knew if I put hands on him again, he'd probably have a heart attack. As I stared at him, he attempted to get to his feet, but only managed to fart again. Lamar got off the cart and helped his fat buddy to his feet. Earl clumsily plopped his oversized behind back down in the passenger seat and gave me a baleful stare.

"By God, I'm going to see to it you go to prison," he threatened again.

I returned his stare with my own. "Listen up, lard ass. You rolled up here on your little golf cart talking down to me, threatened to kill and bury me here, and then you pulled a gun on me. Who do you think will really end up in prison?"

"Our word against yours," he huffed. "You're trespassing. I can kill you for that."

I frowned at his ignorance. "You idiot, you can't shoot a man for trespassing."

"I'm going to have you arrested," he threatened again. I guess he thought if he said it enough, it'd become true.

I ignored his threats and focused on Lamar. "That vehicle," I said, pointing at the Kia, "belongs to a missing person. She's probably been murdered. You two seemed awfully concerned about me looking at it. Why is that?"

Lamar nervously puffed on his cigarette and made a head nod toward Earl, who was staring down at his knees. I snapped my fingers to get Earl's attention.

"Why didn't you want me to look at this car, Earl? Are you hiding something?"

"I ain't hiding nothing. I could see you weren't pulling any parts, so I knew you were up to no good."

He was sweating profusely. The physical activity had put a strain on him. He pulled a dirty rag out of the little tray on the golf cart and rubbed his face. Lamar was frowning at his buddy.

"Earl, you smell to high heaven. Have you shit on yourself?"

Earl hung his head. "I couldn't help it," he muttered.

I kept myself from laughing in disgust and spoke to Lamar. "Maybe you ought to carry him back to the office so he can clean himself up. Earl, the police are on their way. If you want to make a complaint against me, go right ahead."

"I'll do that. You can bet on it," he said.

"Good, and I'll file a complaint on you. Pointing a loaded weapon at someone is a felony. Slapping the shit out of someone in self-defense is not a crime. You figure out how it'll go."

I was done with the fat ass. I focused back on Lamar. "Tell me about this car."

Lamar shrugged. "We found it the other day in the parking lot. Earl told me it must be abandoned and move it into the yard. Tell him, Earl."

Earl was sullen now. "Will you please drive me back to the office? I'm your boss and you should do as I say."

Lamar looked apologetic and shrugged before driving off. I watched them leave, and as they were turning onto the road that led back to the office, a marked patrol car came into view. I gave them a wave, motioning them to come to me. As the car approached, I immediately recognized the driver. Officer Abbigail Severns grinned and waved before parking and jumping out. Her uniform was crisply pressed, and her boots had an excellent gloss. She had the air of a professional law enforcement officer, which is the way all cops should look.

"Well, hello, stranger, what are you doing here?" she asked as she walked up.

I pointed at the Sorento. "Found a car that belongs to a missing person. Are you on day shift now?"

"I am. This is my last rotation. If I pass my final evaluation, I'm on my own."

Last rotation. She was still in training, but about to be promoted to a full-fledged police officer. A dark-skinned woman got out of the passenger side and walked up as we were talking. She was attractive but had a stern expression and looked tough as nails. To enhance that image, her shoulders were broader than a lot of men. Abby introduced us.

"This is my training officer, Sheba Pelletier. Ma'am, this is Thomas Ironcutter. He used to work for Metro."

I extended my hand. "Hi, I'm Thomas. I don't think we've ever actually met."

She shook my hand with a firm grip. "No, we've never met, but I remember you, and I've heard a lot about you." She glanced over at the Kia. "You used to be a homicide detective, so I know you haven't been searching through that car, right?"

"You're correct."

She gave a small nod. "Alright. Trotter's coming and should be here in about fifteen." She then turned to Abby. "Start on a recovered property report, and I don't need to remind you not to touch anything."

"Yes ma'am," Abby responded and walked over to the Kia. The two of us watched as she took a picture of the VIN on her phone and then trotted back to the patrol car.

"On our way over here, we received an update from the dispatcher, saying something about the business owner being assaulted."

I started to say something, but she interrupted me.

"Just so you know, you're the reason she's riding with me. I'm Sory's cousin and he's paying up that favor you asked of him."

I slowly nodded in understanding. Not too long ago I was in a position where Commander Sory Bartlett owed me. I requested he keep tabs on my rookie officer friend and prevent assholes like Ian Poston from taking advantage of her and undermining her career. So, he put her with a female training officer. That was good. Also, this officer exuded toughness and competence. I liked that too.

"Alright, now that you know who I am and that I'm taking care of your girl and training her right, don't be bullshitting me. Did you assault the owner of this business?"

"I was looking over the car when two knuckleheads rode up in a golf cart. The fat one started running his mouth and then pulled a gun on me. I took it away from him." I pointed. "It's over there in the weeds somewhere."

"Did you assault him?" she asked.

"I defended myself. I may have slapped the shit out of him. Literally."

She stared a moment, unsmiling. "Will he need to go to the hospital?"

"Not for anything I did," I replied.

"You carrying?" she asked. I nodded. "If he pulled a gun on you, you could've killed him."

"I could've. I didn't."

There'd been too much death around me lately. Adding Earl to the body count was the last thing I wanted or needed. She stared at me, gauging my response, and after a moment she changed the subject.

"What's up with you and Severns? She talks about you a lot."

"We're friends, nothing more," I said. "How is she doing?"

"A little naïve, but she'll get over it."

I waited for more, but that was it. Obviously, she wasn't a person who felt the need to talk a lot. After a few minutes, Percy's car rounded the corner of junk cars and drove up the dirt path, parking behind the patrol car. He walked to the Kia and gave it a once over before walking over to us.

"I have to ask, how'd you find it?" Percy asked.

"I have this buddy named Bubba," I began and explained how Bubba recruited the other tow truck drivers to actively search for it.

"I put up a reward and Shazam, here we are."

"Clever," Sheba remarked.

Percy nodded in agreement. "Alright, I'm going to take some photographs and then I want it towed straight to the lab. Can you handle that part for me, Sheba?"

"My rookie will take care of it," Sheba replied. "Anything else?"

"No, that'll do it, and I appreciate it," Percy said.

"I'll get her on it and then I'm going to have a talk with that alleged assault victim," she said and gave me a wink before walking away and rejoining Abby.

I overheard her quizzing Abby on the types of forensic evidence that could be recovered from the car. Abby dutifully answered and grinned when she saw me watching. I knew then that Sheba was clearly a good training officer. With her skill and connections, I had no doubt she'd rise in the ranks.

"What assault victim is she talking about?" Percy asked.

I briefed him on my encounter with Earl and Lamar. When I finished, he grunted slightly.

"That's what I miss about you. It's never boring when you're around. Alright, I'll drive back to their office and have a little chat with Earl. Maybe I can convince him he's the one in the wrong and talk a little more about how they came into possession of this car. I need to talk to Pelletier too."

"Oh yeah?" I asked.

"After she finishes training your buddy, she's being transferred into CID and I'm the one who is going to train her to be a high-speed, low-drag detective."

"Did you know she's Sory's cousin?"

Percy stared in surprise. "Really? Well, that explains some things. Alright, if I don't see you before you leave, I'll give you a call. If you don't mind, keep an eye on her rookie, make sure she doesn't mess anything up." He winked when he said it, making me think he too believed Abby and I were more than friends.

I walked over to the patrol car where Abby was typing on her laptop. She looked up when I approached, a hint of confusion on her face.

"Where'd Detective Trotter go?" she asked.

"He's going to interview the people who work here. How's it going with you?"

"Pretty good. FTO Pelletier is a hard ass, but in the short time I've been with her I've learned a lot."

"Good, she seems capable."

"Yes, she is. Are you investigating this missing person too?" she asked.

"Yeah. It may sound weird, but her boyfriend hired me."

She frowned. "Isn't he considered the prime suspect?"

"Yes, he is. He swears he had nothing to do with her disappearance." I shrugged. "If I can help Percy solve it, I'll either help prove he did something to her or prove his innocence."

"Did he pay you a fee?" she asked.

"Yes, he did."

She bit her lip as she looked at me. "Alright, what if you find out he did it?"

"I'll turn the information over to Percy and he'll be prosecuted. I told him as much."

"So, there's no conflict of interest?"

"Normally there would be, but I was clear when I told him if he was responsible, I'd take him down. He agreed to it," I said.

"Oh."

We chatted as she completed the necessary reports. I had the urge to light up a cigar, but I didn't want to smoke in front of Abby. Sheba returned ten minutes later.

"I think Earl has seen the error of his ways, but he doesn't want you on his property anymore," she said.

"I understand. It was good to meet you and please be sure to tell Sory I appreciate everything he's done," I said. She gave a small nod. I faced Abby. "You're looking good, Officer Severns."

She grinned. "Thanks, Thomas."

I thought about Earl while I drove. The fat man might have thought he was simply going to scare me, but when I grabbed the gun, he tried to pull the trigger and shoot me. Yet another close call. Had the curse really been lifted? Maybe it had. If I still had the curse on me, maybe Earl would have succeeded in shooting me. It was definitely a perplexing conundrum. So perplexing, it required the enjoyment of a fine cigar to help think about it.

I found a place to stop on the side of the road and got one out of my little humidor. I had it prepped and lit when Abby texted me.

Are you mad at me or something? I feel like you've been avoiding me.

I bit my lip, not knowing how to explain things to her. Abby was a good person, a sweet kid, and I valued our friendship, but lately I didn't want to be close to anyone I cared about. I gave it some thought before responding.

Not mad. I miss your company but have been extremely busy lately. We'll do dinner soon.

I knew it was a lame excuse, but what was I supposed to say? I suppose I could've been honest and told her everything. I could have told her about the curse. I could have told her how I aided and abetted a burglary in order to get the curse removed from me. I could have told her about the possible pending murder charge.

I could have told her many things, but the best thing to do was to avoid her. I didn't want to be the cause of her budding career as a cop to be tarnished, or worse, my relationship with her to cause her physical harm.

CHAPTER 11

By the time I'd left the salvage yard, it was a little late in the day to start on William's subpoenas. I decided I'd wait and get a fresh start in the morning and headed home. Percy called me an hour later.

"Her prints, her kids' prints, and Art's prints are all over the vehicle, with one exception. The driver's area has been wiped down. Negative on the presumptive blood tests. The CSI tech took swabs for possible DNA analysis, but at the moment we don't have anything."

"There's something suspicious going on though," I remarked.

"Yeah, definitely," Percy agreed. "The surveillance video doesn't show much. The recording shows the car driving in a little after four in the morning. The driver parked at an angle where the camera doesn't record him, or her."

"So, they knew about the camera and its limitations," I surmised.

"Yeah. There is no second car, so presumably the suspect walked off. He, or she, could have gotten into a car that was waiting for them down the road, but I've not found any other surveillance cameras in the immediate vicinity."

"Did the car have an active GPS?" I asked.

"Nope, and the black box data didn't provide much. It indicated there was only one person sitting in the car at the time it was running and the time it was parked and shut off corresponded with the timestamp on the surveillance video."

"That's not much," I said. Percy agreed.

Neither of us were any closer to finding Felicity. The circumstances regarding her car hinted something bad had happened to her, but we had no idea what.

"I would say I'll start back on it first thing in the morning, but it's not going to happen," Percy said.

"No worries, I'll do what I can."

We bounced around a few ideas, but there wasn't much else that either of us could do. I spent an hour catching up on phone calls, emails, and other nonsense before heading out to the shop. I had the engine and tranny pulled in no time and was installing a throw-out bearing when my phone pinged. It was Kalina and she was at the gate. I waited and watched as she drove up in a late model red Mazda CX-30. She exited the vehicle and walked over. She was wearing a short red dress that matched the Mazda. If she had gotten out in the same manner in a crowded parking lot, she would have turned a lot of heads.

"I was wondering when you were going to show up," I said.

"I was running a little late. I have a problem with time management. I'm an artist after all," she said with a smile.

"Nice car."

"It's a rental. Do you have anything to drink?" she asked.

"Sure."

I got her suitcase, led her inside, and showed her the liquor cabinet. She scanned it over.

"What's your pleasure?" I asked.

"Wow, you have some top shelf stuff." She reached for a bottle and looked at it in appreciation. "Pappy Van Winkle. This is expensive."

"Yes, it is," I agreed. "Do you know much about liquor?"

"I do. I work part-time as a bartender at a five-star hotel in downtown Chicago. Do you mind if I fix myself a drink?"

"Only if you fix one for me too. I'll take mine neat," I said.

I got the metal whiskey rocks out of the freezer and plopped one in mine. She did the same with hers and we sat on the couch. I watched as she took a sip and made an expression of deep satisfaction.

"This is awesome bourbon. I've never had it," she said.

"But you're a bartender," I said.

"That doesn't mean management will let me drink high-priced bourbon on the house, and I damn sure can't afford it," she said. She took another sip before speaking. "Can I ask you something?"

"Sure," I said.

"We spent about twenty hours together on the road and yet you barely spoke to me. May I ask why?"

"You slept for about eight of those hours," I said.

"Alright, twelve hours. We spent twelve hours together and barely talked. So, what's the deal?"

"All I wanted to do was to end that damned curse. I honestly thought I'd never see you again after I left your house," I said.

"That hurts, Thomas," she said quietly.

"Why?"

"Because I like you," she said.

I eyed her. "I had a fling with your crazy ass cousin and my actions led to the death of another cousin. Why in the hell would you like me?"

"I'd never admit it to my aunt, but I'm glad Wolf is dead. He was a true psychopath," she said.

"What about Lilith?" I asked.

She took another sip, larger this time. "Lilith was a tragedy living on borrowed time. I wish I could have changed her life, but she was too far gone. Can we go visit her grave tomorrow?"

"Sure."

"You never really answered my question," she said.

"You won't like the answer," I replied.

"Try me."

"I don't trust you. I don't trust anyone in your family. I have this nagging feeling in my gut that I should keep far away from the Ratkovich family and the Gray family. As far as possible."

She stared with those dark eyes. "And yet, when I asked to come visit, you instantly agreed."

"Yeah, I'm stupid when it comes to pretty women," I said.

She smiled and drank again. "I appreciate you letting me stay with you. Money is a little tight and I can't afford to be extravagant with things like getting a hotel room."

"What's going on up there in Chicago where you had to get away?" I asked. Before she could answer, my phone pinged.

"Is someone calling you?" she asked.

"Sort of. Someone's at my gate and pushed the button on the call box." I tapped the icon and was greeted by Abby's face.

"Hi," she said.

"Hey. This is a surprise. Hang on," I said and tapped the icon to open the gate.

I walked outside and greeted her. She got out of her Jeep and stumbled a little, which seemed odd. She had her hair down and was wearing a crop top, showing off a six-pack of abs, and white shorts which showed off her muscular legs. I had to admit, she looked good. When I got closer, I could smell alcohol.

"How's it going?" I asked.

"I think I'm a little bit drunk," she said and stumbled when she tried to walk. I grabbed her hand and escorted her inside.

Kalina was sitting on the couch and when Abby saw her, her expression registered surprise and perhaps some embarrassment.

"Oh, I didn't know you had company. I'll leave," she said and started to turn toward the door.

"It's alright, come in and sit down," I said and introduced them. "Abby, this is Kalina. She's a friend visiting from Chicago."

"Uh, hi," Abby said. "I'm sorry for interrupting."

"You're not interrupting," Kalina said. "Thomas used to date my cousin. I'm in town for a couple of days and Thomas was nice enough to let me stay here."

"Oh," Abby said and glanced at our drinks.

"Would you like something to drink?" I asked.

"I think I'd better stick with water," she said and gazed at Kalina. "I normally don't drink and may have overdone it."

"What've you been doing?" Kalina asked. "You're dressed nice. Were you on a date?"

Abby glanced at me and gave a sheepish nod.

"It was awful," she said. "He was so arrogant and immature it was nauseating, and his friends were just like him."

Kalina sat up. "Oh, I've got to hear it. Come sit down," she said, patted the couch, and looked at me. "Could you freshen my drink, please," she requested and smiled sweetly.

I freshened both drinks and fixed Abby a glass of ice water and then sat with the two women. Abby told us about her date. He was a fellow police officer who was full of himself and defined his manliness by how much alcohol he could put away. Soon, the conversation segued into relationships in general, police work and tattoo work. Kalina had no hesitancy in dropping her dress and showing us her various tats.

There was a point where Kalina and I were talking when I realized Abby had become quiet. Looking over, I saw that she was asleep. Kalina noticed too and emitted a quiet giggle.

"She's been trying to keep her eyes open for the past thirty minutes," she said.

I stood, and gently guided Abby into a supine position on the couch. I pulled her shoes off and carefully laid a blanket on top of her. When I looked up, Kalina was smirking. I made a head motion and led her to the front porch.

"She likes you," Kalina said.

"We're friends," I replied.

"No, I think it goes beyond friendship with her," she said. "When she saw you admiring my ink, I could see a little bit of jealousy."

"I don't know about that. I'm old enough to be her father."

Kalina gave a quiet chuckle. "That's probably why she likes you. You were old enough to be Lilith's father too, remember?"

I didn't know how to respond to that. It was true, when I met Lilith, she was only a couple of years older than Abby is now. I glanced over at Kalina, who was still smirking.

"Oh, hush," I grumbled.

"There's nothing wrong with that. Older men are generally more mature and dependable. Plus, they usually have more money."

I glanced at her again and wondered if she knew about my lawsuit. If it wasn't for the sizeable settlement, I'd still be working from paycheck to paycheck.

"Yeah, well, it's nothing more than friendship," I said. I looked down at my glass, which was now empty. I stood.

"I don't know about you, but I'm ready for bed. I'll see you in the morning."

CHAPTER 12

I smiled to myself when I walked into the den the next morning. Abby was on the couch, sleeping deeply. She didn't wake up until I had the aromas of eggs and bacon wafting through the house. She sat up, stretched, and looked around in confusion a moment before standing and spotting me in the kitchen. Her expression turned from confusion to realization. A hand shot up and covered her mouth in embarrassment.

"Good morning," I said.

"Oh, my God. I am so ashamed of myself," she said.

"Don't be," I replied. "I'll let you in on a little secret; you're not the first person who's slept on that couch due to having a little much to drink. Me included."

"Well, this is a first for me. I guess I should get going."

"Sure. Do you want some breakfast first?" I asked.

She gave a small shake of her head and gestured with her phone. "I better get home. I had my phone on silent and it looks like Mom has called several times already."

I stared at her blankly as the implication sunk in. Abby noticed and chuckled. "Yes, Thomas, I still live with my mother."

"Hey, I didn't say anything."

"Yeah, but I know what you're thinking, I'm still a kid, right?" she asked.

"No. Well, maybe," I admitted.

She laughed again, which caused her to put a hand to her head and groan. I pointed toward a glass of iced water and two ibuprofen tablets sitting on the counter.

"I recognize the symptoms of a morning after headache. Take those."

She thanked me and washed them down. "I should have never caved in to peer pressure."

"That's what people do," I said.

"Yeah, but I'm not a drinker, I've told you that, but I didn't want to seem like a prig. Anyway, I've got to go." She walked up, gave me a hug, and then stood on her tiptoes to kiss me on the cheek before walking out.

The shower started as Abby disappeared down my driveway and Kalina emerged from the spare bedroom fifteen minutes later. Her hair was wet, and she was wearing her silk bathrobe, the one I saw her in back in Chicago, but this time she did not have it tied. She was showing off a lot of cleavage and a pair of lime green panties. I don't know if she was doing it on purpose to tease me, or maybe she simply didn't care.

I forced myself to stop looking and instead thought about Felicity's Kia while I ate. There were two unanswered questions. One: how did it get there? The second question had to do with the actions taken with the car once it was parked at the auto salvage business.

"There's a third question, dummy," I muttered to myself before taking a sip of coffee. Kalina glanced at me.

"What?"

"Nothing," I said.

The third question was: what was I going to do? I was still drawing a blank on how to answer question number one, but I thought I might be able to work on question number two. Lamar and I had always been friendly toward each other, and I hoped our amicable relationship made him approachable.

"Only one way to find out," I muttered.

Kalina stared and frowned. "Are you talking to me or yourself?"

"To myself, I have a bad habit of that," I said and reached for my phone. Finding the number for Big Boy's Auto Salvage, I called. To my surprise, Lamar answered.

"Hey, Lamar. It's Thomas Ironcutter, the guy who found the Kia."

"Oh, hey," he replied. "Yeah, how're you doing? Parts for a Cadillac, huh? What year and model are you looking for?"

I'm not anywhere close to Stephen Hawking in the brains department but I understood immediately; someone else was in the office and could overhear the conversation.

"Yeah, I was hoping we could talk a little more about that car."

"Yeah, I can do that," Lamar said. "It might take a little time though. I was about to go down to the McDonalds down the street and have an early lunch and then I can look up those parts."

"Alright, give me a few minutes and I'll meet you there," I said.

"Yeah, okay bub. I'm sure I have what you need," he said and hung up.

I looked over at Kalina. It was a no-brainer that I did not want to leave her alone in my house. She saw me staring. "What?" she asked again.

"Briefly, I've been hired to investigate a missing persons case. I need to follow-up on a lead. Get dressed, you're coming with me."

"This sounds like fun," she said and hurried off to the bedroom.

Lamar was sitting at a table eating some breakfast burritos and washing them down with a large soda when we walked in. He gave me a head nod and then noticed Kalina. He hastily stood and gestured at the chairs.

"This is Kalina, I hope you don't mind her joining us," I said.

Lamar responded with a grin, exposing nicotine-stained teeth with a few particles of food added in.

"Not at all. I hope you don't have no hard feelings for me," he said.

"None of that nonsense was your doing," I replied. "I'm hoping you can help me out though."

"Sure, but I don't know much more about that Kia than what I told you before," he said.

"Yeah, you told me it was parked in front of the office and Earl told you to move it out in the yard. No business transaction, no paperwork, nothing. That doesn't sound like normal business."

Lamar took a drink of his soda and stared evenly before answering. "You're right. You're absolutely right."

"Is there something else going on?" I asked.

Lamar casually peered around the restaurant and then cast a glance at Kalina.

"This conversation is confidential. Neither of us will tell anyone what you say."

He considered it a moment before answering. He then leaned forward slightly and lowered his voice. "Between you and me, Earl is taking in cars under shady circumstances."

"What do you mean?" I asked.

Lamar looked around again. "Well, I can't prove it, but I think he's letting his nephew run a chop shop operation."

I nodded in understanding. Stealing cars and selling the parts off them could be a lucrative business. All you needed was an adept car thief and good cover, and an auto salvage yard was perfect.

"Is that how it went with the Kia?" I asked.

Lamar shrugged. "I have no idea, but usually when Whopper brings a car in, they don't drop it in the parking lot, they take it directly back into the yard. The cars are then stripped almost immediately."

I perked up. "Did you say Whopper?"

"Yeah, that's Earl's nephew. He's a big fat biker dude. He rides around with some group that calls themselves Satan's Dogs. They're devil worshippers or something."

"Do you like him?" I asked.

Lamar made a face. "Hell no. He's always had a mouth on him and one day he put his hands on me and threatened to kill me."

"Why did he do that?"

"Because I told Earl he needed to cool it on taking in those stolen cars before we all got arrested. Whopper showed up a few hours later. He damn near strangled me to death and told me if I knew what was good for me, I'd keep my mouth shut. Which brings me to something else you don't know about. Earl told him about you."

"Did you hear what he said to him?" I asked.

"Oh, yeah. Earl was all torn up that you made him shit all over himself. Especially after that detective told him he could be arrested for pointing that gun at you. He didn't even bother going home to get cleaned up. He called Whopper and told him all about it. I could hear both of them speaking. Whopper said he knew you and he was going to take care of you." Lamar pointed at my hand that was wrapped around my coffee cup.

"You got scars and callouses on your knuckles which tells me that you can take care of yourself, but you be careful. Whopper's a mean one." He glanced at his cellphone. "I can't think of anything else, and I've got to get back to work or else Earl will bitch and complain the rest of the day."

The three of us stood. I shook Lamar's hand and thanked him.

"Don't mention it," he said. "I hope you find that missing woman."

CHAPTER 13

"Alright, I've got to hear how you made a man shit his pants," Kalina said.

"I'll tell you about it later. Give me a minute, I need to think."

Kalina started to say something, but I held a finger up, shushing her. The mysterious appearance of Felicity's Kia at the salvage yard could not have been a coincidence. There had to be a connection, a nexus, but I couldn't determine what it might be. I was still thinking it over when Kalina decided she needed to say something.

"What is this case all about?" she asked.

"A missing woman. Her name is Felicity Turnbow. The boyfriend is the primary suspect. He's hired me to find her and clear his name. The car Lamar referred to belongs to Felicity and it turned up in the salvage yard."

"That's weird. Is she one of those biker whores?"

"I don't think so," I replied. She didn't do it on purpose, but she caused me to think of the obvious. I called Art.

"Are you and Felicity friends with any outlaw bikers?" I asked him.

"Um, no, why?"

"Has she ever mentioned anyone by the name of Bang-Bang, or Whopper? Or a biker gang called Satan's Dogs?"

"Um, no, don't think so."

"What about Big Boy's Auto Salvage? Do you two have any connection to that place or anyone who works there?"

"That'd be a negative on all of that, why are you asking?"

"I'm following up on some possible leads. It may be nothing. I'll call if anything changes." I ended the call while he was trying to ask me something else and called Melanie. I asked her the same questions and I got the same answers.

"She has her secrets, but she's never said anything about bikers," she said.

I thanked her, thought for a moment, and decided to call Felicity's mother. The tone in her voice when she answered let me know what kind of person I was going to be dealing with. I was as polite as I could be. I told her I was investigating her daughter's disappearance, but I didn't dare tell her that Art had hired me though. It took some sweet talking, but she agreed with my request to meet with her and the kids. I turned to Kalina.

"Alright, you're going to be working with me on this. We're going to visit the missing woman's mother. I'm going to try asking her some questions. You can work with me and play off my cues, but mostly I want you to keep your mouth shut."

Kalina smirked. "Okay, boss man."

We were at her house twenty minutes later. It was a small, older house in the Tusculum community. The home appeared neglected and was in dire need of some home improvement projects. I directed Kalina to wait in the car. When the door opened, I was greeted by a sour looking woman in her late fifties or early sixties wearing a blue Nike sweatshirt and black yoga pants that were most definitely not flattering to her physique. She was clearly annoyed by my presence, but I didn't let it deter me and greeted her with a pleasant smile.

"Hello, Ms. Holloway, I'm Thomas Ironcutter."

She took a moment to look me up and down before responding. "Is this going to take long?"

"I hope not. May I come in?"

For a moment I didn't think she was going to allow me to enter, but after a long second, she opened the door wider and stepped back. The two children were sitting in the front room, I guess it was the den, watching cartoons on TV. They were still in their pajamas and were eating bowls of cereal for lunch.

"Hi, kids. What're you watching?" I asked.

"SpongeBob SquarePants," the girl said.

"That's a funny name."

She turned to me. "That's because he's a cartoon character." After setting me straight, she refocused on the TV.

"I see. You know, I know of some men who have funny names. They're named Bang-Bang and Whopper. Do those names sound familiar?"

Both kids shook their heads in unison. I turned to their grandmother, who also shook her head. I turned back to the kids. "Did your mom have any friends who drove big loud motorcycles?"

The little girl focused on me again. "Like a scooter?"

"Sort of, but bigger and louder."

"Nope," she replied. The little boy, who had been listening, shook his head along with his sister. I turned back to Ms. Holloway, who also shook her head.

"If she did, she probably wouldn't have told me. I detest motorcycles," she said.

"Alright, I was following up on a lead, but it doesn't look like there's anything to it. I appreciate your time."

Grandma Holloway nodded at my effort and started to walk me to the door. The little girl muted the TV.

"Grandma, can we go to Starbucks?" she asked.

"I'm a little short of cash, dear," she replied, and then fixed me with a stare. "Maybe Mister Ironcutter will take us."

It was a shitty little move, but I wasn't going to say so in front of the kids. "Yeah, sure. Let's go."

The little boy didn't want to leave the TV, but his sister wouldn't have it. Kalina stared in confusion as I loaded them up.

"We're going to Starbucks," I explained.

"Oh."

Grandma Holloway gave me directions while telling me her opinion of Felicity's demise.

"It was her ex-husband. It had to be. I always knew he was going to kill her one day," she proclaimed.

"He's got a pretty solid alibi," I offered.

She scoffed. "He hired a hitman."

"Does he have that kind of money?" I asked.

She scoffed again but didn't answer. We rode the rest of the way in mostly silence. I opted to use the drive-thru window due to the kid's attire. Surprisingly, the kids knew exactly what they wanted. Grandma was a different story. She changed her order three times. I ordered a full roast blend for myself. Very dull and normal. Kalina got a cinnamon dolce.

When the barista passed us our beverages through the window, she smiled and waved. The little girl waved back. "Hi, Cassidy!"

"Hi, Emma! As soon as I heard the order, I knew it was you," Cassidy said. "Only you and your mom order a dragon drink with five pumps of caramel."

Little Emma had a hearty giggle over that. I had no idea what was in a dragon drink and why pumping caramel into it was unusual, nor did I care. All I know is I paid over forty bucks for some stupid foo-foo drinks. Driving them back to their house, I gave Ms. Holloway my card and asked that she call if she could think of anything.

CHAPTER 14

My phone rang as we left the Holloway residence. I glanced at the caller ID and saw that it was a federal government number. Whatever the caller wanted, I wasn't in the mood and let it go to voicemail.

"Where to now?" Kalina asked.

"It's time for a more direct approach," I said and began driving toward LaVergne. "I'm going to have a little talk with Whopper."

"Is he the man Lamar was talking about?" she asked.

"Yep."

Kalina stared in concern. "Is this a smart thing to do?"

"Nope."

"Aren't you worried things might get physical?" she asked.

"I'd be surprised if it doesn't," I replied.

The truth was, I was hoping for it. I was sick and tired of people thinking they could come onto my property and attack me, and I was sick and tired of people talking shit about me. It had left a foul taste in my mouth for a while now and today was going to be the day I did something about it. I saw Kalina staring at me out of the corner of my eye, but she wisely remained quiet.

The Satan's Dogs clubhouse was on a dead-end street in a shitty part of LaVergne. It only took us twenty-five minutes to get there from Tusculum. Surprisingly, the security gate was standing open. I drove in and parked.

"I don't think this is a good idea," she said.

"Probably not," I agreed, but I was undaunted. Thinking a moment, I opened the console, unlocked the secure box mounted in it, and pulled out a handgun, a Glock model 43X. I handed it to Kalina, along with the key fob.

"If it goes bad, drive away, if you can. If you can't, make sure your shots count."

Kalina's eyes widened slightly, but she nodded in understanding. I got out of my SUV and began walking toward the house. A grungy young man who was skinny as a rail walked around the corner of the house and approached me.

"Can I help you with something?" he asked.

"Yeah, I need to talk to a lard ass by the name of Whopper," I said.

His eyes widened in disbelief at my lack of respect and looked around for some reason. Maybe he thought he was secretly being recorded for some stupid reality show.

"I don't have all day, squirt. Go get him," I demanded.

He then turned and hustled around back where he came from. After a moment, he remerged. Whopper and another young man were following him. Whopper looked at me and scowled in recognition. As he walked closer, the scowl turned to a smirk.

"The last time I saw you, I was putting an ass whooping on you," he said.

"The last time I saw you, you were squealing like a pig after being shot in the ass," I retorted.

He didn't like that. The smirk disappeared and the scowl returned. "What the hell are you doing here?"

"Two reasons," I said. "First reason; I'm looking for Felicity."

He squinted at me. "Who?"

"Busty brunette, early thirties, she's got a stupid looking tattoo on her neck," I said.

He shook his head slowly. "I have no idea who you're talking about, but if I run into her, maybe I'll slide my sausage down her throat while I'm telling her how I kicked your ass."

"That leads to my second reason for being here."

"Yeah, what's that?" he asked.

"A fat piece of shit by the name of Earl said you were going to hunt me down and take care of me. Well, here I am."

He stared with unease for a moment, but the smirk returned. "You think you can take me?"

"Let's find out," I replied and then waved a finger at the other two men. "I don't know you two, but Whopper here is a coward unless he has at least two other men with him to help him out."

"Oh, they ain't gonna interfere," he said and turned back toward the two men. "Watch and see what a Dog does to a loudmouth pig."

The anger was back, and my adrenalin was pumping enough to cause me to shake. I wasn't going to wait for him to make the first move. That was good if you were going to claim in court you were merely defending yourself, but I was the instigator, and you can't claim self-defense if you're the instigator. I wasn't worried about the legalities though; this wasn't going to go to court. The only thing I was worried about was if I'd bitten off more than I could chew and was about to get my ass kicked in front of Kalina.

Big fat men all had a certain way of fighting. I'm not talking about professional fighters, I'm talking about fat ass street fighters, like

Whopper. Their strong points were their thick heads and brute strength. Their weaknesses were a lack of stamina, coordination, and disciplined training. And predictability. They always tried for a knockout punch with a haymaker or wrestling their opponent to the ground. I'd fought him once before and I knew his skills were limited.

He stepped toward me and was winding up his right fist. I made a quick lunge forward and landed a left jab to the chin. I had a good jab, brought about by many hours of training. It was good enough to knock most people off balance. Not Whopper. It stunned him momentarily, but he didn't even take a step backwards.

No matter, I did not hesitate, took a quick sidestep left to avoid his haymaker and planted a right hook into the side of his jaw. Did I mention I had a good left? I had an even better right. I'd knocked out many men with my right. Not Whopper. The impact of my fist caused a rippling effect across his face, but I had to give the fat ass credit. He didn't go down, he merely grunted and squared up again.

The fight was on now. My skill level was superior, and I was connecting with more punches, but Whopper took it all and dished it right back to me. After a minute or so, he was gassing out. I was getting the better of him but then he connected with a hard right cross which sent a jolt down my spine and stunned me. He immediately dropped and grabbed me in a single-leg takedown attempt. I was out of practice and had never fought professionally, but I was well versed in a move commonly known as the whizzer. I'm sure my execution was sloppy, but it worked. I reversed the takedown and worked it into a full mount on top of Whopper.

"I got you now," I growled.

He tried to buck me off. He couldn't. I responded by raining an onslaught of punches. All he could do now was to try to cover up, but to no avail. My punches were connecting, and they were causing damage. It was exhilarating. It was satisfying.

"Thomas!"

The sound of my name being called caused me to pause. I jerked around to see Kalina standing beside my SUV. The look on her face was both of amusement and concern. She had the gun out, holding it in the general direction of the two young men. She gave me a come hither with her other hand. "Let's go."

I focused back on Whopper and took a moment to admire my work before getting off him. He looked like a freight train hit him. His left eye was already swelling shut and his nose was canted off to the side, bleeding profusely. It made me smile.

When I stood up, I saw the two young men staring at me in a mixture of astonishment and worry, perhaps even a little fear. They looked like drug addicts. Neither of them could have been over twenty. I stepped away from Whopper's supine body and inspected my hands while I caught my breath.

"He's going to kill you for that," one of them said. "The Dogs don't forgive."

I fixed him with a hard stare. "Neither do I. He came after me once and he put the word out he was coming after me again. I told him the first time what would happen. Besides, from what I hear, you boys need to be more worried about the Feds than with me."

"We ain't with the club," one of them said.

"We're hang arounds, about to be prospects," the other one added.

I pointed at Whopper. "Let me guess, you two came here to get a fix from him, right?"

They didn't respond, but the lack of eye contact was answer enough. I started to give them some fatherly advice about how they needed to turn their life around, but it would've been a waste of oxygen.

"Alright, you two, be honest with me, do you know Felicity?"

One of them shook his head. "There's more than one girl who hangs out with us that has a neck tattoo, but I don't think any of them is named Felicity."

"Hang on a second," I said, went back to my SUV, got my phone, and showed them a picture. Both men shook their heads.

"I would've remembered her, she's cute," one of them said.

"And nice puppies," the other one added.

"Alright, thanks," I said and pointed at Whopper, who was conscious now, but had only managed to roll over on his side and spit out blood. "Take care of lard ass. He might need to go visit the ER."

Walking back to Kalina, I pointed at the driver's seat and got in the passenger side.

"Okay, I have no idea where I'm at. You're going to have to give me directions," she said.

"Yeah, start driving, I'll get my phone synced up and plug in directions."

I mentally admonished myself as I synced up my phone to the car's onboard navigation system. I should have done this before. If I had lost the fight, or if it had turned especially ugly and Kalina had to take off, she would've been lost.

I gave my phone the voice command for home, and after a moment, the map illuminated on the display and a disembodied voice started giving instructions.

I pulled down the sun visor as she drove and checked my face in the mirror. I had a few scrapes and bumps. The two noticeable injuries were to my left cheek, which was red and starting to swell, and my right ear, which had a cut and was bleeding. I didn't remember that punch. It too was starting to swell.

"You kept dropping your left, that's how he was able to hit you with that right. I'm surprised he got you, you're pretty fast for a big man," she said.

"I got cocky," I said and pointed at a fast-food restaurant. "Pull in there."

Kalina turned in and parked. I got out and retrieved my first aid kit out of the back. Getting back in the passenger seat, I got some gauze out and dabbed at my ear. Kalina backed out and entered the drive-thru lane. She ordered two large cups of tea and a cup of ice. I dug a five out of my wallet and handed it to her.

"Put the ice on your cheek if you don't want it to swell up," she said. "Are you feeling nauseous?"

"Nope," I replied and gulped down the tea. I was suddenly incredibly thirsty.

"Good," she said. "If you start throwing up, we're going to the emergency room."

"Sounds like you know a little bit about concussions," I surmised.

"Yeah, you might say that."

My phone rang. It was the same federal government number. I ignored it again. Then my phone rang again. It was Abby.

"Hey girl," I said, and caught Kalina smirking at me out of the corner of my eye.

"Hey, what are you doing?" she asked.

"I'm following up on my missing person case. How about you?"

"I've been apartment hunting."

"Great, did you find anything?" I asked.

"Not yet. The rental prices in Nashville are sky high. It's very frustrating," she said.

"You need to find one or two people to be roommates with," I suggested.

"Yeah, I've been talking to a couple of people from work, but I don't know."

I almost blurted out my spare bedroom was available, but then caught myself. If Kalina was right about Abby's feelings for me, asking her to move in would've been a big mistake.

"You know, maybe I can call around and see what I can find. The contractor who built my shop also builds houses. Maybe he knows someone who's renting out a room or something."

We talked a few more minutes before I had another incoming call. I told her I'd call her back later and switched over to the incoming call. It was Bull.

"Is it true?" he said as soon as I answered.

"If you're asking about a certain fat ass, yep."

He let out a loud belly laugh.

"Word travels fast," I said.

"Yeah, it does."

"I'm glad you called. We need to have a face-to-face. Not on the phone," I said.

There was a moment's pause. "Yeah, I understand."

"Come on by the house later, I'll have some beer waiting."

"Sounds good," Bull said and hung up.

CHAPTER 15

My gate intercom buzzed at a little after nine. I checked the camera to ensure it was Bull. It was, and he had Doobie with him. I tapped the icon that opened the gate and was waiting for them when they drove up.

After getting his helmet off and placing it on his handlebars, Bull walked up and peered close at my face. "Looks like he got a few licks in, but I expected you to look worse." He glanced over at Doobie as he jabbed a finger at me. "This old man gave Whopper an ass whipping, and he don't look any worse for wear. That tells you something, don't it?"

Doobie nodded in agreement but remained silent.

Kalina walked outside carrying beers and cigars. "Who wants one?"

"Oh, hell yeah," Bull said, taking a beer and cigar while staring at Kalina's breasts.

Doobie did the same but made a point of not ogling and muttered his thanks. Kalina then focused on me and gave a slight smirk.

"I'm sure you three have important men-stuff to talk about. I'll be inside if you need me. By the way, you two missed a good fight."

"I bet we did," Bull said.

Kalina gave me one last smirk before turning and walked inside. The three of us watched. Once the door was closed, Bull gave a low whistle.

"Damn, Ironcutter. You're always getting the fine women," he remarked.

Doobie glanced at his friend but didn't have anything to add.

I shrugged. "She's in town for a few days."

"Damn, must be nice," Bull said and then changed the subject. "Well, let's hear about this fight. What made you go down there in the first place?"

I led them over to my picnic table and waited for us all to get seated before speaking.

"If you remember, three of them paid me a visit one night; Whopper, Bang-Bang, and some little turd named Zango," I said. "They were looking for information about you guys and made it clear they were going to hurt me to get it."

"Yeah," Bull said and turned to Doobie. "They were convinced that there was this big conspiracy to kill Turk and since Ironcutter here was good friends with Flaky, they thought they could punk him. Those other two didn't know it, but Bang-Bang was in on it the whole time."

I didn't say it, but I wasn't aware of it either. Until now. It made sense.

"So, I'd had a search warrant served on me about an hour before they showed up. The cops had taken my guns and my cellphone. I didn't have a landline at that time, so there was no way to call anyone. The fight was one, but luckily, I had help," I said.

"You got your nose broke and Whopper got shot in the ass. You never did say who shot Whopper," Bull said.

"Nope, sure didn't," I replied. I wasn't going to tell them either. "Anyway, when Whopper got shot, it took the steam out of them, and they left."

I took a swallow of beer. "The fact that they came to my house with the intent to hurt me has been a sore spot for me, but I was willing to let it go."

"What changed?" Doobie asked.

"I don't know how much you guys know about the missing woman case I had, but her car was found at an auto salvage yard over by the Cheatham County line. I went there and was inspecting the car when this fat ass by the name of Earl voiced his displeasure and pointed a gun at me."

"Did you kill him?" Bull asked.

"No, but I made him regret his decision," I said. "I didn't know it at the time, but Earl is Whopper's uncle. So, Earl goes running to Whopper."

Bull interrupted. "Oh, wait, let me guess. Whopper ran that big mouth of his and threatened you."

"Yeah. He did the same thing after he got shot. I'd had enough and decided it was time to settle it," I said.

Bull emitted a belly laugh. "Man, I would have loved to have seen that." He noticed his beer was empty and handed the empty bottle to Doobie.

"Why don't you knock on the door and ask Ironcutter's ole lady for three fresh ones?" It was a request, but Doobie knew better than to say no. He nodded and stood. When he'd walked away, Bull lowered his voice.

"I don't know if you know it, but him and Marti have hooked up. He's a little worried that you'll take it personally."

I grunted. "It's not an issue for me. I hope they're happy together."

"Yeah, I figured you wouldn't give a shit," he said. "Good. Glad that's out of the way."

Doobie came back a minute later with the beers. As soon as he sat, Bull spoke up.

"Thomas knows you're putting the wood to Marti. He's fine with it."

Doobie glanced at me. "Oh, okay. Thanks."

"Alright, let's hear about the fucking fight," Bull urged.

They wanted a blow-by-blow of every detail. I tried to oblige him, but I felt like I was bragging about myself. The two men ate it up though, and Bull was especially cheerful.

"He's had something like that coming for a long time," he said when I'd finished. "He's a loudmouth and thinks he's the cock of the walk."

"Are the Baroques and the Dogs still going to merge?" I asked.

Bull shook his head. "It's club business, so you didn't hear it from us, but it's all on hold since the arrests." He paused a minute, took a long drag off his cigar, killed the rest of the first beer, and then jabbed at me with the cigar stub. "So far, only four of them have been arrested. We've been looking at it and we're beginning to believe they may have a snitch."

"There's been too many suspicious things that's happened. It can't be coincidence," Doobie said.

I thought of Agent Maroney. The man had kept his identity a secret, but it seemed to me he was being a little bit cavalier about it. I didn't like the man. Hell, I liked Bull more than I liked him. I definitely had more respect for Bull, but I was not going to be the person who exposed Maroney's identity. There was something else I needed to say though. I turned to Doobie.

"I've got to say a few things to Bull in private. Why don't you go in my shop and have a look at the car I'm working on?"

Bull held up his beer bottle. "Doobie is acting Veep while Flaky is locked up. Anything you need to say, you can say it in front of him."

"I'd rather not. If you want to tell him later, that's your prerogative," I said.

Bull stared at me a moment before giving Doobie a nod. Doobie didn't protest, stood, and walked over to the shop and walked in. When the door shut, I faced Bull.

"There's only a couple of people in the world I'd tell this to. You wouldn't be my first choice, but I think it's something that you need to hear directly from me, otherwise, you might decide that I'm the snitch."

Bull stared intensely. "Alright, I'm listening."

I started with how I suspected the Satan's Dogs of burning down my shop and went from there. It took about thirty minutes.

"So, you met with Bang-Bang at that bar to ask him about your shop getting set on fire?" he asked.

"Yep. That was it. Nothing else was discussed."

"And some bar fly followed you into the pisser?"

"Yep. He almost got me. I ducked at the last second," I said. "I've never met the man, we didn't have words, nothing. For some reason he decided he wanted to take a beer bottle to my head."

Bull grunted. "Well, that's self-defense."

"I think so too, but I don't want to take my chances with a jury," I said.

Bull grunted. "I can understand that. So, those fuckers are threatening to charge you with murder if you don't snitch for them."

"Yes, they are. It'll only be a matter of time before they decide to try to coerce me to snitch on the Baroques."

"That ain't going to happen," he said.

"You're correct, it's not. I may get arrested, I may not. Either way, you don't have to worry about me."

Bull stared off into the night and took a long minute to think about what I'd told him. Finishing his cigar, he set it in the ashtray and focused on me.

"I'm glad you told me. Like you said, if I'd heard about all this from someone else, I might've thought bad things about you. So, how did the cops put you on this?"

"There's only one person in that bar who knew me, and that's Bang-Bang."

Bull grunted. "He ratted you out. He's looking at some serious time so he's looking to make a deal."

I nodded, impressed that Bull took the time to analyze it and think it through. He continued.

"Just so you know, I ain't going to tell anyone about this. But I'm not sure it's a good idea for us to be hanging out for a while."

"You're absolutely right," I said. "It's possible they may start active surveillance on all of us, and that might even include wiretaps. Feds love wiretaps."

Bull gave a slow nod. "I'll need to call a special meeting and go over this. Well, I guess this'll blow over one day. Until then, it was nice knowing you." He paused a moment before speaking again. "I wouldn't ever admit it to anyone else, but I like you, Ironcutter. Except for that time you served them papers on me, you've done me right more times than I can count, and you've given me good advice when I needed it."

"You've certainly grown on me too," I said with a chuckle.

"It's a shame though. I don't doubt there'll be times when I need advice and you ain't going to be there anymore," he said.

I thought about it a minute. "We can use a cutout if there's a need to communicate with each other."

"A cutout? What's that?"

"A third party go between. If you need to get a message to me, you tell them, and then they turn around and contact me. All we need is someone who nobody will suspect. It'll need to be someone like a mutual friend who isn't under suspicion, but someone who we can trust."

"What about Marti?" Bull suggested.

I stared. "Bull, that's a damn good suggestion. Have Doobie explain it to her."

"Alright." He finished his beer and stood. "I'm going to step around to the side of your shop and drain the monster, then I guess we need to be heading out."

While Bull did his business, I walked in my shop. Doobie was looking over the Sprite.

"I don't think I've ever seen one of these," he said.

"They were only sold in the US for a few years. The MG was too much competition," I said.

"I wouldn't buy one, but I guess there's some people who'd like it," he said.

"Yeah. I think Bull's ready to go."

We walked outside as Bull emerged from behind my shop.

"Alright, I guess we're in the wind. Thanks for the beers and cigars," he said.

"My pleasure. This situation may go on a month of two, but then they'll move on to another investigation and this'll be a memory," I said.

Bull nodded, and then held his hand out. I reached out and shook it. He squeezed a little tighter than he needed, tacitly letting me know he still thought of himself as the alpha male. My hands were still sore from the fight, and it hurt, but instead of wincing, I gave him a smile and squeezed back.

"You know, Whopper will probably try to retaliate," he said.

"I'm aware."

He stared for a moment. "I can round up a few of the boys…"

I interrupted him. "No, it's my problem. I'll take care of it."

He smirked. "Yeah, you probably will."

"Before you go, let me ask you guys something. Hang on," I said and went to my car. Retrieving a flyer, I walked over to the men and showed it to them.

"This is the missing woman I'm trying to find. Have you ever seen her?"

Both men looked it over. "Not me," Bull said.

"Me either," Doobie said.

"If I said I think a member of the Dogs may have had something to do with her disappearance, which one of them would you think of?"

"Freak," both of them said in unison.

"Freak?" I asked.

"He didn't get that nickname for nothing," Doobie said. "He's on the outer fringe of reality, even for a biker."

Bull grinned. "There's something else you should know about Freak."

"What's that?" I asked.

"He's Whopper's little brother. Watch out for him; while Whopper is in your face challenging you to a rematch, Freak will sneak up behind you and shove a knife in your back."

My jaw tightened. "Good to know."

The two men walked over to their Harleys. Bull gestured toward the shop.

"You working on anything cool?"

"An Austin Healey Sprite. I'm doing it for a customer," I said.

"It's called a Sprite?" Doobie asked.

"Yeah."

Doobie looked at Bull and gestured toward my shop. "Hey, Bull, remember that girl that Skeezo brought to the party? She had little cartoon type characters going up both legs. She called them sprites. I asked her about it. They're supposed to be little ghosts or something."

Bull grunted. "She had some big tits."

I looked at the two men and thought about how their minds worked when they looked at a woman. Bull's mind focused on her breasts while Doobie was more interested in her inkwork. It was mildly interesting. I wondered what would have been my primary memory of the woman they were talking about, had I met her at the same time they did.

CHAPTER 16

I watched them ride off and ensured my gate had closed before going back inside. Kalina was reclining on the couch, watching a movie.

"Your phone has been ringing," she said. "Why didn't you take it outside with you?"

"We have a little unwritten agreement. When we're talking, we leave our phones. They put theirs in their saddlebags." My surveillance cameras also had an audio record function, but she didn't need to know that. Bull didn't need to know it either.

"You talked about secret stuff, huh?" she asked.

"Something like that," I said and picked up my phone. I had two missed calls from Ronald. I immediately called him back.

"I've had an episode," he exclaimed. That was our code word for when some kind of traumatic event happened.

"What happened, buddy?" I asked. I was trying to listen, but I became distracted by staring at Kalina's breasts. She was wearing a plain tee shirt, but she had taken her bra off and there was an ample amount to look at. She saw me staring and gave a flirtatious smile.

"And they pushed me down," Ronald said. I'd totally missed the first part of the conversation.

"Are you injured?" I asked.

"I skinned up my hand a little bit," he said.

"Are you at home?"

"I've been driving around. I'm afraid they might be following me. Can I come over?"

"Sure, come straight here. I'm going to be waiting at the gate for you, okay?"

"Okay," he said. "Have your gun with you in case they're following me."

"What's wrong?" Kalina asked after I hung up.

"I'm not sure, I missed part of it. I have a friend who is a high-functioning autistic. He's smart as a whip but he's prone to anxiety attacks and emotional meltdowns. He's coming over."

Kalina may have been disappointed, I'm not sure. She walked with me to the gate and waited. Ronald arrived ten minutes later. When he saw her, I thought he might put his car in reverse and flee. I stepped up to his window and explained.

"This is Kalina, she's visiting from out of town," I said.

"Hi," Kalina greeted.

Ronald stared a moment, and then reacted about like I expected him to. Instead of saying hello, or offering to drive us back to the house, he took off without us. Kalina stared at the taillights before looking at me.

"Well, alrighty then," she said.

"Ronald's social skills are not the greatest," I said and motioned for her to follow me. "When we get back, give him some space, and let him get to know you. I'll try talking to him and getting him calmed down."

When we walked inside, Ronald was sitting at the kitchen table doing something on his laptop. Kalina got us two fresh beers, while I sat across from him.

"Let me have a look at your hand," I suggested. He reluctantly showed it to me. There was some redness and a minor abrasion, but that was it.

"Anything else?" I asked. He shook his head. "Tell me everything again."

He shrugged and it took a lot of coaxing before he said anything. "Some teenagers were picking on me at the grocery store. I tried to ignore them but when I left the store, they followed me. One of them pushed me down and then they all took off running."

"Did they steal anything?" I asked. Ronald shook his head. "Okay, that's good. Let's clean your hand and get some Neosporin on those scrapes."

Kalina volunteered to do it but Ronald almost shouted when he told her no. I'd tell her later that Ronald was extremely uncomfortable with being touched. The only people who he allowed to do it was either Anna or myself. After getting his hand treated, he looked it over and then picked up his laptop and retreated to the spare bedroom. I heard the lock engage as soon as he shut the door. Kalina looked at me.

"All my stuff is in there," she said.

"He won't mess with it. I'm sorry, I should have thought about it sooner. The spare bedroom is his safe space here. At his house it's his basement, but here it's the spare bedroom. He'll be better tomorrow."

Kalina sighed and then put a hand on mine. "Are you going to make me sleep on the couch?"

She was standing close. Close enough for me to smell her perfume.

CHAPTER 17

I didn't object or play dumb when Kalina inferred she wanted to sleep with me. I may have even been suggestive of it myself. I'm not sure what she was thinking, but for me I had developed a strong physical attraction for her. I don't know if it was because I was a little lonely or if she reminded me of Lilith.

I took her by the hand and led her to the bedroom. She wasn't Simone, but I wasn't disappointed. Afterward, we lay on the bed, hot, sweaty, spooning each other in casual comfort.

"Abby would be so disappointed in you," she said and giggled.

"I told you we're only friends," I said.

"She'd claim the same thing, but she's attracted to you. It's obvious. I bet she's still a virgin."

I wasn't sure. In some ways, it seemed as though Abby considered us as nothing more than friends, but then there were times when I caught her staring, and it seemed to be a stare indicating feelings of more than friendship. Kalina nuzzled her hips further into me.

"I don't know how you don't see it. She's got a hero worship thing going on," she said.

"I'm no hero," I mumbled.

"Can I confess something?" she asked after a few minutes of silence.

"What's that?"

"Lilith told me all about you. She kind of hero worshipped you too. I thought it was dumb but cute. But when I saw you fight this afternoon, I saw exactly what she saw and had to have you."

I couldn't help but chuckle. "I guess it's a good thing Abby didn't see the fight then."

She laughed along with me. "Yes, it is. You know, you're the oldest man I've ever been with."

"If you start calling me daddy, I'm kicking you out."

Kalina laughed again. "You don't have to worry about that."

"How old is your father?" I asked.

"If he were still alive, he'd be sixty."

"What happened to him?"

"He was murdered," she said. "I don't want to talk about that. Let's talk about something else."

"Okay, like what?" I asked.

"How's life been since the curse was lifted?"

"Honestly, I don't think it's changed much. It seems like I'm still having bad luck."

I felt her head turn back toward me in the dark. "I'm a little confused."

"How so?" I asked.

"I don't know what's going on in your life to make you feel like that, but you kicked a man's ass today who was bigger and younger than you, and now you're in bed with a younger woman who, if I may say so, is pretty damn cute, and from what I'm feeling pressed against my backside, you're ready to go for round two. Most men would love to be in your shoes. Oh, and don't forget the young virgin whose loins are aching for you," she said with a giggle.

When she put it like that, she made a point. Of course, she didn't know anything about the possible murder charge. And she was right about something else. I was indeed ready for round two.

CHAPTER 18

As I fixed breakfast the next morning, a few words were playing around in my head regarding how I felt about last night. Smug? Satisfied? I certainly felt both of those. Sexually, Kalina was a little hellcat, identical to Lilith.

But there was one word that was also out there in the periphery of my mind. Regret. I had not intended on sleeping with her. After all, I didn't trust her. Back when we went to Atlanta, the place where we were to pick up her precious heirlooms was in an upscale, gated neighborhood. Kalina directed me to park on a side street whereupon she waited for a vehicle to come out of the neighborhood and scurried through the closing gate.

My guess is she wasn't there to simply pick up the heirlooms from someone. She broke into the residence where they were located and stole them. Even though I suspected, I didn't question it and we rode back to Chicago without mentioning it.

Ronald emerged from the spare bedroom dressed in the same jeans he was wearing the day before and a clean blue tee shirt bearing an anarchy logo and sat at the kitchen table.

"Will you make me some toast?" he asked.

"Sure, buddy. How are you feeling?" He responded with a shrug. "I have some sodas in the pantry, you want one?"

"Okay," he said and watched while I poured a can of Coke over ice in a glass and set some toast in front of him. He took a bite before looking over at my closed bedroom door. He motioned for me to come closer.

"Did you beat her last night?" he whispered.

I frowned. "No, of course not. Why?"

"I heard screaming."

I tried hard not to grin. "They were screams of joy, buddy."

"Oh," Ronald said and then he understood. "Ohh," he repeated, smiled, and then lowered his voice. "Does she have a lot of piercings?"

I knew what he was asking and gave him a grin. "Yes, she does."

"Where?" he asked.

"Everywhere you might imagine."

Ronald was speechless and his jaw dropped open. I laughed at him.

Kalina came out of my bedroom ten minutes later wearing one of my tee shirts and nothing else. Ronald couldn't help himself. He practically strained his eyes staring at her breasts.

"Good morning," I greeted. She gave me a small smile and fixed herself a mug of coffee. She then faced Ronald.

"May I use the room a minute? All my clothes are in there."

Ronald looked to me for guidance. I gave him a nod.

"Okay," he said.

She disappeared into the spare room, and I heard the shower going a moment later.

"How long is she staying?" Ronald asked in a whisper.

"That's a good question. I don't know, but you don't have to whisper."

It was indeed a good question. Last night was enjoyable, but I wasn't sure I wanted her to stick around. I couldn't help but feel there was a lot of subterfuge with her, as in there were things going on in her life that she wasn't telling me.

She emerged a few minutes later with wet hair, wearing dark blue shorts and a bright red Nike brand shirt. I noticed she'd put on a bra, which was good. She sat down and gave me a morning smile.

"You want some breakfast?" I asked.

"Coffee is fine," she said and peered closely at me. "Your face doesn't look too bad. How are you feeling?"

"A little sore and I have a mild headache, but that might be from the beer. How about you?"

She smiled again. "I'm feeling wonderful."

Ronald rolled his eyes and finished his soda before closing his laptop and standing. "I think I'm going to go home."

He looked over at Kalina, the first time he'd made eye contact with her. "You scream too loud."

Kalina's jaw dropped open as Ronald walked out. I followed him outside. "Do you want me to come over and hang out?" I asked.

"I'm okay," he said and patted his laptop. "I'm working on a cheat script for an online game. I almost have it figured out, but I need a quiet workplace."

"Okay, buddy. If anything changes, let me know. All I have planned for the day is piddling around in my shop."

To my surprise, Ronald chuckled. "You're going to be piddling alright."

I watched him drive away and was about to go back inside when I saw an unfamiliar car coming down the driveway. He must have waited until Ronald drove out before driving through the open gate. It was a late model red Ford Mustang. I watched as the single occupant parked and got out. He was a muscular man in his early thirties, almost as tall as me, with an overly long goatee and dark hair he had slicked back and tied in a ponytail. He took a moment to light a cigarette before acknowledging me and walking up.

"You're Ironcutter, right?"

"And you're trespassing," I replied. He ignored my admonishment.

"My undercover name is Terry Malone, but I go by Trademark. That's all you need to know for now. Oh, and I'm your control officer."

"You sound like an idiot. Who do you work for, DEA?" I asked.

"You got it, and be careful who you call an idiot," he warned. "Right now, I'm the only one keeping you out of jail."

He was one of those. One of those self-perceived alpha males who thought they were the cock of the walk. Or, as Abraham Lincoln liked to say, he thought he was the buck of the lick. I decided then and there I didn't like the man and never would.

"Did I call you an idiot? I'm sorry, I meant to say you're a fucking idiot, and you're still trespassing," I said.

He gave me a steely eyed stare as he smoked. "I heard about the fight."

"From whom?" I asked.

"Doesn't matter. What matters is I can help you, but you have to help me," he said.

"Help me how?" I asked.

"With the murder charge," he said.

"Are you working under Westlake?"

He took a deep drag off his cigarette and nodded. "You got it."

"Westlake has already said my conviction is guaranteed, so I don't see how you can help me." I thought a moment. "You know what, there is a way you can help."

He continued eyeing me. "Oh, I'm all ears."

"I need Freak's pedigree. His full biography. That'll be a good start for you."

He scoffed now and dropped his cigarette butt on the ground. "That's not how this works, Ironcutter."

"Then I have no use for you, and you can get the hell out of here," I said.

He smirked. "Why don't you put me out?"

I was tired of this guy and his cocky attitude. When I took a step forward, he responded by reaching back and pulling a gun out of his waistband. I stopped and stared at it. A Glock, identical to the one I owned. I was considering punching him anyway. He saw it and smirked.

"Go ahead, boy, make your move so I can go ahead and kill you."

He was smirking as he pointed the gun at that imaginary spot between my eyes, but his arrogance only lasted a second.

"And then I'll kill you."

He instinctively turned toward the voice. It was Kalina. She was standing at the corner of the house and pointing one of my handguns at him. She must have gone out the front door and snuck around.

"That's my Glock she's holding. It's the same model as yours. I've got it loaded with semi jacketed hollow points. I don't know what kind of shot she is, but at this distance it'd be hard for her to miss, and those bullets will cause a lot of damage."

"Tell her to drop that gun or else she'll be spending a lot of years in prison," he snarled.

"Remember when I told you that you were a fucking idiot? If you will look up at the eaves of the house, you'll see one of many surveillance cameras. They're top of the line. The resolution is incredible. The recording will show you committing a felony by pulling a gun on me and then it'll show her defending me. Do you really believe she'll go to prison?"

"Video recordings have a way of disappearing, Ironcutter. Don't you know that?"

"If you feel confident in that statement, then go ahead and pull the trigger. If you don't, then get your ass out of here. You have five seconds before I make the decision for you."

I took another step forward. "Three, two…"

DEA Agent Trademark's tough guy persona disappeared. He was suddenly no longer confident and instinctively took a couple of steps back. The smirk was gone. He lowered his handgun.

"Alright, Ironcutter. You win this time, but you fucked up. I'm the wrong person to cross."

He looked back at Kalina as he tucked his gun in the small of his back. "And I'll remember you too."

While he was making his threats, I pulled my phone out of my pocket. When he faced me again, I took several pictures of him. His eyes widened in surprise and his features tightened.

"You're not allowed to do that," he said.

"Yet another idiotic response," I replied. "Now, get out of here."

He didn't want to. To leave would admit defeat and he was the kind of man with an inflated ego that did not take defeat well, even though he was the cause of it. I followed him as he walked back to his Mustang and sat in it. I closed the door for him. He started the car while he stared at me. After a second, he rolled down his window.

"You've made it harder on yourself, you know that, right?" he asked.

"You sought out this confrontation. You could've handled it far more professionally, but you had to act like a badass and treat me like a scumbag." I held my phone up. "If I get the impression that you're retaliating against me or her, I'll out you. What's the word the kids are using? Doxing? I'll dox you. I'll put your face all over the internet. It'll most likely mess up your ongoing investigation and I bet that won't endear you to your superiors."

He stared in anger, but I could see now that he may have realized he screwed up.

"Why do you want that information about Freak?" he finally asked.

I thought about my response and decided it wasn't too late to get this idiot straightened out.

"Let me ask this first, are you embedded with the Dogs?"

He gave a slight nod.

"I'm investigating a missing person. Her name is Felicity Turnbow. Recently, her car was found in an auto salvage business that's owned by the uncle of Whopper and Freak. If you're interested, it appears the Dogs are stealing cars and running a chop shop. I'm trying to determine if that's what happened with Felicity's car or if they had something to do with her disappearance and used the salvage business to dispose of her car."

He frowned. "A chop shop?"

"I don't know how knowledgeable you are about the industry but used car parts are a lucrative market these days."

Trademark stared at me like he was eyeing a moron. "I'm looking at putting away these assholes on drug trafficking and RICO charges and you want me to investigate them for selling stolen car parts?"

I didn't admit it, but he had me on that one. I could have said that investigating one crime, like the chop shop operation, may lead to the discovery of other crimes, like the abduction and murder of a woman whose car was found in the salvage yard, but I suspected I would've been wasting my breath.

Trademark stared a moment longer before lighting another cigarette. He then started his car and barked the tires as he backed up. He then laid rubber on my driveway as he left.

"Idiot," I muttered.

Kalina walked over. "That was intense. I thought for a moment he was going to shoot you. Are you okay?"

"I'm fine, and I appreciate what you did, but you may have bought yourself some trouble," I said.

"He doesn't know who I am, right?" she asked.

"Good point."
"Then screw him. Can we go visit Lilith's grave now?"
I smiled at her. "You got it."

CHAPTER 19

I asked her about the trip to Atlanta while I drove.

"My boyfriend got arrested a couple of days before you called me," she said. "The original plan was for the two of us to go get the box."

"So, when I called, you saw an opportunity," I surmised.

"Yeah, I guess that's one way of putting it. It wasn't something I felt like I could do alone. I needed muscle in case one of the other Gypsy clans got wind of what I was doing."

I'd been driving with half my attention fixed on the rearview mirror for Maroney and his red Mustang following us. So far, I'd not seen it.

"You've mentioned the boyfriend a couple of times, yet you slept with me. I'm confused."

Kalina answered with a slight shrug. "We've been together a couple of years, off and on. I grew to love him, but it hasn't been easy. Now he's looking at ten to fifteen years in prison. What am I supposed to do, become a nun or something? Besides, you're a handsome man, in a rugged sort of way. I thought that about you the first time we met."

"Point taken," I said. "So, if he's going to prison, what's in the future for you?"

"I'm not sure yet. I want to reopen the tattoo shop, but I'm going to have to relocate it and put it under a different name. I'll probably have to move out of Chicago."

I glanced over at her as I drove, wondering if she was hinting of relocating to Nashville.

"Where were you thinking about?" I asked.

"Oh, I don't know. Maybe Colorado. I like the mountains," she said.

I breathed out slowly. I wasn't sure if I was disappointed or relieved. The thought of her moving to Nashville brought an instant conflict of emotions. She was a pleasant enough person to be around, and I had to grudgingly admit, the sex was exceedingly satisfying. But I sensed something else. I guess it had to do with her family and my history with them. Or maybe I was still gun shy when it came to relationships with the fairer gender.

The cemetery was currently bereft of living souls, which was fine with me. I didn't want anyone to intrude on a personal moment. Besides, it made it a lot easier to spot a tail.

There was nothing unique about Lilith's grave. A simple bronze marker affixed to the plot of ground listing her name, birthdate, and date of death. I walked her to it and then pointed.

"Right there," I said.

She stared a few seconds and glanced at me, probably wondering why I didn't drop a few grand on an elaborate headstone. She didn't complain though and focused back on the grave.

"There's a ritual that's supposed to be performed when one of our own dies. I don't know it by memory. Maybe I should say something, I don't know."

"It wouldn't hurt to say a few words. I'm sure she knows you're here. You know, you're the first family member who has visited her," I said.

She stared with an arched eyebrow. "How do you know that?" she challenged.

"Because, other than the priest and the gravediggers, I'm the only one who knows where she was buried, until now," I said.

When she realized that nobody in her family had cared enough to visit Lilith, her face clouded up. "Yeah, okay, that makes sense. Could I have a moment alone with her?"

I nodded and walked over to a bench that was about fifty feet away and sat. Kalina sat down cross-legged and stared at the marker. At one point she caressed it, but that was the extent of any physical emotion. After about ten minutes she stood and rejoined me.

She gave a small, sad smile. "I appreciate everything you did for her."

I gave a shrug. "I hope she's at peace now. I only wish I could've helped her more than what I did."

"I hope you don't have any lingering guilt about her death."

I paused a moment before answering. "I know it may sound crazy, but I do have some guilt, and I find myself questioning things. You know, what if I'd done this or what if I'd been more attentive instead of feeling sorry for myself, things might've been different for her."

"Why were you feeling sorry for yourself?" she asked.

"Eh, a combination of things. It's unimportant."

She waited for me to explain. I didn't. I wasn't going to explain to her about the depths of depression I was in when my wife was killed and I was suspected of murdering her. I wasn't going to explain how, after meeting and falling for Simone, I truly believed my life was turning around for the better, only to have her and her daughter murdered by her crazy ex-husband.

After a minute she gazed back at Lilith's grave before turning away. "I guess it's time for me to go back to Chicago."

I stared in surprise. "You're going home?"

"Yeah, as much as I don't want to, I have to."
"Okay, when?" I asked.
"Today."

CHAPTER 20

After arriving back home, we had a light lunch, chitchatted, and then we made love again. I couldn't help myself. We then showered together and engaged in superficial conversation while she packed her things. I walked her to her car. We kissed, and then she left. Part of me was sorry to see her go, but my gut kept telling me she was trouble. Trouble I didn't need.

I started tidying up the house, but only got as far as my kitchen before becoming bored. I fixed a tall glass of water and sat down in front of my computer. I was in the middle of reading an email from a potential customer when a crack of thunder startled me. The day had started out pleasant but overcast, now the sky was dark with storm clouds and flashes of lightning were becoming more frequent. Within minutes a torrent of rain had busted loose.

"A real turd floater," I muttered and then chuckled.

It was an idiom an old co-worker used to say whenever there was a hard rain. He grew up in Southeastern Alabama and explained when it rained hard enough, the turds in the outhouse would float. I must have heard that explanation a hundred or more times, and he'd howl with laughter at his own joke. Other than that annoying habit, he was a decent enough fellow.

It took only a few minutes before the storm caused the internet to go out.

"Dang it," I muttered.

I was antsy and wanted something to do, so I braved the rain and ran from my backdoor to the shop. Turning on the LED lights was like turning on the stadium lights for the beginning of the Super Bowl. Whenever I turned them on, I had a feeling of exhilaration and for a moment all my worries disappeared. I'd already assembled my oversized toolbox, which cost almost as much as a car, now it was time to organize my hand tools that were scattered everywhere. I spent the rest of the day on the endeavor, using a label maker to identify the contents of each drawer and then putting away my tools. It was pleasurable and rewarding work, and I had to admit, I spent several minutes opening each drawer and inspecting all my tools to ensure they were organized and sorted properly.

The internet must have come back online at some point because I started receiving several text messages at once. I sat on a stool and started scrolling through them. The first was from an unidentified number. It had a comment with a link attached.

don't make me regret this if you find anything you let me know asap! pw is dogs$$ - tm

The link was to a Google cloud folder. I was dubious at first, but I opened it and after creating an account, I found a decent-sized pdf file on Freak.

"Well, isn't this a surprise. Thanks, Skidmark," I mumbled.

I tapped the print icon and then read my other texts. There was one from Marti, she said that there was something she needed to talk to me about. I texted her back and said I'd come by the bar tomorrow.

There was one from Bubba, confirming our start on the Sprite and said he'd be here in the morning at nine o'clock sharp.

The last text was from Abby, asking if I was safe from the storm. I texted back that I was, and I hoped she was as well. She then asked if Kalina was still here. I responded that she had left and was headed back to Chicago, which brought an instant response from her stating that she did not believe Kalina was a good fit for me. I had to chuckle and texted back that I agreed. I thought it was over, but then she called.

"Alright, I'm bored to death and don't have anything to do," she exclaimed.

"Don't you have to work in the morning?" I asked.

"Nope. I have the next two days off."

"I bet you have big plans," I said.

"Nope, how about you?"

"I'm going to get started on a car project. My mechanic partner is coming over in the morning and we're going to dive into it." I told her about the Sprite and how it was going to be a surprise anniversary present for the owner's wife. She thought it was an awesome romantic gesture.

"I hope I have a husband like that someday," she said.

I chuckled. "I have no doubt you will."

She talked my ear off for the next hour, but I didn't mind. I put her on speaker and continued creating labels while we talked. My guess is she was feeling a little lonely. She finally ran out of things to say but promised to drop by tomorrow and check the car out.

A second round of storms had moved in. I closed up the shop, fixed myself dinner, and then began reading the file Trademark had sent me.

Felton McLaughlin, also known as Freak, was charged with rape when he was a teenager. He was tried as an adult and sentenced to prison. There was a summation of the incident. Freak had attacked a teenaged girl in the girl's restroom at their high school. In addition to raping her, he'd almost beat her to death.

The victim said her assailant had worn a mask, but there was plenty of forensic evidence. When the detectives confronted him the next day at school, he was still wearing the same shoes with bloodstains on them. The semen recovered from the victim was a conclusive DNA match to Freak.

There wasn't a whole lot more. The only next-of-kin listed was his mother. There were no other siblings listed, and only showed his father as being deceased. There was a section on his prison record, but there was nothing remarkable. He had no disciplinary write-ups, which was probably why he got approved for parole.

Interestingly, the parole sheet showed his mother's address as his residence and Big Boy's Auto Salvage as his place of employment. At the bottom of the sheet, it showed the name of the assigned parole officer and her phone number. I gave her a call. She answered after several rings.

"Hello, my name is Thomas Ironcutter. I am calling in regard to a parolee that's assigned to you."

"What's their name?" she asked.

"Felton McLaughlin," I replied and waited as I heard typing on a keyboard. After a moment, she answered.

"Yeah, he's one of mine. Are you looking to hire him or something?"

"No, actually, I'm investigating a possible abduction and his name came up," I said.

"Do tell," she replied. It wasn't the response I was hoping for, but it was better than nothing.

"Yeah, the missing person is an adult female that went missing shortly after his release from prison. At the moment, there isn't a lot of evidence, but he is definitely a person of interest."

"Interesting," she said. I heard more clicking and typing. "He hasn't made an appearance since his first meeting with me."

"That's good enough to violate his parole, right?" I asked.

She gave a derisive chuckle. "I've got eighteen violation requests sitting on my supervisor's desk as we speak and I'm working on another one right this very minute. A couple of them are about three months old. But I'm sure the boss will forget all the others and get right on McLaughlin's if I submit it."

"It doesn't sound like your supervisor is all that great," I surmised.

She gave another derisive chuckle. "Oh, he's a joy to work for. By the way, we have three open positions. You want to come down and apply? I'll put in a good word for you. What's your name again?"

"Yeah, I'll do that. Thanks for your time," I said and hung up. Tommy Boy jumped up on my desk, sat, and stared at me.

"You heard that, right? What a crock of shit, huh?"

My faithful companion meowed in agreement.

I was frustrated. The pdf was informative, but I couldn't say it helped with the case. I was no closer to finding him and therefore, no closer to finding Felicity. I didn't know where he was living or working. For all I knew, he was making his money by stealing cars or slinging dope.

Would a car thief also be abducting women? Those were distinctly different crimes and the type of person who did one generally did not do the other, but anything was possible these days.

CHAPTER 21

I knew it was going to happen sooner or later and Whopper did not disappointment me.

My phone pinged at a little after two in the morning, indicating the motion sensors near the driveway had been activated. The deer used to activate them constantly, but I'd eliminated that problem by liberally spraying deer repellant every week and especially after a rainstorm.

Activating the outdoor cameras, I saw two figures standing beside my gate. One of them had a larger than normal build. It didn't take advanced sleuthing skills to know who that one was.

I was out of the bed in seconds, clad in camo pants and a black tee shirt, I had some slip on shoes ready by the door. Putting them on, I crept outside. I had my Glock compact tucked into my waistband, but the weapon I planned on using was a Marlin Bull-Pup rifle. It was a short barreled twenty-two caliber. When firing subsonic ammo, it was as quiet as a B-B gun.

I also had one other item that was going to work to my advantage, a pair of night vision goggles. These were a high-end brand, the kind you could strap to your head. I'd only ever used them once, and that was when I first bought them. I waited until late at night and tested them out by walking along my trail. They were fairly easy to use and wear.

Tonight was going to be the real deal. I stealthily crept into the tree line near my driveway and waited. Within seconds two shadows appeared. I activated the goggles. Inky night was instantly turned to daylight, although it was more like an overcast day. I adjusted the focus and then watched as they approached. The clarity was good enough to make facial recognition. The big guy was Whopper. I didn't need fancy goggles to know that. The other one was the skinny kid who was present during the fight.

Both were holding handguns.

I stood still and watched as they passed by, got a good position against the tree, and then brought my rifle to bear. It was a little awkward aiming it with the goggles on, especially when I'd never practiced the act, but Whopper was big enough where I doubted I'd miss.

I had several thoughts in the next three seconds. Did I want to shoot them, or should I simply warn them? If I decided to shoot, should I kill them? They were certainly here to kill me. I wondered what Whopper had in mind. Did he plan to torture me first, or simply put a couple of bullets in my head?

I did my best to aim and shot Whopper in the same butt cheek that Eva shot him in a few months ago. Whopper howled in pain and began hopping around like his ass was on fire, which is probably what it felt like. He began firing wildly in my direction, and even managed to hit the tree I was now hiding behind. After several seconds the gunshots ceased. I could hear him cursing a string of profanities as he desperately racked the slide over and over. The other man stood there, frozen in fright, not knowing what to do.

"You two are one second away from getting a bullet in your head if you don't drop those guns," I growled.

The skinny one dropped his immediately. Whopper, being the idiot he was, aimed toward my voice and tried to shoot, only his handgun did nothing but make a clicking sound. Cursing again, he threw it at me. It missed by several feet.

I carefully set my rifle on the ground, removed my night vision goggles, and pulled out my Glock. It had a Surefire tactical lite mounted on it. I activated it and pointed it at them as I walked around the tree.

"I'm done playing nice. Do exactly as I say or the next time I shoot, I'm going to make sure it counts. Understand?"

"Yessir," the little one said.

"Fuck you," Whopper growled.

My light was a Surefire model XCS, which meant in addition to the bright light, it also had a red beam. I adjusted my aim where the beam was now pointed at his right eye. Whopper winced and held a hand up to block the beam. As stupid and stubborn as he was, I think he realized he was beaten. Again.

"Alright, alright."

"Start walking toward the gate. You," I said, waggling my light at the skinny punk, "help fat ass."

The younger man draped Whopper's arm around his shoulders and the two began walking. Whopper knew he had lost yet another encounter with me, but it didn't stop him from running his mouth while we walked.

"You're a dead man, Ironcutter, you know that, right?"

"You've trespassed on my property twice with ill intent, and what did it get you?" I asked. He didn't answer. "You got shot in the ass, that's what it got you. If you try it again, you won't be so lucky. If you know what's good for you, you'll let this go. Besides, you should be worrying more about the Feds. Rumor has it they're about to make another round of arrests on you guys."

I could have said more, but there was no need. Once we reached the gate, I directed them to look away and used the keypad to open it. I stood to the side and watched them walk away. Soon I heard the sound of a car starting. As I suspected, they'd parked down the road and walked up. Thankfully, they were unaware of my surveillance cameras.

I then inspected my gate. I could see some mud smears where they had climbed over. I wanted to incorporate something into the gate that would deter someone from doing that. I saw a driveway gate once that the owner had taken a bandsaw blade and surreptitiously welded it to the top edge. It worked, but unfortunately it was considered a booby trap, which made him civilly liable for the injuries incurred by the would-be burglar when they tried to climb over. It was something I needed to think about.

I was too keyed up to go back to sleep. I went back to the ambush spot, recovered their two handguns along with my rifle, and carried them back to the house. I then went outside, put the night vision goggles back on, and walked around my property. After a while I was getting a little bit of eye strain, so I went back to the house, fixed a pot of coffee, and got comfortable in one of the rockers on my front porch.

It was a little cool but otherwise a pleasant night. My phone showed the temperature in the upper fifties. Everything was quiet and still, which allowed me to reflect on this latest incident. In hindsight, starting the fistfight with Whopper was foolish. One might even go as far to say it was boorishly stupid. Not only did I beat him, but I also embarrassed him. He would be one of those I could add to the enemy-for-life list.

He'd be another reason on that long list that caused me to constantly check my rearview mirror when I drove, sitting with my back to the wall whenever I went out to eat, jumping out of bed with a gun in hand whenever the house would creak.

Bonking Kalina was probably not a good move either. Sure, it was consensual, and I wasn't cheating on anyone, but I had a nagging feeling it was going to come back to haunt me.

My thoughts soon drifted to Felicity. With the exception of finding her car, I was no closer to finding her than I was the night Art hired me. The lack of progress had me doubting my skills. Skills were perishable, after all. If you didn't keep them sharp, they dried up and withered on you, and then you're nothing but a has-been.

I abruptly stood and walked inside. Sitting at my desk, I opened my laptop and began searching through my old case files. Back when I was a real detective, I'd solved a few missing persons cases. My thinking was that if I read over my investigative reports, it'd cause me to remember something that I'd not done on this case.

I read until the sun came up and came up with nothing.

CHAPTER 22

Bubba and I made significant progress on the Sprite. It was a small car with a small engine, and everything was mechanical, so working on it was easy. Abby came over at eleven and she'd brought a big bucket of fried chicken along with a gallon of sweet tea, which immediately caused her to become Bubba's new best friend. She was wearing a pair of jeans with tears and holes, which the designers were calling distressed, and a dark green Carhart brand tee shirt, tucked in of course. She had her hair pulled back in a bun, the way she usually wore it. I wasn't a fan of that hairstyle, but she still looked good.

At one in the afternoon, we'd come to a stopping point. All that was left now was ordering parts for items that needed to be replaced. After Bubba left, Abby sat with me in the garage.

"How's Felicity's case going?" she asked.

"Nothing but dead ends," I replied. I didn't tell her about my late-night visitors. No need worrying her.

"Do you think she's dead?"

"I hate to say it, but it's not looking good," I said.

"You mentioned the two dead women found in Rutherford County. Do you think she might be one of them?"

"No, they've got those two identified, but I have to be honest, I'm wondering if Felicity has met the same fate and she simply hasn't been found yet," I said.

"If that's true, the suspect has expanded beyond Rutherford County," she surmised.

"Yeah, it's possible."

"Has anyone put out any missing person flyers?" she asked.

Her question surprised me. "No, I don't believe that's been done."

"We ought to do that," she suggested.

I looked at her. "We?"

"Yeah, I'll help you out."

I did not answer, at least not verbally. She saw my expression and gave an encouraging smile.

"C'mon, it can't hurt."

"Yeah, okay. I guess you're right," I admitted.

"You've got a picture of her, right? We can make up a flyer here and then go to a Kinkos and get a few hundred printed off."

"Okay, we can do that," I said. When I looked at her, I realized she meant do it now. I led her inside and opened my laptop for her. "You get started on it while I get cleaned up."

Emerging from my bedroom thirty minutes later freshly showered and wearing clean clothes, I saw that Abby had already created a flyer and was waiting for me. She held the flyer out.

"What do you think?" she asked.

I looked it over. She had two pictures, including a closeup of Felicity's neck tattoo, and it had all the pertinent information. "It looks good," I said, causing her to beam with pride.

After getting copies printed off, we posted one in the laundry room of Art's apartment complex and then, at my suggestion, we headed to LaVergne.

"Why LaVergne?" Abby had asked.

"Call it a hunch, but I think her car was taken by a group of people who live there," I said.

"Who?"

"A group of outlaw bikers called the Satan's Dogs."

Her eyes widened. "A biker gang has her?"

I quickly shook my head. "I'm not saying that exactly. I think one or two of them may have had something to do with her disappearance, but like I said, it's only a hunch."

"Isn't there anything you can do?"

My jaw tightened. "I asked them for consent to search their clubhouse, but I was turned down, and there isn't enough evidence for Percy to obtain a search warrant."

"Can't you go to the FBI or something?" she asked.

"They generally don't fool with a case like this unless they're certain it's an abduction or foul play is involved. Besides, that's not my call."

We talked some more as we rode to LaVergne. Within a few hours we'd put flyers in the windows of more than thirty businesses in both LaVergne and their sister city of Smyrna. Eventually, we took a break and stopped in a Starbucks. She ordered some kind of foo-foo drink. I decided to live dangerously and ordered a cinnamon dolce. It was drizzling out, so we sat at a booth inside.

"Do you think we'll get any hits?" she asked.

I shrugged. "Hard to say. I hope so. Some people will actually take the time to look it over."

She considered my response and sipped her drink. "Is this considered regular detective work?"

"Yeah, it's a part of it," I said. "Why, are you aspiring to be a detective one day?"

"I don't know, maybe," she said. "I don't see myself being a patrol officer for the next twenty years. What do you think?"

"Hmm, it's not an easy answer. There are a lot of pros and cons with being a patrol officer and the same with being a detective. Each job plays a specific role, and each job can be stressful. Detective work has a different kind of stress, and let me emphasize, it's not at all like they portray it on TV or in movies. Most of it is boring, mundane stuff. Like going from business to business and repeating your spiel to get permission to put a flyer in their window."

"But you liked it," she countered.

"Yep. I still do," I admitted. "That's why, after I resigned from Metro I became a detective rather than a mechanic. So, you want to be a detective, huh?"

"Yeah, one day. I find it intriguing, interesting, like this case. Are all missing cases like this?"

"No, most of them are cases of people wanting to be missing and the person reporting them doesn't like it. But when a legitimate missing person case comes together, it can be rewarding."

"If I get you a refill, will you tell me how you do it?" she asked.

"How to conduct a missing person investigation? Yeah, sure, I can give you the basics."

She grinned and jumped up like her ass was on fire. "Okay, I have to go to the restroom first, so hold tight."

I chuckled while I waited. Her passion for police work was refreshing. I leaned back in my chair and stretched. Fatigue was catching up with me. While I waited, I couldn't help but overhear a snippet of conversation between two baristas that made me instantly alert. I stood and walked up to the counter.

"Excuse me," I said.

The two girls faced me and stared. They were in their late teens or early twenties, probably college students. One of them smiled and gestured at my cup.

"Would you like a refill?" she asked.

"Yeah, but I thought I overheard one of you say something about an unusual order you just had."

"Yeah, a dude ordered five pumps of caramel with his dragon drink. What kind of goober does that?" she said.

CHAPTER 23

Her co-worker laughed.

"Who ordered it?" I asked. The urgency in my tone caused her grin to freeze and then fade.

"Uh, the dude in the drive thru. Why?" she asked.

I made a hurried scan of the parking lot. "Where is he?"

"I don't know, he paid for his drink and drove off," she said.

"What kind of car? It's important," I asked.

"I don't know. It was gray, I think," she said.

"How about the customer? What did he look like?"

She gave a suspicious frown. "Why are you asking?"

"Look, it's important, okay?" I implored.

She stared and sucked on the piercing on her lower lip before answering. "He was, uh, kind of creepy looking, to be honest."

"How old was he?"

"Thirty, maybe?" she answered.

"What race?"

"He was white."

"And he was alone?" I asked.

"Yeah, why are you asking all these questions?" she asked.

"He may be a person of interest in a kidnapping," I said.

One of the baristas gasped while the other one sucked on her piercing so hard I thought she was going to rip it from her lip and swallow it.

"Okay, take a breath, think a minute, and describe what he looked like," I said.

She stared in confusion and all I could get from her was a repetition of what she'd already said. I gritted my teeth in frustration and then suddenly remembered our flyers. I pulled one out and held it up.

"Alright, let me ask you girls something, have you seen this woman?" I asked. Both girls studied the picture but shook their heads at the same time.

"She doesn't look familiar at all," pierced lip girl said. Her friend agreed.

"Alright, thanks," I muttered. Abby came out of the restroom, and I motioned for her to follow me to the parking lot.

"What's wrong?" she asked.

"C'mon," I urged and started the car.

I sped toward the exit of the parking lot but then had to stop. There were two options, left or right. The road had a moderate number of cars, and it did not take me long to realize I had no idea which way to go or what specific car I was looking for. On impulse I started in the direction of the Satan's Dogs clubhouse.

"What are we doing?" Abby asked.

I tried to explain as I drove. Abby stared in puzzlement as she listened.

"Alright, if I understand you, a man ordered a specialty drink with five pumps of caramel added to it and you believe he might have something to do with Felicity's disappearance," she surmised.

"Yep."

She stared. "That doesn't seem like a whole lot to go on, right? Or am I missing something?"

"You're right and you're not missing anything, but sometimes you have to work with what you have."

"Oh."

When we arrived at the clubhouse, I parked down the road and directed Abby to reach in back and get the binoculars out of my kit. She did so and handed them to me. There were a couple of bikes, a raggedy Chevy Malibu that was mostly black in color, and an old Ford Ranger truck. There might've been other cars back behind the house and garage, but I couldn't see them.

"Anything?" Abby asked.

I gave a heavy sigh. "None of those cars come close to the barista's description."

"What are we going to do now?" she asked.

I put the car in gear, made a U-turn, and headed back toward the main drag of LaVergne. I parked in front of a retail store and called Percy.

"We need that surveillance video," I said after explaining everything.

"I'd go down there myself but I'm currently in Texas working on Poston's big case," he said.

I frowned. "Do you know any detective at Smyrna that could help out?"

"Yeah, I do, sort of. I'll give her a call and give her the information. I don't know her that well, so it may have to wait until I get back," he said.

I agreed and ended the call. I pondered the situation a moment, and even though I didn't want to, I called Detective McAdoo. Unfortunately, it went to his voicemail. I left a message with a brief explanation of what I had and a request for his assistance in obtaining a copy of the surveillance video.

I put my phone down and sighed again. I'm sure it was starting to get on Abby's nerves.

"What next?" she asked.

"There's not much we can do. All we know is it's a gray car and a creepy white man in his thirties driving it."

"Yeah, that's not much. Maybe the surveillance video will show something we can pick up on," she said.

"We, huh?" I asked with a chuckle.

"Yeah, I want to help out on this."

"Okay, sure, but we're done for the evening. I am anyway. I didn't get much sleep last night."

"Why not?" she asked.

"Oh, the deer were active and kept triggering my surveillance cameras," I said.

"You ought to do something about that," she suggested.

"Yeah."

CHAPTER 24

I should have let Abby drive, but I was stubborn and even though I had a little trouble keeping it between the lines, I got us back home safely.

We conversed on the way home and I thought now was as good a time as any to have my talk with her.

"Abby, I need to talk to you about something that's important."

She stared with wide eyes as I tried to explain to her that being friends with me could have negative consequences and even hurt her career, but she shut me down quickly.

"Thomas, what you're saying is preposterous."

I was too tired to argue. In fact, I was so tired, about the only thing I remember once we got back to my place was brushing my teeth and crawling in bed.

When I woke up the next morning, I was still clothed, but at least I had the forethought to take my shoes off before going to bed. Abby had left a note on the kitchen table saying she enjoyed spending the day with me and added a few smiley faces to it. It made me smile, but I was still worried that our relationship would not be in her best interests.

Marti called me at nine. Since she usually only texted, I figured something was up.

"Hey," I answered.

"Hey, can you come by the shop?" she asked.

"Um, well, I have some things planned. Is it important?"

"Very important," she replied. I caught a hint of anxiousness in her voice.

"Alright, I'll be there in about thirty minutes."

Marti was talking with a beer vendor when I walked in. My first thought was this was the vendor that had been double billing her and he needed an attitude adjustment. I was mistaken. As I watched, Marti reamed the guy a new asshole for once again attempting to double bill her and told him she was going to take it to corporate if he didn't straighten up. He seemed duly chagrined and promised to do better.

"You handled that nicely," I said after he walked out.

"Yeah, but that's not why I called. Here he is now," she said and pointed out of one of the plate glass windows. A rider on a Harley turned into the lot and parked next to my SUV. It was Doobie. When he walked in, Marti got her keys, locked the door, and motioned us to sit at the bar.

"How's it going?" Doobie asked as we sat.

"Fine," I replied, wanting him to get to the point.

"You want a beer?" Marti asked me.

"Too early in the morning for me, but thanks," I replied.

She poured Doobie a beer, set it in front of him and then gestured at me. "Okay, tell him."

Doobie took a large swallow before speaking.

"They're going to put a hit on Bang-Bang," he said.

I stared at him a moment, wondering if the two of them were playing a joke. Doobie took another large swallow and then gave a somber nod to indicate he was being serious. I stood, went into the humidor, and got a good, strong maduro blend. Returning to my stool, I took my time with clipping and lighting it before speaking.

"Is this Bull's idea?" I asked.

Doobie squirmed a little. "I'm not supposed to talk about club business to someone who ain't in the club."

"Okay, whoever came up with this lame-brained idea is unimportant, but I'm going to ask another question. If the answer is yes, you can kind of look at Marti and tell her how pretty she is. Since Bang-Bang and Flaky are both in lockup at Rutherford, is he the one who is supposed to do the hit?"

Doobie stared at me a moment and then focused on Marti. "You're looking beautiful today, sweetheart."

I cursed under my breath and puffed a little too hard on my cigar, which caused me to cough. Marti hastily scooped some ice into a glass, filled it with water, and set it in front of me. I nodded my thanks and took several swallows. After a few seconds, I nodded to myself.

"What are you thinking, Thomas?" she asked.

"I swore I'd never do it, but I guess I'm going to pay Flaky a visit. In the meantime, you two need to talk some sense into Bull. This is a horrible idea and will come back to bite all of us in the ass."

"He's hardheaded," Doobie griped. "About the only people I've ever seen him listen to is Duke and you."

I cursed again, not so quietly this time and asked Marti for a notepad. I hastily wrote Bull a note that he'd understand but was cryptic enough to be confusing if it fell into the wrong hands. Finishing, I slid it over to Doobie.

"Alright, give this to him as soon as possible and tell him I'm going to visit Flaky. I've got to go."

Traffic was heavier than normal, if there was even a normal anymore, and it took me almost an hour before I arrived at the Rutherford County Jail. After that, it was another forty-five minutes before I was seated in the visitor's room. Flaky was a trustee now, so I wasn't restricted by the heavy glass partition and telephone. He walked out and paused a moment when he saw me.

He was the same Flaky. His hair and beard were a little longer, and it looked like he'd added a little weight, but otherwise he was the same. He stared a moment longer and I thought he was considering turning around and walking back out the door he came through, but then he walked over and sat at the table across from me.

"I honestly didn't think I'd ever see you again," he said.

That makes two of us, I thought. "And yet, here I am."

He casually stretched and watched out of the corner of his eye as a lone jailer walked through. He then leaned forward and spoke in a low voice. "Rumor has it, this room is wired, although I've cleaned it a hundred times already and never found anything."

I gave him a small nod. "Remember that book I read when I was in lockup, and we discussed it?"

"Which one?"

"Crimson Tide," I said.

Flaky grinned. "That was a good one. It was on TV a couple of weeks ago, did you watch it?"

"No, I missed it, but I'm glad you remember. I want you to think of yourself as the new XO, Lieutenant Commander Ron Hunter, and Bull is Captain Frank Ramsey. Tell me, what did the young XO do to his captain?"

"He defied orders," Flaky said. The grin was gone.

"That's what I want you to do."

Flaky stared a moment with those crazy Charles Manson eyes of his. He then spoke in a voice barely above a whisper. "It needs to be done."

"No, it doesn't. All it will do is open up Pandora's Box. Now I know Bull would have no idea what that idiom means, but you do."

"So, what do you propose?" he asked.

"I'll figure something out. You know I can."

Flaky stared a moment longer and finally gave me a small nod.

"It's good to see you, Thomas," he said and then stood. He stared a moment, and I thought I saw a hint of a grin forming under his beard.

"Did you know, in the story, Pandora's box wasn't a box at all but a jar?"

"I didn't know that," I said.

111

"Pithos. The Greek word describing the container was pithos, which means an earthenware container." Flaky stared a moment longer before walking out of the room and closing the door behind him.

Detective McAdoo called me as I was getting in my SUV.

"I see you walking across the parking lot," he said. "What brings you to our fine facility?"

I looked around and spotted him staring out of a window.

"I'm just visiting someone. You know, I tried calling you. I even left a message," I said.

"Yeah, sorry about that. I've been extremely busy. What did you want?"

"I was going to ask you if you have a suspect or person of interest in those two female homicides."

"Ah, it's an ongoing investigation. Why do you ask?"

"I'm investigating a case of a missing woman and I was wondering if there was any connection," I said.

"What's her name again?" he asked.

"Felicity Turnbow. Her maiden name is Holloway," I said.

"Hmm. Well, all I can say at the moment is her name has not come up in our investigation."

"Do you want to sit down and compare notes?" I asked, already knowing what the answer was going to be.

"I'm afraid I can't do that. Sorry."

"Alright, can you give me the name of the two victims? I'll ask Felicity's friends and family and see if they know them."

McAdoo grunted. "I would, but I'm under orders to keep their names confidential for now. I know what you're thinking and you're right, it's not reasonable, but my hands are tied."

Yeah, that was a load of crap. There was no logical reason to keep the victims' names a secret if their families were already aware of the situation. If they held a press conference and released the names, it could generate leads. I didn't voice this reasoning. I'm sure McAdoo already knew it. I sighed in frustration.

"Alright. Well, if anything changes, please let me know. Oh, and if you're concerned about my credibility due to that idiot co-worker of yours, the police detective assigned to the case in Nashville is Percy Trotter. Give him a call. Maybe you two can help each other out."

"I'll keep that in mind. Thanks, Ironcutter," he said and hung up.

The conversation frustrated me, but at least I'd successfully distracted him from asking why I was visiting Flaky. I left the jail and decided it was time to pay a visit to the McLaughlin residence.

CHAPTER 25

The address for Whopper and Freak's mother was located in a mobile home community in LaVergne. I don't know if it still applied, but it used to have the distinction of being the largest mobile home park in the world.

I turned onto Cliff Barnes Road and did a slow drive-by. When I came to the right address, I turned my dash-cam slightly to get a good video of the mobile home. It was an unnecessary action, but I'd developed the habit from back in the day when I was a real detective. An accurate description of a residence was always needed in order to obtain a search warrant.

But only cops needed a search warrant, and I wasn't a cop anymore, which meant if I decided to go inside that mobile home, I'd need her permission, otherwise I'd be going in illegally.

It was a nondescript, white accentuated with green trim. I could see blinds in the windows, all of them were closed, shutting out the rest of the world. The small drive was empty, but there were oil stains on the concrete, perhaps indicating that the occupants did in fact own a car. I parked a short way down the road, enabling the dashcam a good view of the door.

"Here goes nothing," I muttered, walked up to the mobile home, and knocked on the door.

I had to knock on the door twice before an elderly woman with a cigarette dangling from her mouth opened the door. She looked like she was in her late sixties, or older, plain looking, dark hair with gray roots, a little overweight, and reeking of alcohol.

"Good morning, ma'am, is Felton home?" I asked.

She squinted at me. "Who are you? Are you a cop?"

I could've lied and said I was. It might've intimidated her into being compliant, but I decided on honesty.

"No ma'am, I'm a private investigator. My name is Thomas Ironcutter."

She looked me up and down. "Private investigator, huh? Well, he ain't here. What do you want with him?"

"I'm investigating a missing woman's case and I was wanting to talk to Felton about her. Here, let me show you a picture of her." I pulled the flyer of Felicity out of my jacket pocket and held it out for her to view.

She glanced at it a moment, stared at me, and then inhaled with a raspy wheeze and coaxed a glob of phlegm from deep within the nether regions of her sinuses. I realized what she was about to do about a hundredth of a second too late. She spit out the glob before I could move, and it impacted on the top of my left shoe with a distinct splat.

There have only been two instances in my life when I put hands on a woman. Once was in third grade. McDory Lockett tackled me from behind because I wouldn't give her a piece of my Halloween candy. We tussled around on the ground for a few seconds before I relented and promised her two pieces if she'd get off me.

The second time was more severe. A woman who was high on crack lunged at me with a boxcutter. I instinctively pushed out and hit her square on the chin with the heel of my hand. It knocked her out cold, but not before she'd nicked me on the wrist. The cut wasn't deep, but it bled a lot and required a couple of stitches and a tetanus shot.

This woman was sorely tempting me. If she were a man, I would've already yanked her off the stoop and clobbered her, but she wasn't a man. She was nothing more than a drunken old woman. I stepped back, admired the yellowish globule of spittle, and smiled at her.

"Nice one."

"You assholes ain't gonna frame my boy for some rape, like last time," she declared.

"No, ma'am, I wouldn't dream of it. You have a good day," I said.

She slammed the door as I walked away. Stopping in her yard, I took my shoe off and wiped it in the small patch of grass by her drive. Once I got back to my SUV, I retrieved a container of disinfectant towels and went over my shoe with it. I then used a clean one to clean my hands.

Mrs. McLaughlin didn't know it, but her actions helped me reach a decision of what I was going to do next.

I went home and waited. While I waited, I chatted with Ronald on the computer. He conducted research on the McLaughlins while we talked.

"I can't believe she spit on you," Ronald said. "What if she has COVID?"

"That would suck," I replied.

"You should throw that shoe away, or burn it," he suggested.

"I'll consider it. Have you found anything?"

"I've found the tax records. She owns it. There is no Mister McLaughlin, so I guess she's single or divorced, or she's a widow."

"Could be," I agreed.

"Do you think that's why she drinks?" he asked.

"Because her husband is no longer around? Possibly," I said.

SPRITE

"She's probably very lonely. Do you think she drinks because she's lonely or she has no friends because she's a drunk? You're probably not the first person she's spit on."

"Most likely the second one. She sure wasn't nice to me," I said. I thought of my father. He was a mean drunk, and as a result, he had no friends.

Ronald continued. "I can't even imagine why someone would start drinking so early in the morning. That's true alcoholism, right?"

"Yes, it is," I agreed. "It's going to work to my advantage though."

"I hope you're right," Ronald said.

I was going to pay Mrs. McLaughlin another visit. This one wasn't going to be easy. There were too many unknowns. Freak or Whopper may decide to pay their mommy a visit about the time I was searching through their mother's underwear drawer. I didn't see any security cameras, but that didn't mean they weren't present. There were other unknowns, other variables, but I was committed.

I glanced at the car's digital readout as I slowly drove by her mobile home. It was a little before nine. I was banking on my knowledge and experience with drunks. Someone who smelled like a distillery before lunch was most likely passed out before dark every day. That was usually the case, but there were exceptions. Like my father. There was a time when that man could drink all day and night without missing a beat.

"I'll have to risk it," I muttered.

I found a place to park down the road and walked up to the mobile home. It had a glass storm door and an entry door. The entry door was standing partially open, allowing me to see inside. The TV was on, and somebody was sitting in a recliner chair in front of it. I lightly tapped on the storm door with my fingernail. The figure in the chair did not move. I did it again, louder this time, and still no movement. Peering closer, I could see the side of Mrs. McLaughlin's head canted to one side. I couldn't see her eyes, but I'd bet a dollar they were closed.

Trying the handle, I found it to be unlocked. I slowly pulled it open and watched the woman closely. She was as motionless as a day-old corpse. I held onto the interior side of the latch and let the storm door gently close. Mrs. McLaughlin still did not move, but her loud snoring let me know she wasn't dead.

Stealth was the key. I was careful not to bump into anything as I searched her small home, and took photographs with my phone of anything I thought might be significant. There were a couple of times I had to stifle a sneeze. The place was filthy and reeked of cigarette smoke.

115

It took me about fifteen minutes, but there was no evidence that would lead me to believe Felicity had been here. No younger women's clothing, no panties, no condoms, no pictures, no bondage apparatuses, no decapitated head sitting on the nightstand, nothing.

There were two bedrooms, and although the second bedroom had a bed, it was being used to store old clothes and other assorted junk. There were also no items of men's clothing anywhere, nor were there any men's toiletries in the bathroom. Freak may have this address listed as his place of residence, but he did not live here.

There was an old picture hanging on the wall of the den. It appeared to be a younger version of her and two young boys. No doubt it was Whopper and Freak, back when they were children. Mrs. McLaughlin had her arms draped across their shoulders, a lit cigarette dangling in one hand, a bottle of cheap wine grasped by the other. I guessed her to be in her late twenties at that time. Her hair was long, and she appeared to have been a reasonably attractive woman back then.

Before leaving, I glanced back at Mrs. McLaughlin. She was a worn out, pitiful looking woman. Spitting on my shoe was a shitty thing to do, but I felt no animosity toward her, only pity.

CHAPTER 26

I muted my car's radio and drove home in stoic silence. My brief interaction with Mrs. McLaughlin and that damned picture brought back memories of my own childhood. It made me recall a similar family photograph. It was taken during my sixth birthday. I was sitting in front of my birthday cake surrounded by my mother and father, and Mom had my little sister hoisted on her hip. Everyone was smiling, but I distinctly remember Mom and Dad getting into a heated argument later that day. It culminated in much the same way as the other shouting matches. Dear old Dad would storm out of the house and would not return until long after my sister and I were put in bed.

I wondered if Whopper and Freak had suffered the same kind of childhood. Was the situation different with them? That is, was it their mom who was the abusive alcoholic and their father took off and abandoned them?

There were only two things that probably had kept me out of juvie back when I was a young teenager. One was Uncle Mike. He'd been more of a father to me growing up than my real father. And the second thing was enlisting in the Army when I was seventeen.

I took my oath of enlistment seriously and stayed out of trouble. I was also fortunate enough to be in a unit that had squared away leadership. It was funny. I was in Bravo company, and we were a damn good outfit. Next door was Charlie company, and they were rife with knuckleheads who were constantly screwing up.

My father had no one to blame but himself for how he turned out, but I wondered if the same could be said for Mrs. McLaughlin. Back when she was younger, were there circumstances that prevented her from raising her sons properly, or was she simply a lousy mother and a selfish drunk?

Dear old Dad was like that. He was an ungrateful, selfish prick with a mercurial temper. Perhaps she was no different. I gave a scornful snort. She was the kind of woman my father would've liked; a hussy who loved her booze and cigarettes.

My phone vibrated, reminding me that I had muted the sound before going in the McLaughlin trailer. It was Percy.

"It took more work than necessary, but I finally got some help from a Smyrna detective. He went down to the Starbucks and copied the surveillance video onto a thumb drive. I told them I'd send my partner there to pick it up, and you're the partner, in case you were wondering," he said.

"That's great. I'm not too far away. I'll go get it now," I said.

"Anything new on your end?" he asked.

"I've been snooping around but haven't found anything."

"Pity," Percy said.

"How's the big murder-for-hire case going?"

"I've spent the day getting sworn statements because Poston is going to try to take this federal. I hate to say it but it's a good case and Poston will no doubt try to get one of those real-crime TV shows to make a documentary out of it."

I scoffed. "No doubt, and he'll make himself out to be the star who cracked the case singlehandedly."

Percy chuckled. "Ain't that the truth."

"Alright, I appreciate everything, brother," I said.

"You got it wrong. I appreciate you for staying with it. I thought I had an agreement with Bartlett to leave me alone and let me work my cases, but I think he too is convinced this murder-for-hire case is going to make national news and he wants himself to look good. I'll let you in on a little secret. Rumor has it the Mayor has grown disenchanted with the current chief and will be making changes soon."

"Oh, let me guess, Bartlett is subtly laying the groundwork so he'll be the number one contender for the spot," I surmised.

"Bingo," Percy said. "But that wouldn't necessarily be a bad thing. Those days where he hated the two of us are gone and forgotten, it seems. Anyway. If you need anything, don't hesitate to shout."

A portable flash drive was waiting for me at the information desk, but the little man behind the counter didn't want me to leave with it, nor would he allow me in back to view it on the computer. I asked him to email the data to me, but he didn't know how. I finally convinced him to allow me to swap a spare thumb drive I had with the one containing the surveillance video but not before admonishing me to bring the original back after I had viewed it.

"I know how all you big city detectives are," he huffed. "You think you know everything, and you don't have to play by the rules."

I had no idea what he was rambling on about. After all, I'd given him a flash drive that in fact was of higher quality than the little one I now had in my hand, but I bobbed my head up and down and thanked him for being such a good sport before leaving. At least he didn't spit on my shoes.

CHAPTER 27

Ronald called again as I was exiting the interstate.

"How'd it go?" he asked.

"It was a bust at the trailer, but the Smyrna police had a copy of the surveillance video from Starbucks. I'm going to have a look at it when I get home."

"I want to see it too," Ronald said. "Maybe I can come over."

It suddenly occurred to me that Ronald was lonely. I guess Mrs. McLaughlin had an effect on him as well.

"Hey, I have an idea. Pack an overnight bag and come on over. We'll analyze the video, maybe watch a late movie, and tomorrow we'll hang out, maybe go on a hike or something."

Ronald waited all of perhaps a tenth of a second before answering. "Okay, see you there."

I couldn't help but smile as I tapped the icon to disconnect the call. Ronald had always been sensitive and introverted. Because of that, he only had one or two real life friends. Not too long ago he decided he was perhaps bicurious. He'd started seeing someone close to his age, but it didn't last long. Since then, he'd been kind of lost. His only outlet was me, whom he considered his best friend and I tried to be the best friend he could have, but I wasn't always successful.

I received a text from Marti shortly after I arrived home.

B and F talked. All is good. B said he's counting on you.

I assumed she was telling me that Bull and Flaky had spoken to each other and this idiotic idea of killing Bang-Bang had been called off. I nodded in satisfaction and texted back.

Awesome. BTW, how's business?

I hired a bookkeeper!

"Good deal," I said to myself.

Tommy Boy meowed at me when I walked in the door. He was sitting on the back of the couch staring. I guess he wanted an explanation.

"It's always good when people take your advice," I said. "For instance, a couple of knuckleheads thought it'd be a good idea to murder a man. I talked them out of it. Shit like that is no good and there are always consequences. You see, once you go down that road, you can never go back. Enter not into the path of the wicked and go not in the way of evil men. That's in the Book of Proverbs."

Tommy Boy meowed again. He might've been agreeing with me, or he was hungry.

I thought about what I said to my feline companion while I filled his food bowl. I may be good at doling out sage advice, but I wasn't exactly practicing what I preached.

I sat at the kitchen table drinking a glass of water and reflected on my decisions for the past couple of months. I regretted what happened to Perry Goforth. I mean, after what he tried on me, he deserved a punch, but he didn't deserve to die.

Fighting Whopper came to mind as well. I should have let it go. He's a big, tough boy and he'd heal up, but it was still unnecessary, and his ego was going to remain bruised long after his physical injuries had healed. It didn't help that I shot him in the ass. He'd never forget it.

Same with Kalina. We were two consenting adults enjoying each other's company, right? Yes, we were. But it was superficial. Meaningless. Carnal lust. It made me wonder if I'd ever have a deep, significant relationship with a woman again. Like I had with Simone.

I'd punched out her ex-husband one time, much like I did to Perry. It didn't kill him though. I've often wondered if that was the impetus for him to kill her and their daughter. Thinking of it saddened me to the point where my eyes began watering up. I got up and fixed myself a glass of Scotch with a couple of whiskey rocks tossed into the tumbler. Ronald showed up ten minutes later.

"Have you eaten?" he asked. That was his way of saying he was hungry. I gave him a smile.

"How about I fix up some grilled cheese sandwiches and tomato soup?" I asked.

"That sounds yummy," he replied with a grin of his own. "Have you changed the sheets on the spare bed lately?"

"No, I haven't. You want to take care of that before we eat?"

"Sure," he said and walked down the hall to the linen closet. After a moment he walked back into the kitchen carrying a box.

"What's this?" he asked.

I peered at it and frowned. It was an old wooden box, a little larger than a cigar box, and I recognized it immediately. "Where did you find that?"

"It was in the linen closet hidden under the sheets. What is it?"

"It belongs to Kalina, and I have no idea why she left it here. Let me see it," I said.

Ronald handed it over. I took it to the kitchen table and sat down with it. The first thing I found when I opened it was a sheet of folded notebook paper.

"What the hell," I muttered as I unfolded it and read it.

Thomas, I hope you don't mind, but I need a safe place to keep these for a while. When the time is right, I'll contact you and ask for you to send it back to me. I know I should've asked first. I hope you understand. I'm trusting you. – K

"What the hell," I muttered again as Ronald took the paper from my hand and read it. After a moment, he looked up.

"What the hell?" he said.

"I thought I was rid of this Gypsy nonsense," I said and took a liberal swallow of Scotch.

"Apparently not," Ronald said. "That's what you get for sleeping with her and making her scream like a wild banshee."

I gave him a look, but he was probably right. I watched as he took the items out of the box and inspected them. I pointed at the medallions.

"Supposedly, they're very old and one of a kind. If a Gypsy possesses them, they gain some kind of power, or something," I said.

He nodded and then pulled out the only other item in the box, a book that was obviously old.

"Careful with it, the pages are probably fragile," I admonished as Ronald opened it.

He began going through the pages with delicate slowness. There was old style script writing in some foreign language with drawings intermixed.

"It's all handwritten. Do you know what language it is?" he asked.

"No earthly idea. Is there an app on the internet that can translate it?" I asked.

Ronald considered the question. "Could be," he said and began reaching for his laptop. I stopped him.

"Let's do that after dinner," I suggested.

Ronald nodded, got up, and went back to the hall. He grabbed some sheets, and after a moment, I could hear him pulling the old ones off the bed and replacing them with fresh ones. I stood and resumed preparing supper, but I kept staring at the box and its contents. It was both puzzling and troubling. The medallions and the book certainly looked old but otherwise there was nothing remarkable about them.

Personally, they didn't interest me. My only issue was, if by my having possession of these items, was I going to encounter issues with some crazy ass Gypsy clan?

Ronald and I talked about it over dinner, and as soon as we had finished and cleaned up the kitchen, I tried calling her. The automated message informed me the number was temporarily out of service.

"Send her an email," Ronald suggested.

I did so, but after a few minutes I had one of those automated messages informing me the email address was invalid.

"What do you think has happened to her?" Ronald asked.

"I'm not sure," I said. "She might be in trouble, or maybe she's gone into hiding."

Ronald clucked his tongue and began typing on his laptop. "She's a Zoomer, or close to it. I bet I can find her. What's her full name?"

"Kalina Ratkovich. I don't know her middle name. What do you mean by Zoomer?" I asked.

"Generation Z. Zoomer. Everyone who's a Zoomer has social media accounts. I'll find her," he declared.

I chuckled and watched him as I put the thumb drive in my computer and booted up the Starbucks surveillance video. We each worked on our respective laptops. The video was good quality. Not the highest resolution on the market, but still good enough to see that the car was a gray Nissan Sentra. Unfortunately, the driver was wearing sunglasses and had a ballcap pulled down low. I could tell he was Caucasian, he was unshaven, and he was between twenty and thirty, but that was it.

I played the video over and over. The only thing I saw that was notable were a couple of deep scratches below the driver's door handle and a distinctive dent in the back door on the passenger side. It was a spherical concave dent, almost looked like it'd been done by a baseball. The video showed the car leaving, it only had a temp tag, and there was no footage of the passenger side.

"I'm striking out," Ronald said, interrupting my thoughts. "The only social media account I could find was Facebook, and it's been deleted. If she has an account on anything, it's not under that name."

I had a thought. "Try searching the name Lilith Gray."

Ronald frowned for a second, but then his eyes widened in understanding. "Good idea."

It took him another ten minutes, but then he found an account for Lilith Gray on one of the more popular social media platforms.

"I think you're onto something. The last activity was two days ago," he said. "It says she's going on a trip for a while. Do you think it's Kalina?"

"If you can, send her a message for me and ask that she contact me ASAP," I said.

"You got it," Ronald replied and began typing.

While he did that, I called Skidmark. He answered.

"Does Freak or Whopper own a gray Nissan Sentra?" I asked.

"How the hell should I know?" he replied. "What's this about?"

"I'm following up on a lead. A gray Sentra may be involved in Felicity's abduction," I said.

"Damn it, Ironcutter, you're supposed to be finding information on their drug and human trafficking. I don't have time for this missing woman bullshit."

He then hung up on me.

"Asshole," I muttered.

"Done," Ronald said a minute later. "Hey, while we're at it, I've got some ideas for updating your website."

"Okay, I'm game."

Ronald wanted to add a few case profiles that had successful outcomes and a few more descriptors. Eventually, I started yawning and my head was nodding. The lack of sleep had caught up with me.

"I'm going to bed," I said.

Ronald acknowledged me with a hand wave. He'd found something on the internet that'd captured his attention, and for all I knew, he'd probably be up all night.

CHAPTER 28

I'd slept like a rock and was up at my usual time feeling refreshed and rejuvenated. I went on a five-mile sunrise run and pushed it hard. If Eva were with me, she would have complimented me. After, I enjoyed a hearty breakfast while watching the morning news. Ronald emerged from the spare bedroom as the news lady was speaking about two homicides that occurred over the weekend in East Nashville. He glanced at it as he began making toast.

"What time did you go to bed?" I asked.

"Not too long after you. There hasn't been any response from Kalina yet."

"Figures," I muttered and gestured at the food on the counter. "Coffee, eggs, bacon, toast, and a slice of cantaloupe for me this morning, what do you want?"

"I'll try some of that cantaloupe with my toast," he said.

I grinned at him. "Expanding your pallet, huh? Good deal. Cantaloupe is an excellent source of vitamins A and C."

"I remember Mom would sometimes fix it for breakfast when I was a kid," Ronald said with a hint of sadness. I had to be careful. Sometimes he'd get depressed when he started thinking about his dead parents and it could last for days. I tried to get his mind off of them.

"Is there anything you want to do today?" I asked.

Ronald heaped a glob of butter on his second piece of toast. "What's going on with the missing woman?"

"Not much, I'm afraid. They have Percy tied up on another case, and," I gestured at the TV, "it looks like they have their hands full with these recent shootings, so I doubt they'll have any precinct detectives working on it."

"We could work on it," he said between bites.

"You want to help me?" I asked.

Ronald shrugged. "Sure, why not."

"Okay, cool. Let's eat, get cleaned up, and head out."

"Um, what are we going to be doing, exactly?" he asked.

I chuckled. "We're going to search for that danged Sentra, which means we'll be doing a lot of driving around. I'll run the video for you after we eat."

"I watched it last night after you went to bed. I tried to enhance the man's face, but I didn't have any luck," he said.

"Dang, figures. Well, thanks for trying. So, we're going to start at the apartment complex that Art Bell lives at and we're going to work our way down to LaVergne, Smyrna, Murfreesboro, hell, we're going to ride around everywhere and look for it. That reminds me."

I called Art, and after telling him about the Starbucks incident, I described the Sentra.

"Do you know anyone with a car like that?"

"It doesn't ring any bells," he said.

"Alright, how about this; ride around your apartment complex and see if it's there. Maybe even check out your place of work."

"I can do that," he said. "What if I find it?"

"Call me immediately. I'll contact the police and we'll go from there," I said.

"Alright. If there's somebody in it, what should I do?"

"Good question. Don't confront them. Call me and we'll figure something out."

He didn't like that answer, but reluctantly agreed. He also said he'd search every location Felicity and he had ever frequented and would call if he found anything.

"Good, that'll save us some time," I said to myself after hanging up.

I dressed in jeans and a blue button-down shirt that Simone had given to me. It was my favorite. I left it untucked to hide the handgun holstered on my hip. Ronald wore some old jeans that his mom probably bought when she was still alive and a tee shirt with a Spiderman logo on it. I had to smile; we looked like a father-son combo. We were on the road before nine.

"Let me see if I get this right," Ronald said as I drove. "Felicity's car is found at the Big Boy Auto Salvage, which is owned by the uncle of Whopper and Freak."

"Yep."

"And they belong to the Satan's Dogs."

"Yep," I said again.

"And they aren't related in any way to Bull's biker gang, the Baroques."

"Correct," I said. "At one time they were going to unite into one biker club, but not anymore."

"Okay, and someone told you the bikers are using the salvage yard as a chop shop."

"Yep."

"And one of those bikers was recently paroled from prison for rape."

"You're on a roll," I said.

"And therefore, you believe they have something to do with Felicity's disappearance."

"Yep."

Ronald frowned. "That's it?"

"Yeah, it's not much," I lamented.

"Have you talked to the person who you suspect might've done it?"

"No, I haven't," I admitted.

"Has anyone?" he asked.

"Not that I know of."

Ronald continued frowning. "Alright, what about this gray Sentra. You think it might be involved because the driver ordered some kind of coffee drink with five pumps of caramel in it, just like Felicity and her daughter do."

"Yep."

"Well, what is your link between the Sentra and the bikers?" he asked.

"Other than my gut? I don't have one," I said.

"Hmph," Ronald replied.

I got off the interstate at Waldron Road and used that as our starting point. I drove while Ronald scanned. We went through all the side roads and parking lots that I could find. And although Ronald spotted a plethora of Nissan Sentras, none of them had the distinctive damage of the car in question. I guess we had drawn the wrong kind of attention because a Lavergne cop pulled us over.

"This ought to be interesting," I muttered as the officer exited his patrol car and walked up.

"Good morning, sir," he greeted. "I couldn't help but notice you slow rolling through parking lots. You don't look like thieves, but may I ask what you're up to?"

I identified myself and explained, opting to give a one-minute summation rather than all the details of Felicity's case. He said he understood, asked to see my PI card, and even agreed to look over the flyer that Abby and I had printed up. He eyed it for several seconds before speaking.

"Doesn't look familiar, but I'll be glad to put one or two of these up in the squad room, if you want," he said.

"I appreciate that," I replied and handed him a few extra. I watched him in my sideview mirror as he walked back to his car and casually tossed the flyers in the passenger seat before leaving. I wasn't feeling too optimistic that he'd honor his word.

At eleven, I decided I'd like something to drink and had an idea.

"Let's take a break and go to Starbucks," I suggested.

"Do they have Coke?" Ronald asked.

"Maybe, I don't know. Let's find out."

I went to the Starbucks located in Smyrna, the same one where this all started. The same barista was there. She was a cute girl, but I'm not sure I found the purple-colored hair attractive. She gazed at me when I walked up to the counter, and I doubted she remembered me.

"Give me a bold roast flavor, Colombian maybe," I said.

"What size?"

"Um, large, venti," I replied.

"You want five pumps of caramel in it?" she asked with a small grin.

"So, you remember," I said with a smile of my own.

"Of course, I do. Where's your daughter?"

"What?" I asked, and then I remembered Abby was with me. "Oh, Abby's not my daughter, just a friend. I believe she's at work."

She smiled and asked Ronald what he wanted and then found a table to sit at.

"You know why she asked about Abby, don't you?" Ronald asked in a hushed voice.

"No, why?"

"She's attracted to her."

I frowned. "Are you saying she's a lesbian?"

"Yup," Ronald said with a grin. "I understand though, Abby's nice looking and she looks kind of butch."

"Butch? What the hell are you talking about?"

"Don't get me wrong, she's cute, like I said, but she's muscular, she doesn't wear any makeup, and every time I've seen her, she has her hair pulled back in a bun."

I shook my head. "Well, I could be wrong, but I don't think Abby's gay."

"A lot of female cops are," he remarked.

"I don't know about that," I retorted.

Ronald laughed at my apparent discomfort. I had to laugh with him. When I first met Ronald, he had so many anxieties he had to carry around a suitcase to hold them all. He lived most of his waking hours in his parents' basement with his computers. He'd come a long way since then.

The barista called my name and I walked to the counter.

"Say, has that guy who ordered that drink been back?" I asked.

She frowned now. "Not that I know of, why?"

"I really need to make contact with him." I could have told her more, but I wasn't sure I should. When I saw the other barista working on an order, I leaned forward on the counter and lowered my voice.

"I don't want to get you in trouble here at your job, but if he ever does come back and you were to happen to jot down his tag, or even get a picture of him with your phone, I'd give you a reward."

Her eyes narrowed in puzzlement. She was about to ask something, but a couple of customers walked in and waited expectantly at the counter. She turned her attention to them. I waited for my coffee and when she handed it to me, I put a business card in her hand.

"Call me when you can and I'll explain," I said.

She didn't respond, but she took my card and quickly put it in her pocket before her co-worker noticed. I walked back to the table but didn't sit.

"It's nice out. Let's sit outside and watch for Sentras," I suggested.

Ronald agreed and we found an open table that had an umbrella. It was Ronald's idea. He didn't care to be out in the sun for long periods. We chitchatted while we drank, didn't see a single Sentra drive by, and were about to leave when purple-hair came outside. From the way she was walking and the expression on her face, I got the idea that she was suspicious.

"Alright, what's going on?" she asked.

I briefly explained. "Like I explained earlier, the man who ordered that drink is a possible suspect in the disappearance of a woman out of Nashville. I think I know who he is, but I want to make sure."

"Then what?" she asked.

"I'm going to attempt to talk to him," I replied.

"Talk to him?" she asked.

"I'm going to try, yes."

"You know, the cops have already been here. They downloaded the surveillance video," she said.

"Yeah, I heard that," I replied. "I don't think they were able to do much with it."

"What kind of reward?"

"A hundred for the tag, another hundred if you get a good picture of his face," I said. "If he pays with a credit card, I'll throw in another hundred for that information."

I reached into my wallet and pulled a bill. "Here's a twenty for taking the time to talk to me."

She glanced around before taking it. "Are you a cop? A-C-A-B."

I frowned. "I'm not sure what you're saying."

"A-C-A-B. It stands for all cops are bastards," she said.

Oh, she was one of those. I stifled a groan. "Oh, okay. Well, I'm not a cop. I used to be, but now I'm a private investigator and I've been hired to try to find this missing woman."

"How come the cops aren't looking for her?" she asked.

"They are, but they have other cases to investigate as well. This is my only case, so I can devote more time on it than they can."

"What do you think about gay people?" she suddenly asked.

"I don't have any animosity toward gays. To each their own, you know?"

"I'm pansexual. Do you know what that means?"

"You got me on that one. I'd have to Google it," I said. Ronald snickered. I thought she'd at least smile, but she didn't.

"It means my attraction to a person is not based on their gender or sexual identity," she said.

"Oh." It was the only response I could think of. She pulled my card out of her pocket and looked it over.

"Thomas Ironcutter," she said.

"Yes ma'am, that's me," I replied and made a head nod toward Ronald. "This is my best friend, Ronald."

She glanced at Ronald a moment, and then focused on me again.

"I'll think it over," she said, turned suddenly, and hurried back inside the business.

"I guess it's time to go," I said.

"Yeah," Ronald agreed. "Do you think she'll call?"

"I doubt it," I said.

CHAPTER 29

"I think we've searched the entire city," Ronald said.

He was right, we'd literally been up and down every road in the city limits, and that included driving by the McLaughlin mobile home a few times.

"Alright, let's move south to Smyrna," I said.

We searched in the same manner and came up with the same negative results. We did a slow drive-by of Mona's Paradise, but I did not dare drive into the parking lot. I did not know if it was under surveillance or what, but I didn't want to take the risk.

We had left Smyrna and were heading back to LaVergne with the idea of scanning a location for possibly mounting a surveillance camera around the McLaughlin mobile home when my phone rang from a number I didn't recognize.

"This is Brittany, from Starbucks," she said when I answered.

I eyed Ronald. "Hey, Brittany."

"I've been talking it over with my friend. Her uncle is a lawyer, so she knows all about these things," she said.

"I can assure you I'm not asking you to do anything illegal," I replied.

"I know," she rejoined.

"Okay, good. If you see this man again and get the information, give me a call and I'll pay you immediately," I said.

"My friend said you're legally required to pay me a fee," she said.

"A fee? A fee for what?" I asked.

"For my work. I will be performing a service for you by watching for this man. So, that means I'll be on the clock, and you'll need to pay me for my time," she said.

I frowned, wondering what in the world she was thinking.

"Let me get this straight. In addition to the reward I offered, you're demanding that I pay you simply for watching out for this guy, is that what you're saying?"

"Yep, that's our contract," she said.

"Yeah, no, I'm going to decline that offer. The reward still stands though. In fact, I'll double it, but that's all I'll do."

"Hang on a sec," she said and muted me. After a few seconds, she came back on the line.

SPRITE

"My friend said we've already entered into a contract, and you can't breach it, otherwise I can sue you for a bunch of money."

I didn't know whether to laugh or tell her and her friend they were idiots. I tried for a more diplomatic response.

"Do your friend a favor and tell her that having an uncle who is a lawyer does not magically transform her into a legal expert. If you spot the man I'm looking for and you want the reward, be sure to give me a call. Take care, Brittany."

When I disconnected the call, I glanced over at Ronald. "Did you hear that nonsense?"

"Yeah, she sounds like a nut. I bet she smokes weed."

I chuckled. "That must be it."

We ultimately decided that it would be too risky to put a camera anywhere around the trailer, there was simply too much pedestrian traffic around there. We were frustrated and decided to head home.

"You want anything special for dinner?" I asked Ronald once we arrived back at my house.

"Nah. I'm going to head home. There's a big online event tonight. It starts at nine and will probably go all night, so I better take a nap first."

"Alright, buddy. Have fun with it," I said.

After Ronald left, I cleaned up and spent the next hour on phone calls and emails. I got Bubba to spread the word about the reward for the Nissan and followed up on a couple of potential new clients. Two of those were attorneys, which was a good thing. Attorneys, for the most part, were professional businesspeople who operated above board and paid their fees, which was always a positive trait.

I reached a stopping point and contemplated fixing dinner but decided instead to go out to eat. There was an Outback Restaurant near where I lived that I frequented, and I decided to treat myself to one of their delicious steaks. I was tempted to get a beer, but instead opted for water with extra lemon slices.

The waitress was pleasant, and the food was good. I'd paid my check and was leaning back in my chair finishing my glass of water when my phone rang. I recognized the number as belonging to Brittany the barista. I reluctantly answered.

"Okay, we're following him now," she said.

131

CHAPTER 30

I sat up in my chair. "Wait, what?"

"Your five pumps of caramel dude, we're behind him now," she exclaimed.

"Okay, that's good, but this is probably not a good idea. Get me a tag number and take some photos with your cell, then back off before he spots you," I advised.

"It's a temp tag," she said.

"No problem, get a photo of it and send it to me."

"No way. If we do that, you'll cheat us out of our money," she proclaimed.

"I won't do that. Where are you now?" I asked.

"We're heading down Jefferson," she said, and then her phone started cutting out. She said something else, which I could not understand, and then the signal was lost. I tried calling back a couple of times, but it was a no-go.

I was certain she meant Jefferson Pike, which was a road in Rutherford County that went through the Smyrna city limits, but there was also a Jefferson Street in Nashville. I quickly paid my check and headed back toward Smyrna. I called Ronald as I drove.

"Hey, I've got a cell phone number. Can you find out its location?" I asked.

"I used to be able to, but the phone companies have upgraded their encryption software. None of us have been able to overcome it yet," he said.

"Damn," I muttered and explained.

"The cops may be able to help. Under emergency situations, they can call the phone company and they'll ping her phone," Ronald suggested.

"I'll give it a try," I said and disconnected.

I tried calling the Smyrna Police. It went about how I expected it to go. I did not have any kind of legal standing to declare Brittany was in danger. Hell, I didn't even know her last name or the name of her friend. The dispatcher was rather condescending in her explanation and hung up on me.

So, I had to find them the old-fashioned way. I drove up and down Jefferson Pike, looking for anything unusual, and I continued to try calling her the entire time. It took me almost two hours before I found them.

CHAPTER 31

Jefferson Springs Recreational Area was located on the outskirts of Smyrna and accessed off of Jefferson Pike. It had a picnic area, a walking trail, and a boat ramp into the West Fork of the Stones River. After driving back and forth along Jefferson Pike multiple times without spotting anything, I turned into the entrance to the area purely on a whim.

Surprisingly, there was nobody there. Usually, there were always one or two good old boys doing some night fishing. Places like this also seemed to be a magnet for people who weren't married to each other to meet and have a little tryst before going home.

But tonight, there was nobody. Maybe because it was a weeknight everyone was home, where they should be. I searched the side roads and parking areas, but there was nothing. My bladder was protesting, and I needed to stretch my legs. I parked on the boat ramp, got out, and walked down to the riverbank. The river was quiet, serene, inky black. I walked along the bank for a few yards and looked around to ensure I was alone before unzipping my fly and doing my business. Finishing, I took a moment to stretch before walking back along the bank toward the boat ramp.

My eyes had adjusted to the darkness now, and as I got closer to the boat ramp, I began to see a faint glow in the water. As I got closer, it became more succinct. It took me a couple of seconds before I figured it out.

"That's a car down there," I muttered.

I pulled out my phone and called 911, but I wasn't getting a signal.

"Shit, shit, shit," I growled.

I debated on what to do next. Get back on the main road and keep calling 911 until I got through? Or, go in the water and try to determine if anyone was still alive in the car?

The odds were, if anyone was in that car, they were most likely dead. But then I thought of that story I saw on the news about that man who was found in a capsized boat in the bottom of the Atlantic. He'd been trapped for three days but was still alive when divers went down to salvage the boat. I cursed some more as I began stripping down to my underwear.

"Good thing I peed downstream," I grumbled.

I had a tactical light that claimed to be waterproof. I was about to put it to the test. Walking down the ramp, I paused when the water was at waist level to let my body adjust to the chilly water before taking a deep breath and going under. My light stayed on, and I was soon down by the side of the car. Using the light, I was able to immediately see bullet holes in the windows and there were two figures in the front seats.

I was able to open the driver's side door. Even in the murky water, I could tell it was Brittany, and even though it was blurry, I could see the hole in the side of her head. She was held in place by her seatbelt, as was the person in the passenger seat.

My lungs were about to burst. I pushed off the roof of the car with my feet and headed toward the surface. Unfortunately, the action caused my underwear to slide off. Now I was totally nude. I wasn't all that concerned at first. I had the rest of my clothes sitting on the ground beside my SUV and I even had a couple of towels in the back of my car.

Here was the problem. When I burst onto the surface and was sucking in air, it seemed to be unusually bright. It was then that I realized another vehicle was parked on the boat ramp with its high beams on, as well as flashing blue lights and a spotlight focused on me.

"Shit."

This didn't look good. There was at least one cop out there. If it was some dumb shit like Georgie, this would not end well. A solitary person walked toward me, pointing their own extremely bright tac-light at me.

"Nice night for a swim, huh?" a female voice exclaimed.

Wonderful, I thought. Why did it have to be a female cop? This was going to be embarrassing.

"No, not really, and it's not what you think," I said.

She snorted. "Yeah, my ex said the same thing to me once. I didn't believe him either. Are you alone?"

"Yes, ma'am."

"Alright, come on out of there," she ordered.

I didn't have much of a choice in the matter, so I swam toward the bank until my feet found the concrete ramp and I walked up, stopping when I was about ten feet from her. She was a tall woman, I guessed her at about six feet, and had broad shoulders. She had her light on me and so I could not readily see her features. As I stood there, she directed her light slowly up and down, and let it linger a few seconds on my manhood.

"Well now, aren't you a fine specimen of a man," she drawled. "But enough about that. Why don't you tell me what the hell you're doing out here going skinny dipping?"

I hooked a thumb behind me. "There's a car in the water with two bodies in it. They're both dead, but I'd go ahead and call out the rescue squad anyway. I'd recommend you telling them to hurry, the current is pushing the car deeper into the river."

The officer pointed her light into my face, I guess to see if I was lying to her. The only effect it had was to blind me temporarily.

"Are you serious?" she finally asked.

"Yes, ma'am, I am. It also appears the driver has been shot in the head. I don't know about the passenger, but I'd bet they've been shot too."

She took her light off me and pointed it into the water. After a moment, she gasped. "I see it. Damn, I thought you were lying to me."

She used her portable radio and started calling for assistance. It took her a couple of minutes of explaining, but she finally had a lull in conversation and turned toward me.

"It goes without saying that you can't go anywhere for a little while," she said.

"I understand, but if you don't mind, I'd like to get dressed before everyone else gets here," I said.

She smiled now, showing nice teeth, and glanced down at my nether regions. "I think that might be a good idea. By the way, what's your name?"

"Thomas Ironcutter," I replied. "What's yours?

"Officer Carla Wasserman," she replied.

I peered closer at her badge and uniform. "You're with Smyrna."

"I am," she said and then pointed at a small black box attached to her tactical vest. "That's my body camera. Don't worry. I won't show it to anyone but my girlfriends, and maybe a couple of my gay friends."

"Gee, thanks," I said.

She laughed, but then was interrupted by someone calling her on her radio. I walked over to my SUV, hurriedly dried off, and got dressed. While she was distracted, I retrieved my handgun. I had placed it under my vehicle while I went swimming. Looking up, I saw she was still preoccupied by the radio. I opened my SUV and quickly placed my gun into the lockbox located in my center console.

Ensuring it was secure, I walked over to her while she was on the phone. She did not appear to be happy. After a brief but heated conversation, she hung up and focused on me.

"What's wrong?" I asked.

"There's this one fat ass peckerwood detective with the county. He's exercising his jurisdictional authority."

Now it was my turn to frown. "Don't tell me it's George Thompson," I said.

"The one and the same. You know him?" she asked.

I cursed under my breath. "I'm afraid so." I was tempted to voice my opinion of Georgie's incompetence and my overall disdain for him, decided that it didn't matter and kept my opinion to myself. Besides, she had her body cam on, and I needed to watch what I said. I gestured at my SUV.

"It's parked where the tow truck is going to need to park. Why don't I move it out of the way?"

She gave me a sly grin. "You're not trying to sneak away, are you?"

"Not at all. In fact, maybe when this is all over, I can talk you into taking a dip with me," I deadpanned.

Carla chuckled. "It's mighty tempting, but I don't think my husband will give me permission."

I smiled. Under normal circumstances I would've laughed, but these weren't normal circumstances.

"Alright, I promise I won't sneak off," I said.

I moved my SUV down to the far end of the parking lot and sat in it for a few minutes with the heat on high. After I'd sufficiently warmed up, I got out, lit a cigar, and then sat on a nearby picnic table.

It was time to watch the show begin. Another car with lights flashing and siren blaring arrived in a little under five minutes, not a bad response time. Soon the parking lot was full of cars with their flashing lights.

Most of the officers were not needed here. They merely responded out of curiosity, not to help out. They were doing a lot of standing around and flapping their gums, but no actual investigative work was being performed. The only thing they achieved was cluttering up the scene and getting in the way, especially the two officers that had parked their patrol cars on the boat ramp which was going to block the rescue squad and tow truck. In summation, it was a massive clusterfuck.

"Some things never change," I muttered.

It took about thirty minutes for the rescue squad and tow truck to arrive on the scene, which led to another debacle of convincing the officers to move their patrol cars off the launching ramp and out of the way. During all this, two unmarked cars arrived. The drivers exited their cars simultaneously. The driver of the second car was a young woman with hair pulled back in a ponytail. The other driver was the village idiot, otherwise known as Detective George Thompson.

He took his time lighting a cigarette, and then cast his gaze upon the scene like a king looking over his realm. I'm certain he'd seen a Hollywood actor do it in some kind of stupid cop movie and had practiced it in front of the mirror in the men's room for occasions like this.

Officer Wasserman walked over to him, and although I could not make out the verbiage, I'm sure she was briefing him about the incident. At one point she pointed me out, the witness. When Georgie recognized me, the look on his face was priceless.

CHAPTER 32

Georgie walked around speaking to various officers and trying to look important, while being shadowed by the young woman. I was inclined to think she was an intern due to her age, but a duty weapon was holstered on her hip, along with a badge clipped to her belt. When the rescue squad people activated some portable lights, I was able to get a better look at her.

The first thing I noticed was her strawberry blonde hair. It was an attractive trait, although the Italian in me favored brunettes. She faced me briefly, which confirmed she was young. Attractive, but young. I guessed her at no more than twenty-five. She was wearing a burgundy Polo shirt with the sheriff's department insignia blazoned above her left breast, and khaki-colored tactical pants, the kind you bought on websites that specialized in cop and military gear. She stared at me a moment before walking over.

"Thomas Ironcutter? Detective Thompson needs to speak to you," she said.

"So, he sent you to fetch me?" I asked.

She didn't respond verbally, but the cool stare was enough to know she didn't like it.

"Follow me," she said and turned without waiting for me to acknowledge.

Her snug fitting pants complimented her backside and I'm sure she knew it. There was a group of officers mingling with Georgie, including Officer Wasserman. They all stopped talking as we approached.

"This is Thomas Ironcutter," Officer Wasserman said.

"I know who he is," Georgie retorted and looked around at his colleagues. "Everyone get a good look at this man. Anytime he pops up, there's trouble. You can count on it."

Not to be outdone, I responded. "And everyone here get a good look at Georgie. If he's around, you can count on the investigation to be an unmitigated disaster. Oh, and someone please explain to him what unmitigated means."

Officer Wasserman started giggling uncontrollably. A couple of others laughed as well. No doubt they were well aware of Georgie's investigative skills. Georgie scowled and pointed his cigarette at me.

"You're going down to the jail and sit there for a while. Then, when I'm good and ready, we're going to have a nice long talk," he declared.

"Unless I'm under arrest, the only place I'm going to is home, and your fat ass isn't invited," I retorted.

There was some more laughter. Georgie flicked his cigarette onto the ground and stabbed a finger at me. "Have it your way, Ironcutter." He turned to Officer Wasserman. "Cuff him up and drag his ass to the jail."

"And what would the charge be?" she asked.

Georgie was about to say something but was interrupted by the tow truck driver honking his horn. The car had been pulled out of the water and was now sitting on the ramp, leaking water out of the door cracks. Georgie stopped what he was going to say and walked over to the car. The rest of the group followed. Only Officer Wasserman lingered behind.

"You two don't like each other very much," she remarked.

"He's arrogant, lazy, incompetent, and a walking poster boy for what a detective should not be. On the other hand, I like you though," I said.

"You do huh, why's that?"

"You're an attractive woman, you look good in a uniform, I like your laugh, and most importantly, you didn't mention one thing about shrinkage."

She chortled. "If there was shrinkage, the thought of how it might look normally is making me all giddy inside."

I started to smile, but then I looked down at the car, I could see the outline of Brittany's head lulled to one side. The portable lighting gave it an eerie effect.

"So, do you always go commando?" she asked.

"Heh, no, I don't. I stripped to my underwear before going in the water, but they weren't snug fitting and came off." I gestured toward my car. "I don't have a spare pair with me."

"My current husband is like a boy scout, always prepared. He keeps a change of clothes in the trunk of his car, including a couple of pairs of underwear and a roll of toilet paper. He's old school."

"So, he's older," I surmised.

"Yes, he is."

"An older man who managed to snag you and knows how to plan ahead, he sounds pretty smart," I said.

She chuckled. "Yep, he's pretty smart."

We watched as everyone crowded around the car, peering in, and making comments. One younger officer felt the need to make some crass remarks about Shanna. After a few minutes, the crime scene tech shooed them out of the way and began taking photographs. I saw Georgie talking to the young woman, who nodded and began walking back toward us.

"I wonder what Georgie has told her to do now," I remarked.

She walked over, stopped, and looked me over a few seconds like she was sizing me up before speaking.

"I'm going to need to search your vehicle," she said.

"Certainly, but I want Officer Wasserman to witness it," I said.

She frowned before she could help herself. "Why is that?"

"Because if you're anything like Georgie, I don't trust you."

The frown intensified, but she didn't reply and held an arm out toward my vehicle.

"Fine. After you."

I led the two women to my SUV, unlocked the doors with my remote and stood there with my new friend, Carla. I waited for her to ask me to sign a written consent-to-search form, which was standard detective protocol, but she didn't.

"Is there anything you need to tell me before I find it on my own?" she asked.

I couldn't stand it anymore. "Ma'am, since you haven't bothered identifying yourself, I have to ask, are you a detective?"

She paused and stared at me like the answer was obvious and I was being a dumbass. "Of course, I'm a detective. That is an incredibly stupid question. Now, I'll repeat myself. Do you have anything in the car I should know about? If I find it on my own, there could be consequences."

"Oh dear," I said, took a deep breath, and pointed at her with my cigar. "No, Madam Detective. There is nothing in that vehicle that you need to know about, except possibly for that snake that's been hiding under the seats. He's a big copperhead. I've been trying to get him out of there for a few days now, but he's not too friendly."

Carla stifled a chortle. Detective Hamilton gave us both a dirty look before abruptly turning her back to us and going inside my SUV.

"What is up with her?" I whispered.

Carla leaned closer and whispered back. "I'll tell you about it later."

I nodded, smoked my cigar, and watched. The detective was orderly and methodical as she removed an item and inspected it before going to the next item. When she got to my kits, she set them on the asphalt and carefully removed everything. When she had everything laid out, she took several photographs.

When she was done, she stepped out and pointed toward the console. "What's in there?" She was referring to the lockbox that was mounted inside the console.

"Nothing of consequence," I answered.

"Let's have a look," she said.

"No."

She stared in surprise and even made a Pikachu face. Perhaps she wasn't used to a man telling her no. She was about to say something, but Carla spoke up.

"He's giving consent to search. He can refuse to allow you to search certain things. You'll need a search warrant for that, and you don't have any probable cause."

Carla gave me a sideways glance and winked. Yes indeed, I liked Officer Carla Wasserman. And she was a brunette.

The detective gave Carla a shrewd stare before scoffing. It was a setback for her, but she didn't let it stop her. She pointed at the items she'd taken out of my kits.

"Why do you have all of this stuff?" she asked.

"I call them my detective kits. I don't know if Georgie told you, but I'm a private investigator. At one time I used to be a police detective."

"I know that," she huffed. "Detective Thompson has told me all about you."

"Well then, if you're ever around a real detective, ask them what kind of gear they carry around. You'll find they have a lot of the same things I do," I said and pointed at my equipment. "What does Georgie have in the trunk of his car, besides a blow-up doll?"

She gave me a long stare and then walked off without comment.

"I guess she's done," I surmised and began packing my gear back into the bags. Carla was nice enough to help me.

"You've got a lot of equipment," she remarked.

"I actually use some of it from time to time," I said.

"What about that other piece of equipment? Do you use it from time to time as well?" she asked and then chortled. I laughed with her and changed the subject.

"She seems a little young to be a detective," I remarked.

"Oh, you don't know the half of it," Carla said. "Her name's Nancy Hamilton. She started out as a dispatcher with the county a little under a year ago. Before you know it, she's in the academy. She graduated last month."

I eyed Carla, wondering if she was pulling my leg. "Wait, she's only been out of the academy for a month? And she's now a detective?"

Carla nodded. "Isn't that something?"

"Back in my day, you had to have at least three years of street cop experience before you were even considered to be a detective."

"Yeah, it's still the same way, unless you're sleeping with the chief deputy of the sheriff's department," Carla said.

"Ah, well, that explains things, but he can't like her too much. He stuck her with Georgie."

"The prevailing theory is they're either grooming her to take George's place and then demote or fire him, or it's simply a matter of keeping her away from some of the younger, more handsome detectives," she said.

"Could be both," I said.

"Could be, I guess. She certainly gets a lot of attention. What do you think about her?" she asked.

"She seems attractive enough, the strawberry blonde hair is nice, but I prefer brunettes, like you. You have nice hair. You should let it grow out a few inches though."

She gave a short chortle. "My husband says the same thing. Says he likes pulling on it."

"I can see that," I said and gestured at Detective Hamilton. "She strikes me as a high-maintenance type."

"My husband says I'm high maintenance," she said.

"Yeah, maybe so, but you'd be worth it," I said with a wink, which got another laugh.

We continued talking while I packed my gear and put my bags back in my SUV. Carla suddenly stopped in midsentence and cleared her throat. When I turned around, I saw Georgie and his flunky walking back toward us.

"Detective Hamilton said you're refusing to open up that lockbox in your console," he said.

"That's right," I replied.

"Why not?" he asked.

"Because I don't have to," I replied.

He smirked, as if he'd caught me. "So, you're hiding something. That gives me probable cause to impound your vehicle and get a search warrant."

"No, it doesn't," Carla said.

I chimed in as well. "Georgie, if I was you, I'd rethink your premises. You cannot obtain a search warrant simply because someone does not give you consent."

He didn't like it and it showed. He stabbed a finger at me. "Are you armed?"

"Not at the moment."

Even though he was dumb, he probably suspected I had a firearm in that lockbox, and he wanted it.

Georgie turned to Carla. "When you first ran up on this idiot, did you search him?"

"Nope," she answered.

Georgie arched an eyebrow. "Why not?"

"Because, when I first encountered Mister Ironcutter, he was in the river. He'd risked drowning to go down there and try to see if the victims were still alive. When he came out of the water, he was buck naked. Not a gun on him anywhere. Let me correct myself, the man is certainly packing, but it isn't a firearm, if you know what I mean."

When she said it, she gave Detective Hamilton a knowing wink. Hamilton was confused for a moment, but when she figured it out, she hastened a glance at me before quickly turning away and stared attentively at Brittany's car. They had it strapped down and were now draping a tarp over the entire car and securing it with bungee cords.

It took Georgie a little longer to understand Carla's words, but now he scoffed and lit another cigarette. Taking a deep drag, he stared at me like I was the cross-eyed stepchild that he never wanted.

"Thomas-Fucking-Ironcutter. Do you gals know anything about him? No? Well, let me tell you. Yeah, he was once a detective with the almighty Nashville Police Department. He resigned in disgrace, under suspicion of murdering his pregnant wife. I'm sure I don't know the half of it, but I've heard all kinds of things about him. I do know one thing though, back in June he murdered a man in cold blood, and I'm going to see to it you go to prison for the rest of your life, Thomas-Fucking-Ironcutter."

He waited a moment for a response. When I didn't give him one, he spat on the ground and walked off. The two women stared at me. I focused on Detective Hamilton.

"Since Detective Georgie has decided to act like a buffoon, I won't be consenting to anything else. I'll give you the two-minute version of what I know and my involvement. If that doesn't interest you, then too bad. Either way I'm leaving."

She settled for the two-minute version. When I was finished, she began asking questions, which turned my two-minute statement into ten minutes. I finished by showing her the call history on my phone.

"Here is the first call, from Brittany to my phone. As you can see, it wasn't a long conversation because the signal was lost." I scrolled down. "And here is where I made numerous attempts to call her back. If you feel it's necessary, subpoena my phone records. I'm sure it'll show the cell towers my phone pinged from the moment I left the restaurant until I turned in the entrance to Jefferson Springs, which is about the same time I lost my phone signal."

Detective Hamilton looked it over. "Can you screenshot that and send it to me?"

"Um, possibly. How do you do that?" I asked.

She once again gave me that stare before holding her hand out. I handed her my phone and watched while she fiddled with it a minute before handing it back. Her phone gave off a sound alert, indicating she had texted it to herself. I glanced down at my phone and noticed she'd deleted her phone number.

"Okay, we'll be in touch," she said, turned, and walked off.

I turned to Carla. "Well, this has been a shitty night, with the exception of meeting you. I think I'm going to go home now, take a hot shower, have a drink, and try to convince myself I shouldn't feel guilty for getting Brittany and her friend involved in all of this. It was a pleasure to meet you, Officer."

I started for my SUV, but Carla stopped me.

"I have to ask, all that shit Thompson said, is it true?"

My face tightened and I took a deep breath before responding. "Not in the way he made it sound. As far as that incident back in June, the answer is no, I didn't murder anyone."

I got my wallet and fished out a business card. "If you're interested in the whole story, give me a call sometime. We'll meet for a beer. Hell, bring your husband, I think I'd like to meet him."

Carla couldn't help but smile and waved as I drove off. As I drove by Georgie and his flyweight-sized blonde-headed flunky, I was tempted to flip them off, but stayed civil and kept driving.

CHAPTER 33

Once I got a good cell signal, I called Percy and updated him.

"They didn't ask about Felicity?" he asked.

"One or two questions, that's it. It was the same with Freak. It's like they weren't interested in any information or theories I had, but that's Georgie for you. But, I bet I planted a seed, and if I did, one of those knuckleheads will be calling you in a day or two asking about the case."

"Is she as bad as Thompson?" he asked.

"She's young and inexperienced, but I didn't get a good read on her as a person." I left out the part where she was probably sleeping with her chief deputy. There was no need to spread gossip, and besides, I didn't know it for a fact.

"Alright, thanks for letting me know," Percy said.

"Let me ask you something, brother. Do you think my suspicions have any merit or am I making something out of nothing and blowing smoke up my own ass?"

Percy was about the only person whose opinion I valued, and I knew it would be honest. There was a long pause before he answered.

"Thomas, we've known each other for what, twenty years now? You've always amazed me with your skills and intuition. If you think there's a connection, there's a connection. Stick with it, chances are you'll solve this thing before anyone else does, including me."

"Alright. Thanks," I said.

Once I arrived home, I got in the shower, soaped up heavily, and stayed there until I could no longer smell river water. It gave me time to reflect on what happened earlier. Some might call it a textbook example of the law of unintended consequences. If I had not offered to pay Brittany a reward for spotting the Sentra, she and her friend would still be alive. I knew I tried to discourage her from following the car, nevertheless, she did, and now she's dead. Her and her friend.

Thanks to me.

I put on underwear and a tee shirt before heading to the kitchen. I had poured myself a short tumbler of Scotch, but ultimately, I went to bed without touching it. It took about thirty minutes for me to wind down, and when I slept, I had dreams. I don't recall all the details, but Brittany was in one or two of them.

The next morning, I did my usual routine. When I left the gym, I tried giving Trademark a call. Surprisingly, he answered.

"Have you heard the latest?" I asked.

"No, hang on a minute." I heard people talking in the background before the phone was muted. He came back on a minute later. "I'm at the Dog's clubhouse. Make it quick."

"Two people were killed last night and they were dumped in the Stones River. Freak is a possible suspect," I said.

"How do you know?" he asked.

I didn't bother explaining my reasoning. "Is he at the clubhouse now?"

"Yeah, as a matter of fact, he is. Why?"

"What kind of car is he in?" I asked.

"There you go with the car thing again. He doesn't have a car here. He's on a bike. The club is about to go on a ride, and I've been invited. This is important in case you didn't know."

"Was he there last night?" I asked.

"I have no idea. When I got here this morning, he was already here. What's with all these questions?"

"Indulge me a little bit, okay? Is there any gray Nissan Sentra there?" I asked.

He sighed. "Hang on." I could hear him moving around. After a moment, he spoke quietly. "There's no gray Sentra anywhere around here. You're going to have to do better than this, Ironcutter. You've done absolutely nothing to help yourself out. Since you've fucked yourself with the Dogs, you need to devote your efforts into digging up dirt on the Baroques. You need to get in bed with them and start wearing a wire every time you speak with one of them. Don't call me unless you have something in the form of evidence that we can use to put their asses away. And if you don't call, life as you know it will be coming to an end."

I heard the distinct disconnect signal as he ended the call.

"Asshole," I muttered.

I turned on the television, and no surprise, the double murder was the headline story. As I watched, my feelings of guilt were becoming exponentially greater. Sure, she ignored me when I told her to stop following the Sentra, but I reminded myself that I was the one who put the idea in her head.

I sighed deeply. Bubba was coming over after he got off work and the two of us were supposed to work on the Sprite, but I knew I'd continue to stress over this if I didn't at least try to do something. I called Bubba and explained. It turned out he had been asked to work overtime by his boss, and we agreed to try again tomorrow.

My conversation with Trademark didn't satisfy me and I knew what I needed to do. I dressed with the possibility in mind that I might get in a fight. An older but durable pair of jeans, a plain black tee shirt, and a pair of Red Wing brand steel-toed boots. In addition, I dropped a pair of brass knuckles in my back pocket, put a lock-blade knife in my front pocket, and put a backup gun in an ankle holster.

I texted Ronald and asked him to keep an eye on my GPS in case something happened to me and headed out. The first place I was going to visit was the McLaughlin home. I wasn't too worried about anything happening there. It was the next place on my list that might get me into a sticky situation. Trademark said the club members were going on a ride, and they were inviting others to ride with them, the hang arounds, potential prospects, and maybe a few others. That most likely meant the clubhouse was going to be empty of people. I was going to go see for myself if there was a gray Sentra parked there or not.

Mrs. McLaughlin was sitting out back in a lawn chair under a shade tree as I drove by, a large glass in one hand, a cigarette dangling from the other. If she recognized me, she didn't show it, but it didn't matter. There was no car present.

It was only a ten-minute drive from there to the clubhouse. I drove up to the front gate and pushed the button on the intercom. I had no idea what I was going to do if Whopper answered. He'd probably shoot on sight. But nobody answered.

I wasn't going to risk getting hung up on the barbed wire running along the top of the fence, so I parked down the road and walked around the perimeter. When I got to the backside of the property, I came within a hair's breadth of stepping on a bear trap that was hidden in the tall weeds.

"That would've hurt," I muttered.

I was okay though. I didn't step on it, and from my position, I could now see all the cars parked in back. There were six of them, and none of them were even close to looking like a gray Nissan Sentra.

I carefully retraced my steps and made my way back to my SUV. If there was anyone in the clubhouse, they either didn't notice me or didn't care. There were a couple of surveillance cameras, but I didn't care if I was recorded. What were they going to do, call the cops on me? Pay me a visit in the middle of the night?

I was aimlessly driving around the Smyrna and LaVergne area when I received a phone call from a number I did not recognize.

"Good morning, Thomas, it's Carla Wasserman from last night."

"Hey, good morning. This is an unexpected surprise," I said.

"I hope it's a pleasant surprise," she said lightheartedly.

"After what Georgie told you and Detective Hamilton last night, I was certain you'd want to keep a lot of distance from me."

She laughed. "Oh, I might have, but curiosity got the best of me and after I got off work, my husband and I spent an hour or so reading about you on the internet. That's some interesting stuff."

"I don't know if I'd call it interesting. I'm just now getting my life back to near normal after all of that," I said.

I don't know how much she'd read. The false arrest for my wife's murder was usually the first thing that popped up if one were to search my name. If you kept digging, there were a lot of other things out there that I wished would disappear.

"So, what can I do for you, Officer?" I asked.

"First off, call me Carla."

"Alright, Carla. What's going on?"

"I got a phone call from a buddy this morning. He works for the TBI and apparently a shit storm has been stirred up."

"Over what, the double murder?" I asked.

"Yep. Since the murder took place on state property, the TBI was supposed to have been notified by the investigating agency. It wasn't done and Georgie tried to blame me."

"Wow, that sounds like something he'd do. Did you get in trouble?"

"Oh, no. That got straightened out quick. I've been told there was a conference call early this morning and the short of it is, Georgie has stepped on his dick once again and the sheriff is not happy."

"Good, did he get fired?" I asked. I hoped he did. He was a terrible detective, but also, if he got fired, his so-called murder investigation had a good chance of going away.

Carla laughed. "Nope, not yet anyway, but he was removed from the case."

"Smart move. Who's the primary now?"

"Why, you've already met her," she said and laughed again. "You know, the one whose ass you stared at more than once, Detective Nancy Hamilton. Don't worry though, my buddy is partnering up with her, and he's a squared away dude. He's with her now at the autopsy."

"That's good, I suppose. That case needs a competent detective working it."

"Bob is definitely competent; you can count on it. Which leads me to the reason I'm calling. He wants to do a follow-up interview with you."

"Yeah, I can understand that. Have him call me," I said.

"He will. His name is Bob Thrasher. I've already given him your number. When they're done with the autopsy, he'll give you a buzz. Him and Nancy Drew."

I sighed. "I'd rather not deal with her."

"Oh, Thomas, just take her skinny dipping. You do that and she'll be following you around like a little puppy dog." She then erupted into a giggling fit. "Anyway, I have to go. Oh, I told my husband everything. He's jealous and said we should absolutely get together for a beer."

"That sounds good. Give me a call and we'll make a date," I said.

I'd no sooner disconnected when my phone rang again.

"Hello, Mister Ironcutter. This is Agent Bob Thrasher with the TBI."

"I just got off the phone with Carla. She said you'd call and that you want to do a follow-up interview."

"Yessir, I do. Are you at home?" he asked.

"No, I'm actually in Rutherford County at the moment."

He paused for a moment. "Would you mind meeting us back at Jefferson Springs? It'd be a good opportunity for you to walk us through it all."

"Not a problem, I'll see you there," I replied. He said they'd be there in thirty minutes.

I diverted to a chain restaurant that specialized in fried chicken and tea by the gallon. I arrived at the boat ramp ten minutes later, parked in the same spot I'd parked in when little Nancy Drew searched my vehicle, and ate a chicken sandwich while I waited. Agent Thrasher did not yet know it, but I had an ulterior motive for meeting with him. I wanted to get him and the TBI involved in the Felicity Turnbow case.

CHAPTER 34

The two of them arrived in different vehicles. Nancy had a Dodge Durango, black like Georgie's unmarked unit, and dark tints. Bob's car was a Ford SUV, like mine. He got out of his car and stretched as he looked around. He appeared to be in his early forties, like Carla. He was also about six feet tall, relatively fit, with an earnest expression and dark brown hair that was starting to gray.

Nancy took a moment to check herself in her rearview mirror before exiting. She was a little on the petite side, barely five-three, slender, and her strawberry blonde hair appeared to have been perfectly brushed and tied back. She was young, probably around Abby's age, but this girl looked like she was still in her teens. Hell, she even had a hint of acne that was covered with makeup. She looked every bit as good in the daylight as she did last night.

"I appreciate you meeting with us," Bob said as he shook my hand.

"Not a problem. I was going to come back here anyway."

"Why?" Nancy asked.

I pointed skyward. "It's a sunny day out, which makes it easier to search the scene."

"We've already searched the scene," she rejoined.

"Yeah, during the night," I said. "Plus, I bet nobody walked up and down the road leading here, right? Did you?"

She didn't answer. I had a feeling that was her standard reaction when confronted with something that she overlooked or failed to do, she simply didn't say anything. I held my hands out. "You've probably already thought about it and are getting together a few people to do it, so I won't bother. So, Agent Thrasher, what questions do you have for me?"

He looked around and pointed out the picnic table I sat at last night. "That looks like an excellent spot to conduct an interview."

I agreed. I got the gallon jug of tea out of my vehicle, along with three Styrofoam cups of ice and met them over there.

Nancy looked it over and then stared. "Is that for all of us?"

"Absolutely," I said. "It's been my experience that watching an autopsy, even if you have a mask on, leaves an unpleasant taste in your mouth. This'll help."

Nancy surprisingly gave me a smile and thanked me when I poured her cup. Bob did the same.

He pulled his digital recorder out and opened his A4-sized notepad. Nancy looked a little embarrassed that she didn't have one until I reminded her that her cellphone had a recording function. Once they were set up, I walked them through everything, beginning with Felicity's disappearance, the recovery of her car, and my personal suspicions that at least one member of the Satan's Dogs was involved.

I then told them how I met Brittany and the unusual drink order. Both of them had been taking copious notes. Bob paused and held up his pen.

"Let me see if I got this right. Felicity and her daughter like to drink a Starbucks dragon drink with five pumps of caramel added to it." He paused and read a moment. "And you were at the Smyrna Starbucks recently and the barista was commenting about a man who ordered a dragon drink with five pumps of caramel, and this is an unusual order?"

"It's my understanding that caramel does not go well with the ingredients of a dragon drink. I don't know what's in them…"

Nancy interrupted me. "A dragon drink is a fruity drink. It has mango and white grape juice in it, so no, adding caramel, especially that much, would make it taste weird."

"Interesting," Bob said. "So, it's not something that is commonly done, and yet a short time after Felicity Turnbow goes missing, a man orders the same concoction." He stared at me. "Thomas, if your hypothesis is correct, this would suggest that perhaps he was ordering the drink for Felicity."

"Which would mean she might still be alive," I added. "It doesn't answer the question as to if she is with him willingly or a hostage, but it gives me hope."

He thought a minute and waggled his pen at me. "Thomas, it's not much, but you may be onto something. So, you overhear the victim telling her co-worker about the unusual description. You interview her. This is where you learn of the description of the vehicle in question?"

"Yes," I replied.

"And the vehicle is, let me see." He paused and looked at his notes. "An older model Nissan Sentra with faded gray paint and distinctive damage to the rear driver's side door."

"Correct," I said. "The Smyrna Police have a copy of the surveillance video."

"Excellent. We'll get a copy of it." He turned to Nancy. "Was a statewide BOLO aired?"

"Yes, last night," she answered.

"How often was it repeated?" he asked. Nancy didn't answer, which indicated the BOLO was probably aired only once. "This needs to be aired hourly. Why don't you make a call to your supervisor and have them make that happen, or do you want me to?"

Nancy's face reddened in anger. "Don't blame me. George was supposed to do that."

Bob maintained an even expression. "I'm not blaming. This is the nature of detective work, sometimes things are overlooked."

Nancy calmed down, excused herself, and walked out to the far end of the parking lot, taking her phone with her. Bob refocused on me.

"Okay, where were we?" he asked.

I gave him a summation of my investigation and explained how the recovery of Felicity's vehicle indirectly connected her to the Satan's Dogs.

"Alright, so you suspect Whopper is the one fencing stolen cars, but what about Freak? What has made you suspect him of being involved?"

"He served time for rape and was recently let out. I admit, it's not much," I said.

Bob did not offer any comment and instead jotted it down. "Alright, anything else?"

"I believe you've got the gist of it," I said.

"Okay, if you don't mind, I'd like to video record you while you walk us through your actions last night."

I agreed. He started filming as I re-entered the area and parked my SUV on the boat ramp. After getting out of my car, I narrated the rest.

"I can't explain why I decided to park on the boat ramp. Maybe it was from past cases that I've been involved in. Up in Nashville we've had more than one car driven into the Cumberland River. So, it was dark out, which allowed me to see the faint glow of the lights. They were still on."

"Alright, what did you do next?" he asked.

"At that time, I could not make out anything other than a faint outline of a car. I didn't know if it was Brittany and her friend or someone else. For that matter, I had no idea if the car was occupied. I'm a decent enough swimmer, so I stripped down and went in."

"Did you know what kind of car Brittany was driving?" he asked.

"No, I didn't. So, I had a tac-light with me. I dove under water and swam toward the car. The first thing that jumped out at me were the bullet holes in the windows. I got closer to the driver's side and that's when I saw Brittany. It was obvious she was dead. When I ran out of air, I surfaced. I was going to go back down, but Officer Wasserman had driven up at that point. She had her lights on me and ordered me out of the water," I said.

"Were you nude?" Nancy asked.

"I was," I answered.

She stared but didn't say anything. Bob was smiling. I assumed Carla had already told him about it. I continued.

"I advised her what I'd found. She called in backup, and we waited together for everyone to arrive. Oh, while we were waiting, I dried off and put my clothes back on. Y'all know the rest."

"Alright, Thomas. While I'm recording you, I want to ask a couple of hard questions," he said.

I knew this was coming. "Go ahead."

"Did you have anything to do with the death of these two people?"

"I did not," I said. I left out the part about the guilt I felt, but that was not anyone else's business.

"Alright, you may not be aware of it, but a meeting was held this morning in regard to this case. During that meeting, Detective George Thompson with the Rutherford County Sheriff's Department asserted that you intentionally withheld critical information."

I felt my anger rising. "Like what?"

Bob's face tightened and he gave a pained smile. "He said many things, most of which is irrelevant to this investigation, but he strongly urged us to consider you the prime suspect."

I forced myself to calm down. "Detective George Thompson is an idiot. For the record, I solved one of his previous cases in which he erroneously concluded the murder of a man was a suicide, and when I got up this morning, I was fully prepared to investigate and solve this case on my own. If not for the intervention of the TBI, that's what I would be doing right now." I pointed at him and Nancy. "This case is solvable. You find that Sentra and the driver, this case will come together."

If the driver was Freak, or perhaps Whopper, interrogating them would've been a waste of time. If I got either one of them alone in a room, I could've extracted the truth out of them, if I wanted to take it that far.

I cleared my throat. "I have a question." They stared expectantly. I gestured toward the boat ramp. "What were their full names?"

"Brittany Parkhurst and Shane Maldonado. Shane was transgender and used the name Shanna instead of Shane," Bob said. "We're scheduled to meet with the family members this afternoon at two."

"Has anyone bothered contacting the DEA agent? His name is Terry Maroney."

Bob had already turned the camera off. When I mentioned Trademark, he double checked it to make sure it was off.

"We have. Agent Maroney has echoed what Detective Thompson asserted, that you are a suspect in a murder committed at a bar in June. He also said your arrest is imminent," Bob said, paused, and continued.

"I am not privy to the particulars of that investigation. It's not my case, and I don't see myself becoming involved in it. However, accusations have been made."

"Spurious accusations," I said.

Bob gave the pained smile again. "Perhaps so, but until this case is resolved, the accusations by Detective Thompson will be an issue." He gestured toward the other detective. "Detective Hamilton is the lead investigator for this case, but I believe I can speak for the both of us and formally request that you cease any kind of active investigation into the murder of Brittany Parkhurst and Shane Maldonado."

He seemed almost apologetic when he said it, but I knew he wasn't joking around. I didn't like it, but I had to be honest, it was prudent and logical. I was about to say something when Nancy decided to speak.

"You know, this would be a good time to make arrangements for you to take a lie detector test and clear your name."

I eyed her. "For which case?"

"How about both?" she asked with a smug grin.

"How about no?" I retorted. The grin disappeared.

"Thomas, you can refuse, but how can we eliminate you as a suspect otherwise?" she asked.

"That's a good line, but the thing is, Detective, I don't give a shit if you consider me a suspect in any crime," I replied.

Bob smiled before he could help himself. Nancy was not happy. She didn't scowl, but she definitely did not like my response. I didn't care. I turned to Bob.

"Alright, you're asking me to keep my nose out of this case. I'll try, but I can't promise anything," I said.

"Why not?" Bob asked.

"Because I'm convinced the suspect in this case is also the prime suspect in the disappearance of Felicity Turnbow."

"You have no proof of that," Nancy asserted.

"Not yet," I countered.

Her eyes narrowed at me. She was about to retort, but her phone rang. She glanced at the caller ID and walked away from us before answering.

"She's too young to be a detective," I remarked in a low voice.

Bob shrugged, reached into his jacket, and came out with a business card. "If you find anything that might help with this case, I'd appreciate it if you called."

"I will," I said. "I only hope that you seriously consider Felicity's disappearance when investigating this case."

Bob only responded with a nod. Detective Hamilton walked back to us.

"I have the rescue squad coming to search the area," she said.

"Excellent," Bob said and turned to me. "When we meet with the victims' families, I'll ask if either of the two victims mentioned anything about Felicity or the car."

"I appreciate that," I said.

He turned to Detective Hamilton. "Do you have anything else for Thomas?"

She glanced at me and stared a moment before shaking her head.

Bob turned back to me. "We appreciate your cooperation, Thomas. One of us will be in touch."

"Thanks," I replied.

I knew I was being dismissed. It was understandable. I got in my car and drove off, pausing only long enough to refill my cup of tea. I caught a glimpse of Detective Hamilton in my rearview mirror. I was checking her out again, and when I realized what I was doing, I chastised myself.

"Don't be a dumbass," I muttered.

CHAPTER 35

I pulled my eyes away from the mirror and concentrated on driving. The meeting didn't go exactly as I'd hoped. They knew I had nothing to do with the murders, but they weren't going to say so. Instead, they were going to use it as an excuse to exclude me from the investigation, and I knew they weren't going to give Felicity's case a second thought.

Maybe it was my ego, but I felt like I could have contributed to their case. The mere fact that I mentioned searching the scene again during daylight hours was a good example. I had many other suggestions, but I grudgingly admitted to myself Bob was right. As long as there were suspicions that I was involved in another murder, even though it had nothing to do with Brittany and Shanna's deaths, interjecting myself into this particular investigation could be misperceived.

For a moment I thought about the request to take a lie detector examination. Passing it would be enough to eliminate me as a suspect, but I knew there would be a possibility of opening the door to Perry Goforth's death, and I did not have any desire to talk to anyone about that case.

It suddenly occurred to me that the Smyrna golf course was only about a mile from my current location. Getting in eighteen holes would be a nice way to work off the stress, but then realized I didn't have my clubs with me.

"Shit," I growled as I exited the park.

Ronald called while I was driving down Jefferson Pike.

"Everything okay?" he asked.

"Yeah, no problems. What're you doing?" I asked.

"Not much. I don't know if you've been checking, but Kalina hasn't responded."

"Figures."

"And you have a bunch of emails and voicemail messages," he said.

It was true. I'd not gone through any of them in a couple of days. "Yeah, I'm heading home now. I'll go through them and sort them out."

"I think the Turnbow case is done for," he pronounced.

I let out a sigh without meaning to. "You're probably right but I need to stick with it a while longer."

"What is the expression, beating a dead horse? Oh, wait, I know. It's a Sisyphean endeavor."

I chuckled. "Sisyphean. Good one. And appropriate."

"I'm working on expanding my vocabulary. Do you think I ought to go to college?" he asked.

"Academically, it'd be a breeze for you," I said.

"But you don't think I'd do well in a classroom environment," he said.

"I don't know. Two years ago? Hell no, but you've come a long way."

"I don't know if I'm ready for that, but since COVID hit, a lot of colleges offer online classes. I was thinking about going that route."

"I think that's a great idea. What are you going to major in?"

Ronald chortled. "Computer science, of course."

I laughed. "Excellent choice."

On the way home, I decided to alter course slightly and do a slow drive by of Mona's Paradise. There were only three cars in the parking lot, and none of them were even close to being a Sentra.

"Shit," I muttered.

I was beyond frustrated and decided to drive home. Abby texted me as I drove. I hated people who texted while driving, so I called her through my vehicle's hands-free phone feature.

"What are you doing?" she asked.

"Driving home. What about you?"

"I'm sitting around the house bored out of my mind. You want to hang out?"

"What, aren't there any young men who're trying to charm and woo you?"

She laughed. "It just so happens I've been asked out, but I'm really not interested. Besides, there's something I'd like to do, and you were the first person I thought of."

"Oh yeah, what's that?" I asked.

"There is a Van Gogh exhibit in Green Hills. I'd like to see it before it closes. Then, if you're not bored with me, we can go eat at the Cheesecake Factory."

My first inclination was to turn her down, but I decided spending the day with someone whose company I enjoyed would be a pleasant diversion from all of the nonsense I was currently suffering from.

"That sounds wonderful. How about I swing by and pick you up at four?"

CHAPTER 36

I had a good time with Abby, like I always did. After visiting the Van Gogh exhibit, we had a wonderful meal at the nearby Cheesecake Factory, although we had to wait almost an hour before being seated. I started to tell her of my feelings of guilt about Brittany and Shanna's senseless murders but stopped myself. We were having an enjoyable evening and I didn't want to ruin it.

Instead, I let her talk about police work. She regaled me with a story about her second felony arrest. A man ran a red light, tried to flee, and wrecked. He was found with two hundred grams of heroin and a stolen handgun. The excitement and passion she had when retelling the story reminded me of the days when I was a rookie cop. I couldn't help but smile as she talked. Her company was pleasant, refreshing.

After dinner, I drove her back to her house. We hugged and said our goodbyes. While driving home, I realized I was glad she didn't allow me to end our friendship, although I was worried it'd come back on her one day.

My biological clock woke me up at precisely five forty-five, even though I was still a little tired. I got up anyway and went on a morning run. I'd finished breakfast and was cleaning up when I received a text message from Percy.

Got a voicemail from a Detective Hamilton regarding Turnbow. Who is she?

I gave him a call and explained. "She's the rookie detective I told you about."

"She is, huh? Let me tell you what her message says. She's directed me to provide her with a copy of my Turnbow case file and to deliver it to her at her office at my convenience, but she needed it today, and no later than three o'clock."

I couldn't help but laugh.

"She's sure got some chutzpah, I'll give her that," Percy said.

"Yes, she does. They've got Georgie training her, so obviously somebody down there doesn't like her."

I heard Percy sigh. "Well, normally it wouldn't be a problem, but I could easily put in a hundred hours this week and still not be caught up, and I have about a dozen voicemail messages from people like her making all kinds of demands. This is not a good day."

"Give me her number and I'll take care of it," I said.

"Are you sure? I'll owe you, big time."

After assuring him I didn't mind, Percy gave me the number and thanked me again. I took a moment to decide the best approach. It seemed to me she was overcompensating, or maybe she was nothing more than a self-entitled bitch.

"She'll either be pleasant or not," I muttered and placed the call.

"Good morning, Detective. This is Thomas Ironcutter."

"Oh, hello, Mister Ironcutter. I was about to call you," she said. If she wondered how I got her number, she didn't mention it.

"Oh yeah?" I asked.

"Yes. I hope you've had time to think over what I said to you yesterday," she said.

"Which part?" I asked.

"The part where you are considered a person of interest in a double homicide and a bona fide suspect in another murder."

"Oh, that? Yeah, I'm not worried about that. Remember what Georgie said? Not only have I been considered a murder suspect in the past, but I was also even arrested on that case. It took a while, but the truth came out, as it almost always does. Then the lawsuits start. Are you aware that after I was falsely arrested for murder, I sued the dog shit out of everyone who was involved?"

There was a moment of silence before she responded. "Did you win?"

"You bet your bouncy little bottom I did."

Was it a crass remark? I suppose it was. But I wasn't sure whether or not I liked her and I felt like goading her a little bit. I expected a harsh response, but she surprised me.

"Well, if you won, why are you still a lowly private investigator?"

Now she was goading me back, but it didn't work.

"I like the work, although now I can pick and choose my cases," I said.

"If I got a big settlement, I'd be living on a beach somewhere exotic."

"I'd considered something like that, but I'm good with where I'm at. I like Tennessee and I love my home, especially now that I have a new shop."

"Have you even thought about doing anything else with the money?" she asked.

"Honestly, lately I've thought about doing some travelling. The last time I've been out of the country was back when I was in the Army."

"Where would you go?"

"I thought about Italy. You know, go visit my ancestral home and all that," I said.

"Pfft. The hell with that. I'd go to the Bahamas, or Aruba, somewhere exotic," she replied and then made a dramatic sigh. "Spending the rest of my life in aw shucks Tennessee is not in my plans. One day I'll be gone from here and I'll never look back."

"Good for you," I said. I could've told her the grass always looks greener when it's elsewhere but didn't bother.

"So, back to the double murder. That is the main thing I'm concentrating on at the moment."

"As you should be," I said.

"And you're a person of interest," she said.

"Yeah, you've mentioned that before. Don't the phone records prove my innocence?"

"I've been told you may have manipulated the timeline to make the phone records jive with your claims," she said.

"Sounds like something the idiot would say. Detective, if I may ask, what exactly has Georgie told you in regard to this case?"

"He said you're dirty and you have to be involved somehow." She didn't hesitate when she said it. I wasn't sure if she was being blunt or still trying to goad me. Maybe both.

"You're allowing his bias against me to affect your judgement. That's stupid."

"So, tell me, Thomas. What do you think I should do?"

"Clear your head of any false fallacies from idiots like Georgie. The only absolute thing you know is that Brittany and Shanna were following a man driving a gray Nissan Sentra and ended up shot and dumped in the Stones River."

She interrupted. "I don't know that. You're the only one who is saying a gray Sentra is involved. How do I know that's not a red albatross?"

"Don't you mean a red herring?" I asked.

"Whatever," she huffed. Yeah, she didn't like being corrected.

"Let me ask you, what actions have you taken to either confirm or disprove my claim?" I asked.

I was met by silence. Like yesterday. It was becoming obvious that when you asked her about something that might have forced her to admit she had erred or had not thought of it, she simply did not respond.

"I'll ask another way. According to me, Brittany called me and said she was following the car I was looking for. So, the question is, where were they when they first spotted the car? It's total speculation, but my guess would be at Starbucks."

"Okay, and?" she asked.

"And, Starbucks has surveillance cameras. I'd go have a look at the video footage starting with the time she made the phone call to me and work backwards."

There was dead silence for a solid ten seconds before she finally responded. "What if there is no video footage of Brittany and Shanna leaving Starbucks and following a car?"

"There's only one way to find out," I replied. "Are you going to check?"

CHAPTER 37

Detective Nancy Hamilton never gave me a straight answer, only some vague, rambling response before hanging up on me. Like I said, the girl irritated me. It was getting bad enough to where I was beginning to think of her as a younger version of Linda Kettleworth. Now that woman was a walking nightmare to the police profession. And ugly, that woman was butt ugly. Nancy was far better looking, I'd give her that, but she still irritated the hell out of me.

I think she was trying to be a good detective, but damned if she didn't have some annoying quirks. Being paired with that idiot Georgie certainly didn't help. It also didn't help that she had little to no experience in being an actual street cop.

I spent the rest of the day at my house, multitasking between house chores and PI work. Part of it entailed multiple voicemails that needed tending to. I had one call from a woman who proclaimed herself to be a psychic. She'd seen one of my flyers and said she'd had a vision where Felicity's body was.

"Oh, that's great, what's the address where she's at?" I asked.

"She's near a body of water," was her reply.

Yeah, there were bodies of water all over the southeastern United States. Hell, Percy Priest Lake was on the northern edge of LaVergne. I hung up on her, called William Goldman, and had a conversation regarding my alleged pending arrest.

"Have they made any contact with you?" William asked.

"I've spoken on the phone with Maroney. You know, Trademark. It's the usual threats; I better come through with evidence or else," I said.

"Hmm. I must say, I'm surprised they aren't pressuring you more than they have been. Have you ever determined what they have on you?" he asked.

"I'm fairly certain a member of the Satan's Dogs dropped a dime on me," I said. "His name is Samuel Todd and is the president of the Dogs. He's currently in lockup at the Rutherford County Jail."

"So, they have an allegation from one person whose character is certainly questionable," he surmised.

"Yep."

"Is there anybody else that can put you in that bar?" he asked.

"There were a couple of people in there, but nobody who knows me. Whether or not they can pick me out of a lineup is debatable."

"Hmm, you do tend to stand out in a crowd," William mused. "Alright, my advice is to cut off all contact with them. Westlake, Thrasher, Maroney, Thompson, all of them. That includes anyone that works with them. And, by all means, stay the hell away from that bar."

"You sound more and more like your grandfather every day," I said.

"Thank you," he replied. "If they pull the trigger and arrest you, I'll file an immediate habeas corpus motion. Westlake is smart enough to know I'll do that, so I think you're safe for now. Oh, I don't think I mentioned, the local Bar association is putting on a little shindig this weekend. If Westlake is there, I'll cozy up to him and see if he'll tell me anything. I've got to go but give me a call if anything new comes up."

After hanging up, I went against William's advice and texted Nancy, asking if there'd been any luck in finding the Sentra. She replied back after a few minutes with a one-word response: no. She might have been busy or simply being aloof. I didn't know and tried to tell myself I didn't care, but that was wrong. I cared greatly. More than I should have.

I had one other message that needed to be responded to. A lady had called, said she had seen one of my flyers, and had seen a woman matching Felicity's description living in an apartment in Smyrna. She was kind enough to provide the full address and didn't even mention a body of water. I went to the location and a woman who looked a lot like Felicity answered the door, but it wasn't her.

I ran a few more errands, treated myself to dinner at a local Rafferty's restaurant, and decided to go hang out at Mick's Place for a little while. Marti was working and there were the usual regulars, plus, there were several customers whom I had never seen before. That was good. It meant Marti was attracting a new crowd, which increased sales. She may have been a little naïve about how to run a business, but she was a people person and knew how to treat customers. Mick was a little lacking in that department.

I bellied up to the bar beside Wally and Ebbie, who greeted me warmly.

"Are you working on any mysterious cases, Thomas?" Ebbie asked.

"Not at the moment," I replied.

If I had even let out a whisper of Felicity's case, those two would have pestered me the rest of the evening about it and proffered endless suggestions on how I should investigate the case. All I wanted to do was enjoy a beer or two and smoke a cigar. After a moment, the conversation drifted off to other things, particularly golf. The big screen behind the bar was tuned to a replay of the 2022 Master's, while the other TVs by the recliners and couches were tuned to a soccer game. I smiled in amusement. The younger crowd was fixated on the soccer, while the older crowd, that included me, was ignoring the soccer and watching the golf.

Soon, one of the younger men walked up to the bar and ordered a round of shots for his friends. While waiting, he eyed us. He saw me staring and gave me a head nod. I nodded back.

"You guys seem to really enjoy golf," he observed.

"Yeah, I suppose so," I answered. "Do you play?"

"Nah, my dad does. That's what old farts do, right?"

He was grinning, but I suspected the alcohol was talking and he felt like making fun of us. I smiled back and nodded in agreement. I could have told him that golf was a popular sport among people of all ages, but it wouldn't have mattered. I waited for him to walk away but he wasn't through.

"I guess that's what you do when you get old and are too stupid to do anything else," he said.

I was no longer grinning. "Why do you believe we're stupid?"

He scoffed. "I mean, if you were smart, why would you be spending your golden years hanging out in here, right?"

Ebbie had picked up on the conversation and turned toward the man. "Did you just say we were stupid?"

The young man was still grinning. "No offense. It's only an observation, and I call it like I see it."

Ebbie nodded somberly. "I accept your challenge, sir."

His grin faltered. "What challenge?"

"A challenge of wits," Ebbie replied.

He stared at Ebbie a moment before picking up the tray of shots and walking back over to his friends. After a moment, he came back, with a couple of his friends in tow.

"What's this about a challenge of wits?" one of them asked.

"Simple," Ebbie said. "I have accepted your friend's challenge to see who is indeed stupid. I am of the opinion that there is no dumber creature on earth than a smartass college kid and I am ready to prove it. Sadly, I think your friend is full of bluster and little else. Certainly nothing of a cerebral nature."

The man gave a slow smile. "Alright, is there any money involved?"

Ebbie responded with an open-handed gesture. "If you have money to lose, I am agreeable."

The second man gestured at his friends. "All of us against you?"

"I believe I'd like to join in on this," I found myself saying. "Although Ebbie is fully capable of making mincemeat out of all of you."

His smile broadened. "You're on. So, how about this. We're college students…"

"Hence the arrogance," Ebbie breathed.

The young man paused and eyed Ebbie before continuing. "Vanderbilt students, to be specific. We have our textbooks out in our car. How about we take questions from those textbooks?"

"What are the topics?" I asked.

His smile broadened. "I'm a prelaw student, and Tyler here is a political science major."

Instead of smiling, I frowned. "So, law and political science? Those are kind of hard topics, don't you think?" I looked at Ebbie, who was hiding his grin with his hand. I sighed. "Okay, I guess we're committed."

Two of them practically ran out to their car and retrieved their textbooks. One of the girls who was with them would thumb through one of the books and ask a random question. It was so easy it was ridiculous. I contributed, but Ebbie absolutely dominated and surprised me with his expertise of Constitutional law.

After an hour of torture, the college students were thoroughly humbled. They paid Ebbie's bar tab and slinked out with their tails between their legs. On the way out, the girl who asked the questions paused at the door and gave me a little smile before exiting. That was enough to reward myself with another beer.

At ten o'clock I asked Marti to turn the big screen onto one of the news stations. There was the usual stuff, but to my pleasant surprise, they profiled the double murder and Nancy's interview led off the news. She gave a professional presentation and made a point of mentioning the Nissan Sentra. She also omitted the part about how they were found, which I liked. I was impressed.

"A transgender person was one of the victims?" Wally asked.

"Yep," I answered.

"I wonder if that was the motivation behind it," he mused.

I didn't respond. The answer was probably not, but I was not positive about that.

"If they haven't found that car by now, I doubt they ever will," Wally remarked. "It's been dumped somewhere; you can count on that."

I started to nod my head in agreement, but then I had an epiphany. Wally was probably more accurate in his assessment than he realized. The car may have indeed been dumped and there was a place to dump it where I had not searched, nor had anyone else. I paid my tab and hurried out. There was an auto salvage yard I needed to go visit.

CHAPTER 38

I called Bubba, woke him up, and asked for Weird Harold's number. Unfortunately, Weird Harold's phone was temporarily out of service.

"Probably couldn't pay the bill this month," I remarked, which caused me to once again wonder if I talked to myself too much.

"Anyway," I muttered, put my car in gear and started toward the salvage yard.

I tried to come up with a brilliant plan as I drove, but nothing came to mind. Upon arrival, I did a slow drive by. There were no lights on in the office and no cars in the parking lot. That was good. I found a spot down the road, parked, and got a couple of tac-lights. Shoving them into pockets, I found my pepper spray that was supposedly strong enough to repel a bear and shoved it into another pocket. I then unholstered my Springfield, checked to make sure I had a full magazine and a round chambered, and then started walking.

I already knew about the surveillance camera focused on the parking lot. Besides, the front gate was closed and secured with a padlock.

"Not a problem," I whispered to myself and continued walking down the road that bordered one side of the yard.

I'd walked about twenty yards when I spotted a tree stump that was near the ten-foot-tall fence. It was only about three feet tall, but it gave me enough to get started. Clambering up the fence, I managed to drop down on the other side without injuring myself. I then immediately pulled out the pepper spray and waited for any encounter with a junkyard dog. To my surprise, there was none, which was good. I liked dogs and preferred not to hurt one, if I could.

I walked up and down the rows of cars for a solid two hours, carefully inspecting any Nissan. I struck out each time. It seemed like my idea was a bust. I was getting tired and decided to call it. As I walked back toward the entrance, I walked by a burnt car. It had burned recently which caused it to have a unique smell. That smell brought back more than a few memories. When I was a cop, I'd dealt with many burnt cars.

I had walked ten feet past the car and then stopped. Turning around, I walked back to the car and pointed my light at it. The car was burnt to a crisp, but I recognized the body shape. I stepped closer and walked around to the back. Although it was blackened from the fire, I could still read the logo. It was a Nissan Sentra.

"Could be," I whispered.

I kept my excitement in check until I found the fist-sized dent in the rear driver's side door. It was certainly possible that there was more than one Sentra with a dent like this one, but when I saw that the VIN plate on the dashboard had been removed, I was pretty certain I'd found the car I'd been looking for.

Instinctively, I looked around once again, checking to see if I were being watched. Satisfied I was the only human in the yard, I took several photographs before climbing the fence and getting out of there. It was after five now, and the traffic on the road was picking up. Making it back to my car, I debated on what to do next. Ultimately, I called Percy, woke him up, and explained.

"Alright, I'll head that way. It'd probably be a good idea for you to disappear. I'll say I received an anonymous phone call."

"Do you happen to know Bob Thrasher with the TBI?" I asked.

"I've never met him, but I've heard the name," Percy replied. "Does he have something to do with this?"

"He's working alongside Nancy Drew on the double homicide. I'll text his number to you."

"Great, I'll give him a call and see if he wants to come look it over. Since that VIN plate has been removed, I believe I can get auto theft involved, maybe they can make a case for fencing stolen cars."

The fire had destroyed any chance of finding prints or DNA, but at least the registered owner could now be located. The missing VIN plate was only a minor hindrance. Auto manufacturers were also required to stamp the VIN on the chassis. Different makes of autos had different locations, but it was there. I knew Percy would have that information before the day was over. Hell, he'd probably have it before lunch.

I'd been up all night and was dog tired. If I were a younger man, I would've driven directly to the fitness center and hit the weights, but one glance of myself in the rearview mirror confirmed I was no longer in my twenties.

"A hot shower and bed for you, old man," I muttered.

It wasn't meant to be though. As I drove down the road leading to my house, my phone buzzed. Someone was activating the intercom at the gate.

CHAPTER 39

Back when I had my shop rebuilt, I also had the contractor build a security gate at the entrance to the front drive. It was a nice system; heavy duty steel with an automatic opener/closer and decorative rock walls on either side. I had an intercom, keypad, and surveillance camera installed as well. It was money well spent, but there was a downside. The gate was about twenty feet from the road. I did that so a delivery truck could pull in and park without worrying about being hit by a speeding motorist while they used the intercom.

When I arrived home, there were two unmarked cars parked in that entryway, which prevented me from going in. When Detective Nancy Drew emerged from one of the cars, I was mildly irritated. When Georgie got out of the other car, my irritation turned to anger.

The man looked even more ridiculous today than he normally did. He had a country western theme going on today, complete with a string tie and silver caps on the toes of his pointed shit-kicker boots. All he needed was a ten-gallon hat to make himself look like a side show attraction at a county fair. I could see it now. He'd be on a pedestal and the banner above him would read, "Inbred Dumbass!"

Nancy's attire was starkly different. She was wearing an off-white blouse and a navy-blue skirt with a pair of matching blue leather pumps. She looked nice. I had no intention of telling her though.

Georgie stared me down as he lit a cigarette. The man irritated me. Hell, both of them did, but Georgie was currently carrying an air of arrogance like at any moment he was going to slap the shit out of me. I wished he'd try it. But, then again, in all likelihood he was trying to provoke me. Give him reason to arrest and sue me. I stared back indifferently.

"I swear to God, Ironcutter, every time I come visit, you've been out all night on a bender. You really ought to get yourself into rehab. Or, are you waiting until you go to prison to do it so the taxpayers will foot the bill?"

"Georgie, whatever bullshit you're throwing this morning, I'm not interested. If you don't have a warrant, get the hell out of here."

He took a deep drag off his cigarette before speaking. "Oh, I won't be but a minute. This is only a courtesy visit. I'm going to the Grand Jury

Monday morning for a direct presentment on your ass for murder. This is your last chance to come clean."

"You're wasting your time," I said. I was too tired to argue or make smartassed retorts. Instead, I was about to call the cops on them.

"Suit yourself, idiot," he said, walked to his car, and stared a moment before getting in.

Nancy faced me. "I'd like to talk to you a minute, if you don't mind." She glanced over at Georgie and lowered her voice. "I'll tell him to leave."

I stared at her with tired eyes. I would've told her to scram too, but I was curious about what she had to say. I also wanted to know if she'd been told about the Sentra yet.

"Let's make it quick," I said.

I watched as she walked over to Georgie and spoke to him through the open window in a hushed voice. Whatever she said, he made a show of disapproval. He spoke loudly when he told her it wasn't safe to be alone with me. I heard her respond that she'd be fine and glanced over at me with a reassuring smile.

Georgie continued to loudly disagree, and after several seconds of complaining with Nancy talking to him, he reluctantly acquiesced. He told Nancy, in a tone loud enough for me to hear, it was her time to waste, and started his car. Nancy walked over and stood beside me. We watched as Georgie backed out of the driveway. As he went by us, he made a pistol motion with his fingers and acted like he was shooting me.

"A true-blue idiot," I said.

"I suppose," she said and stared. "You look tired."

"That I am. So, what's this really all about? Because it looked like you and Georgie were putting on a show for my benefit."

She stared at me a moment before speaking. "What do you mean?"

"Please don't continue to insult my intelligence. Georgie didn't drive all the way up here simply to threaten me and then leave."

Her lips formed a small, tight smile. "Okay, I guess it was obvious. George thought the good-cop bad-cop routine would be a good idea and I went along with it."

"Dumb," I said.

"I apologize for the subterfuge," she replied. I could not tell if she was sincere o simply saying the words, but it didn't matter.

"Not a problem, but I really have been out all night. Not in the way your idiot co-worker described, but I've been up since yesterday morning. Tell me what you need so I can get some rest."

She looked around. "Do you want to talk here? How about we go somewhere for a cup of coffee?"

I shook my head. "I'm too tired to go anywhere." I thought about it and then walked over to the console. I punched in the code, causing the gate to open. I gestured toward the house.

"Park in back," I said.

Once she parked, she followed me inside. I motioned for her to sit at the kitchen table and told her to wait a minute while I fed and watered Tommy Boy. Once I'd completed that task, I poured myself a glass of water and sat in the chair across from her.

"Alright, let's save some time. Don't bother asking me any questions that you've already asked. I'm tired and not in the mood for that nonsense."

"I won't," she said and opened a notepad she had, and as an afterthought, activated the record function on her phone.

Tommy Boy promptly jumped up on the kitchen table and began inspecting both her and her pad. Nancy wasn't sure what to do and looked to me.

"He's being a pest because he was left alone all night. Let him get it out of his system and he'll find something else to amuse him. Oh, and keep a hand on your phone or else he'll knock it off the table."

She nodded and waited for me to sit before talking.

"Ready? Okay. First, have you interviewed or questioned any member of the Satan's Dogs regarding Felicity Turnbow?"

"I talked to one of them, briefly," I answered.

"Which one?"

"William McLaughlin. He goes by the nickname of Whopper. He denied knowing Felicity or having any knowledge of her whereabouts. Oh, and there were two hang arounds that were present when I questioned him. I showed them a picture of Felicity, but they denied knowing her."

"What makes you think Whopper was involved?" she asked.

"Because I had an informant advise me that Whopper had possession of Felicity's car. It was later found at a salvage yard over in West Nashville."

She nodded but said nothing about the Sentra. She was either hiding the information from me or she didn't know about it.

"It's the same salvage yard where the Sentra was discovered," I said. Her expression was blank. I had my answer. "Ah, you've been left out of the loop."

She frowned in confusion. "What are you talking about?"

I stood. "I think I'm going to fix some breakfast before I go to bed. You want anything?"

"Do you have any iced tea?" she asked.

"Yes, ma'am, I do," I said.

I got a glass, put some ice in it, and filled it from a pitcher of tea I kept in the fridge. She didn't bother thanking me when I handed it to her. Instead, she fixed me with her rather cute hazel eyes.

"Could you answer my question, please?" she said.

I took a sip of water before answering. "The Nissan Sentra. The one we've been searching for. The vehicle that was most likely driven by your murder suspect. It was found at the salvage yard."

"Are you serious?" she asked. I nodded. "Why wasn't I told this?"

"I don't know. You ought to give Bob a call and find out."

"Bob knows about it?" she asked with raised eyebrows.

"He should by now," I replied. She continued staring. "If you think I'm playing games with you, I'm not. The Sentra has been located. Give Bob a call if you don't believe me."

She grabbed her phone, turned off the record function, and began tapping on the screen. Bob answered after a couple of rings and a rather snippy conversation ensued. I listened while I finished making breakfast. She didn't mince words and let him know she did not appreciate being left out of the loop. After a little more back and forth, she hung up and made another call whereupon another snippy conversation transpired.

By the time she'd finished, I had two eggs cooked over-easy and a couple of pieces of toast that were lightly glazed with butter and grape jam. She set her phone on the table as I sat and stared off into space. I ate my breakfast in silence. After a moment, she focused on me.

"He said he called the department dispatch and they told him they'd forward the information to me. When I called dispatch, they said they left a message taped to my office door. They should have called me," she said, her voice trailing off. She was upset, almost to the point where I thought she might start crying.

"I guess I should head to that salvage yard," she said and began putting her notepad and phone in her purse. She then stood, but I stopped her with a slightly upraised hand.

"You could drive out there, but there's no need," I said.

"Why not?"

"The car's been burnt, so it's highly doubtful any forensic evidence will be recovered, and the VIN plate on the dashboard was torn off. I'm not certain, but there might've been a decal with the VIN on the door jamb, but it was burnt."

She continued staring in disbelief. "Well, how do you know it's the Sentra we're looking for?"

I shrugged and continued eating.

"So, there is no VIN, but somehow you're convinced it's the car," she remarked.

"Yep."

"Why?" she asked in a snide tone.

"That tone indicates to me that you don't take me seriously and you still don't consider me as anything other than a possible suspect in your double murder. Why should I help you?"

She dropped her gaze and stared down at the table. She took a deep breath before speaking. "Honestly, I guess you're all I have on this case. If you're not the suspect, I don't have anything. And nobody else is helping me."

When she said the last sentence, her voice started breaking and I knew she was on the verge of breaking down. I probably should have told her it was time for her to leave, but I guess I still have a weak spot for damsels in distress. I put my fork down, reached out, and held her hand.

"Alright, remember when I mentioned the damage to the car I saw on the coffeeshop video?"

She looked up. "You saw the video? How?"

"That doesn't matter. What does matter is the coffeeshop video shows a moderate-sized dent in the rear driver's side door, almost like it took a hard hit from a baseball. The burned-out Sentra has that same dent in the exact same location. What are the odds of that?"

She stared evenly. I don't know if she was beginning to believe me or not. I continued.

"As far as the VIN goes, they may have torn off the little plate under the windshield, but the VIN is also stamped on either the frame or the firewall. My guess is that they'll tow the car to the crime lab and have a tech find it.

"As far as trying to interview the people who work at the business, I'm sure Detective Trotter has already interviewed them and I'm sure all he got was a whole lot of nobody knows nothing. If there is an official tow record, I'm sure he's got it by now and I'm sure he'll provide all that to you, if you ask him nicely and stop with the attitude."

"You seem pretty certain of all that," she said.

I shrugged. "Yes I am. What can I say, I'm awesome."

"Are you the one who found the car?" she asked.

I shrugged again.

"That's where you've been all night, isn't it?"

I didn't bother answering and resumed eating. She watched in silence. I don't know if she were thinking things through or if she found my eating habits fascinating.

"What made you decide to search that salvage yard?" she finally asked.

"Remember me telling you guys about finding Felicity's car? It was found at the same salvage yard. The owner is the uncle of Whopper and Freak, and I have it from a reliable source that they are using the salvage yard as a front for a chop shop."

"Chop shop?" she asked.

I nodded, but I could see she wasn't familiar with the term. It belied her ignorance. If she were an experienced cop, she'd know what I meant.

"You see, instead of simply buying wrecked and junked out cars, they take it to another level. They'll steal newer model cars and sell the parts off them. It's more profitable.

"I'll give an example. A salvage yard is contacted by a body shop asking if they have a front clip for a 2018 Camaro SS in their inventory. The salvage yard tells the body shop people that they don't have it in stock but check back in three or four days. Then, they send out their people to locate a 2018 Camaro SS and steal it. They bring it to the salvage yard, chop it up, and sell the front clip to the body shop."

Nancy slowly nodded. "I think I understand. What do they do with the car then?"

"They'll sell whatever else they can off the car and then crush the rest and sell it for scrap metal." I finished my breakfast, wiped my mouth with a napkin, and leaned forward.

"If you don't mind me saying so, you've got a lot to learn. Don't forget that."

She started to say something but stopped herself. I assumed it was going to be a smartassed retort, but she thought better of it. I suddenly yawned.

"Alright, I'm beat and need to go to bed, and you've got work to do. Give Percy a call. He'll bend over backwards to help a fellow detective, but only if they're courteous and respectful."

"Alright," she said and stood.

I walked the short distance to the door with her and opened it. She paused at the doorway.

"I'll need to get back with you later. I have more questions." She said it with a hint of a smile before walking out.

I was guilty of admiring her backside as she walked out, but that didn't stop me from watching her car exit the gate and ensuring the gate was closed before heading to bed.

CHAPTER 40

Despite my fatigue, I couldn't sleep past noon. It may have been guilt that woke me up, knowing Bubba was out in the shop working on the Sprite by himself. I fixed a couple of sandwiches with heaping slabs of smoked turkey, American cheese, lettuce, mayo, and mustard, and took them to the shop. After wiping his hands, he accepted one of the sandwiches with a big grin.

"Thanks, brother," he said, took a bite, and then gestured at the Sprite with the sandwich. "I got the new speedometer cable put in. When the rebuilt clutch comes in, we can button it up. All that's left is the high-beam switch and the generator."

"And then we can take it back to Nate for him to paint."

Bubba nodded. "We're way ahead of schedule. That was a lot easier to work on than I thought it'd be."

His phone beeped, indicating an incoming text message. He pulled it out of his pocket and read it.

"Speak of the devil, that's Nate. He's asking if I can come in early." He stretched and glanced over at the Sprite. "I suppose I could. We're kind of at a stopping point anyway."

"Until we get the backordered parts in, there's not much else we can do," I said in agreement.

Bubba nodded. "Yeah, I could use the overtime. The wife wants to enroll our little girl in some kind of dance class, and that shit ain't cheap."

"Before you go, take some pictures of the car and show them to Nate."

Bubba did as I suggested and left ten minutes later. I walked around the Sprite, admiring our work product, when my phone buzzed. Someone was at the gate. When I opened the app, I saw it was Nancy Drew. She drove up a moment later.

I watched her get out, look over at me, and give a small smile. I gave her a little wave and continued to watch her as she walked over. If I didn't know better, I'd say she'd unfastened one or two buttons on her blouse since this morning. I liked her looks, but I still wasn't sure if I liked her or not. There was a part of my brain telling me she was trouble.

"What are you doing?" she asked.

I pointed at the Sprite and told her the story about it. She walked in the shop and looked it over.

"I would've liked to have had a car like this when I was in high school," she said.

"It's too small for me, but it's a cute car," I replied.

"What'd you drive in high school?" she asked.

The question brought back painful memories of the Buick Wildcat. I didn't bother telling her that story. "Oh, nothing but an old truck. So, you still have questions for me."

She nodded and yawned. "Can I have a glass of tea? It's been a long day and I need some caffeine."

I held up my grimy hands. "You don't want me to fix it. Go on inside and help yourself. Fix me a glass too while you're at it."

She gave a slight, cheeky smile. "What's to stop me from snooping around?"

I shrugged. "I've got nothing to hide, but my cat may take offense."

She went inside and stayed there for several minutes while I wiped down my tools and put them away before scrubbing my hands in the shop sink. I was drying off when she walked back out carrying two large drinking glasses.

"I wasn't snooping, I had to use the restroom," she said and handed me one of the glasses.

A part of me doubted her, but I didn't mention it. Instead, I took several large swallows. "That hit the spot," I said and pointed at my picnic table. "Let's go sit there."

As soon as we sat, she pulled out her notepad and activated the record function on her phone. I sat and nodded for her to proceed. She started immediately.

"Where were you when Brittany Parkhurst called you on Monday evening?" she asked.

"I was eating dinner at a restaurant that's nearby. It's about two or three miles from here."

"Can you prove it?"

"Sure, hang on." I opened the credit card app on my phone and showed her the receipt. She dutifully noted the date and time stamp.

"I'm sure their surveillance cameras recorded me coming and going, if you feel the need to corroborate that," I added.

"I probably won't need to. Were you with anyone?"

"Nope."

"No dinner date?" she asked with an arched eyebrow.

"Nope. Oh, I almost forgot. After I lost the phone signal with Brittany, I called the Smyrna Police and requested they do an emergency request with the phone company to ping her location. They declined. I'm sure they have a recording of the phone call."

"Alright, I'll check into it. Next question, did you have any kind of relationship with Brittany other than what you have told us?" she asked.

"I've only seen Brittany in person a couple of times, and that was at the coffeeshop where she worked. Other than that, we've only had a couple of phone conversations, including the one where she said she was following the Sentra. That is the extent of our relationship," I said.

"What about Shanna Maldonado? What relationship did you have with her?" she asked.

I shook my head. "I've never met or talked to… him? Her? I'm sorry, I don't know which pronoun to use."

She jotted something down. I didn't bother trying to read it and sipped my tea. After a moment she looked up and pointedly stared.

"What is the nature of the relationship between you and Officer Carla Wasserman?"

That question surprised me, but if she thought that I had convinced Carla to aid and abet a double murder, it was definitely a valid question.

"I'd never met her until the night of the incident. That's the first and last time I've seen her in person. We had a phone conversation the next morning, but that's been it," I said.

"Are you sure, Thomas?" she asked.

"I'm positive. Why are you doubting that?"

"She's made one or two comments about you to some of her co-workers that would indicate you two know each other a little more intimately than what you're claiming," she said.

"She saw me in the nude when I came out of the water. If you'll remember, she told you and Georgie about it. She had a good laugh about it and probably mentioned it."

"Alright," she said, jotted something, and continued. "What was the telephone conversation about?" she asked.

"She called to tell me about Georgie's latest screw up and that her good friend, Bob Thrasher was going to be taking over the investigation."

"He's not taking over," she snipped. "I'm the primary. He's assisting me."

"Okay," I replied. Obviously, it was a sore spot with her.

She sipped her tea and changed tact. "So, you used to be a detective."

"Some would even say I still am," I quipped.

She gave a slight smile. "Alright, I'll agree to that. You seem to think that Freak or Whopper had something to do with this murder. Why?"

"Have you read the case file for the rape Freak was arrested and convicted of?" I asked.

"I haven't had a chance to," she admitted.

"He was sixteen. The victim was fifteen. He ambushed her in the girl's room of their high school. He beat the hell out of her and then brutally raped her. He wore a mask so she wouldn't be able to identify him, but he apparently didn't understand the science of DNA.

"He was tried as an adult, convicted, and was recently paroled. Prison rarely rehabilitates anyone, especially rapists." I finished my tea before continuing. "Your department has two unsolved murders involving girls who were dumped, right?"

She nodded and frowned. "You think he has something to do with those?"

"It's possible. He needs to be investigated as a person of interest in not only your case, but those cases as well. Anyway, back to my case. Felicity goes missing. Her car turns up at the salvage yard. I was told Whopper is the one who brought it in."

"Is that when you questioned Whopper?" she asked.

"Yes," I answered.

"How did that go?"

I shrugged. "One might say it was a hostile interview. Anyway, he denied knowing anything, and like I told you previously, the two hang-arounds claimed not to know her either."

She frowned and jotted a note. She then looked up in sudden understanding.

"Felicity's car was found at the salvage yard, so you realized that might be where the Sentra was being hidden."

"I figured the murderer would hide the car. The salvage yard seemed like a good place. I was surprised the car was set on fire, although it makes sense. Let me add this, the car still reeked of being freshly burnt, but it was cool to the touch when I found it, so it was set on fire before the evening news aired the BOLO."

"So, you are the person who found it?" she said in a slight accusing tone. I shrugged. "Did you have a search warrant?"

"Search warrants are for cops."

She arched an eyebrow, which I now noticed both were carefully plucked, but not overly so, which accentuated her hazel eyes. "So, how were you able to legally search the salvage yard? Did you have permission from the owner?"

"Detective, as far as anyone is concerned, the car was found by Detective Percy Trotter after he had received an anonymous tip, and as you know, a salvage yard operator is required by law to allow the police access to their inventory."

Nancy stared. "That seems like you're skirting the law."

I shrugged. "I have nothing to do with it. If anyone asks, I'll lie about my involvement."

"You're not a good liar," she surmised.

I stared back. "I'm not, huh? If you believe that, then you should have deduced through your questioning that I had nothing to do with Brittany and Shanna's murders."

After a second or two, she gave a slight smile. "Touché. Alright, let's say I believe everything you've said. Why are you so certain it was Freak who shot Brittany and Shanna?"

I shrugged. "I'm reaching, I know. It could've been Freak driving that Sentra, or it could've been Whopper. It could've been another member of the Satan's Dogs. Not all of them are in Federal custody. I think there are eight or nine that are still out there. That's something you should check on."

She was quiet now and tapped the pad with her pen. After several seconds, she slowly shook her head. "I'm not so sure I agree with your theory. You've taken a few grains of evidence and have made some enormous leaps."

"Look, I know I don't have much, but you have a convicted rapist who was recently released from prison and living somewhere in Rutherford County. Your two dump jobs, my missing woman, and now your double murder have all happened after he got paroled." I leaned forward. "Find out who owns that Sentra. That will be your starting point. And I'll bet the registered owner can be traced to the Dogs."

She looked skeptical. "What's the bet?"

"If I'm wrong, you can ask me anything about anything and I'll answer truthfully."

She continued staring, and then a slow smile came across her face. "What if I ask you about the Perry Goforth murder?"

I shrugged. "Sure, but it's my understanding that Perry Goforth's death has been ruled accidental. The only person calling it a murder is your dumbass mentor."

"He's not my mentor, but anyway, if you're right, what do you want?" she asked.

I put my hand on hers and smiled. She arched both eyebrows now.

"Oh, is that it? You think if you win this bet you get to sleep with me?"

"Hmm, I like how you think, but no. If I win, anytime I call you asking for information, you have to provide it."

She looked incredulous. "You want me to be a confidential source for you?"

"Yep."

She scoffed. "Yeah, right."

"Suit yourself. I don't blame you though. There's no way I'll lose."

"For a man who has nothing more than a few snippets of evidence, you seem awfully sure of yourself," she said.

"I could be wrong. It's happened on rare occasions."

She laughed now. "You're funny."

"I would like to ask about the two female murder victims."

"There's not much I can tell you. Both were found dumped in rural areas of the county on the side of the road. They were both in an advanced state of decomposition, so there was no DNA found on them, if that's what you're wondering."

"Who is the primary on those?" I asked.

"There is a team of three detectives, headed up by Chief Deputy Farmingham," she said.

Ah, the chief deputy, the man she was rumored to be having an affair with. She kept talking.

"You're also trying to get me to believe that Brittany and Shanna were killed merely for following this Sentra, right?"

"Yes," I said.

She frowned and shook her head with a little more vigor. "That doesn't make any sense."

I pointed at her phone. "Turn it off."

She frowned but did as I requested.

"Nancy, it's only the two of us here, so let's be honest with each other. You have limited experience in police work, right?"

Her mouth tightened and she did not answer.

"I'm not criticizing you. I'm only pointing it out because I've been involved in more than a few murder investigations where the reasons given by the suspect didn't always make sense. I once helped another detective in a road rage murder. Do you know why the suspect shot the victim? He said he didn't like the way the victim was looking at him. Crazy, right?"

"So, you think they were shot because they were looking at a person?" she asked.

"No, I think they were shot because the suspect became aware he was being followed and was paranoid." A thought suddenly occurred to me. "Has there been any recent reports of a missing female?"

Nancy gave an exaggerated eye roll. "Now you're really reaching."

"Yeah, maybe. All I'm saying is he might've had a kidnap victim in the car when he spotted the tail. By the way, have you identified the registered owner of the Sentra?"

"I'm not at liberty to say," she replied.

"Really? After all this, you're going to pull that on me?"

She smiled smugly, as if she'd scored a victory over me. She stood then and gathered her things.

"No more questions?" I asked.

Nancy paused and stared. It could have been described as a deep stare, or maybe the question confused her.

"We can pick it up at a later time. I'm tired as hell and will no doubt have another long day tomorrow."

"I'm sure you will," I said.

I was almost tempted to ask her to stick around for an adult beverage and casual conversation, but then the correct head took over the thinking process. I bid her goodbye and watched her leave. When she had exited the driveway, I called Percy.

"Any luck with the VIN?" I asked.

"Yeah, in a way. To begin with, the car was originally registered to a man who lives in Woodbury. He sold it a year ago to a man he described as a scruffy, sawed-off runt."

"I guess that eliminates Whopper," I said.

Percy chuckled. "Yes, it does. He was shown a series a photographic lineups. One for each known member of the Satan's Dogs. He didn't pick any of them."

"Was Freak included?" I asked.

"Yes, he was," Percy replied. "No hits. We even showed it to his niece, who was present when he sold it. She didn't pick anyone out either."

"Damn," I said. "What's the good news?"

"There's a rookie detective in the auto theft unit. You know the type, young and full of piss. He's the grandson of a retired captain. Rucker. You remember him?"

"Vaguely," I said.

"Yeah, so he's young and eager, like I said. It didn't take him long to figure out the salvage yard was running a major chop shop and he's running with it. It'll be on the evening news."

"I'll be sure to watch it. Oh well, I guess that's good," I said.

"Aren't you going to ask about the tickets?" Percy asked.

"Tickets?"

"Yeah, the traffic tickets."

"Alright, what about the traffic tickets?" I asked.

"A month after the man sold the car, a young man was stopped by a state trooper in Rutherford County and issued a couple of tickets for invalid registration. They were never paid, and his license was suspended. Bob has been trying to track him down all day."

"What's the name?" I asked.

"Timothy Davenport," Percy said. "He doesn't have any known arrest record and the address on his license is to an old rooming house over on State Street. It's been torn down and they're building a big complex of offices and high-end apartments where it once stood."

I grunted. I knew all about that building project. After all, I was heavily invested in it.

"Anything else?" I asked.

"That's it for now. We're still trying to track this kid down."

"Let me see if Ronald can help out with that. Text me his information and we'll go from there," I said.

"You got it," Percy replied.

After ending the call, I was almost tempted to text Nancy with the information, and had even started tapping in her phone number, but immediately deleted it. After all, she was an unknown variable. For all I knew, she still considered me an enemy and was simply playing nice in order to catch me with my guard down so that I'd admit to being in the men's room at Mona's Paradise the day Goforth was injured.

But that didn't stop me from having carnal thoughts about her.

"Damnit," I muttered.

I called Ronald, explained it all, and gave him Timothy Davenport's information. He promised to give it a shot and he'd call me back later. I started to piddle around in the shop, but Nancy kept popping up in my brain. I knew how it was when I got like this. The only thing to do, the only sensible thing to do, was go on a long run.

CHAPTER 41

Ronald had texted me while I was out jogging, and I didn't notice it until I'd gotten up the next morning. He'd sent it about two in the morning, and it simply said to check my email. I got around to checking it out while eating breakfast.

It was a picture out of a high school annual. It took me a moment before I recognized the young teen. He was one of the men who was at the clubhouse on the day I fought Whopper. He looked rougher now, like a person who was strung out, but it was him.

"I knew it," I exclaimed and immediately called Percy.

"So, he's with the Dogs," Percy said after I'd explained.

"Yeah, he's a hang-around. I don't know much else about him. He's got an Instagram account, but that's all Ronald could find. Apparently, he hasn't been active on it in a while."

"A hang-around? If they follow biker custom, a hang-around isn't allowed to live in the clubhouse. He can't even be on the property without a full member's consent," he said.

"Which means, it's a hit or miss catching him there," I said.

"Yep, and I already know Bartlett will nix the idea of conducting a stakeout in another county. We're shorthanded enough as it is. Two more officers resigned this month."

"Damn."

The Nashville PD were not immune to a nationwide trend that was occurring. The bad guys had convinced a lot of young people that the cops were the bad guys, and nobody wanted to get involved in law enforcement anymore. It was becoming a successful campaign of undermining the fabric of society. Most people were naïve sheeple. They had no idea what would happen if there were no longer any police.

Percy gave a sardonic chuckle. "Hell, we're hurting for people so bad, they'd probably give you your old job back if you applied."

I laughed back at him, but it wasn't a humorous laugh. "It'll be a cold day in hell before that happens."

"Yeah, I hear you, brother. Alright, so what are we going to do with this information? Do you want me to call Thrasher and update him?"

"That'd be the professional thing to do, even if he did tell me to butt out of the investigation, but why don't you hold off on that for about four hours before calling him."

Percy chuckled again. "Let me guess, you're going to get in touch with Nancy Drew. Okay, see what you can do. Call me later."

It was still early, a little after six. I didn't know what hours Detective Hamilton kept, and I still wasn't certain I'd call her. I waited until after my morning workout before making the decision. When she answered, it sounded like I had woken her up.

"Thomas, what's up?" she asked.

"I have some information about the owner of the Sentra, if you're interested," I said.

There was a moment's hesitation before she responded. "Oh, listen I'm sorry but I can't really say anything about the case."

"Yeah, I understand, but I don't think you heard me correctly. I'm not asking for information. I have some information to give you. If you're not interested, I guess I understand as well."

"Oh," she muttered, and then understanding reached her brain. "Oh! Yeah, absolutely. What've you got?"

We agreed to meet at the Smyrna Starbucks. I'd already eaten breakfast, but I wasn't opposed to having one of those delicious cinnamon dolce lattes. She was fifteen minutes late, which didn't surprise me. She seemed to be one of those people who were always late.

When she got out of her car, even though she had a phone stuck up against her ear, she looked good. She had on dark colored slacks that fitted nicely, and a matching Polo shirt that was tucked in, hinting at a flat stomach. Her hair was freshly brushed, and today she didn't have it tied back. She hung up as she entered the business and walked directly to the counter. As she ordered, I saw more than one customer checking her out. Once ordering, she spotted me, walked over to my table, and sat.

"Good morning," I said.

She huffed. "If you say so. Are you always an early riser?"

"For the most part, yeah. What about you?"

"Oh, I'm definitely a night person. Ten o'clock is my usual wake up time. I'm stuck on day shift until I can wrap up this double murder, then you better believe I'm transferring back to the evening or midnight shift."

She was interrupted by a text message. When she read it, she frowned and hurriedly typed something in reply. Hitting send, she looked up. "Sorry, as if I don't have enough to deal with, I have a sister who's having issues. So, what's this information you're talking about?"

"The Sentra," I said. "I'm sure you're aware the registered owner sold it, and he doesn't know the name of the young man he sold it to, right?"

She eyed me, wondering how I knew this. "Yep. So, it turns out you were wrong. That means you lost the bet." She grinned when she said it. I grinned back.

"So, you agree we had a bet?"

"Yep, and you lost."

The barista called out her name. I waited while she went to retrieve her drink. When she sat back down, I slid the printout over to her.

"It's an old yearbook photograph," I said.

"Who is it?" she asked.

"Timothy Davenport."

The look on her face was priceless.

"So, you know about the tickets," I surmised.

"Yeah, but how do you know?"

I waved off the question and pointed at the picture. "I recognize Mister Dalton. He's a hang around with the Satan's Dogs. You've asked me what the connection is between your case and the Satan's Dogs. There's your connection."

She stared at the photograph a moment before speaking. "How do you know he's with the Satan's Dogs?"

"Before I answer that, I want to know something. Do you acknowledge you've lost the bet?" I asked with a subtle grin.

"No," she answered with a defiant stare.

My grin disappeared. "Oh, well, okay. I guess we have nothing more to talk about." I reached over to take the printout. She grabbed my hand.

"Wait," she said. Her mouth moved silently for a moment and then she stared at the tabletop.

"Go on," I encouraged.

"I can't simply give you confidential information whenever you want it," she said. "That's not a fair bet."

"And yet you wanted me to give you information about myself that would possibly incriminate me, right?" I asked. I then leaned back in my seat. "Alright, let's agree it was a dumb bet anyway."

"Okay," she said, looking relieved.

I tapped the printout. "Let's instead focus on this. He needs to be found. I know I'm going to be left out of the loop. That's fine, but I want you to know I'm not going to sit on my hands and do nothing."

"You shouldn't interfere with the case, Thomas," she admonished.

"Nancy, I've given you viable leads to work with. You've done nothing with it. I expect that kind of behavior from Georgie the Dumbass, but I thought you'd be better."

She narrowed her eyes at me. "I'm much better than him. That's why I'm going to take his place." She then threw her hand up to her mouth. "Shit."

"Let me guess, that's supposed to be hush-hush," I surmised.

"You can't say anything about that."

"Don't worry. Your secret's safe with me. Besides, the sheriff needs to understand people like Georgie are a detriment to the department. He's a lawsuit waiting to happen."

"Oh, I know. Eric's working to get rid of him," she said.

"Eric? Is that Eric Farmingham, the chief deputy?" I asked.

She suddenly looked wary. "Do you know him?"

"I've heard of him," I replied and left it at that. I wasn't going to let on that I knew about her and him, nor was I going to tell her of the time years ago where he was caught trying to bring an underage girl into a swinger's club in Nashville. There were never any charges brought against him. Somehow, he got the investigation quashed.

Her stare lingered a few seconds longer than necessary before she picked up the photo.

"Can I keep this?" she asked.

"Sure. It's not a good quality printout though. I can text you the jpeg if you want."

She gave a nod and was about to thank me, I think, but an incoming text message caught her attention. She responded to it and then looked up.

"I have something that requires my attention. Will you be available later?" she asked.

"I should be," I said. She gave me a pleasant smile, probably the warmest smile she'd given me to date.

I started my SUV, rolled a window down, thought about lighting a cigar, and watched curiously as Nancy walked to her car. Instead of immediately getting in, she stood beside it, watching the entrance, and waiting. After a moment, a black Chevy Camaro that'd seen better days turned in and parked beside Nancy. After a second, a girl with pale blonde hair got out and walked over to Nancy.

"Well, it's a small world," I said to myself.

I recognized Nancy's sister. I didn't know her real name though. When she was a stripper at the Red Lynx she called herself Cinnamon.

CHAPTER 42

My memories of Lilith were bittersweet. She was a sensuous but troubled woman who'd taken a liking to me the moment she saw me. Unfortunately, she killed a man and then fled Nashville. I had gone to her apartment in hopes of finding her. Instead of Lilith, I encountered Cinnamon.

I didn't know it until then, but Cinnamon and Lilith were lovers and when Lilith took off, Cinnamon also went to Lilith's apartment in search of her. That's where we bumped into each other. Unlike Lilith, Cinnamon had taken an instant disliking of me. She blamed me for Lilith ghosting her. I never did learn of her real name; it wasn't important back then.

Back then she had long, multi-colored hair. It was shorter now, and blonde. So blonde, it was almost white. It looked like a big Q-tip. She'd also put on some weight, as in she was pregnant. I was mildly curious, but not curious enough to stick around.

Both women glanced at me as I exited the parking lot. I gave them a wave before driving off. I don't think Cinnamon recognized me, but if she did, I could only imagine the conversation that would've ensued.

I was once again in a dilemma with Felicity's case and began mentally listing what I had and had not done. The second list was short, but it occurred to me that I'd not called Art. I used the hands-free call app while entering the interstate.

"I've been meaning to call you. I haven't seen any Sentra running around with the damage you described."

"Okay, don't worry about that anymore. It's been found. Do you know of a man by the name of Timothy Davenport? He's a younger guy, I'd guess no older than twenty or twenty-one."

He paused a few seconds before answering. "No, I don't think I've ever heard of him. Why?"

"He's the owner of the Sentra," I said.

"Did he have something to do with Felicity?" he asked.

"I'm not certain. I saw him once, not too long ago. He's skinny as a rail, looks like he's got some drug abuse issues going on. I definitely want to talk to him."

"Where's he from?" Art asked.

"Smyrna. That's where he went to high school."

"Alright, I'll ask around, maybe somebody I work with or hang out with knows him. Is there anything else?" he asked.

There was a time not so long ago where I would've said no and hung up, but Art had kind of grown on me these past few days. I filled him in about how I had been searching for the Sentra, how I had enlisted Brittany's help, and how it had ultimately cost her and her friend their lives.

"Oh, man, that sucks a big one," Art said when I'd finished. "I'm surprised it ain't on the national news since her friend was one of those trans girls."

He had a point, and I was wondering if I could somehow make that happen. If there was enough publicity, it'd be easier to locate Davenport. I thought about that cute news anchor with the head full of thick auburn hair that had tried to interview me a few weeks ago. She'd given me her business card.

"I've got to get back to work, but please call me if there's anything else," Art said.

"I will."

Hanging up, I looked around in my wallet and found the card. Shelly McRae. She didn't know it, but after meeting her that one time, I'd become a fan of her evening newscast. I left a message, and she called me back within a minute.

"Hi, Shelly. I don't know if you remember me or not," I said.

"I do remember you, Thomas Ironcutter," she replied. "You're the one who was kidnapped by that guy who'd murdered four other people."

"That's me," I replied.

"You know, after you refused to be interviewed by me, I was intrigued," she began.

"Intrigued? I like the sound of that," I said.

"I did some research on you and found some old video footage of you from back in the days when you were a homicide detective."

"That couldn't have been easy. I try to avoid news cameras."

She gave a pleasant laugh. "I could tell. You certainly have an intriguing history. Anyways, what can I do for you?"

I gave her a synopsis of the double murder.

"That is interesting. When we interviewed the detective, he made no mention of one of the victims being transgender, and he said nothing about the suspect's vehicle," she said.

"So, I hope it's interesting enough for you to do a follow-up story on it."

"Are you involved in the case?" she asked.

"Only on the periphery. The lead on the case is Detective Nancy Hamilton with the Rutherford Sheriff's Department. I'll give you her number if you want it."

She agreed and took down the information. "Does this mean I can list you as a source now?"

"If you'd like, but I don't know if I'd be much value," I said.

"I don't think any of the other news stations have this information. So, if Detective Hamilton comes through, I'd say you definitely have value and I'd like to be friends with you."

"I'd like that too. I'll be watching the evening news," I said.

After hanging up with Shelly, I decided to drive over to Mona's Paradise. I got as far as the parking lot, circled it, and then exited. I was being stupid and reminded myself I needed to stay as far away from her and her business as possible. My life, figuratively speaking, depended on it.

I spent the next few hours running errands. I needed to visit a couple of auto salvage yards in search of some parts for the Sprite, and I went by a business to pick up paperwork for a case that I was possibly going to take on. I was parking in front of the Publix for my last errand of the day when I received a call from Nancy.

"I just got off the phone with Shelly McRae. Did you put her up to it?" she asked.

"I did. You're not upset about that, are you?" I asked.

"No, I guess not. She wants to interview me for a spot on the evening news. She'll be here in thirty minutes."

"That's great," I said. "I bet it'll generate some leads."

"I'm nervous," she admitted.

"That's to be expected, but I don't think you'll have any trouble at all. Besides, you're photogenic. You looked nice today."

There was a pause. "Do you think so?"

"I do. You're pleasing to the eye, but I suspect you already know that."

She gave a light laugh now. "Yeah, I know. Next time give me a heads-up though. I'll take a little extra time putting on my makeup."

"You got it and I'll look forward to watching it."

I was back home, busying myself with tidying up the house and was deciding on what to fix for dinner when Nancy texted me.

The interview went great!

I smiled to myself. Everyone I've ever known secretly wanted their fifteen minutes of fame. I guessed Percy and I were the only exceptions to the rule. I texted back.

Awesome. I'm glad it went well. No doubt Georgie will be beside himself with jealousy, which makes it even better.

"Yep, that little fat ass with his pointy-toed boots will be beside himself," I gleefully muttered. Nancy texted back seconds later.

Maybe we should celebrate. Yes?

I didn't know if she was being sincere, or if she had ulterior motives, as in playing nice and attempting to get me to incriminate myself. Although I was suspicious, I had to admit, I had an attraction to her. That thought led to the next question I had for myself; did I really want to do this? I stared at my phone for a full thirty seconds before sending a text.

Sure, what did you have in mind?

CHAPTER 43

We met at an upscale restaurant in Murfreesboro that specialized in fish plates. I felt like this was more than a casual dinner where she was going to be questioning me about the double homicide. Or perhaps I was reading more into it. I took another shower, dressed in slate gray slacks, a dress shirt that the sales lady called shrimp color, but I thought of it as pink, and one of my newer sport coats. I finished the ensemble with a pair of Sperry shoes that didn't get worn too often.

When Nancy arrived, I saw she had not changed, which probably meant she'd come directly from work. She greeted me with a smile, and we walked through the rotating door together.

We were seated immediately, and the waitress was standing there within seconds.

"Can I get either of you started with a cocktail?" she asked. I glanced at Nancy.

"I could sure use one," she said.

"Sure," I replied.

Both of us ordered one of their specialty cocktails; I ordered their Smoked Old Fashioned and Nancy opted for a fruity cocktail named a Coral Reef Punch.

"Hard day at work?" I asked.

"You don't know the half of it," she answered.

"Any progress on the case?"

She made a face and shook her head. "It's going absolutely nowhere."

"Has there been any feedback from your interview?" I asked.

"Not yet, but you were right. I passed by George in the hallway, he made some kind of snarky remark. I asked him to repeat it, but he only glared at me and kept walking."

I grinned. "Good, that makes my day. By the way, I was right. You looked good on TV."

"Thanks," she replied, giving her own smile.

"So, nothing at all on the case, that sucks," I remarked.

"Yeah. In addition to George behaving like an ass, I asked a co-worker to go pick up the surveillance video from Starbucks. She said she would but when I asked her about it, she acted like it'd slipped her mind." Nancy shook her head. "Did you ever have problems with co-workers like that when you were a detective?"

"Yeah, once or twice," I said.

"How did you handle it?" she asked.

I gave a small chuckle. "I wasn't very professional about it. There was one person in particular. His name is Poston. He still works for Metro. After one particular incident, I confronted him and told him what I thought about his behavior. I guess you could say we've been enemies ever since. My advice, be more tactful than I was."

"Easy for you to say," she replied as the waitress set our cocktails down. She picked hers up, took a small sip, and then took a much larger one. "This is delicious."

I took a sip of mine. The bourbon was definitely not anything close to Pappy Van Winkle, but for a restaurant bar, it was good enough.

"So, tell me about yourself," Nancy suggested.

"I think you know all about me," I countered.

"Tell me anyway," she said with a small smile.

"Alright, Reader's Digest version. I joined the police department when I got out of the Army. I worked hard and put myself through college while working the graveyard shift. That's where I met my wife. We eventually got married. I made detective and she was murdered. It turns out she was having an affair and was pregnant with his child. He killed her and made it look like a suicide."

"You were arrested for her murder," she remarked while staring.

"Right you are. On that particular night, I was called away from the house. When I returned, she was dead. I was in an unusual situation where I had to lie about where I had gone, so I made up an alibi. When it was discovered to be false, it made me look like a murder suspect. I had an uncle who worked on the department and there was a great deal of animosity between him and an assistant chief. That particular person took my false alibi and used it to conspire to have me framed for her murder. Once the truth came out, I was freed, and I sued. The rest is history."

"Why did you have to give a false alibi?" she asked.

"I was helping out somebody and if the truth had come out, it would have ruined some lives."

She took another drink and gave a small smile. "Dare I ask you to tell me?"

I gave her a small smile in return. "That one will go to my grave. Enough about me. What about you?"

"There's not much to tell," she said.

"Sure, there is. Where are you from originally?"

She stared a moment. "I don't tell this to many people, but I'm originally from a little dent in the road called Junction City, Kentucky. I moved out as soon as I graduated high school and ended up in Murfreesboro."

"Murfreesboro is a nice city," I said.

She scoffed. "There's still too many backward rednecks for me."

"There was a time when Nashville could be described like that, but it's fairly liberal now."

"Yeah, and now the crime rate is outrageous. As soon as I get a year or two under my belt, I'm out of here."

"You've mentioned that before. What are your plans?"

"I'm either going to go into business for myself as a private investigator, like you, or apply at a federal agency, like the FBI. Either way, I'll be living on the coast somewhere. I love the ocean."

"Anywhere in particular?" I asked.

"California, maybe."

"Nice," I said.

"Have you ever been to California?" she asked.

"Yeah, but only to Los Angeles. That was a few years ago."

"How'd you like it?"

I gave a small shrug. "I didn't get to see much. It was a working trip. The biggest thing I remember is the traffic and the smog."

"Yeah, I was thinking possibly San Francisco, but lately I've been thinking more and more of Key West."

I nodded in appreciation. It was good to aspire. I hoped it worked out for her.

"Did you see any combat when you were in the Army?" she asked.

"Does being hunkered down in a bunker count?" I asked with a lighthearted laugh. I was not inclined to tell war stories.

She laughed as well. "Chief served a tour in Iraq. He's a decorated veteran."

"Chief?" I asked.

"Our chief deputy. He recently got promoted to Colonel in the National Guard."

"Is he the one who got you transferred to the detective's division?"

She smirked. "Yeah. He saw my potential."

I bet he did, I thought. She went on for a few minutes about her apparent hero. Despite that, I found myself enjoying her company and she was a good conversationalist. That is, until the entrée arrived. That's about when the text messages started. It wasn't one or two, she was being bombarded with them, and for some reason she felt the need to give each text an immediate response.

The content of the texts changed her demeanor. She'd taken one, maybe two bites of her lobster before she was sidetracked and her meal was soon forgotten, and I was seemingly forgotten as well. After five minutes of nonstop texting, she suddenly stood.

"Something's come up and I have to go. Thanks for dinner."

She didn't wait for me to respond and left the restaurant like her ass was on fire. The waitress noticed and approached the table.

"Is everything alright?" she asked.

"Yeah, it's fine. My friend has irritable bowel syndrome and sometimes it catches up with her."

The waitress made a face and walked off. I finished my lobster and then helped myself to Nancy's. I was going to have to put in some extra time at the gym to burn off the extra calories, but I'd be damned if I was going to let it go to waste.

I gave the waitress a generous tip and left the restaurant, disappointed in how the date turned out. The most disappointing part was that we never even got into the case. I figured this was my prime opportunity to get her to open up and share details about her investigation. Anything I learned could have perhaps helped me find Felicity, but it was not to be.

And there was the physical aspect. I wouldn't admit it to anyone, but I found myself attracted to her. But there was another part of my brain telling me I'd dodged a bullet, but damned if I didn't find myself wondering what could have happened.

As I drove, I forced myself to stop thinking about Nancy and focused on Felicity's case. I wasn't making any progress, and I knew there was a point in time where I was going to suspend my investigation and move on to other cases. The big question was at what point do I call it?

"Yeah, maybe it's time to move on," I mumbled.

CHAPTER 44

There were only a few regulars in the gym and Danica wasn't present to pester me, so I was able to have a solid workout without interruption. After, I showered in the locker room, purchased a smoothie, and headed straight to LaVergne.

It was a pleasant day, overcast and in the low seventies. I was dressed in jeans and a casual Carhartt brand tee shirt. When I left the fitness center, my first inclination was to go play a round of golf. It was a great day for it. But Felicity's case was still nagging me, and I wasn't yet ready to let it go.

I went directly to the mobile home park and did a drive-by of Mrs. McLaughlin's residence. There were no cars parked in the drive and everything appeared buttoned up. She might've been inside sleeping one off, or she had gotten a ride to the liquor store. It could've been either. I turned around, parked on the side of the road, and knocked on her door. I tried for a solid five minutes without a response. She either wasn't there or she wasn't going to answer.

Sighing in frustration, I went back to my SUV and sat in it, trying to come up with some kind of plan. I'd noticed a neighbor eyeing me when I first drove up. She was now trying to act nonchalant as she swept her driveway. I decided to take a chance that she wasn't a spitter, got out, and walked over.

"Good morning, ma'am," I greeted.

"Good morning yourself," she retorted. "If you're friends with that hussy, I don't think I want to talk to you."

I glanced over at the McLaughlin trailer and lowered my voice. "I'm not friends with any of them. In fact, I think one of her sons is a murder suspect."

She narrowed her eyes at me. "What are you talking about?"

"Did you happen to hear about that double murder over at Jefferson Springs?" I asked.

Her eyes widened now. "I saw something about it on the news. You think her son was involved?"

"There's not a lot of evidence at the moment, but yeah, I think that," I said. "Have you ever seen a gray Nissan Sentra parked there?"

She continued frowning while giving a slow shake of the head. "Can't say that I have. That big fat son of hers is usually riding one of those loud motorcycles, but sometimes he'll be in a car. Can't say I remember a gray Sentra though, and I know what a Sentra looks like. I worked at Nissan for twenty-nine years before I retired. I must've helped build ten thousand of those damn things. Now all I have to show for it is an awful case of carpal tunnel. You know what that is?"

"Yes ma'am, I do. I hope your health insurance is taking care of you."

She scoffed. "Don't even get me started on them. So, that fat ass is a murder suspect."

"Actually, it's his brother. His name's Felton, but his nickname is Freak," I said.

She frowned again. "She's mentioned him, but I've never seen him around. I saw you here the other day speaking to the old hag. Was she hospitable?"

"She wasn't," I said. "In fact, she ended up spitting on me. She was drunk too."

She responded with a snorting chortle. "Yep, that sounds like her. She tried that on me once and I gave her a good poke in the ribs with my broom handle."

"Good for you," I said. "I bet she doesn't mess with you anymore."

"Nope, but that fat son of hers came over a few days later and threatened to take a knife to me," she said. "I called the police, but they didn't do anything."

"Sorry to hear that. The next time I run into him, I'll have a word with him about threatening women. Thanks for your time."

I got back into my SUV and drove off. My level of frustration had not abated. I was out of leads and had nothing to show for it. I'd not made any contact with Freak, and I had no idea how to find him. Same with Timothy Davenport. Simply driving over to the Satan's Dogs clubhouse and asking for them was not an option any longer. Beating the shit out of Whopper had ensured I'd never be welcome there.

I could have spent another day driving around in circles, hoping I'd bump into one of them, but that would've been stupid and a waste of gas. I texted Percy to see if there were any developments. He replied that there was not. He said he'd spoken to Detective Hamilton, but it was a waste of time.

"That woman could use a lesson or two on professional courtesy," he growled.

So, there was nothing for me.

Felicity had been missing since last Thursday. I was grounded in reality, and the reality of it was, she was most likely dead. Lying in a ditch on a rural road somewhere, waiting to be found. It was a dismal thought, but like I said, I'm a realist.

I turned into my drive, only to have to stop for a Fed Ex delivery van. I frowned in confusion a moment before I realized the delivery must be the parts to the Sprite Bubba and I had been waiting on. I grinned and waved at the deliveryman as I parked.

"Hey, I was just about to push the button," he said.

I took the two boxes, thanked him, and then backed my SUV out of his way so he could get on with his business. The boxes put me in a slightly better mood, and the plan was to get to work on the Sprite, but I was going to eat lunch first.

I was in the middle of prepping a pasta salad when my phone rang. I looked at the caller ID. It was Nancy.

"This ought to be good," I muttered and answered.

"Hi," she greeted. "I wanted to apologize for last night, I got called into work," she said.

It was a lie, but what was she going to say? Confess that she had to leave because her married boyfriend was jealous because she was out on a date with a dashingly handsome Italian man? Of course not. Why tell the truth when you can lie, right?

"They're working you to death," I replied. It was hard, but I kept the sarcasm out of my voice.

She scoffed. "You're telling me."

"I hope it was something big. Was Davenport found?" I asked.

"Who?"

"You know, the owner of the Sentra," I said with a slight amount of scorn. She didn't notice.

"Oh, him. No, he hasn't been found yet. So, let's try it again one evening. It'll be my treat," she said.

"Yeah, that sounds great. Looking forward to it. I've got to let you go, I have a delivery van at the gate," I said.

She directed me to call her later and told me to have a great day before hanging up. I ate lunch, grabbed a cigar out of my humidor, and headed to the shop with Tommy Boy tagging along.

I'd only got as far as opening one of the boxes and pulling out the parts when the gate intercom buzzer was activated. I tapped the camera app on my phone and saw two cars. I recognized both of them, but I did not understand why those two particular people would come to my house together.

Abby was in the lead car, her beloved Jeep. Trademark trailed behind her in his undercover red Mustang. They both parked and got out. Abby walked over to me looking apprehensive. Trademark got out and made a show of lighting a cigarette. His mannerism reminded me of Georgie. My level of respect for him dropped down yet another notch.

"Do you know him?" I asked Abby.

"We met for the first time a couple of hours ago. He had a lot of things to say about you."

I stared at her. She stared back. There was a mixture of concern, puzzlement, and perhaps even some wariness in her expression. Trademark walked up and stared with a smirk.

"Yeah, we had a nice long talk. You've been keeping secrets from her," he said and gestured at me with his cigarette. "Go ahead. Ask him. Let's see if he tells the truth."

"He said you've murdered someone," she said. "You ambushed a man in a restroom and killed him in cold blood."

"Well, Ironcutter? Are you going to tell the truth to your buddy, or are you going to lie to her too?" Trademark asked. He was still smirking, like he'd backed me into a corner. "By the way, where is that little filly who pointed a gun at me? Is she your side piece when Abby isn't around?"

"Watch your mouth, idiot," I growled.

Trademark grinned like he'd scored additional points. I glanced at Abby again. She was still somber, apprehensive.

"What's your game here, Skidmark? Are you trying to play Abby against me in the hopes that I'll confess to a murder that I've not committed? Or maybe you're hoping I'll knock that smirk off your face and then you'll have me arrested on some kind of silly ass federal charges."

His smirk broadened. "Oh, I've got one better." He pulled his phone out of his pocket, tapped on it with his index finger, and eyed me. "I've got it on speakerphone so we can all hear."

He then waited. After a couple of rings, a man answered.

"Hello, Hayden," he said.

Hayden, as in Hayden Westlake, the Federal District Attorney who was threatening to have me arrested and wanted me to be his snitch.

"Hello, Agent Maroney. What's your status?"

"I'm here with Ironcutter, and I've brought Officer Severns along," he replied.

"Excellent. Thomas, can you hear me?" he asked.

"I can. What is the purpose of this?"

"I would think that it's obvious to you, Thomas. This is a wake-up call. I've been patient with you, but my patience is at an end. You have done nothing to help yourself. You have been disrespectful to Agent Maroney, and you have not given us one scintilla of evidence that can be used in the furtherance of prosecution against the Satan's Dogs, nor the Baroques," he said.

"It sounds like you rehearsed that little speech," I said. "Have you spoken with William? You know, my attorney? The one who told you to have no further contact with me without his consent?"

"Thomas, if you want to hide behind your attorney, that is your right to do so. But I want to emphasize what I am about to say; the gloves are off. We are going to continue to reach out to your friends and associates, people like Officer Severns, and let them know about the murder you committed. We will continue this action until you decide to cooperate. What do you think of that, Thomas?"

I glanced over at Abby. "Well, it's a good thing I don't have any friends."

I heard Hayden make a tsking sound before speaking. "Your sarcasm is duly noted. Now, what shall it be, Thomas? Shall we continue with this until your reputation is completely ruined? If that happens, I doubt your PI business will survive, nor do I think any reputable businessmen will include you in any future venture capital investments."

"Venture capital investments? What's that?" I asked.

Hayden tsked again. "Do you really think I haven't performed my due diligence? I know all about your investments, down to the last penny. I must say, I am impressed. You are creating a nice portfolio out of the settlement from your lawsuit. Oh, by the way, if I were you, I'd make sure you have all your paperwork in order. The IRS may be paying you a visit soon."

"Ah, yes, the IRS audit threat. You're pulling no punches, Hayden," I said.

"Yes indeed, Thomas. So, you can continue to be recalcitrant, or you can sit down with Agent Maroney whereupon he will instruct you on what you should do and how you are going to do it. What's it going to be?"

It only took me a half-second to respond. "I've thought this over long and hard since you and that fat idiot came to visit me. And the question I have to ask myself is this; how in the hell am I being accused of murdering someone I've never met, and never talked to? Here's your answer, Hayden. A man by the name of Samuel Todd, commonly known as Bang-Bang, has made up a story in an effort to keep himself from going to prison. When he and his attorney met with you, the little devious wheels in your head began turning. You found a dupe by the name of George Thompson and set your plan in motion. How close am I?"

I paused and waited for an answer. Hayden stayed silent. Trademark eyed me.

"Alright, I'll answer for you. Other than Bang-Bang's accusation, you have nothing on me. No eyewitnesses, no physical evidence. Now that we have that out of the way, let me tell you this, Hayden. I've been trying to find a missing woman and I have reason to believe that one or more members of the Satan's Dogs may have something to do with her disappearance."

Trademark interrupted. "You don't have one iota of evidence pointing to the Dogs."

"I have a few pieces of circumstantial evidence which I am the first to admit is not much, but I could've used some help from the two of you."

"I helped you when I could," Trademark said.

"It wasn't much, but you did help, I'll give you that. I had hoped that maybe we could have succeeded in putting together a case against them, until you pulled this nonsense. So, I'm done with this game. Fuck off, Westlake, and fuck you too, Skidmark."

CHAPTER 45

DEA Agent Terry Maroney gave me a baleful stare after my proclamation. He was about to say something, but I heard Hayden call out to him on the phone. He disabled the speaker function and then walked around his car, putting it between us. Abby walked over to me as Maroney spoke in a low, hushed voice.

"You shouldn't use profanity," she whispered.

I almost chuckled at the admonishment. After several seconds, Skidmark hung up and walked back over to us.

"Well, Ironcutter, you have royally screwed yourself. You know that, right?"

"If there is nothing else, Agent Maroney, you can get the hell out of here," I replied.

He sniffed and then glanced at Abby. "C'mon, let's get out of here. I'll spring for lunch."

"No thank you," Abby said.

He stared at her, as if he could not believe she was rejecting him. He stared a moment longer before scoffing and getting in his car. He backed up, turned it around, and drove away without spinning his tires, which was a surprise.

"What brought this on?" I asked.

"Agent Maroney called me this morning. He introduced himself, said he was assisting a sheriff's detective with a murder investigation, and asked to meet with me."

"Let me guess, that detective was a fat ass by the name of George Thompson."

She nodded. "Yeah. I met them at the Rutherford Sheriff's Department. They took me back to an interview room and proceeded to tell me you are the prime suspect in a murder. Then they asked the usual questions, which also included asking me if I'd be willing to wear a wire."

"Let me guess, that was Maroney's idea?" I said.

"Yep. I told them no immediately," she declared. She saw me staring and probably thought I wasn't believing her. "I'm not wearing one now, if that's what you're wondering. Do you want to see?"

"That's okay, I believe you," I said, and it was true, I did believe her, but even if I didn't, I had no intention of saying anything that would incriminate me anyway. "So, how did it go and why did you come here?"

She frowned. "It was a short interview. I cut it off when that fat detective started saying horrible things about you and making threats that I could be arrested along with you. He honestly thought he was being clever and scaring me. I got up and walked out. Maroney followed me to the parking lot and said he was going to come pay you a visit and that I should join him. So, here I am. I wasn't sure what he was going to do and to be honest, I wasn't sure what I was going to do either, but here I am." She huffed in exasperation and stared down the driveway, as if she were wondering if Maroney was going to return.

"Are they going to arrest you, Thomas?" she finally asked.

"I don't think so. They would have already if they had any proof. I'm not sure how they made the connection between us, but I'm sure they were hoping you'd have something on me that they could use," I said. "And, of course, like Westlake said, they're going to start pestering everyone associated with me in the hopes of causing me enough stress that I'll do something stupid."

"Detective Thompson said you ambushed a man in the bathroom of a bar and beat him to death," she said. "You don't seem like that kind of person, and I said so. Tell me I'm not wrong."

"You're not wrong."

She stared off into the woods now. I don't know if she saw it, but a deer was peeking out at us from behind a tree.

"There's more. When I said you weren't that kind of person, Detective Thompson said that it's highly possible you murdered your wife and that your friends in the department covered it up and made it look like that rogue FBI agent did it. He also said you killed the agent and covered that up too."

I glanced over at an old oak tree in the back. Henry's headstone was near the base. I swear to goodness I felt tears coming and quickly wiped them away, ashamed of myself. I had more love for that dog after he died than I did when he was alive. I caught Abby staring at me.

"What?" she asked.

"I'll tell you all about it, but for now, let's focus on you. This nonsense that happened today is only the start. It's the exact reason why you and I need to cool our friendship. It's only a matter of time before Detective Thompson or Agent Maroney has the idea of making a phone call to the Office of Professional Accountability and stirring up trouble. Once that happens, OPA will be required to conduct a formal investigation."

"Do you mean they'll investigate me?" She scoffed. "Let them. They won't find anything. I've done nothing illegal, nor have I violated any department policy," she said.

I was tempted to remind her about driving over here the other night when she had no business behind the wheel.

"Even if they rule any allegation as unfounded, the complaint will stay in your personnel file for the rest of your employment. The mere fact that you associate with me may even stigmatize you."

"But you're a good person, Thomas," she said.

I sighed. "Abby, I'm not the saint you think I am. There are details about that case that you don't know about and I'm not going to tell you. Plus, there are things I've done in the past that you would never do or condone."

"Like what?" she asked.

I grunted. "Maybe, one day, I'll write an autobiography and you can read it. In the meantime, I think you can see why we should not be close."

She once again stared down the driveway, and after a minute turned to me. "Do me a favor, finish this line. As iron sharpens iron…"

I gave a small smile. "So shall a friend sharpen the countenance of a friend. Or something like that. Are we resorting to the book of proverbs now?"

She smiled back and stared deeply. "That's why I like you, Thomas. You're a true friend and a Christian man."

"I may know a little bit about the bible, but I'm the first to admit I'm a sorry excuse for a Christian," I replied.

She gave a small, patient smile. "We're all sinners, right? The important thing is that you're a good friend and I value that. It doesn't seem like many people are like that anymore."

I couldn't help but smile back. "I guess that's true."

"Do you have any true friends in your life, Thomas?" she asked.

"Not many. One or two," I said and glanced over at the old tree. "Come with me. I want you to meet somebody."

I walked Abby over to Henry's grave. "This is Henry. He belonged to a neighbor, but they died and he kind of adopted me. He was a true friend. So, let me tell you a little bit about Henry and a little bit about myself."

She listened attentively while I told her about my wife, how I could not give an alibi, her affair, her death, and the fatal confrontation with Special Agent Enrique Hernandez. I summarized a lot of it, but I didn't leave out how Henry had saved my life. The whole story took over two hours. By the time I was done, the sun was going down. I pointed down at Henry's grave.

"I didn't realize what a true friend Henry was until after he'd sacrificed himself to save Anna and me. So, I guess I shouldn't do that with you, right?"

She grinned. "Absolutely right." She stretched and rubbed her tummy. "I'm famished, what about you?"

We went to an authentic Mexican restaurant where we ate and talked until closing time and then said our goodbyes. When I arrived home, I poured myself some Scotch and carried a chair over to Henry's grave. My recitation to Abby brought a lot of feelings to the surface and I needed to process them before I went to bed.

I also had a lot of thinking to do about Abby. Remembering what Kalina said about her, I found myself thinking what kind of relationship would the two of us have if we took it further and then immediately quashed those thoughts.

"Short and simple, it'd never work," I muttered.

I knew it from the bottom of my heart. She needed to find herself a good man, a man with the same values, a man of stalwart character, and a man closer to her own age. I glanced at the grave and thought back to when he was alive. Those memories brought a smile. I held up my glass in a small salute.

"Goodnight, boy. I hope I get to see you again, one day."

CHAPTER 46

Nancy called me as I was about to head to the gym. I wasn't sure I wanted to talk to her and debated on letting it go to voicemail, but ultimately answered.

"I thought I'd let you know, a corpse was found this morning, and we're pretty certain it's Timothy Davenport," she said.

My ears perked up. "Really?"

"Yep, so I thought I'd let you know."

"Hold on, don't drop this on me and hang up without telling me the circumstances," I said.

She huffed, as if I had suddenly become a big inconvenience. "There's not a lot to tell. He was found in a ditch by a farmer in the southern end of the county. There aren't any physical injuries, so it may be an overdose and then whoever he was doing drugs with dumped him. The autopsy is in an hour, and we'll know more then. Anyway, after having to leave so suddenly at dinner, I figured I owed you one. I've got to go."

She hung up on me, which was no surprise. She probably knew I was about to pepper her with more questions and that's why she cut the conversation short. Even though I understood her thinking, it still irritated me. I texted her.

I appreciate you telling me about Davenport. If you don't mind, give me a call when you learn more. Thanks

I then texted Percy to update him because I had no doubt neither Nancy nor Agent Thrasher would do it. After I'd done that, I fixed a pot of coffee and sat at my kitchen table, wondering what to do next. I would not be allowed to watch the autopsy and I had no idea where specifically he was dumped. At some point Tommy Boy had walked in the kitchen. He was now sitting a few feet away, staring up at me.

"Two murdered women dumped in ditches on rural roads, and now Timothy Davenport is found under the same circumstances. Coincidence? I highly doubt it, but nobody's asking my opinion. Can you believe that shit?"

Tommy Boy's only response was a flick of his tail. I grunted. "I guess that's a no."

The detective in me wanted to get involved in Davenport's investigation, but I knew that was a party I wasn't going to be invited to.

After a good workout, I went to Home Depot and then worked on the Sprite most of the day while waiting for Nancy to call me back.

She didn't.

As the afternoon sun started casting shadows, I put some gas in the tank, hooked up the battery, and coaxed the little gal to life. The puny four-cylinder engine was only capable of about fifty horsepower, so it did not emit a throaty growl of a muscle car, but it was still music to my ears.

I took a video of me revving the engine and sent it to Bubba. I then shut the engine down and checked my phone for any voicemail that I might've missed. Nancy still had not called, but Bubba responded to my text with a bunch of smiley-face emoticons.

I supposed it was possible that Nancy was too busy with her double murder to call me, or she was simply avoiding me. Whatever the reason, it irritated the crap out of me.

I was once friends with a person who still worked at the medical examiner's office, Doctor Holly Gross. I couldn't say we were friends anymore, maybe acquaintances, but that was it. I was tempted to call her and ask about Davenport's death, but then dismissed the notion. Like I said, we weren't that close anymore.

I ate dinner with Tommy Boy being my only company. I then poured myself a small amount of Scotch, sat in my easy chair, and finished reading a book I'd been reading off and on for over a month. I then used the remote to surf through the channels on TV, but there was nothing that interested me.

I was tempted to pour myself some more Scotch, chose not to, and aimlessly wandered around my house. I ended up in my bedroom. After a moment of staring at my bed, I pulled the mattresses aside and opened my safe. Retrieving Kalina's box, I carried it back to the den and sat back in my easy chair.

"What's so damned important about this stuff anyway?" I muttered.

I looked at the medallions first. They had intricate detailing, but otherwise I didn't see anything remarkable about them. After inspecting them for a few minutes, I set them aside and picked up the book, or journal, or whatever it was.

The cover was a dark leather, old and not with a few hairline cracks. The papers had a yellowish tint, which I assumed was also a result of aging. I don't think the paper was papyrus, but it was coarse, not like regular paper. I tried a couple of translator apps in an effort to decipher what was written but was not successful.

I rifled through the pages to see if anything was written on the edges. I think I saw that in an adventure movie once, but there was nothing. The paper was definitely old. The ink used for the writing and drawings had the appearance of being old as well, although I was only speculating.

One of the drawings was fairly simplistic. It was of a man staring down into a well. That was it. He had a knife in one hand, but there wasn't much else.

"Knives have unique designs, I learned that on TV," I muttered to myself. If I could identify the style of the knife, that might give a time period or location where the book was written. I had one of those magnifier apps on my phone. I activated it and used it to look closer at the knife. To my surprise, I could see faint writing underneath the drawing.

"Interesting," I said and began inspecting the other pages. There was faint writing on all of them. My brain had a faint spark, and it only took a minute on the internet to find the appropriate term.

"I'll be," I muttered as I stared at the book. "It's a palimpsest. I wonder if Kalina knows that?"

I stared at it a few minutes longer before putting everything back in the box and securing it in my safe. Crawling under the covers, I instinctively knew that box of Gypsy trinkets was going to eventually bring me trouble. Lots of trouble.

CHAPTER 47

Bubba and I tapped our glasses of sweet tea together and stared admiringly at the Sprite. It had not been painted yet and there were primer spots all over it, but still, I thought she looked awesome.

"That went better than I expected," Bubba remarked.

"Yes, it did. We finished it ahead of schedule and below budget." I swallowed some tea before speaking again. "I have something to say."

"What's that?" Bubba asked.

"I've been pretty much a loner the past year due to everything that's happened to me. This," I said as I gestured toward my shop with my glass of tea, "was to be only for me. I had no intention of sharing it with anyone. I was uncertain about our partnership and how we'd work together. But standing here looking over this Sprite, I think we make a good team."

I think my speech stunned Bubba. He gave a surprised look and took a few seconds to respond.

"I appreciate that, Hoss. I have something to say too. The only person who stuck by me when I was arrested was my wife. I had what you call fair-weather-friends. Once I got out, I've been extra careful with who I hang around with. My wife likes you, so that's a plus too. She's a mighty tolerant woman, but she makes me toe the line these days, you better believe that."

I chuckled. "That's a good thing."

"Well, anyway, before either of us get all kinds of warm fuzzies, I'm going to head on home. Nate has promised us cash on delivery, so that'll sure help things."

After Bubba left, I tinkered around my shop and daydreamed about new tools I could buy. My phone pinged as I was sweeping the floor. Someone was at the gate. Looking at the screen, I could see it was Nancy.

"Well, this is a surprise," I murmured and tapped the icon that opened the gate.

When she got out of her car, the first thing I saw was the swollen lip. Her eyes were also puffy, like she'd been crying. She saw the glass of tea in my hand and gestured at it.

"Is that tea?" she asked.

"Yeah, you want a glass?"

She shook her head. "You have anything stronger?"

"Yeah, sure."

I led her inside, sat her on the couch, and chose the Jack Daniels. She was not yet worthy of the Van Winkle. I dropped some ice in a tumbler and filled it with a double shot. She took a large swallow, coughed when she swallowed it, and then took one of the ice cubes and held it up to her lip.

I sat on the couch and faced her. "Do you want to talk about it?"

The tears came quickly. She tried to hide it with a quick wipe of her hand and another swallow of whiskey. After a moment, she shrugged.

"There's not much to say. I called my boyfriend a lying, two-faced, piece of shit and he backhanded me."

"You should file a police report," I said. Her response was an immediate shaking of her head. "Why not?"

"It's complicated," she said.

"Complicated? How?" I pressed.

"Because he's the second-in-command at the sheriff's department and it would jeopardize his career."

I scoffed. "If a man hits a woman because she called him a few names, he has no business being a cop."

She eyed me. "You've never hit a woman?"

"Not under those circumstances, no."

She scoffed, as if she didn't believe me, and took another drink before speaking. "Well, there's more to it."

"So, tell me what happened."

There was a long pause. Nancy finished her drink and looked around. She spotted the bottle sitting on the counter and nodded to herself. Standing, she waked over to it, poured herself a generous helping and plopped back down on the couch.

"You've heard me mention the chief deputy," she said.

"Eric Farmingham, yes. I take it he's the boyfriend in question?"

"Do you know him?" she asked.

"I've heard of him, but I don't know him personally," I said.

"Well, we're involved, but nobody else knows about it."

I kept a straight face, but I didn't see how she believed nobody else knew of the two of them.

"Anyway, it's complicated. He's married but she's a crazy bitch and all that. At least, that's what he told me. I thought we had a connection, but about two hours ago I found out he and my sister have been having an affair behind my back."

The tears returned and she didn't try to hide them now. Instead, she sipped some more whiskey. I left the room briefly and returned with some tissue.

"Thanks," she murmured and began dabbing her face.

"How did you find out?" I asked.

"She told me. You see, she's pregnant. At first, she told me the father of her child had taken off and ghosted her. I kept pushing her to give me all his info so I could track him down and make him pay child support. She kept avoiding the issue, but today she decided to confess to me that Eric is the father of her child. I confronted him and here's the result," she said, pointing at her lip.

"That sucks," I said.

She rolled her eyes. "You think?"

"What are you going to do now?" I asked.

She eyed me with what she probably thought was a seductive stare. "I'm going to get drunk and fuck."

I gave a small, patient smile. "You can sit here and get drunk if you want, but I'm not going to sleep with you."

Her eyes widened in surprise. "Why not?"

"Because two people who you care for have betrayed you deeply and you're in a lot of pain. I'm not going to take advantage of you," I said.

She scoffed. "How very fucking noble of you. You know you want to. I've seen the way you look at me."

"Right now, what I want doesn't matter. Your life has been suddenly turned upside down. Sleeping with me, or anyone else for that matter, won't make the pain go away."

She broke eye contact and the tears started flowing again. I reached over and held her as she began loudly sobbing. She'd occasionally say something, but I couldn't understand her, so I continued to hold her, telling her it was going to be okay. Eventually, the sobbing ebbed enough where I was able to get her some fresh tissues.

"Thanks," she said as she dabbed at her eyes. "I don't know what the hell I'm going to do now. Any suggestions?"

"If you haven't done it already, tell him it's over. If he argues with you about it, tell him you'll expose and prosecute him."

"Yeah, I'm done with him. I have a feeling that he'll make my work life hell."

"Don't allow it. There are hostile work environment laws to protect you from something like that."

She eyed me. "He's smart. He'll find a way."

"Begin by documenting everything, and I mean everything. Dates, times, places. Take a few photographs of that lip. Conduct a controlled call and ask him incriminating questions."

"What do you mean by that?" she asked.

"Tennessee is a single-party consent state. You can record any conversation between the two of you without him knowing he's being recorded. Prepare a scenario with a list of questions that are designed to get him to admit his culpability, and the next time he calls or confronts you, record it."

She'd fixed herself a third drink while we talked, and then a fourth. Four bourbons was enough to make me shitfaced and I weighed significantly more than her. I was amazed she stayed conscious as long as she did, but eventually she nodded off in the middle of a sentence about her mother. I got a pillow and blanket and made her as comfortable as I could. I watched a moment as she breathed deeply in drunken slumber. She looked like a child who had cried herself to sleep. The ice cube she'd held to her lip had kept it from swelling too much, but it would still be noticeable for a day or two.

I took one last look at her before locking up and turning off the lights. It wasn't yet ten o'clock, but I went ahead and turned in. Lying in bed, I thought about Nancy. I was still uncertain what my feelings were toward her. Was she a naïve, small-town girl who'd been duped by a man who'd used his position of power and status to manipulate her? Or was she the manipulator?

Whatever the case, my gut was telling me to keep it on a platonic level, the same as Abby. Tommy Boy had jumped up on the bed and was making himself comfortable at my feet. When I sighed to myself, he gave me a questioning meow.

"Go to sleep, you," I said, as much to him as to myself.

CHAPTER 48

When I was a younger man, I never would have imagined I'd have frequent overnight female guests. Especially when I was in my forties. When I walked into my den the next morning, Nancy was sprawled out on the couch, snoring contentedly. I gave a small, silent chortle. Jack Daniels could make anyone snore.

She woke up while I was cooking breakfast, sitting up in confusion and looked around. Much like Abby had done recently. Spotting me, she stood, looked down at herself and then walked into the kitchen and sat at the table. I placed a glass of tea in front of her.

"I'm guessing you prefer tea rather than coffee," I said and pointed to the pill bottle sitting on the table. "There's some Ibuprofen if you want any."

She nodded, picked up the glass, and took several swallows before working a few pills out of the plastic container. She washed them down and finished off her tea. I poured her some more.

"Thanks, that hit the spot," she said.

"No problem. How're you feeling?" I asked.

"My head hurts a little, but I guess I'm okay," she replied.

If that was the extent of her hangover after drinking the amount of whisky she'd had, I strongly suspected she was no amateur when it came to alcohol. I gestured toward the stove.

"Are you hungry? Breakfast will be ready in a few."

"What are you fixing?" she asked.

"Spanish omelets, yogurt, brioche, and good strong coffee. Oh, and I have plenty of tea if you want more."

"That actually sounds pretty good. I haven't eaten since lunch yesterday," she said. "If you don't mind, I'd like to use the restroom first."

I pointed her in the direction of the guest restroom and had everything plated when she came out a few minutes later. Her hair was brushed and her face slightly damp. I didn't say it out loud, but she looked cute. She resumed her seat and looked everything over.

"Looks yummy," she said.

"I guarantee a high level of yumminess," I said and took my own seat.

She took a tentative bite of yogurt, purred her approval, and dug in.

"I've never had a man cook breakfast for me," she said between mouthfuls.

"I enjoy cooking," I said. "Back when I was a teenager, I cooked for me and my dad. After I got married, the wife was perfectly fine with me running the kitchen."

"My mom was a good cook, but I never picked up the knack. She tried to teach me, but it was useless. Who taught you, your mom or dad?"

I grunted. "Neither. Mom took off when I was a kid, and the only thing Dad really taught me was how to work on cars."

"Self-taught then?"

"Mostly. When I was in high school, I took a home economics class. It was taught by Mrs. Esposito, an Italian woman who had taken an instant liking to me. Boy she could cook. I learned the basics from her and went from there."

"Did you two have something going on?" she asked with a mischievous grin.

I chuckled. "Nothing like you're thinking. Mrs. Esposito was in her fifties and severely overweight. She was a nice lady though. I liked her."

"Well, since you brought it up, I'm guessing we didn't have sex," she remarked.

"No ma'am, we didn't. You drank quite a bit of whiskey and dozed off on the couch," I said.

After a moment, she nodded slightly. "That's good, I guess. Not that I didn't want to. I came over here with the intention of sleeping with you. I wanted to get back at Eric."

"You mentioned that," I said.

"I did?" she asked. I nodded. "And you didn't do me?"

I smiled. "I was tempted, but I didn't want to take advantage."

She stared at me for several seconds. "Well, okay. I'm not sure if you're bullshitting me or what, but I guess it was good that we didn't."

She seemed to want to say more, but her face darkened, and the tears started again. I moved my chair beside hers and held her. It took several minutes, but the sobbing eventually ebbed, and she used her napkin to blow her nose.

"I'm sorry about that," she said.

"It's totally understandable," I replied.

"Why do you say that?"

"Because two people you care for deeply betrayed your trust," I said. "I've no doubt you're hurting and uncertain how to go forward from here."

She croaked out a chuckle. "Well put. I'm guessing you've experienced something similar."

"Yeah, you could say that," I said.

She scoffed at herself. "Oh yeah, I remember now. Your wife cheated on you."

"Yeah."

"Yeah, and I remember George telling me that he was certain you'd killed her and got away with it." She wiped her face and smiled. "Don't worry, I don't believe him. He's full of shit, but you already know that."

"Yes, he is."

"I'm sure it's a hell of a story though. You'll have to tell me all about it one day," she said.

"I will, but it's all old news. Let's concentrate on you and your situation."

"My situation, yeah, that's one way of putting it," she said.

"Don't misunderstand, I'm not suggesting it's your fault. In fact, you're the victim here."

That seemed to sink in. "Yeah, you're right, I am the damn victim here."

After a few minutes, and a fresh napkin, she was better. We resumed our breakfast. She complimented me several times and suggested perhaps I could fix her a gourmet dinner one night. I chuckled and said I'd be glad to. Finishing, she stretched and glanced at the clock above the stove.

"I'm officially late to work," she said. "I don't want to go in."

"Call in sick," I suggested. "You deserve it."

She pursed her lips as she thought about it. The action caused her to feel her lower lip, which was still swollen. "You know what, I think I will. Have you seen my phone?"

We found it in her car. It was turned off. Looking at it, she gave a sardonic smile.

"I bet I have a few dozen texts from both my sister and the asshole," she said.

"No doubt," I agreed. "Do yourself a favor and call dispatch. Tell them you're taking a sick day and then activate your do not disturb function."

She frowned. "Good idea, but it won't work. I'd bet my paycheck he's sitting in my apartment, waiting on me and stewing. Both him and Nina."

"If he is, be careful," I said.

"Oh, if he tries to put hands on me again, he'll regret it, and he better not have put hands on Nina."

"Don't shoot him," I said half-jokingly.

She grinned. "I'm not promising anything." She thought a moment as she stared at her phone. "You know what? I'm going to send him a text and tell him if he's anywhere near my apartment, I'm going to shoot him in the balls. That ought to scare him away."

"Maybe, but be careful what you text, it can be used against you," I suggested.

She sighed. "Yeah, you're right. I guess I'll threaten to call the sheriff and tell him everything. That might scare him off."

"Yeah, maybe," I said, thought a moment, and then took a breath. "There's something I think you should know."

"What's that?"

"I've met your sister before," I said.

She frowned in puzzlement. "You know Nina?"

"Yep. I saw her the other day when you met with her at the coffeeshop and recognized her."

Her frown deepened into suspicion. "Where do you know her from?"

"Long story short, I briefly dated a stripper by the name of Lilith. Her stage name was Midnight. Did you ever meet her?"

She nodded slowly. "That was Nina's girlfriend."

"Yeah, I gathered that. So, I don't know how much you know, but Lilith got herself into a situation and fled Nashville. Anyway, when I realized that she had left, I went to her apartment looking for her. That's when I bumped into your sister. She told me her name was Cinnamon. We talked a little bit about Lilith, and that was it."

Nancy nodded slowly again. I expected her to say something, but I think I stunned her. I continued.

"So, that's how I met your sister," I said.

She stared off into space a moment before focusing on me. "I want you to be honest. Have you slept with her?"

The question took me by surprise. "What? No, absolutely not. In fact, the one and only time I spoke with her was that chance encounter at Lilith's apartment. I gave her my business card. She wadded it up and threw it on the ground. She didn't like me."

She stared for several seconds. "Okay, I guess I believe you." She shook her head in a mixture of sadness and frustration. "You see, Nina left Kentucky as soon as she graduated high school and followed me here. For some reason, she decided to be a stripper. Don't ask me how or why, but she did. She made decent money, more than me, but the lifestyle was awful. She got involved in all kinds of bullshit. And then she hooked up with Midnight."

"She seemed to have strong feelings for her," I said.

Nancy scoffed. "She was head over heels in love with that girl. Were you?"

"No, I can't say that. I liked her, but I can't say it went any further than that," I said.

"Well, good for you. Nina was all torn up when Midnight disappeared. The club burned down around that time. Did you know that?"

"Yeah," I said. I don't know if she was aware the Red Lynx was owned by the Baroques and a rival biker gang had burned it down. That was a conversation for another time.

"Anyway, she quit stripping. I got her a job as a receptionist at an assisted living facility, and she was living with me. I guess I'm stupid because the two of them were having an affair right under my nose."

She wiped her eyes. "I'm not going to cry again, I promise."

"There's nothing wrong with crying," I said.

"No, I'm done crying," she declared. "Okay, is there anything else you need to tell me, Thomas?"

"I can't think of anything at the moment," I said. "What about you?"

"Yeah, I forgot to tell you, they expedited the toxicology tests on Davenport. He died of an overdose. Heroin and Fentanyl."

"I see," I said and wondered if Skidmark knew, and if he did, did he make the connection? I was about to mention it, but Nancy interrupted my thoughts.

"There's something else."

"What's that?" I asked.

"Timothy Davenport was Eric's snitch," she said.

I felt my eyebrows arch. "Really?"

Nancy nodded. "There's more. Timothy called Eric the evening before he was found dead and told Eric that Freak had often borrowed Timothy's car because they had fake tags on it. He had borrowed it Tuesday night, and when he didn't bring it back, he told Timothy to forget all about that car and if anyone asks, he sold it to some Mexican dude."

"When did he tell you all this?" I asked.

"The day before yesterday," Nancy answered.

"And he sat on that information the whole time?" I asked.

Nancy nodded. "He said it wasn't important and the car had nothing to do with my double murder."

"Do you believe that?" I asked.

Nancy shrugged. "I don't know what to believe anymore. Listen. I have to go." She grabbed both my hands with hers. "I appreciate everything, Thomas. If not for you, I'm not sure what I would've done. I'd give you a kiss, but I haven't brushed my teeth."

"That's okay, I'll take a raincheck on that kiss, and on that other thing," I said with a grin.

She smiled back. "You can count on it."

I stepped back from her car and watched her drive away. The funny thing was, as I watched her leave, I couldn't help but feel a sense of relief, like I had dodged a bullet. I wasn't having any lustful thoughts toward her anymore. I don't know if it was her situation, or if I had subconsciously picked up on something. Whatever it was, I was glad I kept junior in my pants.

But I was mad too. Mad at Chief Deputy Farmingham. Almost everyone had been scoffing at my theories. Nobody was taking me seriously. Percy was a possible exception, but I kind of suspected he didn't put much credence to them either.

"What's worse is the man sat on the information and now Davenport is dead," I declared out loud, but nobody heard me. Nobody was present to hear me explain how Davenport could have been the key to get a search warrant on the bikers' clubhouse and perhaps develop a case. They might have even found physical evidence linking them to the dump jobs, to the double murder of Brittany and Shanna, like the murder weapon, and perhaps there could have been evidence recovered that would lead to Felicity.

But that wasn't going to happen now. I sighed in exasperation. I wanted a drink. I wanted to hit something. Instead, I changed into my running gear and headed out to my trail.

I was so engrossed in deep thought I lost track of the number of laps I ran. My guess was six miles. I'd not run that far in a couple of years. It felt fairly good, but my back started aching. It was a byproduct of being slammed onto hard asphalt not too long ago. My pinky finger was aching too. I don't know how running caused it to hurt, but it was.

I got my phone and called Percy as I walked a slow, cool down lap.

"Eric Farmingham, yeah, I met him once, a couple of years ago. He seemed like a decent guy, but there was something about him. He talked a good game, but never followed through on a couple of things. At least, not with me."

He was interrupted by someone talking to him. After a minute he came back on the line. "It's too bad about that Davenport kid. If he could've been talked into wearing a wire, it could've broken things wide open, especially that double homicide."

"Yep, it could have. Now she doesn't have anything," I said.

After hanging up with Percy, I sat at my kitchen table wondering what I should do next.

"So, back to square zero," I muttered.

After clearing away the dishes, I got out a notepad and jotted a few notes that I was going to suggest to Nancy. Her case was difficult, but not impossible to solve. It occurred to me she had made no mention of following up with Starbucks and inquiring about the surveillance video on the night that Brittany and Shanna followed the Sentra. I jotted it down.

I noted other possible leads. The death of Davenport would enable her to identify his next-of-kin, friends, place of employment, all of which could possibly provide information. I received a text as I was writing. It was from Nancy.

Thanks again for everything. I may be out of touch for a day or two, I have a lot to think about and sort out. Also, I forgot to tell you, a missing person report was filed yesterday on a woman. I'll try to get the details when I go back to work.

"What the hell?" I muttered, wondering why something like that casually slipped her mind.

I tried calling her, but it went to voicemail. I then tried to call Detective McAdoo to see if he would tell me anything about the missing woman. Again, it went to voicemail. I searched the news websites, but there was nothing reported. It was frustrating.

I got my kitchen cleaned up and then went out to my shop. There wasn't a lot to do, so I busied myself with sweeping and tidying up. When I rebuilt this shop, one of the things I'd promised myself was that I would always keep it clean and organized.

I had everything cleaned within thirty minutes. I needed something to work on and realized it was time for a new project. I wanted to rebuild a roadster. I loved old Cadillacs. I loved Buick Roadmasters, but it was getting increasingly more difficult to rebuild old cars. The parts were becoming rarer to find, and when you did find them, the prices were through the roof.

I needed a truck too. Not an antique, I needed one that was dependable, one that I could use as a daily driver and tow stuff. I decided to peruse the internet while I ate lunch.

Going inside, I fixed a couple of sandwiches, poured myself a large glass of filtered ice water, and sat down in front of my laptop. Logging on, I thought I'd check my emails first. I had four in my inbox. One was spam, two were from former clients. The third one was from an unknown email address. When I opened it, I almost choked on a bite from my sandwich.

It was from Kalina.

CHAPTER 49

Hey, it's Kalina. I hope you're okay. I'm not. Things are uncertain but I hope to see you soon. Please continue to be my friend.

That was it. Five measly ambiguous sentences. I prepared a response, changed the wording a few times, and hit send. After a few minutes I got the automated daemon response saying there was a delivery failure. In other words, that email address no longer existed.

"Well, shit," I grumbled. It was a day of frustrations and there didn't seem to be anything I could do about it.

I briefly considered giving Percy's daughter, Vadoma, a call. Her mother was a Gypsy, and she was in possession of one of the medallions. There are supposed to be five of them, and I now had two in my possession.

"I better call Percy first and make sure it's okay," I muttered and opened my phone. I briefly explained with a story that only had a few elements of the truth in it. The fact was, I didn't want anyone to know I had those things sitting in my safe. Percy agreed and said he'd have her call me. I was surprised when she called a few minutes later.

"Hi, Vadoma," I greeted.

"Hello, Thomas," she replied. She was only a teenager, but her voice sounded older. I'd only met her a couple of times and the conversation between us was limited, but it was safe to say she wasn't what you'd call a normal teenager.

"I don't know what your father told you, but I'll try to explain. I have a client who has a medallion that is similar to yours," I said.

"Have you seen it?" she asked.

I hesitated a moment before answering. "I've seen photographs. It looks a lot like yours."

"I see. What would you like to know?" she asked.

"Are they valuable?"

"They are priceless. There is a long story about how they were made. Do you know it?"

"Only the basics. Long ago, a mysterious man showed up in a village in India and he hired a man to make the medallions out of some ore he'd brought with him."

"Five medallions from five separate pieces of ore. The story describes the pieces of ore as coming from the sky, which probably means meteors. The medallions are much sought after by some Gypsy clans. It is believed they bring power. Be careful, Thomas, there are people who would kill to obtain them, and they would willingly sacrifice their lives for them."

The line disconnected then. I stared at my phone and confirmed the kid had hung up on me. I guess she was done talking, but I still had questions. And that one sentence she said. She said people would kill to obtain them. Did she know I was in possession of two of them already, or was she merely referencing the medallions collectively? I wasn't sure, but it sounded like she was giving me a friendly warning. Even so, I felt like I may have made a mistake by calling her.

I should've kept it to myself.

"I ought to take that damn box and throw it in the Cumberland River," I muttered.

I was tempted. It'd be one less issue I'd have to deal with. But even as I thought it, I knew I'd keep the box and everything in it safe and sound until Kalina came back.

A thought came to mind. What if she never came back? What the hell would I do then?

I don't know if it was kismet or what, but my phone rang two minutes later, and it wasn't a social call.

"Is this Thomas Ironcutter?" the man asked.

"It is," I replied. The man had a faint accent and I suspected it was going to be a spam call. I was mistaken.

"This is Special Agent Camper with the FBI," the voice said.

"What can I do for you, Agent Camper?" I asked.

"Kalina Ratkovich," he stated.

I waited for him to continue speaking, but there was silence. I think he was waiting for a response, a confession, or something. I'm not sure if he thought this was a sly tactic, but if he did, he was mistaken. After waiting for almost thirty seconds, he spoke again.

"Hello?"

"I'm still here, Agent Camper. I'm waiting for you to tell me what you want," I said. I was tempted to simply hang up, but this was slightly amusing.

"You need to tell me where she is," he said.

"I don't know where she is," I replied.

"You wouldn't lie to a federal agent, would you, Ironcutter?" he asked.

"I'd say no, but how would you know I'm not lying about not lying?" I rejoined.

There was a moment of silence. I'd confused him. Something was off here. Some FBI agents were good at their job, some not, but this was an odd way of attempting to obtain information. It was amateurish.

"I'm going to give you a chance to come clean, Ironcutter. Tell me where Kalina Ratkovich is."

"I think before we go any further, I'd like to know your full name, employee number, and what office you work out of," I said.

There was a brief pause. "I work out of the Chicago office, but it wouldn't take much for me to get a warrant on you down there in Nashville for obstruction," he said.

"As I said, I have no idea where she is. Now then, are we through here?"

There was another pause. "You're playing games, Ironcutter. This won't be good for you. We'll be in touch."

The line disconnected. Something didn't seem right, and after a moment, I scrolled through my contact list and made a call to Special Agent Carter Pike.

"Hey, Thomas. How are you?" he greeted.

"I'm doing well. How about you?" I responded. After the pleasantries were out of the way, I got down to business and explained the phone call.

"I don't know, Carter, but something seems off to me," I said.

"Hmm, well, why don't I give him a call?" he offered.

"That'd be great. Do you know him?"

"Honestly, I've never heard of him, but we have a lot of agents. Let me look him up."

I heard his keyboard clacking and at least one grunt of seeming confusion.

"I'm not finding an Agent Camper. Are you sure you heard the name correctly?" he asked.

"Fairly sure," I replied.

This time, he paused. "Alright, I have an idea. Don Luttrell is a buddy of mine and he's currently assigned to Chicago. Let's give him a call."

Carter put me on three-way and called his friend. As I suspected, there was nobody named Camper working in the Chicago office. The closest was a female agent named Kemper, but she was out on maternity leave.

"Is there anything I can do to help?" Carter asked.

"I'm not sure yet," I replied. "It may be nothing."

"Alright, Thomas. Let me know. I definitely owe you one or two favors," he said with a chuckle.

After Carter confirmed this Camper asshole wasn't an FBI agent, one would think I'd be relieved, but it seemed to have the opposite effect on me. It confirmed to me that Kalina was being sought after, and whoever was looking for her had found me.

That was concerning. Concerning enough to amp up a higher level of paranoia than I normally walked around with.

I stood and walked directly to my bedroom. It only took a couple of minutes to move my bed, open the safe, and retrieve the box. Carrying it to my shop, I wrapped it in three trash bags and then sealed it all with a roll of rubber tape.

Then I buried it. With Henry. I knew he'd protect that stuff far better than a safe.

The digging had me hot and sweaty. I grabbed the pitcher of tea that was in the fridge and carried it with me outside to the picnic table. I didn't bother using a glass and drank with gusto. After I'd settled a little bit, I began making phone calls. It took around forty-five minutes and brief conversations with a few people to confirm what I already knew.

Nothing was being done.

I checked their social media sites. No mention of the missing woman. I called the Smyrna Police Department, and they referred me to the Rutherford Sheriff's Department.

The lady who answered the phone seemed to be confused and referred me back to Smyrna. I asked to speak with someone in charge. She said she'd take a message.

Detective Nancy Hamilton's phone was turned off.

Detective Ricardo McAdoo's phone went to voicemail.

Nobody was doing jack shit. While I was sitting at my desk, cursing under my breath, Tommy Boy jumped up and made himself at home on my laptop.

"Not even Jack is doing jack shit, and I have no idea who Jack is," I said to him. He meowed in agreement.

CHAPTER 50

I had thought it over, weighed the pros and cons, talked it over with myself and Tommy Boy, and made a decision. Art answered on the second ring.

"I've got something I'm going to do, and I need someone that'll have my back and is not afraid of the possibility of violence."

"When?"

"Tonight."

"Does this have anything to do with Felicity?" he asked.

"Yes."

His response was without hesitation. "Then I'm in."

"It might mean jail if we're caught. That's why I'm not asking any of my police friends," I said.

"I'm no stranger to jail or prison. If it gets Felicity back, it'll be worth it."

"Alright," I said and gave him directions. "We'll meet at midnight. I'll explain everything when you get here."

"You got it," he said and hung up.

Our meeting location was a church parking lot about a half-mile from the Satan's Dogs clubhouse. He arrived ten minutes early. When he got out of his truck, I could sense the adrenalin pumping in him. He was wearing jeans, a black tee shirt, and a black ballcap, which was good. I was wearing similar clothing. He looked up at the sky as he walked over to me. There was distant lightning and the rumble of thunder.

"We have bad weather moving in," he said.

"It'll work to our advantage," I said.

He gave a nod. "So, we're sneaking up on someone?"

"Yeah," I said and explained it all.

"Outlaw bikers huh? Alright, not a problem. Where's their house at?"

I pointed. "About a half-mile that way. We're going to walk from here. If we get separated, get back to your truck as quick as you can and take off. Don't wait for me. Obey all traffic laws and go directly home. I'll call as soon as I can, and I'll have us an alibi if we need it. Are you armed?"

He pulled out a lock blade knife and held it for me to see. "Good enough?" he asked.

"It's a start." I handed him a snub-nosed revolver, along with a tac-light and some black nitrile gloves.

"If you have to use it, dump it as soon as you can. Toss the gloves too, but don't toss them with the gun," I instructed.

"Got it, but what if they find the gun?"

"Make sure you don't get any of your DNA on it. They'll never trace it back to either of us," I said.

He smiled slightly. "Got it."

"Any questions?" I asked.

His expression was intense, like he was about to erupt. I wondered if he'd bumped a line of coke on his way over here. He pointed at me.

"If Felicity's in there, I can't promise I won't hurt anyone."

"If you want to knock some teeth out, fine, I may even help you, but don't kill anyone unless there's no other way. I'm serious about this."

He stared off into space for a long moment before making eye contact again. "You seem to have thought this all out, so I'll go along with it. But if my baby is in there, and she's hurt..."

He left the sentence unfinished. I gave him a singular nod of understanding and put on my own pair of nitrile gloves. "Let's get going."

I started us off at a slow jog. It was at that time the rain hit, and it hit with a fury. The heavy rainfall and multiple close lightning strikes indicated the storm cell was right on top of us. One bolt of lightning was eye blinding, and the thunderclap made us both jump.

"Fuck almighty that was close," Art exclaimed.

I agreed and pointed around. "Look, everything's dark. The power got knocked out. That'll work to our advantage."

"Yeah, let's hope it stays that way for a while," Art said.

I gave a silent prayer asking not to get struck by lightning and kept jogging. Art kept up, although he was breathing hard after only a couple of hundred yards. I could've admonished him for smoking so much but didn't bother. One way or another, after tonight I doubted there would be any further interaction between us. Honestly, I didn't know what the hell we were going to find, but if I didn't check it out myself, it would be something I'd regret for the rest of my life.

CHAPTER 51

Another bright bolt of lightning lit up the sky and the thunderclap hurt my ears. It was one of those nights where sane people were buttoned up snug in their homes, wrapped up in a blanket and watching a movie with someone they loved. I thought of Simone and me in that scenario. She would have fixed us some hot chocolate and we would've been watching one of our favorite black and white film noir movies.

It was a sad, lonely thought. I shook it off and focused on the mission at hand. Lightning illuminated the area enough to confirm that we were close now, perhaps another two hundred yards. I glanced over at Art. He was breathing heavily. It wouldn't do for him to be gassed out if we encountered trouble, so I tapped his arm and slowed us to a walk.

"Not far now, catch your breath," I whispered. He gave a head nod in understanding.

The street had a few houses, mostly old and reflective of lower income inhabitants. Most likely they were owned by some sleazy slumlord and being rented out to illegal migrants who only wanted to have a decent life. I saw the dim flicker of a candle emanating from within one of the homes, but otherwise there was no sign of people. They weren't stupid enough to be out in this weather. I stopped Art when we were about fifty feet from the gated driveway.

"There's a surveillance camera pointed at the gate," I warned and pointed us in another direction.

We veered off the road and made an approach to a section of the fence that I had walked along not too long ago. As far as I could determine, there were no cameras covering this sector and I didn't think there were any bear traps hidden in this section.

I hoped.

Crouching beside it, I looked around, trying to determine if we were being watched. Art read my mind.

"I can't see any further than ten feet, which means if anyone's keeping lookout, they can't see us."

I nodded in agreement.

"This is where it becomes illegal. If you're having second thoughts, now's the time to let me know. You can wait here."

Art took a moment to spit before responding. "I'm all in."

"Alright, remember, you're here to cover my ass. No John Wayne bullshit."

"Yeah, yeah," Art said.

The fence was five feet tall, not much in the way of security, a fence of that height was mostly for pets, but the strands of barbed wire running along the top added another foot in height. Art pointed at it.

"That won't be easy to climb over," he whispered.

"Yeah, I planned ahead for that," I said and pulled out a small pair of Klein brand wire cutters out of my pocket.

He took them from me, crouched down, and started cutting. After a few minutes he had a hole in the fence large enough for us to crawl through. Once on the other side, I pulled out my handgun. It was my Glock Model 43X with the Surefire light mounted under the barrel. It wasn't my favorite handgun. That would have been my Springfield, but this one was compact, and the light was plenty bright.

I checked the magazine one more time and performed another press check. Art pulled out the handgun I'd loaned him. He opened the cylinder, gave it a quick inspection, and closed it quietly. When he gave me a nod, I gestured toward the house and led off in a quiet but deliberate walk.

It was dark and eerily quiet, the only noise being the drubbing of the rain and an occasional clap of thunder.

It was an older, one-story house, built of brick and Masonite siding. It looked like the windows had blinds, and they were closed. The front door was also closed, and I assumed it was locked. I led us around to the back. There was a detached garage that was also dark and silent. There were no cars or bikes parked here. The place appeared to be unoccupied. The side door to the garage was standing open. I peeked in and scanned it with the light. Save for some junk and a few motorcycle parts, it too was empty.

I pointed at the back door of the house and the two of us walked to it. We stood to the side of it, and I gently checked the doorknob. It was locked, no surprise. I holstered my gun and started to pull out my lockpicking kit, but Art had other ideas. His foot flew by my head and the door frame sprayed me with splinters. I reminded myself to slap the taste out of his mouth later as I dropped my kit and drew my weapon.

I activated my light and Art did the same. The interior turned from night into day and the room we were looking in proved to be the kitchen. There was an overflowing trash can in the center of the floor and used takeout containers littering the counter. It smelled awful, but there was nobody standing there pointing a shotgun at us, which was a good thing.

We carefully walked in and made our way to another doorway, which went into the den, but it had been turned into a party room. There was a bar at one end, a pool table that'd seen better days, and even a disco light hanging from the ceiling. There was more trash, but no people.

There were two restrooms and a bedroom off to the side, but the next room was obviously the meeting room. There was a long conference table and chairs. All rooms were trashy, but there were no people.

"Nothing," Art grumbled. "What now?"

"Let's take a better look in that garage," I suggested. Art nodded and led off.

It was an open garage and we searched it easily. Besides the trash, there was nothing. No bikes, no cars, no tools. Nothing but oil stains on the floors and trash. We walked back inside the house and stopped in the den.

"It was a good idea, Ironcutter, but it looks like we struck out," he said.

"Yeah. They don't have anyone living here. Hell, they don't even have anybody guarding the place." I suddenly realized something. "Have you seen any surveillance monitors?"

Art shook his head. "Does that mean the cameras are fake?"

"Either that or they've packed up everything and left," I said. "There's no TV, no tools in the shop, nothing. They're gone."

Art had a few things to say about that. His expletives drew another crack of thunder, which even caused me to jump. I stumbled on a whiskey bottle and put a hand against the wall to steady myself. When I did so, it gave slightly under my weight. I didn't think anything about it at first, but then I used my light to look it over. It was a paneled wall, the type that was popular back in the seventies. Art saw me looking it over.

"What is it?" he asked.

"There's something not right about this wall," I said and pushed on it again. It gave way some more. I kept messing with it and then realized it slid open.

"What is that, a hidden door?" he asked.

I pointed the beam of my light in and saw an opening. Peering further, I saw steps leading down.

"Basement," I whispered, although I don't know why. If anyone was down there, they would have already been alerted to our presence.

We slowly walked down the stairs. SWAT teams had a special tactic for going down a flight of stairs. If there were gaps in the risers, someone could lie in wait and shoot out our feet. We weren't using that tactic, but we made it to the bottom unscathed. When we got there and shone our lights around, Art gasped at what he saw.

A partially clad woman was slumped against the far wall. Chains were manacled to her wrists and the chains were affixed to fasteners in the wall.

CHAPTER 52

"What the fuck?" Art uttered. He started to rush over to her but stopped when I pointed my light and gun at the man seated in a chair in the far corner.

My old cop training kicked in. "Get your hands up!"

The man didn't move, and I repeated my command. He still didn't move. In fact, he was slumped over and appeared to be sleeping. Art marched over to him with a clenched fist and was about to punch him, but he paused and peered closer.

"I think he's dead," he said.

I walked over, a bit more careful than Art, and inspected closer. He was dead alright. The evidence, a burnt spoon, a rubber strap wrapped around his left bicep, a syringe still stuck in a vein, all indicated an overdose.

"Who the fuck is he?" Art asked.

My light was bright enough to allow me to easily identify the dead man. Felton McLaughlin was his name, also known as Freak.

"He's a piece of shit who deserved to die. Check on the girl," I said as I scanned the room.

Much like the rest of the house, the room was filthy. It wasn't large, maybe fifteen feet by twenty feet, but I wanted to make sure there were no additional hidden rooms or traps. Finding only trash and dirty needles, I walked over to Art and the girl. She was on a mattress, but due to the chains she wasn't able to lie fully supine. A jug of water and a five-gallon bucket sat beside the mattress. Judging by the smell, the bucket served as her toilet. A couple of empty dog food cans were also sitting there. Art had knelt down beside her and gently moved her head so he could see her face.

"Is she alive?" I asked.

"Yeah, but I'd say she's on her last legs." He stared at me in concern. "It isn't Felicity."

She was filthy. Her hair was possibly blonde, but it was too dirty for me to be sure. It looked, and smelled, as though excrement had been smeared all over her. She also had numerous cuts and bruises. Her right arm was swollen and looked as though it'd been broken. I initially thought there were bruises up and down the sides of her legs, but when I used my light and peered closer, I saw they were tattoos. I dropped to one knee and looked closer.

"Do you know her? You're looking like you know her," Art asked. He stared at me pensively, worry etched on his features. I'd never seen this side of him.

I stood and inspected the brackets the chains were secured to. I even tried to yank on them, but it was going to take more than brute strength to get her free. I pulled out my phone, but I wasn't getting a signal. I thought quickly and faced Art.

"Alright, you need to get out of here," I said to Art.

"No way, dude. I'm going to see this through," he replied.

"You're a convicted felon. They won't treat you the same way they'll treat me, and stop calling me dude."

Art clenched his teeth. "She might know something about Felicity."

"She might, but she's in no shape to talk right now."

He cursed and grabbed me by my shirt. "She may know something about Felicity!"

I holstered my weapon and placed a hand on top of one of his. "She can't talk right now. All we can hope for is to get her to the hospital as soon as possible. You've done all you can for her right now, and now you've got to get scarce. In a short time, I may or may not be in cuffs. No need in it being both of us."

My words calmed him a little. He nodded and let go of me. "Okay, I get what you're saying."

We hustled up the stairs and outside. My phone had a signal again and I called 911. After hanging up, I faced Art.

"I'll call you later and let you know how it goes," I said.

He nodded, handed over my handgun, and disappeared into the heavy rain. I watched him go and then suddenly thought of something.

I hurried back down the stairs and took as many photos as I could until I heard the distant wail of sirens. I knew once the cops were on the scene I would not be allowed back in the house. I then searched Freak. He had a wallet with a fake identification in it and a key ring with a half dozen keys on it. He also had a handgun tucked into his waistband in the small of his back. I left it where it was and quickly took a picture of the ID before wiping my prints off it and putting it back in his pocket. I then hustled back up the stairs.

CHAPTER 53

An ambulance and a marked patrol car were at the gate as I came running up. I worked through the keys until I found one that opened the padlock and pulled the gate wide. Both vehicles splashed me as they sped through, and I ran along behind them.

"Alright, follow me," I said once they'd exited their vehicles and led them down the stairs. The two-man EMT crew wasted no time and hustled to the woman. The officer spotted Freak and started to warily approach him.

"He's dead," I told him. He stared quizzically at me for a moment before focusing back on Freak.

"Yeah, I'd say you're right," he surmised.

I handed him the keys. "One of those keys might fit those padlocks," I said and pointed at the locks on the chains.

He needed no further urging and after a couple of attempts, had the chains off her. Her wrists looked like raw meat. I didn't wait to be told and walked out. I found a spot under an eave, but it didn't matter much. I was soaked to the bone and shivering uncontrollably.

The place was swarming with cops before I knew it. All of the flashing strobes reminded me of a discotheque and it was hard on the eyes. I was considering making an Irish exit when a familiar voice called out my name.

"Lordy, Lordy look who it is," she said. I looked up to see Officer Wasserman walking up. She was wearing a reflective rain jacket and a ball cap was pulled down low, but there was no mistaking it was her. She also had a cup of coffee in one hand.

"Hi, Carla. Please tell me that coffee is for me."

Her smile disappeared as she looked me over. "Oh honey, you're soaked to the bone. Here," she said and handed me the cup. "It's tea, not coffee, but it'll warm you up."

"Thanks, beautiful," I replied and took a tentative sip. It would not have been my first choice of beverage, but it was good and hot, which is what I needed.

"What's going on, Thomas?" she asked.

I filled her in as best that I could. "Do you know who'll be investigating this?"

"That'd be me."

I turned around to see who said that. It was Detective Ricardo McAdoo. He had somehow blended in with the crowd, although he was the only one with an umbrella. He was dressed casually, jeans and a Polo shirt with the department's insignia emblazoned above his left breast and his name embroidered on the other side. His shirt reminded me of the first time I laid eyes on Nancy. She was wearing a similar shirt.

"Detective, good to see you. I know now that this'll be a professional investigation," I said.

He smiled, revealing his perfect white teeth. "I appreciate that, Ironcutter. Now, I only caught a little bit of your statement to the officer. I'd appreciate it if you'd start from the beginning and repeat yourself."

I was about to repeat myself but paused when some of the rescue personnel emerged from the house with the gurney and their patient. She was strapped down securely and had a blanket covering her. She looked like hell. Not even the rain hitting her face caused any kind of reaction. We watched as she was loaded onto the ambulance and within a minute, the driver was driving off. He was courteous enough to wait until he was down the road before activating his siren.

I turned to McAdoo and gave him a brief synopsis. He waited until I finished before speaking.

"What in the world made you come here in the middle of the night?" he asked.

"I'd grown frustrated, bub. Frustrated at the lack of action by law enforcement. This should have been done at least a week ago."

"So, you came down here by yourself? You didn't have any help?" he asked.

I nodded. He eyeballed me like he didn't believe me but didn't press it.

"So, you decide to come down here in the middle of the night. What's the first thing you did?"

"It was dark, so I pressed on the intercom to see if anyone would talk to me. Nobody answered. I thought I heard a woman screaming so I became concerned. I walked around the fence line and saw a hole cut in it, so I crawled through and hurried up to the house."

"How did you find that hidden entrance?" he asked.

"Like I said, I heard cries for help," I replied.

He continued eyeing me, but I guess he knew I wasn't going to change my story.

"Okay, we'll get into the rest of that later. Did she say anything to you?"

"No, she was incoherent by the time I got to her," I said.

"Do you know either one of them?"

"I don't know the woman. I'm fairly certain the man's name is Felton McLaughlin. He's commonly known as Freak. He's the one I've been saying should be looked at as a suspect from the start, and now he's dead."

"So, the victim isn't Felicity?" he asked.

I shook my head. "She could be rotting in a ditch somewhere, for all I know."

Detective McAdoo rubbed his chin in thought. After a moment he looked up at me. "Alright, we'll talk more at a later time. One more thing, have you removed anything from the crime scene?"

"I got keys out of Freak's pocket to open the padlock on the gate. I gave them to one of those paramedics."

He nodded. "Alright, anything else?"

"Nothing I can think of. Oh, there is one other thing. Rumor has it there are one or two bear traps hidden in the weeds around the fence. You might want to tell your people to be careful."

He smirked at me. "Lord only knows how you're aware of that. I'm thinking the more I get into this, the more questions I'm going to have, but we'll save all that for later."

"You have my number. I think I'll go home now, unless you're going to do something like tell me I'm not free to leave," I said.

Detective McAdoo smirked. "Why, I'd never do anything like that with you, Ironcutter. You're a cooperating witness, right?"

I stared a moment before focusing on Carla. "Thank you for the hot tea, Officer Wasserman."

She gave me a worried smile. "You get yourself out of those wet clothes and get warmed up."

"I will, thanks."

The rain had stopped, and the walk back was filled only with the lights from the patrol cars and the only noises were from the police radios. I saw a few people staring out of their windows, but that was the extent of their curiosity.

When I reached the parking lot where my SUV was parked, Art was there, waiting on me. He was smoking a cigarette and drinking out of a pint bottle.

"Hell of a night," he said.

"Yeah. What're you drinking?"

"Jim Beam," he replied and held it out. I took it, wiped the top off, and took a hefty swallow. It burned all the way down, but it felt wonderful.

"Appreciate it," I said, handing it back to him.

"Do you think she's going to live?" he asked.

"I hope so."

"So, what's next?"

"They'll be out there the rest of the night and probably all day tomorrow. At some point they'll call me in for a formal interview. I told them I was alone. So, let's stick with that story."

"Fine by me," he said. He took a long swallow and then cleared his throat. "Felicity is probably dead, isn't she?"

"I don't know, but it's not looking good," I replied. I could have thrown out some platitudes, like he shouldn't give up hope, but that's not the kind of person I was.

"Are you done looking for her?" he asked. When I made eye contact, I could see sadness, perhaps there might have been a tear or two, it was hard to tell due to the rain.

"No, I'm not done. I'm out of ideas at the moment, but I'm not finished."

"Alright. For what it's worth, I appreciate everything you've done," he said. I gave a small nod of acknowledgement. "I suppose I need to pay you another grand."

"That won't be necessary," I replied.

Art stared. This time he was the one who gave a small nod.

"Did you see the tattoos on that girl's legs?" he asked. "My first wife had a couple almost exactly like those. Hers was above her right breast. They're called Sprites."

"Sprites?" I asked.

"Yeah."

"How about that," I muttered.

"They probably still consider me a suspect," he said and suddenly yawned.

"I don't think so, not anymore," I said. "Go on home and get some sleep. That's what I'm going to do. I'll be in touch tomorrow."

"Alright," he said. "Please give me a call if anything about Felicity comes up, even if it's bad."

I watched him get in his truck and drive slowly away. I had a couple of towels in my vehicle. I got them out and gave them a whiff. As I suspected, they smelled a little musty. I used them anyway and wiped myself off the best I could. The storm front had moved away, and it was a little cooler now. I turned the heat on high and sat a moment, decompressing and watching the lightning in the distance. They were faint red flashes, high in the atmosphere.

There was a part of my brain that seemed to be programmed to memorize useless trivia. My late wife, Marcia, had often joked that I should compete on game shows. One of those useless trivia tidbits came to mind now. Those faint red flashes of lightning were known as sprites.

The irony was not lost on me.

CHAPTER 54

I called Percy on my way home, apologized for waking him up, and filled him in on the night's events. The only thing that upset him was the fact that I had not asked him to join me. The truth was, I felt his game had been off lately. He had a few things taking up all of his time; an overwhelming workload, Anna, and his teenage daughter. I didn't blame him; it was a part of life.

I used the do not disturb function on my phone so I could get some uninterrupted sleep, but I still tossed and turned throughout the rest of the night. I awakened at my usual time, tried to go back to sleep, and finally rolled out of bed at seven. I might've, but Tommy Boy was lying on the pillow beside me with his ass pointed toward me. He made sure I knew he was there by flicking his tail in my face.

I did my usual morning routine. It was a beautiful morning out with the temperature in the mid-sixties. I wanted to play a round of golf, but I knew that wasn't going to be a possibility.

As soon as I turned off my do-not-disturb function, my phone let me know I had numerous texts and voicemail messages. One of them was from Harvey Wilson directing me to call him immediately. I did so, and we had a ten-minute conversation.

"I owe you big time," I said when he was finished.

"I know," he replied with a clipped chortle and hung up.

I was trying to take a sip of coffee when my phone rang.

"I'm Mister Popularity this morning," I grumbled as I peered at the caller ID. It was from a Rutherford County government number. I wondered if it was possibly Nancy who was calling. It wasn't.

"Good morning, Ironcutter," Detective Ricardo McAdoo greeted.

"Have you gotten any sleep yet?" I asked.

"Not a wink. How about you?"

"Slept like a baby," I replied.

"Smart ass."

"How's the girl?" I asked.

"Critical but stable. She'll live. It'll be a day or two before I can have a proper interview, but she confirmed it was Freak who abducted her."

"Good. Did he have an accomplice?"

"Apparently he did, but she is uncertain who it was. Enough about her for now, let's focus on you. I want to have a sit down with you and talk about all this."

"Am I considered a suspect?" I asked.

"In this particular thing? No. In fact, I'd go as far as to say you're the hero of the day, but we'll get into that when you come on down here for a formal interview. Are you going to lawyer up on me?"

"Probably not. It depends on whether or not you and your co-workers behave yourselves. I'll be there in an hour," I said.

"Alright, I'll see you then," he said and hung up.

I opted to dress in a pair of gray slacks, a pressed white shirt, and a darker gray sport coat. I completed my ensemble with one of my Fedoras. I admired myself in the mirror a moment. I'd not worn one of my hats in a while now, and I missed it.

Also, when wearing a hat, proper footwear was required. I opted for a pair of Allen Edmond black wingtips. I took a minute with a rag to spruce up the sheen before walking outside. I resisted the urge to wander into my shop and hang out there the rest of my life and headed to Murfreesboro.

McAdoo had a junior detective waiting for me in the lobby. She gave a terse greeting and escorted me to a plain but clean interview room.

"Detective McAdoo will be with you shortly," she said and walked out, closing the door behind her.

"You could've offered me a cup of coffee," I muttered to the empty room.

Ricardo didn't keep me waiting long and he wasn't alone. TBI Agent Bob Thrasher was accompanying him. I expected Nancy to join in, but she was nowhere in sight. I said hello to Bob and shook his hand. He gave me a polite smile, but it was clear he was here on business. The three of us sat, and after a couple of preliminary statements for the benefit of the recording, the formal interview began.

"Okay, Thomas, since we're on record, can you start from the beginning of your investigation with Felicity Turnbow and how it led up to you going into the Satan's Dog clubhouse last night?"

"Certainly, but I think in order to put everything in proper context, I should start a little bit earlier in the timeline, if that's not an issue," I replied.

Ricardo waved a hand. "By all means."

I started with my first encounter with Felicity and the fight I had with Art. The two men seemed a little surprised but did not interrupt and let me keep talking. I segued my storyline into the evening Art approached me about Felicity being missing and how I agreed to take the case. I then led them through the course of my investigation up to last night. I did not go into a lot of detail unless I thought it was necessary and helpful.

The whole spiel took about thirty minutes. They seemed satisfied, not only with my narrative, but my sincerity, and I did not get the impression that they thought I was attempting to deceive them. When I was finished, the two men glanced at each other a moment before facing me again. Agent Thrasher led it off.

"Thomas, I am in admiration of your investigation. It wasn't too long ago that you only had wisps of information and a gut feeling. I think I said as much."

"You did. You were more polite than others," I said. "Some people chose to listen to the opinions of a certain idiot and let it cloud their judgement, right, Detective?" I gazed at Ricardo when I said it. His only reaction was a grin.

"Let me also compliment you when I say you are a well-spoken, articulate man. I bet when you testified in trials, you had the jury eating out of your hand," Bob said.

"Well, I appreciate that," I said.

"So, that brings about a nagging question I have."

"What's that?" I asked, already sensing what he was about to ask.

"When Detective McAdoo asked you why you decided to go investigate the bikers' clubhouse in the middle of the night, all you said was that it was a gut feeling and frustration on what you believed was a lack of action from law enforcement."

"That's right," I said.

His small smile returned. "I'm not buying it. I mean, sure, you seem to have great intuition, but I think there's something more. Something you don't feel inclined to share with us."

"I've voiced my suspicions about the Satan's Dogs, and Freak in particular, almost from the beginning. I said it to both of you." I pointed at Ricardo. "I left more than one voicemail, and you didn't respond to a single one. I voiced my suspicions to the idiot and to Detective Hamilton. I've even tried to get Agent Maroney of the DEA to investigate. Nobody gave my suspicions any credence. Now, it may have been because Detective Georgie has named me the prime suspect in some bullshit alleged murder, but that should not have been an automatic disqualifier to my assertions."

As I spoke, I realized I was getting myself worked up. I took a deep breath to calm myself and continued.

"Gentlemen, I'm not some Sherlock Holmes wannabe. I am a seasoned detective with years of experience. You two haven't said it, but I'll point out the obvious, for the record. By going into that biker club, I saved a woman's life and quite possibly cleared at least four, maybe five homicides in your jurisdiction."

"Five?" Ricardo asked.

"Yep. Here, I'll list them for you," I said and began with my first two fingers. "Those two female murders that you're investigating, Ricardo. I never did get their names, but I guess it doesn't matter now." I extended two more fingers. "Brittany Parkhurst and Shane, I mean Shanna Maldonado, and," I extended a fifth finger, "Timothy Davenport."

Bob raised his eyebrows. "Davenport?"

"I don't think Timothy Davenport died of an accidental overdose. I think it was intentional because he knew too much. Perhaps he was the accomplice that your victim mentioned. He may have even been involved in the other murders." I sat back in my chair. "Call it a gut feeling, but I bet I'm right."

Bob slowly nodded. "I'm not going to disagree with anything you said, Thomas, but tell me why you decided to do this in the middle of the night."

Ricardo held up a finger. "Before you answer, I want to let you know we found where you cut the fence to get in."

I sat back and gave them a small smile. "I don't know anything about that, but in answer to your question, it was because of you, Detective McAdoo, that I chose to go to that clubhouse in the middle of the night."

He frowned. "How's that?"

"I called you and left a message inquiring about the missing woman. You didn't respond, remember? Every minute that I waited for you to call, my stress level increased. It got to the point where I couldn't stand it anymore. I felt like I had to do something, and it's a good thing I did, otherwise that woman would be dead." I leaned forward in my seat. "That's what my lawyer will say in the press conference if somebody decides to charge me with burglary, or some other trumped-up bullshit. Do we understand each other?"

I could have said more. I could have told them about how I knew Davenport was a snitch for Chief Deputy Farmingham. I could have told them that Farmingham knew about the Sentra and knew that Freak was the one who was driving the Sentra on the night Brittany and Shanna were murdered, but to do so could have put Nancy in a tight spot. There was no need for that. At least, not yet.

The two men stared at me. I felt the sudden tension in the air. Ricardo then grinned.

"Good one," he said. "You've thought this through, I'll give you that." He glanced over at Bob and made a head gesture toward the door. "If you don't mind, please excuse us for a minute."

"Of course," I replied. "But first, I have a few questions."

"Like what?" he asked.

"What is the status on the other bikers? Specifically, William McLaughlin. Has he been located?"

"No," he replied.

"Why not? He lived in the clubhouse," I said.

"Currently, the remaining members of the Satan's Dogs are under covert surveillance," McAdoo said.

"Let me guess, by Agent Maroney, right?" I asked.

The two men stared but didn't answer. I emitted a long sigh of understanding. As far as they were concerned, the case was closed due to the death of the offender. They weren't going to pursue it any further. Not actively. If at some point somebody came along and volunteered some incriminating information, then maybe something would be done.

"Do you have any other questions?" Bob asked. I shook my head.

The two men stood and exited the room. I sat back and relaxed. They were employing a common tactic; they went to a nearby room, probably the room where the monitors and recording equipment were located, whereupon they would compare their thoughts. I'm sure my veiled threat would be discussed as well.

I wasn't too worried. They weren't going to charge me with anything. After all, who was the victim? Who actually owned the clubhouse? Was it in Bang-Bang's name? I grunted to myself. I didn't see them going to Bang-Bang and asking him to sign a warrant against me. If he did, he'd have a lot of explaining to do about what'd been going on in that clubhouse.

Nah, I wasn't worried about getting charged with breaking into the clubhouse.

After a minute, McAdoo opened the door and stuck his head in. "I think we're at a good stopping point. Let's get you out of here."

He escorted me down the hall toward the lobby. When he opened the door, the first person I spotted was Georgie, who was sitting in a chair and pointedly staring at me. A woman was seated beside him. I turned to Detective McAdoo.

"If you need anything else, give me a shout," I said and stuck out my hand.

Ricardo shook my hand and stared a moment before glancing over at his co-worker. I glanced over as well.

"What's Georgie up to?" I asked.

Ricardo smirked slightly, as if I'd swallowed the bait, hook, line, and sinker. "Let's go find out."

I followed him as he approached his co-worker and the woman who was sitting with him. Most people knew her as Mona.

"Good morning, George, what're you up to this morning?" he asked.

George was exuding smugness as he hooked a thumb toward Mona. "Why, I'm interviewing a witness to a murder. Go ahead, Mona."

Mona stared at me a moment and then faced Georgie. "Go ahead and what?"

Georgie suddenly appeared flustered, and he huffed a couple of times before speaking. "Remember what we talked about?"

"Yeah, you had me come down here to point out a man I saw at the bar the day Goforth busted his head in the bathroom," she said.

Georgie licked his lips and glanced at me. "Well, go ahead."

Mona frowned at him. "What do you mean, go ahead?"

Georgie appeared confused and he cleared his throat a couple of times before speaking. He pointed at me. "Don't you know him?"

She stared at me again, confusion etched on her face. "Who is he?"

"Miss Mona, this is Thomas Ironcutter," McAdoo said. "Do you recognize him?"

Mona's frown deepened. "I've never seen this man in my life. What kind of shit are you trying to pull?"

Now it was my turn to frown. "What's going on, Detectives?"

Georgie's agitation grew exponentially. He reached out and grabbed Mona by the arm. I could see his grip tighten. "Don't you play games, lady. This is the murder suspect, and you know it. You need to properly identify him."

I heard McAdoo sigh. He knew now that any identification made by Mona could and would be suppressed due to Detective Georgie Thompson's remarkable ineptitude. It didn't matter though. Mona jerked her arm out of Georgie's grasp.

"Don't you be grabbing me, you fat fuck." She angrily stood. "This is ridiculous and a waste of my time. A drunk slipped in his own piss, fell, and hit his head. That's all that happened. There wasn't any kind of murder, and you know it." She glared a moment at Georgie and then stabbed a finger at him.

"Don't you call me or come around my bar anymore. I've got to get back to work." She then turned and stormed out of the lobby.

I looked back and forth between the two detectives. Both appeared to be in disbelief.

"I don't know what's going on here, but whatever you're trying, it looks like you screwed the pooch. Gentlemen," I said and walked out. It was then I caught sight of that junior detective. She was standing at the far end of the lobby with a video camera. I smiled and waved before putting my hat on and exiting through the glass doors.

As I walked through the parking lot, I saw Mona leaned up against a car, smoking a cigarette and watching me. When I got close, she spoke. "Hey."

I walked over to her. She eyed me up and down with eyes that'd seen a lot of bad times and sad times.

"So, you're Thomas Ironcutter," she said.

"That's right."

"Well, Thomas Ironcutter, did you know Harvey was the love of my life? We went to high school together. He was a year older than me, and I thought he was the cutest boy I'd ever seen. One night after a football game there was a party. I messed up and had a one-night stand with another boy. I ended up getting myself pregnant. I was seventeen. When I confessed to Harvey, he was devastated. He broke up with me and started seeing another gal. They got married a year later and they've been together ever since."

I nodded, not knowing what to say. She took a long drag off her cigarette. "Funny how you can do one stupid thing and it'll mess up your whole life."

"That's true," I said.

She dropped her cigarette on the asphalt and stepped on it. "Perry Goforth was a no-good son of a bitch. About this time last year, he smacked a man in the back of the head with a pool cue because he didn't like it that he lost a game of nine-ball."

She paused and fished out another cigarette. I lit it for her.

"Thanks," she said and took a deep drag. "I banned him but ended up letting him come back because he was a regular who spent a good amount of money. That's the only reason I let him back in my bar. And I'd lay down my life for Harvey. Take care, Thomas Ironcutter."

I watched as she got in her car, a Nissan Altima that had seen better days, and drove away.

I got in my SUV and started it up. She didn't know it, but Harvey had already called me and gave me a heads up. Still, I was thankful for what she did.

I'd smoked a cigar last night, which was my self-imposed limit, but I desperately craved one now. I found a nice Montecristo in my travel humidor, prepped it, and lit it. I rode home in silence while I smoked. I didn't even have the radio playing. My phone rang as I parked. It was Percy.

"What's up, brother?" I asked.

"How'd the interview go?" he asked.

"About how I expected it to. It's all good. What are you up to?"

"You're not going to believe what I'm about to tell you," he said.

"Alright, whip it on me."

"Felicity is alive and well," he declared.

I almost dropped my cigar in my lap.

"She is? Where'd you find her?"

"I didn't. She walked in the front door of her mother's house about an hour ago like she'd only been out for a casual stroll. I just came from there. She's pale as a ghost and has lost some weight, but otherwise she seems fine. I tried to talk to her about it. All she would say is she's fine and is not a victim of a crime. I tried to press her for details, but she told me to leave her alone."

"Wow," I said.

"Yeah. I left my card and told her to feel free to call if she wants to talk about it, but that's all I can do for now."

He was right. There was nothing more for him to do.

"I'll give Art a call and let him know," I said.

"I appreciate it. Alright, I'm officially closing this one unless she tells me otherwise. Hey, I'm going to grill out with the girls tomorrow evening. Anna told me to be sure to invite you and Vadoma even said she'd like to see you. Why don't you join us? Bring someone with you if you want."

"I believe I'll take you up on that," I said. I wasn't sure who I'd bring. Abby came to mind, but I didn't want people to think we were dating.

I called Art and gave him the news. He was incredulous and hesitant to believe Felicity had not called him.

"Is she hurt or anything?" he asked.

"She didn't go to the hospital, but other than that, I don't know," I said.

Art said a few more things before deciding he should give her a call and hung up.

When I got home, I realized I had one last official act to do with her case. I sent a text out of courtesy to Marley and Mel. They deserved to know Felicity had returned home. I knew they'd have a lot of questions and suggested they go pay her a visit.

I brought my laptop outside and finished my cigar while I wrote up a final report on the case. There were many unanswered questions, but I swore to myself I wasn't going to get dragged any further into her nonsense. That woman was trouble.

"I seem to find a lot of those types," I muttered.

244

I had a bite to eat before going into town and buying some welding supplies. I then spent the rest of the day in my shop with the do not disturb function activated on my phone.

CHAPTER 55

When I parked my SUV and got out, I was immediately attacked by Grace. She still had the mentality of a puppy, but she was a big girl now, seventy pounds and still growing. I dropped to a knee and let her jump on me and run in circles, barking in excitement.

Abby laughed at her antics. "She really likes you."

"Yeah, I've missed her," I said.

After a few minutes I stood, and the two of us walked around to the back of the house where everyone else was. Percy was at the grill talking with Sheba and her partner, a tall girl named Lacey. Anna and Vadoma were sitting in lawn chairs, wine glasses in hand. Both were dressed similarly, in jeans and hoodies. I hoped that meant they were getting along now. Anna was as beautiful as ever and Vadoma, although still skinny, was also a cute teenager.

"Hey, everyone," I greeted.

"What've you got there?" Sheba asked Abby, who was holding a large party-sized bowl.

"That is my famous pasta salad," I said. "You didn't think we were going to show up empty handed, did you?"

Anna walked up, gave me a friendly kiss on the cheek, and took the bowl. "I'll take care of that," she said and walked inside.

We made small talk until the food was ready and we all sat at the kitchen table. It took me a moment until I realized, the last time I visited, Percy only had a small table for two. This table was new, and it could now easily seat six or more. Percy saw I noticed. I said nothing but grinned. The man had spent years being a lone wolf and living as a bachelor. Now, with Anna and Vadoma living with him, it looked like he was well on his way to becoming a sociable family man.

After we ate, Percy got a fire going in the chiminea and we all sat around it, enjoying its warmth. All the ladies drank wine, Percy and I had beer.

"What's the latest on your case?" Anna asked.

"The ballistics from the gun that was found on Freak matched the projectiles in the double homicide, so they've cleared that case."

"What about that woman who was abducted? What's the story on her?" Lacey asked.

I shrugged. "She had a lot of injuries, including some head trauma, so she didn't remember a lot. She said something about a party at the clubhouse and the next thing she remembered was being chained up. Freak had mistreated her pretty badly."

"Wasn't there an accomplice?" Sheba asked.

I nodded. "There was, but she was unable to identify who it was. They asked her about Freak's brother, but she couldn't say."

"That's terrible," Lacey said.

"They've decided that the hang-around punk, Timothy Davenport, must have been the accomplice, so they're clearing her case too," Abby said.

Lacey frowned. "Cleared? What does that mean?" She then looked at the rest of us. "I'm sorry. I work for a nonprofit and don't know any of this police jargon."

I was about to explain but Abby spoke up and gave a detailed explanation of the FBI standards of how a case can be cleared. When she finished, Sheba gave her a little smile.

"Not bad, rook."

Abby beamed at the compliment.

"I have a question," Anna said. "Did anyone ever figure out the motive behind the double murder? I mean, why did he shoot them and how did it happen?"

I shrugged. "The short answer is no. The only bullet holes in the car were the driver's side window. That would indicate the shooter was standing outside the driver's door. If I had to guess, I'd say he turned into the Jefferson Springs Rec Area, stopped, and walked back to their car. Brittany might've frozen in place, not knowing what to do."

"So, he shot them and then drove her car into the water?" Lacey said. "That's horrible."

I had a sudden memory. Brittany's car door wasn't even locked. Did that mean she didn't feel threatened or was she simply naïve? It was one of those questions that'd never be answered.

Vadoma, who had been mostly quiet the entire time, stood and walked over to me.

"May we talk in private?" she asked.

"Sure," I said and stood.

She led me inside and into the den. Sitting on the couch, she motioned for me to sit with her.

"Have you heard from Kalina?" she asked.

"She sent me an email back in September. I haven't heard from her since."

She frowned. "Me either. Nobody has. I chat with a lot of people in our community, and nobody has heard from her."

"Do you think something has happened?" I asked.

She frowned. "I don't know. There's something you should know. My sense of intuition is more acute than others."

"Like a psychic?" I asked.

She shook her head. "I don't claim to be a psychic, but I sense things. Not always, but it does happen."

"But you don't sense anything with Kalina?"

She frowned again. "No, and that's strange. But I do sense something with you, Thomas. I sense impending danger with you."

"What do you mean?" I asked.

"I'm not sure how to explain it so that it makes sense, but as soon as you parked your car, I sensed some kind of impending danger surrounding you."

I nodded thoughtfully, unsure of where this was going. "Alright, I'll bite, what should I do?"

Vadoma gave a small smile. "You will survive. You always have and you always will. You have that gift in your bloodline."

"I don't know about that," I said, thinking of my mother and father. My mother died of cancer, and my father had a plethora of health issues, mostly because he was a chain-smoking alcoholic. "I'm curious, did you and Kalina talk much?" I asked.

"We used to Snapchat each other all the time." She gave a small smile. "She told me how much you were bothered by the curse, but pretended you weren't."

"Well, that curse is supposed to have been lifted, but if you say I'm in impending danger, maybe it hasn't been."

"It has been," she said. "Oh, and there's something else. Abby has something important she wants to talk to you about," she suddenly said.

I frowned. "Did she tell you that?"

Vadoma shook her head slightly. "No, but I can sense it."

"Do you know what about?"

She shook her head again. The truth was, I'd kind of sensed it as well. We'd been hanging out on occasion and were getting along, but it'd been platonic. In other words, we weren't sleeping with each other. On the ride over, she seemed to want to talk about something, but was reluctant.

"Alright, anything else?" I asked.

"Only this, protect the medallions," she said. "They may not mean that much to you, but they are sacred to my mother's people."

"What makes you think I have any medallions?" I asked.

Vadoma didn't answer. Instead, she pulled a necklace out from under her shirt and lightly stroked it.

"Do you recognize it?" she asked.

"Yes, I do."

She smiled. "It's priceless to me. I would die if it were taken from me."

We rejoined the others, and the wine soon had the girls peppering Percy and I with questions and asking us to tell police stories. We obliged them, but by tacit agreement, the two of us glossed over some of the darker stuff we'd witnessed and experienced.

When it was after eleven, I gave Abby a nod and the two of us bid everyone goodnight. I'd managed to keep it down to only three beers over four hours, so driving home wasn't a problem.

"I need to tell you something," Abby said when we were about a mile down the road.

"What's that?" I asked.

"I've kind of been seeing someone."

I glanced over. She seemed nervous. Maybe she thought I'd feel like she betrayed me or something. Honestly, I was relieved. I smiled.

"That's great."

CHAPTER 56

It was a crisp Christmas morning and there was a hint of snow in the air. I hoped it would. It didn't snow too often on Christmas in Nashville. The fitness center was closed, so after a cup of coffee, I bundled up and went on an early morning run.

Today's goal was five miles. Maybe six. I'd not run more than five miles at once in a few years, maybe today was the day. I started off with an easy gait. It felt good and I got to thinking that maybe I'd jog for five and then do some wind sprints. I was in a good mood.

I thought about my plans for the day as I jogged. Abby was coming over in a little while. I promised to fix her brunch and I'd even bought her a present. She didn't know it, but she was going to be the proud owner of a Glock handgun. We'd gone to the gun range with her new boyfriend the weekend after Thanksgiving and she loved shooting my Glock. I waited and waited for the new boyfriend to get the hint. I even asked him what he was going to get her for Christmas, but his only response was a shrug of the shoulders.

So, I bought it. If my gift was bigger and better than whatever he bought, too bad for him.

After she left, I was going to Mick's Place to spend the evening. Marti was going to open the bar, and all the regulars agreed to bringing potluck. I would be surprised if anyone other than the usual gasbags showed up, but I didn't mind. Hell, I'd more than likely buy the first round of beers for everyone. I even bought Marti a present. It was a gift card for a couples massage at an upscale spa. I doubted Doobie would have appreciated it, but Marti certainly would.

I was on my second lap when I noticed one of my shoelaces had become untied. I made a quick stop and began to bend over when I felt something impact with the back of my head, like somebody punched me only much, much harder.

And then, everything went black.

The End

www.ingramcontent.com/pod-product-compliance
Lightning Source LLC
Chambersburg PA
CBHW060422180626
46817CB00007B/2633